IMMORTAL

Name: Brian Marotto, author/editor/illustrator

Title: Immortal

Description: First Edition

Identifiers: ISBN 979-8-9987824-1-1 (ebook) | ISBN 979-8-9855207-9-8 (paperback) | ISBN 979-8-9987824-0-4 (hardback)

Printed in the United States of America

First Printing Edition - 2025

Thank you to everyone who has supported my writing journey, especially my family. Your support means a lot, and it keeps me going. This would also not be possible without my readers, who tell me how much they've enjoyed my books and ask when my next book will be out. It's a wonderful thing to hear, thank you!

IMMORTAL

BRIAN MAROTTO

CHAPTER 1

It was an early, brisk October morning as Adam drove his vintage, black 1967 Chevy Impala down the interstate. His original plan was to stay on the interstate to arrive at his destination, not too far east of Charlotte, North Carolina...but fate had other plans for him today. Back in Virginia, he noticed a red Ford pickup truck following him. He made various efforts to be sure his hunch was correct, including slowing down to let the truck pass him and making multiple lane changes. Adam even abruptly took an exit and drove on the local roads for a while before jumping back on the interstate, but the truck was always a few car lengths behind him. It didn't take someone who lived as many centuries as he had to realize that whoever the mystery person was, they didn't care to conceal their actions. At this point, he knew he needed to confront this person in a more secluded area.

He wasn't in North Carolina long when he decided to take the Blue Ridge Parkway. As he drove down the Parkway, Adam couldn't help but admire the beauty of the fall colors surrounding the road. Yellow, red, and orange leaves were quite prevalent on and off the trees. The weather was colder than usual for this early in the month, but he didn't mind.

The further he ascended the mountain, the more he noticed the decreased volume of visitors admiring the scenery. He knew it was because the higher altitude brought even colder temperatures, which caused more leaves to fall. The barren trees were not picture-worthy to most people. Unfortunately, he wasn't there for sightseeing but to unveil his stalker.

Adam carefully maintained his speed but slowed down when he felt his "friend" was beginning to fall behind due to other vehicles pulling in and out of the sightseeing areas. Eventually, it dwindled to just him and the red truck. Adam continued further up the mountain until he was certain they would be alone. His blue eyes narrowed as he peered into the rearview mirror while he ran his hand through his short, messy, yet styled, dark-brown hair. He couldn't get a good enough view of the driver, so once he felt confident it would be just the two of them, he slowly pulled off the road and into a space within the viewing area. Sure enough, the truck pulled in a couple of spaces down from him.

Adam sighed while he rubbed his clean-shaven, lightly tanned face. "I'm sure this is going to go smoothly," he sarcastically said to himself. He then turned the car off, put the keys into the pocket of his blue jeans, and stepped out. He closed the door and was thankful he wore his hiking-style boots after he saw the ground covered in damp leaves. By the time he began to walk toward the back of his car, the man in the truck was already walking toward him. The stranger had a dual-edged battle-axe resting on his shoulder.

"I thought you were never going to pull over. I may be immortal, but time is precious to a guy like me," the man announced as he casually strolled toward Adam.

"Drustan, I presume," Adam responded.

"You know who I am? I'm impressed," Drustan responded with a deep voice as he began to smile.

2

"Well, you do have a reputation," Adam said while he smirked. Even with Adam's six feet, four inches of toned, yet muscular body, Drustan made him seem small in comparison.

Drustan was easily a few inches taller than Adam, but was bulkier due to a combination of fat and muscle. His head was shaved, but he had a full, brown beard. Adam could see the chaos brewing within his brown eyes. He wore a dark flannel shirt with the sleeves torn off and a pair of jeans that had rips around his knees. For a big man, he walked softly in his black combat boots. What caught Adam's eye was the multitude of immortal markings scattered over his chest, stomach, and arms from the ones he had killed. Regardless, Adam stood near the back of his car, unfazed.

"I'm sure I do. I have slain so many of our kind that I make it look easy. In fact, I have grown to enjoy it immensely," Drustan responded as his smile grew. He stopped within ten feet of Adam.

Adam's brow creased as his muscles tensed. "I know a lot of people who would like to see you dead, especially friends of mine that you have hurt over the centuries. Mortals, immortals...it's all the same to you."

Drustan responded with a smug look and a shrug. Adam could feel his anger boiling inside him as his fists clenched and his brow furrowed. He then took a few steps toward Drustan.

"You enjoy being a monster, don't you?" Adam said through his teeth.

"First off, 'monster' is a relative term. To a worm, a bird is a monster. Besides, is it wrong to enjoy being so proficient at killing? The strong prevail, and the weak perish. It's just how it is," Drustan calmly replied.

A smirk appeared on Adam's face. "You are right about one thing. The weak do perish, especially today." He began rolling up his thin, white sleeves when Drustan started to speak.

"You really think you can defeat me, boy? I am much older than you, and I would venture to say a vast number of more markings than you as well. Besides, you don't look much like a warrior."

As Adam pulled up his second sleeve, he detached a black hilt from a band wrapped around his forearm. The grip was seamless black leather that covered the entire hilt. At one end of the hilt, an emerald the size of a quarter was encased in a metal, black skeletal hand. At the other end of the hilt, where the blade would begin, was nothing except the cross-guard, which was folded onto the hilt.

Drustan scoffed. "And they say I'm the crazy one. Don't you realize you're missing the most important part of the sword?"

Adam grinned and, within his mind, willed the blade to come forth. As quick as the thought entered his mind, the cross-guard snapped forward, and the blade appeared. A light-green, almost transparent, dual-edged blade emerged from the hilt. The blade was almost three feet long and had a flame-like, dark green smoke around it. Toward the hilt of the sword, on the blade itself, were ancient symbols. The emerald, which was dormant, became alive and was bright green as if a light appeared within the gem. Adam raised the blade toward Drustan.

"You think you are going to hurt me with that toothpick?" Drustan mocked.

"I plan to do a lot more than just hurt you," Adam countered as his eyes narrowed.

Drustan's face hardened, and his brow furrowed as he took his axe off his shoulder and tightened his grip around the brown leather straps. Then, the steel of his axe became ablaze while he shifted his shoulders to get into his fighting stance. Adam didn't react to the fire around the blade, but inside, he knew he had to be cautious and more strategic in how he would battle Drustan. Without knowing the full extent of the axe's powers, he needed to be mindful.

Drustan bellowed as he lunged forward and swung his fiery axe down upon Adam with both hands as if he were going to split him down the middle like a log. Surprised by how quickly the large man could move, Adam barely sidestepped the attack. As his axe broke the pavement, Adam swung his sword, but Drustan moved his head just enough to narrowly avoid his blade. Drustan swung his axe toward Adam's midsection, but he blocked the powerful counterattack with his sword.

He continued his relentless attack against Adam, but his swings became more controlled and precise. His strikes aimed at a different part of Adam's body each time. Luckily, Adam was quick and agile enough to deflect each strike as he walked backward and past the tree line. Every time Drustan attacked, Adam could feel the heat emanating from his axe. The ground was wet from the downpour the night before, so he had to be careful of his footing and not slip on the fallen, wet leaves. He knew he couldn't overpower Drustan, so he needed to be patient and remain defensive until Drustan made a mistake.

Drustan sadistically smiled as the clangs from their weapons echoed throughout the woods. Adam remained focused and stayed on the defense, either by dodging or deflecting Drustan's attempts to end him. He was now beginning to realize how Drustan had killed so many other immortals.

Finally, Drustan became frustrated and yelled as he swung for Adam's head. Adam quickly ducked under his attack and drove his sword forward with a powerful thrust into Drustan's stomach. Drustan yelled in agony but was still able to swing his axe downward at Adam. He saw this and quickly removed his blade while he darted past him. As he did, Adam held his sword so the blade would trail behind him and let it slice Drustan along his ribs. Drustan growled as he grabbed his wound and swung his axe wildly while he spun around. Adam had already pivoted, and his blade was on its way to slice across Drustan's chest.

However, Drustan's powerful swing almost knocked Adam's sword from his hand as he stumbled backward. Then, in a surprise

5

move, Drustan thrust his axe forward. To counter, Adam placed his blade horizontally in front of him and put his hand on the flat edge of the sword. This allowed him to absorb the impact of the axe as he slid a couple of feet back across the leaves. Drustan continued to push the axe forward as he smiled. Adam clenched his teeth and his muscles bulged to the point that his arms began to tremble. He could feel the heat from the flames as they grew closer to his face.

Then, Adam's eyes widened as he noticed the flames began to grow and the temperature became hotter. Instinct kicked in as he pushed away and dove off to the side, but it was too late. The fire projected from the axe and seared his left shoulder, side, and back as he landed on the ground. He yelled from the intense pain he felt, and for good reason. From what he could see, some areas of his skin were burned and some were charred. He glanced around and didn't see anything else on fire since everything was still wet. Adam grunted as he staggered to his feet.

Drustan slowly approached Adam with a smug look. "Very impressive. I thought this was going to be an easy win, but you are more of a warrior than I anticipated." Drustan took a moment and looked at his wounds, which had already begun to heal. "It was a valiant effort and honestly…fun, and who knows…maybe in another century from now you would have won. Nevertheless, this ends now."

His smile became sadistic again as he lifted his axe in the air. Adam noticed the flames were growing again, so he raised his sword and stood his ground. Sure enough, Drustan sent a fireball toward him. Adam dodged the fireball and thrust his sword forward, but Drustan was too quick and deflected his attack. With one fluid motion, Drustan swung his axe back and sliced Adam across his chest. He winced, grabbed his chest, and watched the top of his white shirt turn red before the blood poured over his hand.

Adam weakly raised his sword in defense, but Drustan swatted it out of his hand with his axe. His sword landed, blade first, into the ground a handful of feet away. Drustan followed up with an overhead swing, but Adam stopped it by grabbing the handle with both his hands. His body trembled from exhaustion, and he yelled from the immense pain that coursed through his body while Drustan tried to push the axe closer to him.

Drustan then yanked him forward and sent a knee crashing into Adam's stomach. When he doubled over, Drustan punched him in the back of the head. Adam crumbled to the ground. He shook his head to rid himself of the dizziness he felt. As he looked up, he saw Drustan, well…what looked like two of him, raising his axe high in the air. Adam closed his eyes tightly for a moment to regain focus, and when he opened them, Drustan was about to add him to his collection of kills. At the last moment, Adam reached up and shoved his hand into the wound that still wasn't healed on Drustan's stomach. He put enough power into it that his fingers disappeared inside the cut.

Drustan's bellow could be heard throughout the woods as he dropped the axe to the side of them and grabbed Adam's hand with both of his. He noticed that the flames around the axe ceased as soon as it left Drustan's hands. In one motion, Adam stood up and rammed his shoulder under Drustan's sternum and drove him a few feet from his axe. He then followed up with an uppercut that landed on Drustan's chin, which sent him toppling to the ground.

Adam took advantage of this and scurried back to the axe behind him. He knew he had to act swiftly since Drustan had already sat up. Drustan shook his head, and then his eyes widened when he noticed what Adam was doing. He glanced around, located Adam's sword, staggered to his feet, and bolted toward it.

Adam reached the axe first and lifted it off the ground. It was heavy but manageable. The fire didn't ignite, and he didn't know how to activate it, but it didn't matter. He had a plan. It had to work because he didn't know how much longer he could last if it didn't. Adam focused on Drustan and not the intense pain he felt. He

7

summoned every ounce of strength that he could, gripped the axe with two hands, and charged toward Drustan. He covered the distance between them quickly as he screamed. When he was within range, Adam raised the axe and swung it toward Drustan.

At that moment, Drustan grabbed the sword, pulled it from the ground, and swung around to defend against Adam. However, the blades never connected. The sound that should have been metallic was replaced with the loud crunch of the axe being driven into Drustan's chest. Adam was able to put enough power behind his swing that the blade embedded horizontally into Drustan's lungs and heart. Drustan didn't make a sound, but Adam could see the confusion in his eyes while blood trickled from his mouth. Drustan looked down, and the blade had disappeared. His eyes slowly drifted back up to Adam's face.

"The spectral sword only works in my hands," Adam commented while he breathed heavily from the adrenaline. A defiant smile then formed on Adam's face.

To Adam's surprise, Drustan smiled before his eyes closed, and his body became limp. He eased up to allow Drustan's body to fall to the ground. Adam put his foot on his chest, pried the axe out of Drustan, and reached down and recovered the hilt of his sword. He walked a few steps away from Drustan and waited for what was to come next.

All the immortal markings on Drustan's body began to emit a bluish light before they all converged onto Drustan's original immortal mark, disappearing as they did. Adam waited to see where Drustan's mark would end up on his body, and sure enough, he felt a burning sensation on his right side about halfway up his ribcage. The more intensely Drustan's mark glowed, the more his side burned. Then, the blue, flame-like glow encased Drustan and Adam, with blue, electrical-like beams connecting them. Adam felt like he was being branded, a feeling he was accustomed to over his long life. Still, he couldn't hold back anymore as the pain became intense enough, so he yelled. After a minute, the blue flames and electrical-like beams vanished, and Adam dropped to his knees. The woods were silent. He pulled his shirt up and sure enough, Drustan's mark was now a part of him. It was the size of a half-dollar and black, like all immortal marks, but of course, the design was slightly different. The mark coiled around itself but then tailed off, with little spikes at the end of it. His original mark was similar, but not as tightly wound, and he had swirls besides spikes. He looked over at Drustan, and as expected, Drustan's body converted to his true age. Even though he had seen this multiple times, he still grimaced at the sight of the skeleton with just enough rotted flesh to cover the bones.

Adam held up his sword, and the blade extended again. "Thank you," Adam whispered before he retracted the blade. He lay down on the wet ground, his body and mind worn out from the battle that had just taken place. He made sure to keep his eyes open because he didn't want to pass out, but he needed to rest long enough until his strength returned and his body healed.

About thirty minutes passed before he sat back up, and his wounds had healed but were still tender, especially where he was burned. They healed quicker than usual, but that was typical when an immortal received a new mark. He felt more revived and could feel the added power that dwelt within him from the kill of an immortal. Unfortunately, it was accompanied by Drustan's rage. He also now acquired the knowledge of how to activate the axe. Something he would have figured out, but the kill granted him the knowledge quicker. To activate it, similar to his sword, it had to be willed; however, the intent had to be for violence. He looked around and saw a bird off in the distance.

He tried to turn it on, but it wouldn't obey him until the thought of burning the bird entered his mind. Once that happened, the axe became ablaze. He quickly dropped the axe, which made it go dormant again. For fear of losing his connection with his sword, Adam didn't want to become too familiar with the axe. Also, he feared his mind would become corrupt since he knew magical weapons could influence anyone who wielded them. He didn't want to take that chance, especially since he needed to deal with Drustan's rage now brewing within him. It would take some time, but he would gain control and become more like himself again.

Adam performed some breathing exercises to center himself before he stood up. He reconnected his hilt to his forearm, picked up the axe, being mindful not to activate it again, and walked over to Drustan's body. Their battle led them deep into the woods, and with the body already decayed as it was, it would not raise too much suspicion about what had transpired today. To be safe, he piled some rocks and leaves over the body and glanced over the area to make sure he hadn't missed anything before he headed back to his car.

As he was almost out of the woods, Adam abruptly stopped. Something didn't seem right. He couldn't place it, but he didn't feel alone anymore. He slowly looked around and could faintly hear the leaves rustling, but it didn't sound like it came from an animal.

"I know you're out there. Show yourself!" Adam demanded as he slowly spun around. Nothing but silence answered him. He exited the woods and was back in the parking area. Only the truck and his car were there. He surveyed the area, and there was still no sign of anyone else. He sighed and rubbed his eyes. "Pull it together, Adam," he said to himself as he walked back to his car. He opened his trunk and put the axe inside it. As he reached for his duffle bag full of extra clothes, he felt the chill of cold steel under his chin.

CHAPTER 2

Adam sighed and rolled his eyes. "It's been a long morning, so whoever this is, I hope you have a better plan than this." He dropped his duffle bag in the trunk and stood straight up. He could feel the stranger angle their body to adjust for his movement. He presumed it was to guard against a possible countermove.

"Maybe if you paid more attention to your surroundings, you would not be in this predicament," the man commented. Adam's brow creased. The voice sounded familiar to him. "You can't just rely on your perfect little square jaw to get you through life. Contrary to popular belief, you're not that handsome. Especially when compared to me," the man added as the knife moved a couple of inches away from his throat.

Adam scoffed in disbelief, followed by a smile. "Oliver," he said as he gently pushed the knife away and turned around. Standing before him was a good friend he had known for a few centuries. Oliver was clean-shaven and stood a couple of inches shorter than him. He had brown eyes and brown, medium-tousled-styled hair. His body wasn't as muscular as Adam's, but it was toned, and he wore dark jeans with a gray V-neck T-shirt.

Oliver sheathed his knife near his waist, and their smiles grew. They gave each other a firm handshake and patted each other on the shoulder. Oliver took a couple of steps back and glanced over Adam.

"Wow, mate. You look terrible. Now, this may come as a surprise, but you'll live," Oliver teased.

Adam scoffed with amusement. "Yeah, I'm pretty much fully healed now."

Oliver's smile vanished, and his eyes grew wide. "Wait a second. Did you fight Drustan?"

"Yeah...how did you know?" Adam cautiously asked.

"Did you kill him?" Oliver quickly asked.

"Yes, but again...how did you know?" Adam inquired.

"Because I was tracking him! You know what he has taken from me. The pain that he had caused. The lives he took. How could you do that to me?" Oliver countered.

"Gee, thanks, Adam, for killing the man that tormented me and so many others," Adam sarcastically responded. Oliver scoffed, but Adam continued before he could speak. "Besides, it's not like he gave me much of a choice. He followed me, challenged me, and nearly killed me." Adam then gestured at his appearance.

The two glared at each other momentarily until Oliver's face relaxed. "Sorry mate, you're right. It's hard to stay rational when it comes to him. Thank you for finally dispatching such a foul person."

Adam's face relaxed, and he put his hand on Oliver's shoulder. "No worries. If it helps, I got you a gift." Adam turned around, reached into the trunk, and retrieved the axe. He turned around and presented it to Oliver.

"Drustan's axe. Are you sure? You did earn it," Oliver said as his eyes fixated on the axe.

Adam grinned. "Yes, I am sure. I may have earned it, but you deserve this after everything he has put you through. With this axe, those feelings of anguish can be put to rest. Just make sure you don't keep it near anything flammable."

Oliver grinned. "Thank you." He then reached out and took the axe from Adam and examined it.

While he was doing that, Adam turned back around and quickly grabbed a black T-shirt from the duffle bag and replaced it with what remained of his shirt. He then took a swig from his water bottle before wetting a washcloth and wiping as much of the dried blood as he could from his body. After he finished, Adam put everything away and closed the trunk before glancing around the surrounding area. It was still just the two of them. He also listened intently and didn't hear any vehicles in the area. The only sounds he heard were the wind rustling the leaves and some birds chirping off in the distance.

"Did you portal here? If so, how did you know what location to pick?" Adam inquired.

"You know it's hard to use portals when it comes to tracking. I got myself at least in the area, and then I…borrowed the motorcycle that you can't see because it's on the other side of the truck." Oliver responded as he lowered the axe.

"Borrowed? As in stole?" Adam asked with a raised brow.

Oliver sighed. "Yes, stole."

"Oliver, really?" Adam huffed.

"If it helps ease your troubled mind, the guy had it coming to him," Oliver countered. He smirked and patted Adam on his shoulder as he walked toward the truck.

Adam scoffed in amusement and then followed behind Oliver. "What do you think we should do about the truck?"

Oliver opened the door and climbed into the truck. "If I were a betting man, Drustan probably stole the truck and maybe even killed its owner." He paused as he searched the inside of the truck. Adam patiently waited outside the door before he noticed Oliver pull a wallet from the center console. "Yep, this truck belonged to someone else, and of course, all the cash is gone. I wouldn't be surprised if he also used the credit cards." Oliver paused and closely examined the wallet. "It's tough being both this handsome and intelligent, but I was right. There is blood on the wallet." He then tossed it back into the center console.

Adam shook his head. "Well, if there is nothing on the bike or in the truck that links anything back to our kind, I say we leave everything here, take my car, and leave. Drustan's body is deep in the woods, decayed beyond recognition, and covered by leaves and rocks. As for the vehicles, once the ranger sees and reports them to the authorities, they will presume it is just a place to dump the stolen vehicles. Case closed."

Oliver nodded in agreement. They searched the truck and motorcycle to make sure they were safe to leave. Once they finished, they headed back to the car. Adam opened the trunk so Oliver could place the axe inside.

Oliver scoffed. "If I didn't lose him on the highway, I would have reached him first, and our paths would have never crossed."

"You lost him on the highway?" Adam asked.

"Yeah, it was going smoothly until he abruptly took an exit, and I was stuck behind some slow person, so I couldn't follow him. I had to take the next exit and backtrack. I don't understand why he did it," Oliver commented as his brow creased while he rubbed the back of his neck.

Adam closed the trunk. "It's a mystery." He felt it would be best not to inform Oliver that Drustan took the exit because he was following him.

The two entered the car and drove off. Once they reached the interstate, Oliver turned to Adam. "So, where are we headed?"

"I'm headed to the manor, but I can drop you off anywhere you would like," Adam responded while he kept his eyes on the road.

"I haven't been there in over seventy years. I think it's time for me to make an appearance," Oliver said in a positive tone.

Adam slightly turned his head toward Oliver. "You do realize that Eva will be there?"

"Even more reason to go!" Oliver replied as his smile grew.

"You do remember she recently tried to kill you, right?" Adam commented.

"That was seventy years ago," Oliver countered.

"Yeah…recently," Adam said as he smirked.

"You've got to stop living in the past," Oliver responded. His smile continued as he leaned further back in the seat.

Adam laughed. "It's your head."

After a brief ride in silence, Oliver turned to Adam again. "Why are you driving?"

"Would you rather be walking?" Adam quickly replied.

"You know what I mean. You obviously are driving from somewhere up north, all the way down to an area outside of Charlotte. A trip that is not quick by any means. You could have been there in a few seconds if you used a portal, yet you chose to drive. Why is that?" Oliver inquired as he raised one eyebrow.

"Sometimes, I like taking the long way to enjoy the scenery. Besides, I enjoy driving my car." Adam was coy with his response as he side-eyed Oliver.

"Bloody hell, do you still get portal sickness?" Oliver asked, trying not to laugh. Adam clenched his jaw. Oliver then burst into laughter. "You do. That's funny."

"I swear I must be the only immortal who becomes nauseous after traveling through a portal," Adam grunted.

The comment only made Oliver laugh harder. Once he composed himself, he turned back to Adam. "No worries, mate. You still got your health." The two simultaneously began to laugh. Once they settled down, they spent the remainder of the drive catching up on decades of stories.

When they were within a few miles of the manor, Adam turned his head toward Oliver. "Are you sure you don't want me to drop you off somewhere…anywhere?"

"Yes, I'm sure. Besides, didn't you smooth things over after I left?" Oliver asked.

"As much as I could. You did steal and then gamble her most prized weapon away," Adam responded.

"Which I later recovered for her after I saw the error of my ways. May I remind you that her way of showing gratitude was attempting to skewer me like a kabob," Oliver countered.

"Well, for your sake, I hope time does heal all wounds," Adam commented.

"If not, I do have my irresistible charm to fall back on," Oliver said as he put his hands behind his head.

Adam chuckled. "The same charm that you used on her before. What did she say again when you made an advance?"

"I don't recall," Oliver said in a low tone as he lowered his hands and fidgeted in his seat.

"Ah, yes…I remember. 'I will go on a date with you, but only if you come to Spain with me so my parents can approve of you first.' That would be impressive considering they have been deceased for over six hundred years," Adam added as he smirked.

Oliver sighed. "Yeah, I remember that now." He then cleared his throat. "So, why haven't you made a move on her?"

"You know why. She's like family to me. I would say she is like the sister I never had, but it's more than that. More than just my mentor. It's hard to explain, but we have bonded at a unique level, and I know she feels the same way." Adam explained.

"After that explanation, are you sure she doesn't see you as a sister?" Oliver teased.

Adam smiled. "Shut up."

As Adam finished talking, they could see the manor in the distance. He pulled up to the large wrought iron gate with gold-swirled accents throughout it. Adam stopped and reached out to punch in the code Eva had given him before his trip. Once it was entered, the gate slowly opened, creaking as it did. He drove through the gate and proceeded slowly down the tan paved driveway.

Regardless of the numerous times he had visited the manor, he was always in awe of the property. The grass, bushes, and trees were well-kept and manicured throughout the vast acres of land. If the three-story building had a tower, it could pass as a castle. The L-shaped stone building was grayish-white with a reddish-brown roof. On the left side of the house was a large stone chimney, and the wooden front door had a U-shaped archway. Other structures were situated around the house, further down the property, but at a much smaller scale. Each building had a unique purpose.

Adam pulled into the giant circular driveway in front of the manor and drove around so that they would be closer to the front door. He put the car in park and shut it off before he sighed and turned to Oliver. "I think it would be better if you stayed in the car."

"I'm not going to hide from her," Oliver replied.

"I didn't say that, but I think it would be a good idea if I paved the way first. She has no idea that you were coming," Adam calmly said.

"It will be fine. Besides, I'm not scared of her," Oliver countered. Adam raised his brow as he continued to stare at Oliver. "Okay, maybe a little."

Adam grinned. "Just give me a few minutes before you make your grand entrance." Oliver nodded.

Adam exited his car, and by the time he closed the door, Eva was standing at the front door. She wore black leggings and a white, long-sleeved crop top that showed off her toned stomach while her long-wavy black hair gently blew in the wind. Her brown eyes lit up, followed by a large smile when her eyes locked onto Adam. He smiled and spread his arms out. She ran over to him, threw her arms around his neck, and embraced him. Eva stood on her toes since he was a foot taller than her. As Adam hugged her back, he was glad his footing was established, or else he might have fallen over.

Eva stood up on her toes more and kissed Adam on his cheek. "It's so good to see you! What has it been…ten years?"

"It's good to see you, too, and yes, it's been about a decade," Adam responded as he slowly stepped back from Eva.

She slapped him on his shoulder. "Nine years too long!" Eva commented before she smiled. Adam scoffed with amusement before he smiled and nodded in agreement. Eva's personality always brought a smile to his face. Over the centuries, they became close, so Adam felt instantly comfortable in her presence. Each time they met, he was reminded how much he missed being around her.

"You're typically not late. What took you so long?" Eva asked.

"Drustan," Adam responded.

Eva's eyes widened. "Drustan! I've heard the horror stories about him. What happened?"

"Long story short, he followed and confronted me. It didn't go as he planned," Adam replied. He then lifted the side of his shirt to reveal Drustan's mark.

Eva put her hand on his chest. "I'm so thankful that you are alive. From what I've heard, he has killed many of our kind."

"For a moment, I thought I would be added to his list," Adam commented. Eva gave him a sympathetic smile while she lightly patted his chest.

Eva's eyes narrowed. "There's something else you want to tell me, isn't there?"

Adam sighed. "Yes…and I can explain." Before Adam could continue, he heard the car door open and shut.

"Hello, luv," Oliver announced. Adam sighed again and slowly shook his head.

Eva's brow furrowed. "You didn't." Before Adam could speak, Eva's eyes became wild as she stormed around him. He then noticed that she reached for her bracelet. Oliver and Adam panicked as their eyes grew wide.

18

"Whoa, whoa, whoa. Hold up just a moment," Adam quickly, yet calmly said as he gently grabbed her arm. She stopped and looked at Adam, then her eyes drifted to her arm. He swiftly let go of her and whispered, "Please." She huffed, and the anger remained on her face, but she stopped her advance toward Oliver. Adam let out a sigh of relief.

"Yeah, calm down. We're all friends here. Besides, it's all water under the bridge," Oliver commented as he smiled. Adam lowered his head because he knew Oliver had just made things worse.

Eva's head whipped back toward Oliver, and she glared at him. "Don't tell me to calm down, and definitely don't tell me how to feel!" Oliver, with his palms upward, raised his hands to shoulder height in surrender. She then turned back to Adam. "Why did you bring him here? You know how I feel about him."

"He was tracking Drustan and showed up shortly after I killed him. I told him where I was going and how it would not be wise for him to come, but he still insisted." Adam explained.

"That doesn't explain why you brought him here besides leaving him behind," Eva countered.

"Because, despite his many…many flaws, he is still my friend. I guess, deep down, I was hoping the two of you could mend what was broken." Adam replied. Eva pressed her lips together and fidgeted, so Adam placed his hand on her shoulder and continued. "The idea of this manor was to be a haven for our kind. For the ones who wanted peace and a place to stay."

"Fine," Eva huffed as she crossed her arms. "I will do this for you, but I'm not making any promises regarding how civil I will be."

"Thank you," Adam said as he rubbed her shoulder.

Eva turned to stand side-by-side next to Adam. She had a look of disdain on her face. "He will stay in the guest quarters out back."

"Really, I can't stay in the manor itself?" Oliver protested.

Eva walked a few steps closer to him. "It's either that or you could stay in the manor and risk me splitting you in half." She then reached for her bracelet again. The bracelet consisted of two silver snakes, about an inch wide, linked together by their tails on the underside of her wrist. The heads curled around the top of her wrist and faced each other. Between their mouths was a small, engraved silver bar. To the common eye, it was a unique antique bracelet. To the few who knew, it was a deadly weapon.

"As kinky as that sounds, I will opt for the guest house," Oliver replied with a crooked grin. Eva rolled her eyes and walked past Adam and back into the manor.

Adam approached Oliver. "Please try not to aggravate her."

"I'm not aggravating. I'm charming. Oh, by the way…thanks for the 'many, many flaws' comment," Oliver added with his hands on his hips.

"Relax. You are alive and allowed on the property. If anything, you should be thanking me," Adam protested.

"Don't tell me how to feel," Oliver mocked.

Adam smiled. "You are here. That's a step in the right direction."

"You're right. Thanks, mate. I need to get my stuff. It shouldn't take me long before I return," Oliver said.

"Don't forget the axe," Adam said. He then briskly walked over to his car and retrieved it.

"Can't forget this beauty," Oliver commented as he took the axe. He placed it on the ground and leaned the handle against his leg.

Oliver reached into his pocket and pulled out a glossy, cylinder-shaped moonstone. It was only a few inches long and the width of a quarter. The cylinder had black, wavy, thin lines in various directions on the surface. He pressed his thumb down on the bottom of the cylinder and held it down momentarily. Then, a small one-inch-long moonstone blade emerged from the top. He sliced his hand with the blade, which made the black lines glow. Oliver extended his arm and used the moonstone to draw a half-circle in the air. A thin, red line half-circle now floated in front of him. He continued by drawing a couple of wavy lines from the center of the half-circle downward and then a straight line on top of the circle, with a slight curve at the end. With the completed red symbol floating in front of him, it began to glow and pulsate. He then slashed at the symbol from top to bottom, creating a glowing red rift, about the size of Oliver, in front of him.

"See you later," Oliver said over his shoulder. Before Adam could reply, he picked up the axe, walked into the portal, and vanished. A few seconds later, the portal dissipated.

CHAPTER 3

Adam strolled to his car and retrieved the rest of his things before he headed inside the manor. There were only a few bags since he already had an abundance of his belongings in his room. Eva allowed him to have a permanent room inside the manor. She wanted to make sure it always felt like home to him, for which he was grateful.

He navigated the hallways with ease until he reached his room, and it was just as he had left it. The room was a mix of gray and neutral colors, with memories of his travels situated throughout his room. Paintings of cities and landscapes, trinkets, weapons, and pictures of him with his closest friends put him at ease as he sat on his bed. His eyes then drifted to a small cedar chest on his nightstand. It was where he kept his most cherished memories of people he was close to, and lost, that he didn't want to forget. It wasn't a box he enjoyed opening much, since even though it brought him joy to relive the memories, it was also a painful reminder of what he had lost. Unfortunately, today, he needed to open the box. He reached into his bag and pulled out a picture of someone close to him that he had lost recently, and placed it into the box. He did it quickly because he didn't have the strength to look at the picture again. As soon as he closed the box and right before his eyes began to water, there was a soft knock at his door.

"May I come in?" Eva asked with a soft smile.

Adam ran his hand over his face and smiled as he turned around. "Yes, of course. Please."

"Is everything okay?" Eva asked. Her brow creased as she walked over and sat next to him.

"Yes. Just settling into my room," Adam quickly responded.

Eva put her hand on his knee. "You really think you can fool me? What is it?"

Adam scoffed. "I never could hide my feelings from you."

"Nope. Not now and not ever. Especially not when I took all your money in blackjack," Eva said. She had a smug expression when she motioned over to the picture of them, a couple of hundred years ago, at a saloon in the Wild West.

Adam laughed. "Yes, apparently I can't even have a poker face with you." Eva laughed along with him.

She stopped laughing and looked at him with sympathetic eyes. "Do you want to talk about what's bothering you?" Adam looked down and shook his head.

"The last few years have been hard for you, haven't they?" Eva inquired. Adam didn't look up. He simply nodded. He wanted to talk to her. He knew he could, and she would be there for him, but he just wasn't ready yet. With how quickly he could physically heal, emotional damage always healed in its own time frame. Even then, some would leave scars that would last for an eternity.

"That's fine. You talk to me when you are ready. You know I am here for you." Eva said. She leaned her head on his shoulder and put her arm around him.

"Thanks. I will," Adam responded. He leaned his head on hers and put his arm around her.

The two of them sat in that position for a couple of minutes before Eva stood up and walked to the other side of him. She

23

squeezed between him and his pillows and leaned back on them while lying her legs across his.

"So, what do two single people, like us, do now?" Eva playfully flirted. She then bit her lower lip while she ran her hands through her hair.

"We could always…play charades," Adam joked.

"You read my mind," Eva sarcastically replied. They tried to keep a straight face, but it didn't last long when they laughed simultaneously. Her plan of switching the mood in the room worked, and he welcomed it. The two of them reminisced about some of their more memorable and funny adventures together. What seemed like minutes turned into over an hour as they laughed and talked.

"As much as I would like to monopolize your time, I know there are others who would like to see you," Eva said as she got up.

"Who else is in the manor? I presume Caleb is one of them," Adam said as he stood up.

"Of course, and Paul is here too," Eva replied.

"Oh, that's good to hear. I presume Caleb still hasn't taken a step off this property," Adam commented.

"Nope. He feels safe here, so I am not going to push it," Eva responded.

"Understandable. I'll search for them now," Adam said. The two of them left his room and went their separate ways.

Adam wasn't sure where they would be, so he had to make his best guess. Caleb would most likely be outside somewhere quiet and writing in his chronicles. He looked forward to seeing him. His innocence and enthusiasm were always refreshing. As for Paul, he was glad he was there, too. Paul was in and out of the manor a lot. They would talk from time to time and had been on some adventures together, but lately, he was more his training buddy. Regardless, he still considered him to be a good friend. He ventured outside, and the warmth from the sun embraced him, even though the temperature was cool.

He walked over to one of Caleb's spots, and sure enough, he found him sitting on a stone bench near one of the large oak trees. Adam stopped closely behind Caleb, but he didn't notice him. He was too busy scribbling in his book with his trusted quill and ink. Occasionally, he would run his hand through his short brown hair and then scratch his head while he searched for the correct word to use. Propped up against the bench was his shield. It was a round Viking shield about two feet in diameter. It was comprised mainly of wood with iron around the borders. In the middle was a large, black Viking ship with a large sail.

"I don't know how you can sit on that awful bench for so long," Adam teased.

Caleb almost jumped off the bench, startled, as his head whipped around. Once he saw it was Adam, a huge smile appeared as his green eyes lit up. "That's because my butt is immortal too."

Adam laughed while Caleb put his stuff down, ran around the bench, and hugged him. Being shorter in stature, his head ended up buried in Adam's chest. He didn't mind Caleb hugging him since Adam viewed him as his little brother. He was eighteen when he became immortal over a century ago, and was the youngest immortal he knew. He hadn't heard of anyone else becoming immortal after Caleb.

"How are you doing?" Caleb asked with excitement.

"I'm doing well. How about yourself?" Adam asked.

"Doing great. Staying busy," Caleb answered. He then walked back to his book.

"Looks like you will be done with that one soon. Another book to add to your impressive collection," Adam commented as he followed him.

"Somebody has to keep our legacies…our stories alive." Caleb stopped, and his eyes widened. "You have been gone a while. Do you have any stories for me to add?"

Adam grinned. "I just may have something small for you to add."

"That's great! Tell me!" Caleb exclaimed. He then turned and retrieved his notepad and pencil from next to his book and quill.

"I defeated Drustan today," Adam calmly replied with a smirk. He knew he didn't have to explain who he was since Caleb was an expert in all things immortal and magical. He learned all he could through his studies and research while at the manor and from his travels before he moved in.

"Drustan! That's wonderful news! All the chapters dedicated to Drustan have nothing good to say about him. Can I see?" Caleb asked as his eyes scanned Adam's body.

Adam grinned and raised his shirt to reveal Drustan's mark. Caleb quickly sketched the mark on his notepad, followed by some notes. Not only was Caleb an amazing writer, but also a talented artist.

"Tell me everything that happened!" Caleb blurted out while he had his pencil and notepad ready. He always took notes before he wrote anything into his book. Adam nodded and told Caleb everything that had happened, making sure not to leave out any details since Caleb thrived on them.

After spending a long time talking with Caleb about his battle and other fun facts about his travels over the past decade, he excused himself so he could find Paul. He didn't feel bad about it since Caleb was already eagerly reviewing his notes and about to start writing in his book. Adam smiled while he watched him write before he turned around and headed back into the manor. As he walked toward the manor, he glanced over at the outside training area. With the absence of walls due to the type of training performed there, it was easy for him to see that no one was there, so he continued inside.

If Paul wasn't outside, he had a good idea of where he would find him, so he went to the indoor training room. Sure enough, when he reached the room, he saw Paul practicing his sword techniques.

The large room did not have any thrills to it. The walls and floor were stone, and either side of the room had a long rack full of non-magical weapons. Since non-melee weapons were located outside the training quarters, these weapons consisted mainly of swords, knives, axes, staffs, spears, and maces.

Near the weapons were some free weights, and at the back of the room was a steel gate that separated the training room from the unclaimed magical items. This is where Eva kept all the magical items that anyone had found or won that weren't kept for themselves. That, or the item was either too dangerous or unknown. The more common magical items were there for anyone who needed them, but the rest were not to be touched. Only Eva and Caleb had keys to unlock the gate, and of course, Caleb had cataloged everything.

Paul had his back to Adam as he strolled into the room. His shirt was off, and he wore a pair of black mesh shorts. His dark-tanned body was ripped since he spent a lot of time training. He always felt it was important, especially due to the type of lives they lived. Adam couldn't argue with his logic. However, he did feel it was extreme.

"Careful, you don't want to mess up your hero hair," Adam teased. He kept enough product in it that if a gust of wind came through, it wouldn't have moved much.

Paul quickly spun around and lunged his sword forward. The tip of the short sword came within inches of Adam's throat, but he only leaned back slightly. Paul's green eyes narrowed as he held the blade pointed toward Adam. "You should be more worried about your well-being than my hair."

"I went too far with the hair comment, didn't I?" Adam asked rhetorically.

Paul lowered his sword and ran his hand through his brown hair. "It was a low blow. You know I take pride in my hair."

Adam smiled. "It's good to see you."

Paul returned the smile. "It's good to see you, too." The two of them firmly shook hands.

"I'm surprised you weren't outside training with your wrist crossbow," Adam commented before he glanced down at Paul's arm. From his wrist to three-fourths up his forearm was a golden brace. On either side of the brace were golden wings that were folded inward and flush against the brace itself. The top of the brace had space enough for where the bolt would appear and a U-shaped lever near the wrist for him to pull and activate it. Adam admired not only the design but also how it was situated on his arm, giving him full movement of his wrist.

"I've practiced with this so much that I could use it with deadly accuracy with my eyes closed. Care for a demonstration?" Paul asked with a devious smile.

"I'll take your word for it," Adam responded while he put his hands up to either side of him.

"I need to be just as deadly with a sword in case I am unable to use my crossbow," Paul added.

"Do you mind if I help you in your endeavor? Don't worry, the weapons here are not magical, so you will be safe," Adam joked.

Paul grinned. "You know I will never turn down a chance to spar. Besides, I would be more worried about your safety than mine."

Adam smiled, removed his shirt, and tossed it on the weapon's rack. "Good. I could use a good sparring session right about now. Especially after my kill from this morning. I need to make sure I'm used to whatever I inherited."

"Anyone I know?" Paul asked, unfazed.

"Drustan," Adam responded while he glanced through the swords.

"Drustan…never heard of him," Paul commented as he made his way across the room to prepare.

"Then you would be one of the few," Adam said as he pulled out a short sword similar to what Paul was using. He then walked up to within a few feet of Paul. "Ready?"

28

"Always," Paul replied with a smug look. They did not raise their swords. Instead, they stared at each other, waiting for one of them to make the first move.

Paul thrust his sword forward, which Adam moved to the side and swatted it down. Then, in one motion, he swung his sword toward Paul's chest. He leaned back, narrowly avoiding being sliced. The two then exchanged melee attacks, each being deflected as they stayed around the same spot from when they started. During one of Paul's attacks that Adam blocked, he surprised Adam by throwing a punch that slammed into the side of his face. While dazed, Paul slashed upwards and sliced Adam's shoulder. Then, he followed up with a front kick that connected with Adam's chest, which sent him falling to the ground.

"Is someone still tired from this morning?" Paul teased.

Adam grimaced from the pain, but the wound on his shoulder healed almost instantly. Suddenly, Adam felt an unfamiliar surge of rage. He surprised Paul when he shot up and rammed his shoulder into his chest. He kept his momentum and drove Paul into the wall. Adam immediately followed up with an upward slash that sliced Paul from his stomach to his chest. Paul grunted as he grabbed his chest, and since Adam struck with the handle up, he followed up by ramming the sword down into Paul's leg.

He screamed while he fell to the ground, holding his sword up in defense. Adam wasted no time by raising his sword in the air and bringing it down hard against Paul's sword. He aggressively continued the move several times, and each time, Paul had to weakly raise his sword back up to block the next attack. Finally, with all his wounds healed, Paul stabbed Adam in the stomach. Adam yelled as he took a few steps back, breathing heavily as he did.

"Focus!" Paul directed.

Adam shook his head and tightly closed his eyes, followed by a deep breath. "Sorry."

"It's okay. We've all been there. It just takes some time. Hours or even days to adjust after a kill. That's why we are sparring, and if needed, you could meditate later," Paul explained.

"I know. It's been a while since I felt rage," Adam commented.

"That immortal must have been pretty evil to make you feel like that," Paul added.

"Apparently so," Adam said before he hung his head.

"I can feel the added strength you now have. Just stay focused. Remember your training," Paul voiced as he raised his sword.

Adam took another deep breath and lifted his head. He then raised his sword and nodded. At this point, his wound was already fully healed.

The two swung their swords at the same time, forcefully clanging between them before they continued. Adam went on the offensive, sending multiple strikes toward different parts of Paul's body. He was nimble and deflected all of Adam's attacks, and during one of his advances, Paul ducked around the sword and elbowed Adam in his temple. He quickly followed with a slash that cut across Adam's side.

Adam grimaced while he stumbled back, keeping his sword pointed toward Paul. He could feel the rage beginning to bubble inside of him again, but he took a deep breath, and as soon as his wound healed, he thrust his sword toward Paul's chest. He swatted it away, and once more, the two began their battle, but this time, Adam took more of a defensive approach. He kept slowly backing up after each time he blocked Paul's attack. When the timing was right, Adam swatted away Paul's sword, leaned in, and smacked Paul on the forehead with the bottom of the sword's hilt. Before Paul could react, Adam had his sword to Paul's throat.

CHAPTER 4

Paul froze as the cold steel lay across his neck. Adam's eyes narrowed with intensity as his muscles bulged. Paul glanced down at the sword before looking back at Adam. At that moment, Adam winked.

"Do you yield?" Adam asked as he grinned.

Paul sighed, "I yield." He then lowered his weapon, shook his head, and pinched the bridge of his nose.

Adam lowered his weapon and patted Paul on his shoulder. "I can't believe you let me sucker you in."

"That makes two of us. I guess I was still expecting your aggressive style, so I didn't notice the change," Paul responded as they walked toward the weapons rack.

"You were the one who told me to focus," Adam said while laughing.

"I know, I know," Paul huffed. The two returned their swords and grabbed a towel to wipe off their sweat.

"I guess you need to train more," Adam teased.

"Don't get cocky. If we were keeping track of all our sparring sessions, I believe I would be in the lead," Paul countered.

Adam scoffed with amusement. "I'm off to get cleaned up. I'll see you later." He grabbed his shirt, flung the towel around his neck, and headed back to his room.

On the way there, he took a detour and went to the kitchen first to grab some water. He grabbed a bottle of water from the refrigerator and gulped down half the bottle before he closed the door. As he turned around, Eva entered the kitchen. Her eyes roamed over Adam's body as a flirtatious smile formed.

"Not that I mind, but why are you standing half-naked in my kitchen?" Eva asked while she slowly approached him.

"I just finished sparring with Paul, so I figured I would grab some water before I get cleaned up," Adam responded.

"That explains the blood stains on your body. How did it go?" Eva inquired.

"It was rough at first, but Paul helped me with my control," Adam responded.

"That's good. The sooner you work everything out after a kill, the easier it is to get your old self back," Eva commented.

"True. I presume you are here to cook us up a feast, so I'll let you be," Adam teased.

Eva laughed. "Yeah…no, unless 'cooking a feast' means deciding what restaurant we are all going to."

Adam laughed. "Pick us out a good one." He winked, left the room, and made his way to his bedroom. There, he showered and put on clean clothes. It was just a T-shirt and mesh shorts until he knew what the plan would be later.

He decided to meditate since he knew they wouldn't eat dinner for a while. He wasn't going to at first, since the sparring session was quite helpful, but he wanted to be certain his mind was right. He pulled out a small mat, sat down on it, and took a few deep breaths to settle his mind. It didn't take long until he achieved a meditative state.

About an hour later, he slowly emerged from his meditation. He took a deep breath and felt calmer and like himself again. Adam stood up and was startled when he looked across his room and saw Oliver sitting in a chair.

"I was beginning to wonder when you were going to snap out of it," Oliver casually said as he one-handedly rolled his coin over his fingers.

"That's not creepy at all," Adam remarked. "How long were you sitting there?"

"Long enough to draw a mustache on your face," Oliver responded as a devious smile appeared. Adam's eyes widened as he touched his lip.

"Relax, mate. I'm just joking," Oliver added as his smile grew.

Adam scoffed with amusement and shook his head. "Does Eva know that you are here?"

"She does, and as you can see, I am still in one piece. I call that progress," Oliver replied with a smug look.

"I call that she gave you a task to complete," Adam quickly responded, with a smirk.

Oliver's smug expression melted away. "Actually, she did want me to relay a message from her." Adam crossed his arms and grinned while he stared at him. Oliver rolled his eyes. "She said to dress nicely, but don't overdo it. We are all going out to eat dinner, and then we'll see where the night takes us afterward."

"Including you?" Adam asked.

"Progress," Oliver responded as he winked, pocketed his coin, and left the room. Adam smiled and proceeded to get ready for tonight.

He knew the type of places that Eva liked to go to, so he had a good idea of how to dress. He wore black jeans, black dress sneakers, and a gray button-up, collared shirt. Since his shirt was short-sleeved, he lifted his pant leg and concealed his spectral sword near his shin. Adam walked toward the foyer and met Paul and Oliver, who were dressed similarly to him. However, Paul wore a long-sleeved shirt to cover his wrist crossbow. They chatted for a few minutes before Eva made her appearance. She wore a tight, white dress that came to her mid-thigh. It had a low but tasteful neckline with a silver pendant to match her bracelet. To finish off her look, she wore white-laced three-inch heels. Draped over her arm was an elegant black trench coat.

"The driver should be here soon," Eva commented as she put her coat on.

"I know he prefers it and is fine, but I always feel bad leaving Caleb behind," Adam mentioned.

"Yeah, but like you said, he prefers it. He's fine. Right now, he is playing video games in his room and will raid the fridge later," Eva said.

"Then, he will ask us if there was any 'immortal action' when we return," Paul added. Everyone chuckled at his comment before they left.

The driver was waiting outside in front of the limo. As they approached, he opened the door and greeted everybody as they entered the vehicle. Eva liked to mix it up. At times, she enjoyed staying inside or going out somewhere more low-key. Other times, she wanted more, and tonight appeared to be one of those nights. On the drive to the city, despite Oliver's best efforts, Eva sat next to Adam while Paul and Oliver sat across from them. The driver was new, which wasn't surprising since Eva switched the service she used periodically. That way, people wouldn't start to wonder about their true nature.

The limo pulled up in front of a fancy restaurant, and the driver got out. He walked around and opened the door to allow everyone to exit the vehicle. Eva tipped the man, and the four of them entered the restaurant. Inside, they were seated, and shortly after, a bottle of wine was brought to the table. The four of them shared stories and laughed as they quickly drank the first bottle of wine and moved on to a second one. It wouldn't have surprised Adam if they made it to a third or fourth bottle. Not only were their tolerances higher due to centuries of practice, but it also took more alcohol for them to feel anything due to their immortal nature. Their body would fight off the effects of the alcohol the same way it would fight off a disease.

They moved from the variety of appetizers they ordered to the main course, where they enjoyed steaks and lobster tails. After eating the feast and sharing four bottles of wine, Adam was quite full and a little buzzed. He knew that feeling wouldn't last long, so he enjoyed it while he could. Once they had paid the bill, they left the restaurant.

"Where to now?" Paul asked.

"The night is still young. I say we go to a club and have some fun," Eva responded.

"That sounds wonderful, luv. Do you have a particular club in mind?" Oliver inquired.

Adam had a feeling Eva would mention a club. He didn't care for them much and knew Paul felt the same way, but he was sure Eva would make the adventure fun. Normally, Oliver was more of a bar person, but he figured his motivation to go to a club was standing in a white dress.

It was now nighttime, and the air became brisker. While the others chatted, Adam glanced around and noticed a person who seemed out of place. He was in a navy-blue business suit with a fedora hat to match it. Even though they were in the nicer area of the city, he was still overdressed. He was by himself while standing in front of a shop, admiring the items inside; however, Adam noticed a couple of times that his eyes wandered in their direction. Adam directed his attention back to his friends, but was going to be mindful.

"Is everyone ready to have some fun?" Eva asked as she perked up. The rest of them smiled and nodded. "Excellent. Let's go." She then turned to Adam. "Would you please escort me?" She smiled as she moved closer to him.

"Of course," Adam replied. When he extended his arm, Eva wrapped her arm around the crook of his before they left. They strolled in front of Oliver and Paul as they continued down the sidewalk. Even though their destination wasn't nearby, it was a nice night for a walk.

"You look lovely tonight," Adam commented.

Eva smiled. "Why, thank you. You look dashing as always."

Adam smiled. "Thank you. I must admit, I am impressed with how well you've tolerated Oliver."

"Tolerated being the key word. I swear if he calls me 'luv' one more time," Eva said through her teeth.

Adam chuckled. "I think he says that to all the women. Now that I think of it, he may have called me that before."

Eva laughed as she leaned into Adam. "It helps that you are here. If not, I think I would have sent Oliver away. In a car…in a casket…one way or another, away."

"Tonight has been nice. It's been a while since I have allowed myself to just relax and have fun," Adam commented.

"I figured as much, hence the club," Eva replied.

"I'm sure that wasn't all for me. I know how much you enjoy dancing," Adam nicely countered.

"So I am a little selfish; shoot me," Eva said.

"It wouldn't do any good. You'd just come back to life," Adam joked. Eva burst out into laughter, which caused Adam to laugh as well. After about a fifteen-minute walk, they arrived at the club.

As they entered the club, Adam could see it hadn't changed much from the last time she took him there. It favored an upscale crowd, as some were dressed the same or more formally than themselves. However, people were also dressed more casually. The club was dark and vast, but the lighting was what made it match the vibe of the music, which was a version of techno. There were white lights scattered about, but other areas had red lighting, and one wall had various colors flashing against it. The dance floor filled most of the space and was contained within a metal railing. Outside this space, semi-private U-shaped couches lined the walls, and a bar was at the back of the building. The bar, the front entrance, and other select locations had a light fog floating around them.

Eva put her arm back around Adam's as the group snaked through the dancing crowd to a reserved couch halfway down the dance floor. While Adam was focused on not accidentally bumping into someone, Eva was smiling and had a slight dance movement to her walk. They eventually made it to the couch and ordered drinks. Eva removed her coat, and everyone sat down. Shortly after, the drinks arrived. No one spoke. They simply relaxed, enjoyed their drinks, and people-watched. Adam scanned the club a few times for the mystery man he had previously observed, and to his relief, he did not spot him.

"It's time to get out there, boys," Eva announced. Adam and Paul's eyes drifted away from Eva and the dance floor while Oliver's eyes lit up.

"Oh, come on. Live a little. I would go out there myself, but I want to spend my time dancing and not fending off random sleazy guys," Eva added.

"I'll be your plus one, luv," Oliver said as he extended his hand toward her. Adam and Paul looked at each other before their eyes refocused on Oliver and Eva, curious to see the outcome.

Eva grinned and gently took Oliver's hand. Oliver's smile grew until his face began to tense up. Adam noticed Eva's grip was tightening, but her facial expression never changed.

"There is no number of drinks that would ever make me say yes," Eva replied while she dangled her empty glass in front of Oliver. The grin never escaped her face. Oliver was able to slide his hand away from Eva's grasp and shook it for a moment once he did.

"Progress," Adam mouthed the word when Oliver looked at him, followed by a wink. Oliver mockingly smiled back at him.

"Well, you know where we'll be if you decide to join the fun," Eva said as she grabbed Adam's hand.

"We?" Adam asked as his brow crinkled. His question was answered by the tug that Eva gave him while she was sliding down the couch to get up.

"Have fun," Paul said with a crooked grin. Adam rolled his eyes as he followed Eva off the couch and to the center of the dance floor.

There, her body began to slowly flow to the music as a flirtatious smile formed. The people around them were dancing faster to the beat, but Eva's movements remained unchanged as she found the tempo within the tempo to dance to. Adam lightly bopped to the beat while Eva danced close to him. As always, Eva was able to convert something that wasn't enjoyable to Adam into something fun. Adam lost track of time while they both smiled and danced together. Eventually, Eva was ready to take a break, so Adam held her hand and escorted her back to the couch. When they were almost off the dance floor, Adam caught a glimpse of the stranger's fedora hat within a crowd on the other side of the club.

They reached the couch at the same time Paul and Oliver came back from the bar, each with a beer in their hand. After each of them slid back into their spots, Eva released a deep breath and smiled. "I haven't been dancing in years. It felt so good."

"It's good to have a fun night like this from time to time," Paul added.

"I hate to burst everyone's bubble, but the fun night is about to change," Adam said, but he maintained his smile.

"What do you mean?" Oliver asked.

"And if it's bad, then why are you smiling?" Paul inquired. Eva turned her head to mask her concerned expression while she looked at Adam. Paul and Oliver continued to smile even though it began to look fake.

"Because we are being watched," Adam replied.

"Bloody hell," Oliver huffed before he sipped his beer.

"Who?" Eva asked.

"I didn't recognize him. He is wearing a navy-blue suit with a fedora hat to match," Adam said while he kept his eyes on his friends.

"Immortal?" Paul asked.

"I presume so, but it was difficult to see if he had any markings," Adam responded.

"It wouldn't be the first time an immortal sent a mortal to gather intel before they made their presence known," Eva commented.

"I say we go over there and see what his intentions are," Oliver said as his smile disappeared.

"No. He would see us coming and vanish before we even got close to him. We need to be strategic about it," Paul said as he placed his hand on Oliver's shoulder to settle him down.

"We don't know if he wants all of us or just one, and it will look obvious if we all suddenly split up individually. I suggest we split up into pairs and see who he follows. Then, after we narrow it down, that pair splits up again, and then we will know for sure," Eva suggested.

"This has been a long, rollercoaster of a day," Adam commented while rubbing the bridge of his nose.

"My life was normal until I ran into you this morning," Oliver said before he took another swig from his bottle.

"You're the one who wanted to tag along," Adam said while he shrugged.

"Since we were already on the dance floor together, Adam and I will head to the bar. You two go toward the entrance and mingle with the large group of ladies I noticed when we first walked in. I'll leave my coat behind so we can return here in about ten minutes," Eva directed.

"Be safe, everyone," Adam said.

"Be safe," everyone else said in unison. Then, each of them slid back and proceeded accordingly to plan.

39

Eva and Adam strolled over to the bar, ordered a drink, and strategically stood in an area that would work to their advantage. After they received their drinks, they leaned against the bar and faced each other. As they sipped their drinks, they scanned the room for the stranger.

"Still having fun?" Adam asked.

"Always," Eva responded as her smile grew.

"I didn't know being stalked by an unknown person with ill intentions was considered fun to you," Adam remarked.

"It's like playing a mystery game. Who do you think he is after? My bet is Oliver. I'm sure he has irritated many people throughout his travels," Eva said. She then glanced in the direction that Paul and Oliver went.

"Bet or hope?" Adam asked as he raised one eyebrow.

"Either one works for me, and before you give me that look, it's not like he wouldn't have us three to assist him if needed," Eva defended.

"You would help Oliver?" Adam asked in amazement.

"Of course, I would. After I finished my drink," Eva said as she took a sip and looked away.

Adam laughed. "You're terrible."

Eva put her hand on his chest. "Yet you still can't get enough of me." She followed with a wink, which caused the two of them to laugh.

"Adam?" The voice from behind him made Adam gasp. His eyes widened while he froze in place. He felt as if the air had left the room because he not only recognized the person's voice, but it was someone he never expected to see again.

CHAPTER 5

Eva's smile left her as her hand moved from his chest to his shoulder and pulled him closer. Her brow crinkled while she stared into his eyes. She mouthed the words, "Who is it?" Adam didn't respond. He took a deep breath and slowly released it, which helped remove the elephant that he felt was sitting on his chest. His face relaxed before he turned around, regardless that his stomach was still in his throat.

"Kaylee," Adam calmly said.

She stood half a foot shorter than Adam, with bright blue eyes and light blond hair with loose curls that came to the upper part of her back. She wore a fitted black see-through T-shirt with patterns and a white tank top underneath it. Her pants were black with rips down her thighs, complemented by black, stylish boots. Her brow furrowed, and her eyes became glassy once Adam turned around. From experience, he knew she was hurt and angry...and for good reason.

Kaylee crossed her arms. "Well, it's nice to know you're still alive."

"I'm sorry, but I can explain everything," Adam said. Before he could continue, Eva placed her hand on his back and leaned in.

"The stranger is watching us," Eva whispered. He sighed. As much as Adam desperately wanted to talk to Kaylee, he knew the stranger had to be dealt with.

"Well?" Kaylee asked. She pursed her lips, and her face tensed.

"But I just can't do it right now," Adam responded.

Kaylee's eyes drifted over his shoulder to Eva before they returned to him. "Don't bother. I hate to ruin your date." Her eyes became glassier before she stormed off.

"Kaylee!" Adam called out, but she continued her way through the crowd.

"You're going to have to explain that to me later," Eva commented.

Adam began to follow her, but Eva stepped in front of him and placed her hand on his chest. "Don't," Eva calmly said.

"But I need to talk to her," Adam quickly said as his eyes tried to locate her within the crowded dance floor.

"If you care anything about her safety, then you won't pursue her," Eva added.

Adam's worried eyes returned to Eva. "Why?"

"Because the stranger has taken an interest in her and is slowly moving away from us. I think he is debating who he wants to follow," Eva explained.

Adam shook his head to focus. He needed to find a way to keep her safe. "We need to regain his attention."

"What do you suggest?" Eva quickly asked.

Adam rifled through his mind until finally, an idea popped into his head.

"Do you remember Paris?" Adam asked. Eva paused momentarily, then a smirk formed, and she nodded.

"She meant nothing to me!" Adam yelled.

"Oh, I bet she didn't. Like all the other girls!" Eva yelled back.

42

"You make it sound like there were so many others. It was just a dozen...or two, and it was when we first started dating. Why do you have to live in the past?" Adam loudly continued.

Eva scoffed. "You make me sick! I can't be around you right now!" She then stormed off toward their couch.

"Fine!" Adam screamed.

"Fine!" Eva screamed back.

Adam glanced around and realized he had the attention of the entire bar area, with multiple disgusted looks coming from the women nearby. On the contrary, the group of single men at the bar laughed while giving Adam the thumbs-up. As his eyes scanned the area, he noticed the stranger's attention had left Kaylee. Now, he was looking back and forth between him and Eva. He felt relieved that Kaylee was safe for the moment, but now he needed to find a way to determine who the stranger was after.

Adam lowered his head, put his hand on his forehead so it semi-shielded his eyes, and pretended to be embarrassed as he headed toward the restrooms behind the bar. He veered toward the exit right before he reached the restrooms. When he was close to the door, he glanced around and left the building when no one was looking.

From what he could see, the back of the club didn't have much. There were a couple of delivery vans parked, some empty crates, pallets along the wall, and a garbage dumpster on the opposite side of the door. The parking lot had enough space for about ten more cars, but it was vacant. The area was gated off with a chain link fence with barbed wire on top of it, and the sliding chain link gate had a lock on it.

He kept his head down and walked toward the furthest van before he turned around. Just as he thought, there was a camera above the door. It seemed to him that its coverage was more around the door than the entire lot, which made sense since there wasn't much of anything with value, and the lot was secured with a fence. He removed the hilt but didn't activate his sword. Instead, he lodged

43

it in his back pocket for easier access and then leaned sideways on the van. All he could do now was wait to see if the stranger followed him.

As he waited, his mind began to wander to Kaylee. The emotional wall he built to hold back his feelings toward her began to crumble as memories started to flow back. He felt horrible for how he had left things and could only imagine how she felt toward him. The thought was too petrifying to entertain as a knot formed in his stomach. Suddenly, the creek from the door regained his concentration as his eyes shifted toward the sound. It wasn't who he expected…it was Kaylee.

Adam's eyes widened. "What are you doing out here?"

"I saw you leave and decided that I wasn't going to let you off the hook that easily. The bigger question is, why are you out here?" Kaylee asked while approaching him.

Adam abruptly stood up and briskly walked toward her, his eyes scanning the area for the stranger. His mind flooded with various responses, but unfortunately, they were all lies. As desperate as he was to tell her the truth, he still felt he needed to shield her from his true nature. More importantly, he needed to get her far away from here, from himself, to keep her safe from the stranger.

"I needed to clear my head," Adam blurted out when he finally reached her.

"And you chose the back of the club instead of the front?" Kaylee inquired as she crossed her arms and furrowed her brow.

"It's quieter here," Adam quickly responded.

Kaylee slowly nodded. "Did your soul-searching include me?"

"Yes, it actually did," Adam softly responded.

"And…what did it reveal?" Kaylee asked while her brow eased.

"I would love to tell you, but not here," Adam replied.

"What?" Kaylee said while she crinkled her face and took a step back. Adam knew she wouldn't like his response, but he had no choice. It pained him to utter those words to her, but every second they stood there increased the chance of the stranger finding them.

His mind scrambled for a reason to tell her. "Yeah, I'd rather we go somewhere else. Somewhere…quiet where we can sit down and really talk. Not in the middle of a lot." Kaylee sighed and rolled her eyes. Before Adam could continue, he was startled by a loud sound off to his right. Kaylee and Adam's heads whipped in the direction of the sound. He saw the stranger tuck something inside his suit jacket, with the broken video camera dangling above him. To Adam's dismay, the stranger had found him.

Adam turned his head to Kaylee, whose brow lowered as her mouth slightly opened. He had no time to settle her confusion. "Let me do the talking," Adam quickly whispered.

Kaylee shook her head. "Is this the real reason you were out here? It wasn't about me, was it? No, you had to meet whoever this guy is. Who is he? Drug dealer, mobster, or let me guess, a buyer interested in one of your antiques?" Kaylee loudly whispered while she glared at Adam.

Adam sighed. "At this moment, I would prefer any one of those options." Kaylee's head tilted as her brow crinkled. Adam turned around and put his hands on her shoulders, which made her cringe. "Please. I know you don't like me now, and you have no reason to listen to me, but if there is just the slightest ounce within you that still trusts me, please follow my lead and allow me to handle this. I will explain what I can later. Please," Adam quietly whispered while he stared into her eyes. Kaylee sighed and nodded. With that, Adam turned back around and stepped in front of Kaylee.

The tall, slender man with an olive complexion strolled toward him with his hands in his pants pockets. The stranger observed the area as he continued and stopped about twenty feet from Adam. He glanced at Kaylee behind him before returning his attention to Adam.

"James," the man said as he grinned and tipped his hat. When he did, his sleeve came down just far enough for Adam to see an immortal marking.

"Adam," he said as he slightly nodded.

"It's a nice night out, isn't it?" James commented as his eyes scanned around.

"It was," Adam said with a deadpan expression.

"Well, that's not fair. You don't even know what my intentions are," James politely countered.

Adam sighed. "From my experience, when someone like us waits for you to be alone before they approach you, it tends to end with only one person leaving the encounter."

James's smile grew slightly. "Technically, you are not alone, but I see your point, and it is valid."

"What is it that you want?" Adam sternly asked.

"Where are my manners? May I ask what your name is?" James smiled as he leaned to his side to see behind Adam.

"Her name is no concern to you," Adam coldly responded.

"Kaylee," she loudly said as she stormed to the side of Adam.

"Pleased to make your acquaintance, Kaylee," James said. His smile grew as he tipped his hat toward her.

"What is going on here?" Kaylee demanded.

James's brow lowered as his smile disappeared. Then, a few seconds later, a grin slowly appeared before he turned his attention to Adam. "You said 'people like us' earlier. As in you and me. She is not like us, is she?"

"No, she is not, and as you know, our encounters are not for public display," Adam replied as he stepped forward.

James scoffed with amusement. "Even better, she has no idea what you are."

"Don't talk like I'm not here! I want answers! Starting with what you said earlier, 'not like us'…what do you mean? What is going on here?" Kaylee loudly asked while her eyes bounced between James and Adam.

"Please," Adam said as he stared at Kaylee. She huffed before she looked away.

"Listen. I am simply looking to gather some intel for my employer. Once I have what I need, everyone can walk away. No fuss…no violence," James explained. Adam could only imagine Kaylee's facial expression after that comment.

"Who is your employer?" Adam inquired.

James's smile grew even bigger. "You wouldn't believe me even if I told you."

Adam's brow crinkled. "Okay…so what information do you need?"

James removed his hands from his pockets while he slowly circled Adam and Kaylee. "A stash of mythical weapons and items. All housed in one central location. My employer believes they are in the area, and since I discovered multiple of our kind loitering around here, that solidifies his theory." He had one hand on his hip while the other hand moved about while he talked.

"He wants the entire stash?" Adam asked. He was trying to gain as much information as possible before James caught on.

"Actually, just one particular item," James answered before he stopped walking.

"And that item is?" Adam inquired as his hands raised to waist height.

"He didn't reveal that information to me," James responded.

"Sounds like trust issues," Adam provoked while he grinned.

James's smile left his face. "Sounds more like you're stalling. Are you hoping your friends will come to your rescue?"

Adam smiled. "I don't need any help. From what I gather, you are young for our kind. How do I know this? Well, let me explain. Your clothes, while nice, indicate that you are still holding onto the era in which you grew up. You are also working for someone, which

47

leads me to believe that whoever the person is, who obviously must be a lot older than you, convinced you to do their dirty work. Finally, any of our kind with any form of experience would not approach one of us that they were not familiar with, alone. Especially, when they are unsure how much older and stronger that person is."

"Some styles just never grow old," James said as he smiled and ran his fingers along the front of his jacket. "I must ask…what made you think I was alone?" His eyes then drifted to the van.

Adam's brow rose as his head whipped around. He saw a man come around the other side of the van. In his hand was a scimitar. The curved steel weapon didn't seem to have any markings or odd additions, not even in the plain leather and steel hilt. If it was magical, he figured it must have been something minor. Regardless, he had to be mindful. It was already going to be difficult enough to protect her from James, but from two immortals, it would be much more troublesome. He now feared for Kaylee's safety.

"Garrett, at your service," the man announced as he mockingly bowed. Garrett was pale, short, and stout, with a red beard and messy red hair to match. Garrett wore faded blue jeans and a white tank top. His attire allowed Adam to notice he had a few immortal marks, but not many. He stopped within ten feet of them and stood there while he fidgeted. Adam noticed he kept squeezing the grip of his sword while he glared at him, as if he was hoping that James would permit him to attack.

"Both of you need to back off before I call the police!" Kaylee threatened while she pulled her phone out of her back pocket.

"Put the phone away," Adam directed as his eyes bounced between James and Garrett. He chose not to draw his weapon, hoping to defuse the situation.

"The man has a sword, and who knows what the other guy has," Kaylee countered, her voice trembling with fear.

"I would listen to the man, little girl," Garrett said while his hand caressed his blade. A sinister smile formed while he approached her. Kaylee looked at him with disgust while she held her phone.

"Trust me," Adam added as he took a few steps closer to her.

"I hope you know what you are doing," Kaylee commented before she put her phone back in her pocket.

"So, do you have the information I need, or do we need to try an alternative plan?" James inquired as he unbuttoned his jacket. He reached inside his jacket, and with both hands, he pulled out two dual-edged throwing axes. The handles were wrapped in brown leather, and the steel blades had etched zigzag lines throughout them. The blades indicated possible magic, but he wasn't sure to what extent. Especially since the axes were typically thrown rather than used in hand-to-hand combat.

"Adam," Kaylee muttered.

"It will be okay," Adam said without looking behind him.

"I don't know about that," Garrett said. Adam noted that he had stopped within striking distance of them.

"I have no idea what you are talking about," Adam lied. He wasn't about to give up Eva's home to whatever evil these men were up to.

James scoffed with amusement. "You see, the beauty of my plan is that your friends will eventually find you. I would wager that they are actively doing so as we speak. However, I want them to find us." Adam's brow crinkled. James grinned and continued. "You see, they will arrive to witness a dead mortal and their friend, who is injured and about to die. Desperate to save your life, I'm sure one of them will suddenly have the information I seek."

There was silence. Adam's face hardened with determination. He wasn't about to allow Kaylee to die or even be injured, especially if it was because she got dragged into his world. As for his secret, he wasn't sure if it was going to last much longer. While he awaited their next move, he noticed James's smile slowly go away as his eyes narrowed in on Adam.

"Oh, great," Adam muttered to himself. Then, from the corner of his eye, he saw Garrett raise his sword and begin to slash at Kaylee.

Adam quickly grabbed his sword and activated it as he extended his arm toward Kaylee. She screamed, closed her eyes, and raised her hands while she helplessly stood there. Her eyes slowly opened after she heard a clang. The greenish glow of his sword highlighted her face. Kaylee's jaw dropped, and her eyes widened at the sight of Garrett's sword, as well as Adam's spectral sword, a foot from her head. Her eyes slowly followed the spectral sword until they reached Adam's hardened face. Kaylee's expression remained the same as she looked at Adam, speechless.

"Stay behind me, and if you get a chance, get out of here," Adam directed. His muscles bulged before he swiped Garrett's sword away from her. He couldn't decipher what she said after that, but he couldn't worry about that now.

"I like using the weapon of the previous person I've killed, and I will admit, I can't wait to use yours," Garrett said as he steadied his sword.

"Sorry to disappoint you, but I don't plan on dying today," Adam replied as he smirked.

Adam stepped forward and swung his sword, which met the blade of Garrett's, but as soon as their swords collided, he felt a hot pain flow across his back. He yelled and reared up from whatever happened to him. Adam looked to his left and saw James standing with one of his axes pointed in his direction, covered with electrical currents. He was only able to look for a couple of seconds before his attention returned to Garrett, whose sword was bearing down on him. Adam raised his sword just in time to block his attack, but he was out of position, which caused his sword arm to be swatted away.

Garrett didn't waste any time and slashed Adam diagonally down across his chest and then laterally across his right thigh. Adam could hear Kaylee scream his name over his agonizing groans. As he dropped to one knee, Adam raised his sword vertically to block Garrett's next attack before it tore through his side. Aware that it was two against one, Adam glanced over in time to see James point both of his axes toward him and send another bolt in his direction. Luckily, he was able to roll out of the way. The bolt crashed into the side of the van and left a scorch mark close to where most of his first attack landed. Adam stood up but grimaced as he held his side, confused.

Garrett smiled. "Hurts, doesn't it? Take it from me, that stinging sensation won't go away any time soon."

Before Adam could respond, fear engulfed him when he saw James turn his attention to Kaylee as he directed one of his axes toward her. She was in the area since she had loosely shadowed him while he fought Garrett.

"Is that all you got, little boy?" Adam provoked, but with a purpose. Garrett's brow lowered, his lip curled, and his eyes narrowed as he glared at him.

Adam clenched his jaw, pushed back the pain he felt, and sprang forward. This caught Garrett off guard, so Adam was able to smack his blade off to his side and ram his shoulder into Garrett's midsection. The two crashed to the ground, but Adam kept his legs moving, scurried off Garrett, and ran toward James. He hoped Garrett was hot-tempered enough that his plan to humiliate him would work. Adam wished Kaylee would take this opportunity to take cover behind the van.

As Adam charged James, he was thankful that Garrett took the bait as he heard his footsteps behind him while he grunted. At the same time, James raised his brow as he redirected his axes toward Adam, which he also hoped would happen. He stayed the course as he continued to run toward James, his eyes fixed on the two axes with electrical currents flowing between the blades. As soon as the currents projected from his axes, Adam dove to the side. He could feel the heat of the electricity as it zipped by him and into Garrett. Unfortunately, Garrett was running at a different angle than him, so the bolts only hit his left shoulder.

He noticed Garrett was slightly dazed as he shuffled across the ground to pick up his sword. Adam wasted no time and quickly got up and charged at James. Adam was too close for James to fire off another bolt, so he readied his axes. James blocked the first couple of his attacks, but Adam could tell he was uncomfortable with melee combat.

Adam adjusted how he held his sword so that the blade was pointed downward. James swung his axe toward his ribs, but he was able to block the attack and then quickly slice James across his stomach. He grunted in pain, but before he could react further, Adam sent a strong front kick that landed on his chest. The force behind his kick sent James flying back into the second van.

He quickly turned around after he heard Garrett yelling as he charged him. Keeping the same sword position he had just used with James, he blocked Garrett's slash. With his entire body now defenseless, Adam went from blocking with his sword to thrusting it down into Garrett's thigh. When he screamed and looked down, Adam yanked his sword straight up, allowing the hilt to ram into Garrett's chin. As he stumbled back, Adam slashed Garrett across his chest.

"Now, we are even," Adam said and then winked. Garrett's face cringed with pain while his hand covered his chest.

"You're a dead man," Garrett snarled. Adam's plan worked since they were both fixated on him, but unfortunately, Kaylee never hid. Instead, she stayed in the vicinity. He saw the worry painted all over her face, but he wished she had hidden behind the van, or even better, escaped.

James and Garrett circled Adam. He raised his sword and did his best to ignore the pain he felt as he watched the two of them. Garrett swung first, followed by James. Adam deflected them both quickly as the onslaught continued. Adam dodged and deflected as they tried to get past his defenses. He knew he couldn't keep it up forever, just long enough for one of them to leave an opening for him to exploit. The problem was, they were attacking so quickly that all he could do was defend.

Adam raised his sword horizontally as James's axes slammed into it. James pushed with all his might as he attempted to overpower Adam. While this was going on, Garrett sent his sword barreling down on him. He reached up and grabbed Garrett's wrist, but now Garrett was also trying to overpower him. Adam's face strained as he struggled to hold back both of their attacks. His muscles bulged and his arms trembled as he dropped to one knee. Between the pain, exhaustion, and their power combined, he wasn't sure how much longer he could hold them off.

"Run!" Adam called out to Kaylee. Moments later, he heard a thump, followed by a grumble from Garrett, while he grimaced. Adam turned his head enough to see Kaylee standing behind Garrett with one of the loose wooden boards she must have found near the pile of pallets. The board also had random nails protruding from it. Without stopping his attack on Adam, Garrett sent a sidekick to Kaylee's stomach. She cried out as she stumbled to the ground.

"No!" Adam yelled. He then screamed again as he mustered all his strength and began to push their weapons away from him while he stood up. Unfortunately, it didn't last long. He clenched his teeth and tried to hold them off, but he could feel his strength leaving him as he dropped back to one knee.

"You're strong, but you're not that strong. Not enough to take on both of us," James said while he smiled.

Suddenly, James's brow lowered, and he looked to his left. At that moment, something hit James, and he stumbled back. Seconds later, the same thing happened to Garrett. That is when Adam noticed a golden bolt stuck in James's left side and Garrett's right shoulder.

Adam quickly looked toward the door and saw Paul. His arm was extended, his sleeve pulled up, and the wings of his crossbow extended on each side. He let out a sigh of relief as he smiled. Paul nodded and smiled back.

James loudly groaned as his face squinched when he pulled out the bolt and threw it away. "Remember, we need him alive if we are going to get any information from him." He then pivoted toward Paul and let out a stream of electricity toward him. Paul dove out of the way and quickly fired a couple of bolts in return, both striking the van where James took cover.

"I think I am way past letting you live," Garrett said as his face tightened when he pulled out the bolt and tossed it aside. Adam took a deep breath to steady his breathing and slowly stood to his feet. He still felt the pain from both of their attacks, but James's attack was beginning to subside. "Now, I want my trophy," Garrett added before he looked at Adam's sword.

"Come and get it," Adam responded before he raised his sword.

"With pleasure," Garrett replied and then attacked.

Their swords collided once more, over and over, as the two of them moved about the lot. Adam stayed on the defensive, looking for an opening, especially since the more they fought, the more he could tell that Garrett was inexperienced at wielding a scimitar. Garrett's sword was made for slashing, so whenever Garrett would thrust his sword at him, he easily deflected it and followed up with either an elbow or a fist to his face. Adam tried to send a quick sword strike afterward, but Garrett dodged each attempt. After the third time, Garrett fell for the same move, he screamed and charged Adam before he could swing his sword again.

Garrett's shoulder rammed into Adam's chest as he picked him up and carried him a handful of feet before slamming Adam into the side of the other van. While Adam was dazed, Garrett raised his sword, but Kaylee jumped on his back and started clawing at his eyes. Garrett stumbled back and, in one motion, grabbed Kaylee's shoulder, turned around, and flung her over his shoulder. She grunted when she landed on the ground, but scrambled to her feet.

"You stupid little girl," Garrett remarked. He then swung his sword at her. She defensively held her arms up, and his sword sliced her left forearm. She yelled and grabbed her arm while she took a few steps back.

Adam became enraged and screamed when he ran toward Garrett. He turned around just in time to defend himself against Adam's attack. Adam continued by holding his sword with two hands and slashing down at Garrett. His attacks were so powerful that Garrett almost lost his sword each time he blocked.

Knowing he had to control himself after his last strike, he quickly slashed up and cut Garrett across his chin. He then sent another powerful front kick that connected with Garrett's chest, but as he fell backward, a golden bolt emerged from his chest.

Adam's brow lowered, and his head tilted, confused. He looked over and noticed that Paul and James were in the same locations as before, but they had both stopped and looked toward Garrett, in shock. Garrett coughed up blood as he looked down and then slowly wobbled as he turned around to see Kaylee standing right behind him. Her hands were covered in blood as she stood there with her mouth open and horror in her eyes.

"Cassian will avenge me," Garrett gargled before he took a few more steps toward her and then crumbled to the ground.

"Another time," James announced. He then created a portal and escaped. After that, Paul sprinted toward Adam and Kaylee.

"What have I done?" Kaylee muttered. A tear ran down her cheek while she stared at Garrett's body.

"You defended yourself...all of us," Adam replied. Kaylee didn't respond. She only shook her head in disbelief. "You will be okay," Adam gently added as he approached her.

"No, no, it's not okay," Kaylee replied as she wept. She stepped back and raised her hand to signal she didn't want Adam to go near her. "I killed someone."

At that moment, Paul arrived, and all eyes were now on Garrett's body as his immortal markings began to emit a bluish light. Then, they started disappearing as they converged onto Garrett's original mark.

Adam's brow crinkled as he scanned his body. "I don't feel anything. Do you?"

Paul mirrored his reaction. "I don't feel anything either."

"Something is burning on the back of my shoulder," Kaylee cried out.

CHAPTER 6

Paul and Adam's jaws dropped. They looked at each other but were speechless. Kaylee twisted her head and reached behind her to see what was the cause of her pain, but she couldn't see or feel anything. She cried out in pain as the burning sensation continued.

"That's impossible," Adam muttered as his eyes reconnected with Kaylee's frightened eyes.

"What's happening to me?" Kaylee called out, looking back and forth between Paul and Adam.

Kaylee's eyes met with Adam's, but as much as he wanted to help her, she had to endure what was to come. "Just breathe through it," Adam softly said. Kaylee's brow lowered from the weight of confusion.

At that moment, the blue, flame-like glow encased Kaylee and Garrett, with the blue electrical beams connecting them. Kaylee clenched her jaw during the process and only screamed toward the end, right before the bluish flames disappeared. Kaylee stumbled a few steps forward before she stopped and took a few deep breaths.

"What just happened?" Eva called out from behind the gate. Oliver stood next to her, confused as well.

Adam deactivated his sword. "I honestly don't know."

"We need to get out of here. We have already pushed our luck as it is," Paul commented.

"What just happened to me?" Kaylee muttered.

"You're right," Adam responded. He then turned to Eva and Oliver. "We'll meet you back home after we clear the area."

"What just happened to me?" Kaylee repeated, but louder this time. Adam ignored her again. He felt bad, but time was not on their side, and they needed to leave.

"Okay. Hurry up," Eva shouted. Oliver quickly created a portal, and the two of them went through it.

"Clear your arrows, and then I will help you with the body," Adam instructed. Paul nodded and lifted his arm. A golden glow appeared on the wings' underside as he moved his arm slowly around the area. As he did, the arrows turned to dust.

"What just happened to..." Kaylee screamed, but she couldn't finish her sentence. Her eyes became fixated on the decayed corpse that used to be Garrett. "I killed someone...I killed someone." Her eyes roamed everywhere as she slowly backed up and began to hyperventilate.

Adam rushed to her, put his hands on her shoulders, and stared into her frightened, glassy eyes, as they frantically looked around. "Kaylee. Calm down before you pass out." He calmly insisted.

"Don't tell me to calm down! I just witnessed a medieval showdown that resulted in me taking a life. Then, some weird and painful light show happened to me, and I have no idea what any of this means! What is going on here? Why does he look like that?" Kaylee loudly asked as she shrugged Adam's hands off her.

Before Adam could say anything, Paul spoke. "It's time to dispose of the body."

Adam sighed. He wanted to console Kaylee; however, they needed to finish clearing the area before they could leave. "Okay, any ideas where?"

"I backpacked through a portion of the Congo over a decade ago. I say we drop him off there," Paul suggested.

"Works for me," Adam said as he quickly turned around and grabbed Garrett's legs while Paul created a portal.

"What's he doing?" Kaylee asked as she observed Paul's actions.

"He is creating a portal so that we can put Garrett's body in a place where no one will find it, at least for a long time," Adam answered.

"Oddly enough, not the strangest thing that has happened tonight. Why?" Kaylee asked.

"Too many unanswered questions for the authorities could lead to trouble," Adam replied. At that moment, the portal opened, and Paul turned around and grabbed the body under its shoulders. They counted to three before they tossed the body into the portal. Moments later, the portal closed.

Adam pivoted back to Kaylee. "We need to get out of here."

"How?" Kaylee cautiously asked as her brow lowered. She then saw Paul dangle the portal key behind Adam as he shrugged.

Her eyes darted back to Adam. "No! I am not going anywhere until I get some answers. I would call the police, but my phone was damaged when I was knocked down earlier! So, in that case, we will stay here until you explain everything to me! As far as I'm concerned, you're a stranger to me."

"I understand this is a shock to you, but you must trust me. I promise I will explain everything later, but we must leave now," Adam responded.

"I trusted you earlier, and what did that get me…killing somebody, so no! Answers first!" Kaylee scolded before she flashed her bloody hands at him. She then crossed her arms and glared at Adam.

"Now is not the time to be stubborn. Please, just take my hand and follow me," Adam firmly replied. Kaylee didn't respond and continued to stand in defiance. Adam turned to Paul and nodded. He nodded back and began to make a portal.

Adam huffed. "Fine, you want answers?"

"Yes, I do," Kaylee firmly responded.

"Okay, you will have your answers. On the other side of that portal," Adam replied. He then quickly put her over his shoulder and ran toward the portal.

"Adam, stop!" Kaylee demanded as she pounded on his back.

He didn't listen and raced toward the portal. His action wasn't ideal, but he felt that there was no other choice. When he got close to the portal, Paul turned, grabbed Garrett's sword, and entered it, with Adam and Kaylee close behind him.

They emerged onto the grass near the circular driveway at Eva's manor. Adam quickly put Kaylee down and took a few steps away. He felt dizzy, as if he had just spun in circles for hours. He tried to fight it, but he was so nauseous that he bent over, put his hands on his knees, and vomited bile. Once that was out of his system, he spit twice before he shook his head to rid himself of the dizziness. Soon after, he felt better…minus the embarrassment and frustration.

"Bloody hell mate, I knew you said you still would get portal sickness, but I thought it had at least improved some," Oliver remarked while he smiled.

Adam let out a long exhale. "Nope, still just as annoying and unpleasant as before."

"Where am I?" Kaylee inquired while her eyes roamed around the property.

"This is my home…our home," Eva responded from behind her. She smiled softly at Kaylee while she gestured at the rest of the group.

"It's also where you'll find the answers you seek," Adam added.

"Okay, I'm listening," Kaylee said with a deadpan expression.

"Sure, let's go inside and talk," Adam said as he turned around.

"No, now! I have done everything you have asked. To add to this horrible, insane night, I've been kidnapped and brought through a portal to a stranger's house. I cannot handle any more unanswered questions, especially after everything that just transpired." Adam turned around but didn't say anything as his mind searched for where to begin. "What are you?" Kaylee asked as she put her hands on her hips.

Adam glanced around at everyone else. There was no response except for Eva, who slightly nodded her head. He sighed before his eyes met with Kaylee's. "I...we, are immortal."

Kaylee scoffed. "Really? I'm supposed to believe that you and your friends are a bunch of immortals? I know I saw some crazy stuff back there, but this...come on now. Be serious."

"When he said we, he wasn't just referring to us," Paul commented.

Kaylee chuckled in disbelief. "What, me too? I'm immortal. I think I would know if I was." She looked back at Adam, but his gentle expression did not change. Her smile left her as her brow lowered. "You're serious, aren't you?"

"You saw everything that happened back there, especially what happened after you killed Garrett," Adam calmly said as he walked toward her.

"Yeah, but still. Immortal...you must be mistaken," Kaylee replied.

Adam sighed and pointed at her arm. "Your wound is fully healed, is it not?"

Kaylee lifted her arm, and as she inspected it, her eyes widened. It was stained with blood, but the laceration was fully healed. "I don't understand."

"You will. We all will, together...inside," Adam said with a reassuring smile. He then gestured for her to walk with him toward the house. She nodded while her hand rubbed where the cut used to be.

61

"Hey! I was starting to wonder where everyone was. Did you run into any immortal…" Caleb stopped speaking. His eyes narrowed when he saw Adam and Paul's blood-stained clothes that were also cut and burned. His brow then raised at the sight of Kaylee.

"Immortal action…yeah, that would be an understatement," Adam remarked.

"Caleb, please lead them toward the kitchen and put on a pot of coffee," Eva instructed.

"Sure thing," Caleb responded. The group followed him inside and down numerous hallways until they reached the kitchen.

As they walked in silence, Adam noticed Kaylee taking in her surroundings. He had so many questions running through his mind, but he also knew Kaylee must have had just as many, if not more. If she truly didn't know she was immortal, then he could only imagine how scared and confused she was. It was something he hoped to remedy tonight, and it took all his strength not to hold her hand or hug her to help put her at ease. However, between how she acted toward him, how things were left all those years ago, and the time they spent apart since he left, he didn't know where he stood with her. He presumed nowhere close to how they used to be. The guilt from those thoughts alone made him zone out. It wasn't until Caleb nudged Adam that he snapped out of it.

"Do you want any coffee?" Caleb asked.

"Sorry. Yes, please. It's been a long day," Adam responded.

"I can imagine. You started by battling Drustan. Then, after you won, you drove all the way here, caught up with us, trained, went for a night out on the town, and then had to deal with whatever happened tonight," Caleb rehashed.

"Yep…just your typical day," Adam sarcastically remarked.

Caleb scoffed. "How are you still awake?"

"Your guess is as good as mine. I'm sure I won't be awake once the adrenaline wears off," Adam joked.

Caleb's brow raised as he let out a long exhale. "I'll make yours extra strong."

Adam grinned and patted him on his arm. "Thank you."

They pulled the wooden chairs from the large oak table and sat down while Caleb handed them their coffee. Eva and Oliver sat at each end of the table while Caleb and Paul sat beside each other. Kaylee and Adam were on the opposite side of them. After a few sips, Caleb spoke.

"So, what happened?"

"Before we get to that, I think Kaylee deserves the right to ask whatever she wants to know," Adam interjected. Caleb nodded and sipped his coffee.

"How did this happen to me?" Kaylee muttered while she stared at her coffee.

No one spoke up, for they all knew how it happened. Adam glanced over to Eva, who kindly gestured toward Kaylee. He sighed and turned his head to Kaylee. "Did something terrible happen after I left?"

A tear ran down her cheek while she pressed her lips firmly together. She began to talk but became choked up and briefly paused to regain her composure. She let out a long exhale and wiped her cheek, but her eyes never left her coffee. "Um…well, about eight months ago, I was driving to the grocery store, and apparently elsewhere, a guy mugged a woman at gunpoint. The cops were chasing him on foot and as he darted across the street…" Kaylee became choked up again.

"You accidentally hit the guy with your car," Paul added.

Kaylee cleared her throat. "No, I didn't hit him. I hit the elderly lady he ran into as he looked back to see where the cops were. The impact sent her flying forward and into the path of my car." Kaylee paused again as more tears escaped her eyes. "I can still hear her scream and the sound of the impact when I hit her." She wiped the tears from her face and, with unsteady hands, sipped her coffee.

63

Adam carefully laid his hand on her shoulder, but removed it when she cringed. He desperately wanted to take the pain away from her, or at the very least dull it, but there was nothing he could do. He hated that feeling.

"The courts ruled it an unavoidable accident, but that didn't make me feel any better. I moved here shortly after, since everything there reminded me of that terrible day," Kaylee added.

The rest of the group glanced at each other before Adam spoke. "That terrible day is when you became immortal."

"That explains the mark," Kaylee softly said as she stared into the distance. Her fingers gently rubbed her heart as she did.

"The first mark always appears over your heart when you trigger the curse," Eva commented.

"Curse?" Kaylee questioned as her attention was diverted to Eva.

"Wait, what ran through your mind when that mark painfully appeared across your heart?" Oliver inquired.

"At first, I thought it was from the seatbelt strap, and after that, my mind was occupied by the lady I just killed. Afterward, when I finally saw it, I didn't know what to think. I checked the internet, but I couldn't find the mark or anything related to it. I tried to talk to my friends about it, but they couldn't see the mark. I thought I was losing my mind due to the heavy guilt I felt," Kaylee said as her eyes drifted down.

"Only immortals can see the markings," Adam added as he lifted his shirt to his chest. Kaylee's eyes widened as she scanned his body.

"There are so many. They were there the entire time we knew each other?" Kaylee inquired.

Adam slowly nodded his head. Then, Eva pulled up the side of her shirt, Paul rolled up his sleeve, Oliver pulled his shirt past his stomach, and Caleb pulled his shirt down to reveal the one over his heart. Kaylee's eyes bounced from person to person as they showed some of their markings.

Kaylee gawked until she shook her head. "At least I'm not insane. So, what about this curse?"

Caleb cleared his throat as everyone fixed their shirts. "From my research, the curse originally started with six, how should I say, unpopular people, but it didn't end with them. Their immediate and distant family members were cursed as well, including all their descendants. The curse is indefinite, but is only triggered once that person kills someone. If they don't kill anybody, then they live a normal life. If they do kill someone, accident or not, then the curse is triggered, and they become immortal."

"Good to know, but why is immortality a curse?" Kaylee asked.

"On one end, you cannot die unless you are killed with a magical weapon. Wounds from non-magical weapons heal quickly, whereas magical injuries that aren't mortal wounds do heal, but take longer. You also can never get sick or grow old," Caleb responded.

"Struggling to see the negatives here," Kaylee remarked while she shrugged and grinned. "So, I stay youthful while not worrying about dying or even getting sick…ever. Think of everything I can accomplish without the burden of time stalking me. I will be able to see and experience so many things. Is the negative side the fighting that goes on? Like, what just happened a while ago?"

"There's that. The more immortals you kill, the more powerful you become, which some immortals crave. However, there is more," Eva replied.

She then took a deep breath and gazed upon Kaylee with sympathetic eyes. "You are doomed to continuously watch your mortal family, friends, and loved ones die. Even worse, you can't stay with them the entire time because they will notice that you never age. Sometimes, you may even have to pretend that you died so they will stop trying to see you. That means, in the short amount of time you spend with them, part of your mind will be thinking of that. You will also worry if another immortal will use them as a pawn or harm them. It makes it difficult to be close to anyone except another immortal, and that isn't a safe bet either. You may be close friends with another immortal for centuries, just for them to be killed in the blink of an eye. Losing someone, regardless of whether they are immortal or not, is tough, and time doesn't heal all wounds. It only teaches you how to cope with their loss, but the pain doesn't fade."

"Once the fun of exploring the world and experiencing new things wears off, it can be a lonely and emotionally straining existence," Paul added.

"Unless you find creative ways to keep your immortal life from being such a bore," Oliver commented, followed by a wink. Kaylee's grin vanished, and her eyes drifted to the table. She remained silent while she took in what everybody had just mentioned.

"There is something else. Another negative aspect," Adam mentioned. Kaylee turned her head toward him, awaiting his response. Adam went to continue, but the words were too painful to say.

"What is it? What are you afraid to tell me?" Kaylee asked as her eyes narrowed. Adam fumbled around with his words but couldn't formulate a sentence. He knew the news would devastate her.

"Just say it," Kaylee pleaded while she fidgeted in her chair. She put her coffee mug on the table and stared at Adam.

Adam slowly breathed in as he gathered the courage to deliver the bad news. After he slowly exhaled, he finally spoke. "Immortals...can't have children."

CHAPTER 7

Kaylee's eyes widened, and her jaw dropped. "Are you sure? I mean, how else would people become immortal today if it weren't for the ones before them being able to bear children? How else are descendants made? I presume they don't magically appear."

"They don't. The descendants are from a dwindling population of people who carry the curse but have never killed someone," Caleb answered, but with his eyes diverted from Kaylee.

"Yeah, even though the curse is indefinite, I actually thought there were no more new immortals until tonight," Paul added.

"I'm sorry. I know how much that meant to you," Adam commented.

Kaylee looked at him with tear-filled eyes as her lips quivered. "I need some air." Before anyone could say anything, she quickly stood up and left the room. Adam scooted his chair back to go after her before Eva interjected. "I will talk to her."

"Are you sure?" Adam asked.

"I think she needs to talk to a woman who has gone through the exact same thing as her. Besides, no offense, she doesn't seem too fond of you," Eva explained. Adam nodded his head and repositioned his chair back to the table. As much as he wanted to chase after

Kaylee, Eva was the better option. She gently rubbed his shoulder while she walked past him and out of the room.

"What did you do to ruffle her feathers?" Oliver inquired as he smiled.

"It's a long story. One that I am sure everyone will hear at some point tomorrow. For now, I think I've had enough fun for one day, so I am going to bed," Adam replied as he stood up.

"Before you go, what about the sword that Paul brought in? Do any of you have an idea what makes it magical?" Caleb inquired as he looked at it lying next to Paul's feet.

"All that I know is that when Garrett sliced me with it, I felt a stinging sensation. Something above and beyond the normal pain." Adam explained.

"Was it poisoned or something?" Caleb asked.

"No, I am fine, and everything has healed. If anything, it may have taken slightly longer to heal, but that was it," Adam replied.

"May I?" Caleb asked as he pointed to the sword.

"Sure. Have fun with it," Adam said. He smiled since Caleb looked like a kid who had received a present.

"Thanks! I will record it and set it in our inventory. You will have to tell me more about that night so I can add it to the chronicles," Caleb responded as he picked up the sword.

"Of course, but tomorrow. For now, I can leave you with a teaser…there was another immortal there with twin throwing axes that shot lightning. Paul can fill you in, but as for me, I am off to bed," Adam added.

"Goodnight," Caleb said, and immediately turned and looked at Paul.

"Goodnight," Adam responded. He looked at Paul and Oliver, who both gave him a nod. He reciprocated before he headed to his room.

By the time he reached his room, the exhaustion finally hit him. He changed his clothes even though he was still dirty, but he at least washed the dried blood off his arms, hands, and face before he collapsed into bed. His mind didn't dwell too long on what Eva and Kaylee were talking about or how Kaylee was doing. He couldn't. Adam was physically and mentally drained and fell asleep quickly.

Adam woke up the next morning to the abundant sunlight in his room. He sat up, stretched, and then rubbed his eyes. Once his eyes refocused, he became startled by Eva sitting in the same chair as Oliver the previous day.

"I really have to start closing that door," Adam mumbled before he sat further up in the bed.

"Good afternoon, sunshine," Eva said as she smiled. Adam's brow lowered before he turned to look at the clock. He noticed it was just past noon.

Adam's brow lowered. "You're in a good mood."

"Why shouldn't I be? We have a new member of this household," Eva proudly responded.

"You convinced Kaylee to stay?" Adam asked.

Eva stood up. "That's right. We had a long talk last night. It took time, but she has come to terms with not being able to have kids and even her new life…at least she claims she has. Anyway, she is willing to stay here to learn from us and to have a safe place to live."

Adam got out of bed. "That's great. I'm glad you were able to help her."

Eva's eyes narrowed as she approached him. "What is it?"

Adam sighed. "I meant what I said. Really. I am happy you helped her, but I feel bad that…"

"That you weren't the one to do it," Eva added as she raised her brow.

"Is that selfish of me?" Adam asked.

"Not at all. It shows that you care about her, but it also shows something else. Fear." Adam's brow crinkled at Eva's comment.

"You're afraid she will hate you forever if you don't fix whatever you did. That's hard to deal with, and that fear is magnified since the two of you are immortal," Eva continued as she stepped within a couple of feet of him. Adam's head lowered before he nodded.

Eva gently put her fingers under his chin and slowly lifted his head until his eyes met hers. "What happened between you two?"

"It's a long story," Adam remarked as he walked a few steps away from her.

"Well, it's a good thing we're immortal," Eva commented.

Adam turned back around. "It was about ten years ago. I was eating at this local bagel shop in California, and once I was done with my food, I went to refill my coffee. As I was standing in line, this woman, Kaylee, turned the corner and rammed into me. Not only that, she spilled her coffee all over me." Adam paused when he saw Eva smile. "Their coffee was always served at the nice hot temperature of the Sun."

Eva giggled. "Sorry, sorry…go ahead."

"Anyway, after she apologized numerous times, we shared a table and talked for over an hour. At that time, she was a freshman in college for creative writing and graphic design. I told her I had just graduated from college with a degree in Fine Arts to help carry on the family legacy of dealing with antiquities. Afterward, we decided to go to a nearby boardwalk. There, we talked, played games, went on rides, and tried some of the more interesting fried foods we came across. We even got our pictures taken in one of those photo booths, which she didn't want to do at first. She said we didn't need evidence of the large coffee stain on my shirt. She added that pictures of her without makeup, hair pulled back, and mismatched clothes weren't needed. I convinced her that she already looked beautiful and with her smile, nobody would notice anything. She smiled and reluctantly agreed to take the pictures with me. We spent the rest of the day talking and enjoying the sunset before we parted ways. It was an amazing day. I haven't felt a connection like that for centuries, if ever."

"I presume you two became a couple soon after," Eva said as her smile grew.

"No, we didn't," Adam replied. Eva's brow crinkled, and her head tilted.

"We discussed it. It made sense. We spent a lot of time together, and our connection was great. However, we decided to hold off on dating and intimacy until after she graduated from college. She recently left a horrible relationship, and she wanted to focus on her studies, but she didn't want to lose what we had. So, we decided to keep going exactly how we were and to revisit the idea once she graduated. I was on board with it because I also didn't want to lose what we had, and it gave me time to decide what I would do next. Either stay with her and reveal my true nature, or find an excuse to leave and slowly phase her out. You know, to shield her from everything that comes with being with an immortal."

"Is that why she is mad at you? Because you decided to phase her out?" Eva asked.

"No. I was actually going to tell her about myself. We spent almost every day together throughout college and planned on starting a relationship the day after she graduated. I rehearsed the entire conversation in my head about what I would say to her. Even the part about me being unable to have kids, and the alternative ways to have children, like any other couple. I planned on telling her the day after her graduation because I didn't want to taint her special day if the conversation didn't go well. I remember feeling so nervous about that conversation. I could barely eat for days. I was more nervous about that talk than the other issue I had going on," Adam said before his eyes drifted away. Memories of what led up to her graduation began to fill him with sadness.

"What issue?" Eva cautiously asked.

Adam's eyes redirected to hers. "A couple of months before graduation, I had an immortal begin stalking me. His tactic was to mentally wear his prey down to the point that they do something stupid. Then, he capitalizes on their mistake and makes the kill. He had many weapons within his arsenal to carry this out. One of them was to hurt, or even kill, the loved ones of the immortal he stalked."

Eva's brow rose. "What happened?"

"Long story short, he found out about Kaylee and began stalking her, so I had to find ways to protect her around the clock. That immortal and I eventually fought on the day of her graduation, and even though I won, I felt as if I had lost," Adam said as he teared up. Eva frowned and held his hands.

"I realized something that day. If I brought Kaylee into my life, I would be subjecting someone I cared deeply for to a life of constant danger. As much as I wanted to be with her, I couldn't do that to Kaylee. So, I disappeared. No word, no trace. I knew she would be confused, hurt, and angry. It was one of the hardest things I ever had to do, but I had to do what was best for her," Adam explained as he wiped his eyes.

"I know that had to be hard for you, and you know I love you, right?" Eva gently asked. Adam nodded. Eva then slapped him hard on his shoulder. He grabbed his shoulder as his brow crinkled.

"How stupid are you?" Eva shouted and then slapped him again on his shoulder. Adam stood there, bewildered. "I would have thought that after so many years, men would get it. That they would finally understand women, but no! Apparently, even after hundreds of years, men still don't get it!" Eva exclaimed and then slapped him on his shoulder once again.

"Get what?" Adam asked as he raised his hands in defense.

"That you can't make a decision that involves the two of you. Especially something as serious as that. If you care, trust, and respect someone enough, you tell them what's going on and let them decide what to do. If she was willing to accept the risk, then that was her decision. Instead, you denied her that. I can only imagine what went through her head when you vanished." Eva stood firm in front of Adam while she glared at him.

"I…I didn't think about it like that," Adam responded as his eyes drifted off. He began to question all his motives that day. He then felt like there was a brick in his stomach from the realization of how bad a decision he must have made.

Eva approached Adam, stood on her toes, and kissed him on his cheek. "Now, shower, and then make things right with her."

Adam nodded and then glanced over his body. "Yeah, I was too tired last night to do that."

"That, and it doesn't help to have another girl's lipstick on you when you reconcile things with her," Eva teased before she left the room. Adam scoffed with amusement and then showered.

Once he was done and had changed into something casual, he left his room and searched for Kaylee. She wasn't inside, so Adam left the manor and walked around for a while before he found her on Caleb's bench. Her back was to him while she sat and stared off into the distance. As he walked, the butterflies in his stomach grew. He had so much to say to her, but ironically, he didn't know what to say or where to begin. Even more frightening, he wasn't sure how she would react once the conversation ended. He never imagined he would have the opportunity for a second chance with her, but would she even entertain it, he wondered.

"Hey," Adam softly said when he arrived at the bench.

"Hey," Kaylee replied.

"Do you mind if I sit?" Adam asked as he pointed to the opposite side of the bench as her. She nodded while she gestured for him to sit. He sat down but made sure he wasn't right next to her.

He glanced at her, and then his brow crinkled. "Those aren't your clothes from last night, and they can't be Eva's clothes. You're so much taller than her, it would be like wearing kids' clothing. Did you go shopping?"

A faint smile appeared. "No. After Eva and I worked out early this morning to help remove the restlessness that apparently can happen when you kill another immortal, she taught me how to create portals. That way, I could retrieve my stuff quicker and safer."

"To avoid other immortals, especially the one from last night, and the police until your identity is wiped from the government's systems," Adam commented.

"Yep. Standard new immortal procedures," Kaylee sarcastically remarked.

"I presume she was quite thorough with her teachings," Adam said.

"Definitely. She went over all the aspects of using a portal key. The design, the importance of visualizing where you are going, and everything in between. Eva even discussed the mechanics, like how it only works with immortal blood. No detail was missed, which is good. The more I know, the better," Kaylee replied.

"I agree. Knowledge is one of the key aspects of survival in our world. Change of subject…I'm surprised you found this bench. Caleb uses this bench often to write and ponder," Adam said as he turned his head and looked off into the distance.

"I ran into him earlier, and we ended up talking about how we both like to write, so he recommended this bench," Kaylee responded.

"He doesn't recommend his bench to just anyone, so you must have left a good impression," Adam said. He saw her slowly nod out of the corner of his eye. "He talked your ear off, didn't he?" Adam turned his head and smirked.

"Yeah. He is definitely a talker," Kaylee responded and then smiled.

Adam smiled. "He tends to do that, but he's a good kid."

"He seemed like one," Kaylee said as she turned her head toward Adam.

"I'm glad Eva could help you this morning," Adam commented.

"Me too. She is really easy to talk to," Kaylee added.

"Did you talk longer with her than Caleb?" Adam teased.

Kaylee grinned. "Believe it or not, yes. We focused more on the feelings running through my head about becoming immortal, especially a female immortal."

Adam's head lowered slightly, and his eyes drifted to the ground. His grin left him as he did. "I'm glad she could be there for you."

"It wasn't all immortal talk. We did talk about you as well," Kaylee added.

"I don't think I want to know how that conversation went," Adam remarked. His eyes were still focused on the ground.

"It wasn't a long conversation. She said that you would find me, so we could talk. She also mentioned that I should listen and try to work things out because, and I quote, 'his heart is usually in the right place even though his brain was stupid' end quote." Adam smiled. "Did she say something like that to you?"

Adam sat up straight and turned his attention back to Kaylee. "Yeah, something like that." He then rubbed and moved his arm around from where Eva had slapped him earlier. They both smiled, and then there was silence. A few moments later, Adam broke the silence. "I'm sorry." Kaylee's face became neutral, and she looked straight forward.

Adam swiveled his body to face her. "I'm sorry, and I am ready to explain myself and talk about whatever we need to discuss." The lump in his throat grew. He did a hard swallow to push back the anxiety of how the conversation would go.

Kaylee swiveled her body to face him. "I'm listening." Her face was deadpan.

"A couple of months before your graduation, an immortal confronted me. One with a reputation for finding ways to wear down his opponent before they fought. A popular tactic he used was to hurt or kill the people his opponent cared for. The nightmare started when he somehow found out about you. I noticed that he discovered your usual routes and places you went to, so I stayed with you as much as possible. Then, when I would leave your place, I didn't always go home. There were plenty of times that I actually staked out your place to make sure he wouldn't go after you once you were alone. I was so tired. I barely slept. I felt even worse when I had to lie about why I was not feeling well when you asked why I looked so worn down and distant. Then, you started to think it was because we decided to become a couple after graduation, and I reassured you that wasn't the case. Finally, on the day of your graduation, I noticed he was following you, so when he walked away after you went inside, I told you I had to grab something and that I would be right back. I left the building and followed him to a metro station, and once I had walked further down the tracks, he confronted me. Apparently, that was his plan. I was exhausted, and my mind was also preoccupied with your graduation. We fought, and even though I won, I felt as if I lost," Adam said as his eyes became glassy.

"Why?" Kaylee asked in a low tone. Her eyes then became glassy.

Adam paused to compose himself before he continued. "Because that was when I realized that I was being selfish for having you in my life. No matter how deeply I cared for you or how much joy you brought me, I couldn't risk your well-being. I don't know what I would have done if anything bad had happened to you. Your life outweighed my happiness, so I decided to leave."

"You didn't just leave…you vanished. With no explanation. Do you have any idea what that was like for me? The mental anguish that I went through for years after you left. Therapy didn't even scratch the surface of the walls I put around myself. All to protect myself from ever being hurt like that again. I basically withdrew from people for years, and even when I did interact with anyone, I was so guarded that no one wanted to be around me. Not only was I scared of being devastated again, but I felt as if I had no self-worth. Heck, I even blamed you for the death of that old woman that I killed because I wouldn't have still been living in the area. We were supposed to leave after graduation. For someone that I thought would never hurt me, you did…right down to the core. You should have talked to me first," Kaylee said with a broken voice as tears ran down her cheeks.

Before Adam could react, Kaylee continued. "Do you know what's even worse? After everything I just mentioned, I became excited when I saw you at the club. It was brief, but still. How pathetic is that?"

Adam wiped the tears that were already rolling down his face. "It's not pathetic, and I'm sorry. For all of it. All I wanted to do in that moment was protect you, and I did the exact opposite. I thought the pain I felt every day after that was just another part of the curse of immortality. I've lived for many centuries, and I could honestly say that the pain I felt when I walked away from you was one of the worst pains I've ever experienced. I have been stabbed, burned, crushed, shot, and so much more, but those pains paled in comparison to the loss of you. Today, I realized that wasn't the worst pain I had ever experienced. It's second to what you just described. I only did what I thought was best, and I realize that I was terribly wrong. I should have talked to you first, and we could have decided our fate together. Instead, I stole that right from you. I'm so sorry for all the pain I caused you."

The two sat on the bench for a few minutes, sniffling and not looking at each other, before Adam spoke again. "I came out here to give you the explanation you deserved, but also with the hopes that we could start over again. I already knew it would have been too much to ask for us to pick up where we had left off, but I hoped we could be friends again. But now…I can't imagine why you would want anything to do with me, and for good reason." Adam stood up and wiped the tears from his face. "I will leave you alone. No contact, nothing. I will even move out of the manor if need be, but I don't want to be a constant reminder of the pain I caused you. However, I will only do that if you want me to. I already made the worst mistake of my long life by deciding something that involved us without you. I don't want to do that again."

Kaylee sat for a moment before she stood up and wiped her face. "Your absence doesn't erase you from my memory. I tried to move on without you, but failed miserably. I understand your reasons, and I even forgive you, but it doesn't change what happened. With that said, I would like to start over. I don't know if we will ever reach the same level we were previously, but I am willing to try."

A smile formed on Adam's face. "Your kindness holds no bounds. Thank you. It's something that I don't deserve, but it's something that means the world to me."

Kaylee nodded. "So, how do we even start from the beginning?" After a few moments of awkward silence, Adam spoke up.

"Hi. My name is Adam. What's yours?" He said as he extended his hand.

Kaylee rolled her eyes. "Really. That's kind of lame." Adam didn't respond. He kept his hand extended and smiled. Kaylee sighed before a smile formed as she shook his hand. "Pleased to meet you. My name is Kaylee."

"The pleasure is all mine. Would you like to go get some coffee with me?" Adam asked.

"Sure. That sounds good," Kaylee said. They then proceeded back to the manor.

"I hope nothing happens to this shirt; it's brand new," Adam commented.

Kaylee chuckled. "It would be a shame if you got coffee on it."

CHAPTER 8

The two walked in silence for a minute, and as they did, Adam couldn't help but feel a swell of hope and positive energy within him. So much that he hoped she didn't notice the goofy smile he had because of it. To have Kaylee back in his life, in any capacity, was a breath of fresh air. It was like a terrible weight had been lifted. One that he didn't know the extent of until just now. Still, he hoped they would emotionally find their way back to where they were during college.

"So, tell me about yourself. The real you this time," Kaylee said as she raised her brow.

"Believe it or not, most of everything I told you was true. It's just some aspects had a slight exaggeration behind them," Adam responded with a crooked grin.

"Like how you were twenty-five," Kaylee mentioned.

"That would be one of them," Adam replied.

Kaylee stopped walking. "Wait, you mentioned something about centuries before. How old are you?"

"I was twenty-five when I became immortal, over five hundred years ago," Adam responded.

Kaylee's jaw dropped. "Wow, and I thought I was daring when I wanted to be with someone seven years older than me."

"The ironic thing is that now, from a mortal viewpoint, you are older than I," Adam teased.

Kaylee scoffed with amusement. "Great, I'm the cougar now." She then paused as her brow crinkled. "So, the stories you told me…the ones passed down from generation to generation, were your own?"

"It was my way of telling you about me without giving away too much," Adam said as he shrugged.

"I can only imagine the life…lives you lived. You will have to tell me about them sometime," Kaylee said.

"Of course, but it wasn't all glitz and glamour. Being immortal comes with the good and the bad. I may have traveled the world, met many great people, and experienced the rise of so many things…but I have also witnessed the worst humanity has to offer," Adam responded.

"Such is life," Kaylee countered. "Speaking of life, how do you support your lifestyle? Are you really in the family antiquity business?"

"Not so much. I occasionally sell artifacts I come across or weapons that are non-magical from time to time, but I like to diversify. Safe investments and other passive activities that generate income are always helpful. If you are creative, you can find other ways to build your wealth. For example, leave items that gain value in a will for your descendants to inherit, meaning yourself. That way, you have money in case you need it without the legal hassles or questions about your age. It's about finding opportunities when they present themselves. Look at Paul; his weapon fires bolts made of pure gold. When he needs money, he just fires off some of them, melts them down, and sells the bars."

Kaylee nodded her head as she took it all in. "Since we will all be living together, tell me about your friends here."

"There is a lot of history behind each of them…better told by them, but I can try to give you some insight," Adam responded.

"Fair enough. Go ahead," Kaylee said.

"Where to start? There's Paul. I've known him for a couple of centuries now. He's a straight-up, good man. He's about a century younger than me, but around my mortal age. He focuses mostly on his training and fighting skills. Mainly because of the life we live, but also because he almost died a couple of decades ago. Before that, he traveled the world. That was actually how we met. We were both in the same boat. I was headed to Greece, and the boat stopped to pick up a person off one of the neighboring small islands, which is where he discovered his crossbow. You can imagine the surprise on our faces. Two immortals on a tiny boat…one with a brand new weapon that he wasn't sure how to fully use yet."

"I bet that was nerve-racking," Kaylee commented.

"To say the least. At first, tensions were high. However, by the time we reached Greece, we were laughing about it. Because of his travels, I didn't see him much afterward. Just here and there as our paths crossed, and during those times, we embarked on an adventure together. Then, like I said, a couple of decades ago, he almost died. It was because he relied too much on his crossbow that he almost lost his head when another immortal was able to get within close range. Literally, the blade sliced his neck, but not deep enough to kill him. Paul managed to get a shot off and won, but since then, he has been mainly at Eva's manor, training to avoid something like that again."

"A couple of decades seems like a long time to train," Kaylee commented.

"I guess a near-death experience will do that to some people. Besides, he does leave the manor. It's just his travels have been more confined to this continent lately," Adam said.

"At least he isn't scared to leave the estate," Kaylee remarked.

Adam sighed. "And that leads me to Caleb."

"Oh no. What happened to him?" Kaylee asked.

"The opposite of Paul," Adam replied. Kaylee's brow crinkled. "Before you, Caleb was the youngest immortal we knew. We even figured he may have been the last one. He's only a little over a century old, and his mortal age is eighteen. I have known him for around seventy-five years, and during that time, he has become like a little brother to me. An excitable, energetic, and curious younger brother."

Kaylee smiled, but only briefly. "Wait, has he been here for seventy-five years?"

"Yep, and he has never left the grounds," Adam replied. Kaylee's brow rose. "You see, about five years after he became immortal, he had his first kill. The problem is that he is a pacifist. Caleb met another immortal not too long after he turned, and that person explained what being an immortal entailed. He thought he could live his new lifestyle, but after his first kill, he realized he could not. So, he tried to vanish by seeking out remote places to live. Unfortunately, that tactic only works for so long because, as time goes on, more and more people settle in those uncharted regions. He finally lucked out when Eva crossed his path. She offered him a home at her manor, and he has been there ever since. Caleb is at ease here. He has chronicled, researched, and cataloged everything regarding immortals and magical weapons. When he is not doing that, he is reading or playing video games."

"As long as he is happy and staying true to himself. I'm glad Eva found him," Kaylee said as the two continued their walk.

"Me too. Next is Oliver," Adam mentioned.

Kaylee scoffed. "We can maybe skip him. He seems too cocky for his own good."

Adam laughed. "That may be, but there is more to him. He is over eight hundred years old, which makes him the oldest one here. Few immortals are around his age or older, at least, that we are aware of. Mortal age-wise, he is a little older than I. When I entered the country formally known as Great Britain over three hundred years ago, I heard about a thief who was impossible to kill. One who would steal by using any means necessary. I investigated, and as you guessed, I ran into Oliver. We fought, and at one point, I had his back against a brick wall, but before I made my next move, something caught my attention. It was a small child…an orphan. Dirty and rags for clothes, the child's lips quivered as he stared at Oliver with his puppy-dog eyes. I immediately backed away from Oliver because no one, especially a child, needed to see an immortal fight. Oliver slowly took some bread from his jacket pocket, handed it to him, and told him it would be okay. The kid smiled and ran off."

"Let me guess, you spared his life," Kaylee remarked.

Adam chuckled to himself. "Yes, even though if Oliver told the story, he spared my life. Anyway, after a long talk with him, it seemed that he originally started off living a life of killing and taking what he wanted because that was how he was raised. He eventually wanted to change after he witnessed multiple acts of kindness over the centuries. So, he would steal from people he felt were 'not the best citizens' and give back to the children. Oliver never told them how he procured the items he gave them because he wanted them to grow up differently from him. As for the people he killed, he justified that the death of one had prevented the death of many."

"Well, I guess that's one way to start a friendship," Kaylee sarcastically said.

Adam scoffed with amusement. "Over the years, I feel like we have learned from each other. To be able to view things from various points of view. I don't know. I guess I'm one of the few who can see his goodness through all his other not-so-redeeming qualities."

"You must have excellent eyesight. So, that leaves Eva," Kaylee said.

"Yes, it does. We have a lot of history, and we are very close. She is like an older sister to me, even though she is a little younger than I in mortal years. However, she is about a hundred years older than me. We met when I traveled through Spain about a year after I became immortal. I had no idea what was happening to me, and I had no home to go to. I was alone, wandering. Then, I met her while working as a blacksmith at a neighboring village to hers. I noticed one of her immortal marks, so I asked her what it meant and showed her mine. That is when she took me in. Not only did she teach me what being an immortal was about and train me, but she also taught me how to survive. Not just survive, but to live. After about fifty years, we finally parted ways, but we made it a point to try to see each other often. As you already know, she likes to help people, especially other immortals. Hence, one of the reasons why she built this manor. Also, with the numerous changes an immortal can experience throughout their life, it's good to have something that remains a constant. This manor is that for not just her, but for all of us. That, and an excuse to see us as well."

Kaylee slowly nodded her head. "Yeah, she definitely seems like a good person. Selfless and generous to say the least. She is easy to talk to, and I could see myself being good friends with her." Kaylee went to say something else, but stopped.

"That's good, and to answer what you were about to ask, we were never a couple," Adam added.

Kaylee smiled. "Funny, that was one of the first things she told me."

Adam laughed. "I'm sure it was."

At this point, they arrived at the manor, but before Adam could reach for the door, Kaylee stepped in front of him. "Do you mind if I ask you something personal?"

"You can ask me anything you want to," Adam replied.

"How did you become immortal?" Kaylee cautiously inquired.

Adam looked away at first. He let out a long exhale before he spoke. "I killed a man trying to steal from my family's shop. He drew his dagger first and attacked me when I confronted him. I was unarmed, so when he came at me, I grabbed his arm and we struggled. I was able to get the blade from him, but when I pushed him away from me, he tripped and fell. His head smacked against the anvil that our shop used."

"I'm sorry," Kaylee said with sympathetic eyes.

"Thanks, but that wasn't even the worst part. The worst part was when my parents and siblings came in to see what the commotion was about." Adam paused and pressed his lips together to keep his composure. "They witnessed the mark form on my body and were convinced it was the sign of a greater evil at work, so they banished me. That night, I had to leave our little village in Italy with whatever I could carry and never come back…and as much as that devastated me, I honored their wishes. Heck, even I thought I was marked by evil, so the least I could do was stay away to protect them. Getting over that was one of the first things Eva helped me with." Adam's eyes welled up, but he quickly wiped them. "It's all in the past," Adam said with a fake smile.

Kaylee began to reach for his hand, but the door abruptly opened, which startled them both. "Sorry, didn't mean to frighten anyone, but we are meeting in the training room in just a bit," Paul announced and then held the door open. Kaylee and Adam nodded and followed him down to the training room.

Everyone else was already there when they entered the room. Oliver was browsing through the weapons on the racks while Eva and Caleb were talking inside the magical supply room. Once Eva noticed they had entered the room, she walked over to them.

"Glad you guys could make it. I'm sure all is well," Eva said as her playful stare lingered.

"Yes, it is," Kaylee replied. She fidgeted, looked the other way, and fixed her hair as she walked past Eva.

"Thank you," Adam mouthed when Eva looked back at him. She winked in return.

Eva cleared her throat. "To catch you both up, Paul described his fight with the other immortal and the bits and pieces he saw of you fighting as well. Oliver and I were searching for you, so by the time we arrived at the back of the club, we witnessed the tail end of

Kaylee receiving the mark." She stopped when she saw Kaylee partially raise her hand. "It's not school. You can just speak."

Kaylee shyly smiled. "Sorry, I didn't want to be rude. Those marks…is there anything else about them that I should know? You previously mentioned it's when I receive the other immortal's power, but is there anything else?"

"It's more than just receiving that immortal's power, luv. It's their power plus all the immortals they killed," Oliver said as he leaned against the wall. He then took out his coin and twirled it between his fingers.

"That's why all the marks turn blue and then converge on that immortal's original mark before it is transferred to you," Paul added.

"From my research, the victor not only gains power but at times can even take on the personality of the fallen immortal," Caleb eagerly said.

Kaylee's eyes widened. "Really?"

"It depends on how strong their personality traits are, how old and powerful, and so forth. Even if you do, it doesn't last long. Usually, you're good once you have a good workout and meditation session. Sometimes, maybe that plus time…one to three days before you are back to normal. The more experience you have with it, the easier it is," Adam explained.

"But the power stays with you. Strength, speed, agility, dexterity, and even knowledge of certain subjects. The immortal would have to be quite old and powerful for their personality to stick with you. At least, that's the rumor." Eva added.

"Depending on the age and power of the immortal will dictate how much of a difference you will feel afterward. For example, we presume the one you killed yesterday was on the younger, less powerful side. When I say powerful, I mean the number of marks they've acquired. Therefore, you won't feel as much of a difference in yourself as you would if the immortal were more powerful and older. Regardless, after last night, that kill enhanced you," Paul explained.

"I guess I know what you mean. It's hard to tell since that was the first immortal I killed, which still sounds weird to say out loud. Some things feel different, while others…not so much. I'm still processing it all. Still, it's too bad you can't pick where the mark goes," Kaylee teased as she rubbed behind her shoulder.

"Remember, luv, most immortals' fashion sense doesn't include the location of their newly acquired marks. They crave power, and that is their singular driving force to kill as many of us as they can," Oliver interjected.

"I didn't mean to mock it. I was just joking around about the mark," Kaylee countered.

Oliver smirked. "Joking around or not. You now have a permanent bullseye on your head. Even more, since in immortal years, you are just a baby. Some prefer the easy kills."

Kaylee sighed. "That's reassuring."

"I think we have gotten a little off-track here. Let's get back to the matter at hand…intel on those immortals," Eva announced.

"I guess I'm up," Adam said as he took a few steps forward. "James is the one with the axes, and Garrett was the one with the sword. I know I already described the sword, and Paul has described the axes. To add to anything else that Paul may have mentioned, they both seemed to be young immortals. James commented on a magical item his employer was looking for, but he didn't know what it was. He was aware of a location in the area that housed magical items and was adamant about finding it for his boss."

"Well, that gives me a sick feeling," Eva commented.

"Anything else?" Oliver asked.

"James was aware of the rest of us, but just of our existence. I don't think he knew anything personal or even where we lived. I had no idea Garrett was there until the last moment, so who knows how many people are working for this unknown boss," Adam replied.

"Or what this person wants with the magical item that we may or may not have," Paul added.

"Cassian," Kaylee softly said.

"What did you say?" Caleb inquired as his brow lowered.

"Cassian," Kaylee said louder. "Garrett mumbled his name before he died."

Caleb's brow raised as a smile appeared on his face. "No way!" The rest of the group's brows crinkled as they looked back and forth at each other.

"Should we know this person?" Eva asked.

"Not many do, but this guy is a legend," Caleb excitedly said as he quickly walked toward everybody.

"Some of us are not as well-read as you. Care to fill us in?" Adam asked as he grinned.

"Absolutely! He is one of the original mortals cursed with immortality, which makes him thousands of years old."

Kaylee's brow raised. "One of?"

"Exactly!" Caleb took a deep breath to steady himself before he began. "To go into detail from what I mentioned before…legend has it, there were six people, of great importance from the known providences, summoned to a central location. The temptation of riches beyond imagination was too much for them to resist. When they arrived, a warlock greeted them. He then went into detail about the violence each of them brought upon their lands. They didn't care, so when they demanded their riches, he cursed them. Each of the six has some legend attached to them, but I figured at this point either they perished or it was only a legend."

"Great. One of the most powerful immortals in the world wants something that I may or may not have," Eva huffed.

"Maybe we can have a civil conversation with him. Work something out," Paul commented.

"I doubt it," Caleb chimed in. "The stories say that after the six were cursed, Cassian wanted to redeem himself. So, he helped others as much as he could, including defending against evil, especially evil immortals."

"How exactly is that a bad thing?" Oliver asked.

"It wasn't until he turned his attention to evil immortals. After killing so many of them over thousands of years…it turned him." Caleb said as he trailed off.

CHAPTER 9

Kaylee's brow rose. "Turned him. Do you mean he became evil? Please tell me you are joking. That can really happen?" She stood up while her eyes bounced from one person to the next.

"It's plausible. If one kill can temporarily change an immortal, imagine killing hundreds of evil immortals over such a long span," Paul mentioned.

"That's a myth," Adam said as he folded his arms.

"So is Cassian, yet here he is," Caleb added. "And now, for as long as anyone could remember, he is as evil and powerful as they come. With that, his original motives have been twisted to less noble ones, to say the least."

"Is there a way to reverse it? Like, purge all the evil he took in?" Kaylee inquired.

"Theoretically, he could kill a bunch of good immortals," Oliver said with a crooked grin.

"Not funny," Kaylee quickly countered.

"He may be on to something," Caleb said as he rubbed his chin.

"Focus, people. We need to figure out what he is looking for," Adam said as his eyes drifted to the magical supply room.

"We also need to stand guard. Keep an eye on this place and each other. Who knows if he will find our home or continue to pursue any of us, but I'm not taking any chances," Eva voiced as her brow furrowed.

"We will do our best," Adam said as he approached her and placed his hand on her shoulder. Eva softly smiled and nodded.

"It's my home, too, so I am willing to help," Kaylee added. She then walked toward the magical supply room.

"What are you doing?" Eva asked.

"Getting a weapon," Kaylee responded.

"Whoa, whoa, whoa," the rest of the group said in unison.

"What?" Kaylee asked as she came to an abrupt stop.

"You can't just go in there," Caleb said as he rushed to the gate.

"Why not?" Kaylee asked.

"Well, for starters, luv, you could die," Oliver said as he grinned. Kaylee's brow crinkled.

"He isn't exaggerating," Adam added.

"How?" Kaylee inquired.

"Without the proper knowledge, so many things could happen. You could become injured or even die if you incorrectly activate a weapon. Not only that, you could grab the wrong object, handle too many of them at the same time, or even have the wrong combination of items and weapons. Any of those could cause harm, physically or mentally," Caleb explained with haste.

"Young immortals are more prone to these negative outcomes," Paul added.

"Okay, okay. I won't stroll into the supply room of horrors. So, how do I get a weapon?" Kaylee asked.

"First, I will train you. Luckily, your toned little body has been to the gym, so we have a baseline to start from, but to survive out there, you will need to push yourself," Eva instructed.

"Cardio is key to your survival," Oliver commented.

"It's true. If you run out of gas before your opponent, you're dead," Adam added.

"Good to know. So, working out more. Got it," Kaylee said.

"It's more than that. I will also train you on how to use all the weapons you see in this room. This will help determine which magical weapon you will inherit. Also, experience with multiple weapons will aid you in combat if you must use a weapon that isn't your primary," Eva explained.

"Depending on you and the weapons, sometimes you could carry more in case you need backup," Caleb said.

"Or, like with the battle I had with Drustan, I used his axe to kill him," Adam mentioned.

"True, but to be fair, I think anybody could use an axe. Don't get cocky over there," Oliver teased. Adam cut his eyes at him while Kaylee giggled.

"Fair enough. May I see what your weapons do?" Kaylee politely asked.

"You already saw mine in action. It's a spectral sword," Adam said as he activated it. Kaylee watched the greenish flames float around the sword. She even waved her hand behind the blade to see how much of her hand she could see. "I found it through my travels within an old crypt in France. It only works for the person it is designated to, and it is connected to my thoughts. The sword can only be used by someone else if its owner dies or if the owner transfers it of their own free will. In addition to that, the blade is rumored to be indestructible since it is from another realm."

"What are the markings on the sword? They almost seem like a language," Kaylee commented.

"That's because it is a language, or at least that's what Caleb and I think. The language is unknown to us. When I first activated the sword, I noticed the symbols changed, but never again until Caleb and I ran an experiment. I transferred the sword to him. Once he activated it, the symbols changed. He turned it on and off, and the symbols remained the same. However, when he transferred it back to me, the symbols reverted to what they were originally with me. Our theory…the symbols represent the owner's name," Adam explained.

"That's so interesting," Kaylee remarked. She paused for a few moments before she looked at Paul. "What about you?"

"Like Adam, you have seen my weapon in action as well," Paul said as he extended his arm. The wings then sprang open. "I found this on an island off the coast of Greece. Everything, including the bolts, is made of pure gold, and it operates on thoughts and commands. Also, it produces an infinite number of bolts. In addition to that, I can also command it to make the bolts crumble to dust. Here, consider this a welcome gift." Paul grabbed a bolt and tossed it to Kaylee. She flinched, but she still caught it.

"While you're feeling generous, you mind tossing one over to me, mate?" Oliver teased. Paul scoffed with amusement.

Kaylee laughed. "Thank you." She then turned to Oliver. "What about you?"

"Show her the coin first," Caleb interjected with excitement.

"You mean this little trinket that I discovered during a stroll through a cemetery in Greece," Oliver said with a smug expression as he flashed the coin toward Kaylee.

Adam leaned toward Kaylee. "Stroll as in grave robbery."

"Where else will you find one of Charon's coins? Besides, someone else hid it there for safekeeping. It's not my fault they did a poor job of hiding it," Oliver said with a crooked grin.

"Charon…the ferryman that carries souls across the River Styx to the underworld?" Kaylee asked.

"Impressive. Probably learned it from watching movies, but nevertheless, you are more than just looks." Oliver's comment made Kaylee roll her eyes. "Anyway, yes…the ferryman, who won't let you cross unless you pay him an obol. The term 'Charon's obol' was misused within texts because he didn't make the coin; he just received the coin as payment. The real Charon's obol is two obols fused together." He held up his coin for Kaylee to see. It was an old silver coin that was not perfectly round. Each side had a raised profile of a soldier's face wearing a helmet with a strip of fur running from the front to the back of the helmet. The coin was about the size of a quarter. "It is said that Charon crafted these coins to allow someone to come back from the underworld. Basically, payment for the ride there and the ride back, besides just a one-way trip."

"That looks so interesting. Can I see it?" Kaylee asked as she extended her hand and took a few steps toward Oliver. The rest of the group loudly cringed. Kaylee stopped. "What?"

Oliver performed a quick sleight-of-hand, and the coin was gone. "Sorry, luv, but no one other than myself will ever touch this coin."

"Some magical anti-theft defense?" Kaylee inquired.

"More like a child who doesn't want to share his toys," Eva commented.

"That's not fair," Adam retorted.

"You're right. I am sorry, Oliver," Eva said. Kaylee's brow crinkled at Eva's quick retraction.

"Thank you, Adam. I went through a lot to acquire this. The coin and I have a history that I currently prefer not to discuss. I will never part with it," Oliver solemnly responded.

"What does it do?" Kaylee asked.

"I thought it was obvious, but apparently not. Whoever has this coin on their person when they die will be brought back to life. However, it can't bring someone back to life who is already dead. The person must be in possession of the coin when they die for it to work, and it only works once," Oliver explained.

"An immortal needs an immortality coin?" Kaylee asked as her face crinkled.

"We are not as immortal as you think, especially when it comes to magical weapons," Oliver countered.

"Fair enough. Any other trinkets you'd like to share?" Kaylee inquired.

Oliver shrugged, pulled out his knife, and casually held it. The dual-sided steel blade was around six inches long, and the hilt was wrapped with brown leather, with burned cross marks scattered about. "A few hundred years ago, I killed an immortal and found this beauty in his backpack. At first, I didn't think I would like it, but if used properly, it's brilliant."

"I know I am new at this, but it must have been something special for you to want to use…that," Kaylee commented.

"Never judge a book by its cover," Oliver retaliated as he dangled the knife. "Adam, would you be so kind as to help me with a demonstration?"

Adam nodded, grabbed a mace, and strolled over to Oliver. He knew what the special ability was, but he could see she was intrigued, so he positioned himself so she could get a better view. He then noticed Oliver glance at Eva, who shot him back an intense stare. Oliver mouthed the words "I know," and Adam understood why. Fighting with magical weapons was prohibited in the training room. However, Adam knew Eva would be fine, provided Oliver didn't go on the offensive.

Oliver gripped his knife and held it in front of him. As he raised the knife, Adam lifted the mace over his head and swung it down, hard. However, the mace stopped within a foot of the knife. Adam's eyes glanced over to Kaylee, whose jaw had dropped.

"Without any thought or command, the knife will generate a small, invisible shield in front of itself whenever the person who wields it is attacked. However, it only works on melee attacks. It won't stop any projectiles. It's a good way to confuse your opponent or surprise them as you 'magically' punch their weapon aside and go in for the kill. Not only that, it absorbs the impact as well," Oliver explained before sheathing his knife.

"I can now see why you use it," Kaylee remarked.

"My turn," Eva announced and then flashed her bracelet.

"I meant to tell you earlier that I love your bracelet, but I didn't realize that was your weapon," Kaylee said.

"Thank you. It's like me, deadly and beautiful," Eva replied. Adam couldn't help but smile. Eva walked toward Kaylee and removed the bar between the two snake heads. Within the blink of an eye, the tiny bar became a six-foot double-bladed spear. The entire spear, including the blades on either end, was silver, and the central section of the spear was textured. Adam noticed Kaylee's eyes widen and remained that way as Eva twirled the spear around her body a few times before she stopped and held it in front of herself. He couldn't blame her reaction. He had seen Eva's spear countless times and found it impressive each time.

"Wow…there are no words to even describe how awesome that is," Kaylee remarked.

"Thank you again. I picked this up during my trek through China. It's made of pure silver but is much more durable. Each dual-edged blade is extremely sharp and never needs to be re-sharpened. It's as if once it reverts to bracelet form, it repairs itself. I can also control the length of the spear. It's in its longest form now, but I can make it shorter if I choose to," Eva explained. It then shrank to its original size before she placed it back into her bracelet.

"I guess that finally wraps up this show-and-tell," Oliver commented as he stood up.

"Wait, what about Caleb?" Kaylee asked. She then turned to him. "Adam mentioned to me that you don't like to fight, but I'm sure you must have some interesting magical item I could see."

"Really? You want to see it?" Caleb stuttered.

"Of course I do," Kaylee responded as she smiled.

Caleb smiled from ear to ear. "Great! Yeah, I got something cool I could show you." He then reached behind a table and grabbed his shield. Adam couldn't decide what made him happier. Caleb's reaction or Kaylee's kindness. He found himself staring at her, thinking about their past as he did. Eventually, she felt his stare and looked at him, so he swiftly turned his head. Now, he wondered if she had caught him staring.

"I'm from New York, but after I killed my first immortal, I left in search of remote places to live. However, there was a time when I did live with a Native American tribe. They allowed me to live among them only because I saved one of their children from a mountain lion. The tribe didn't truly accept me until I picked up this shield. I don't know how they came into possession of it, but they knew it held great power. They just couldn't figure out how to harness it. I held it, and in one of my attempts to make it work, it shot out a gust of wind. I became the tribe's protector, and for many years, I did that, and I really grew to love them. They seemed unbothered when I didn't age or if a wound healed itself. Once again, I learned the harsh reality of immortality when I couldn't protect them when they were attacked from all sides. I did my best to hold their attackers off, but I took a bullet to the head. When I woke up, the entire tribe was dead." Caleb stood in silence as his eyes drifted. Kaylee quickly stood up and put her hand on his shoulder.

"I'm sorry. I didn't mean to make you relive such a horrible memory."

"Just part of the curse that we all must live with," Caleb commented and then cleared his throat. Adam thought he heard a slight sniffle as well. "Anyway, afterward, I did some research and discovered a legend about a Viking's shield. It said it was used to make their boats go faster by blowing the wind into the sails. Also, the wind was used to repel invaders. With practice, I went from only generating strong winds to almost any type of speed. Check this out." Caleb grinned and held up the shield. A dark cloud formed and began to twirl on the face of the shield. A slight breeze projected off the shield, which caused Kaylee's hair to gently move. She smiled and closed her eyes.

97

"That feels nice," Kaylee remarked. Her eyes opened when she heard the scuffling of everyone else moving behind Caleb. "What?"

"It won't be a cool breeze for much longer, and there is no wind behind the shield," Adam said. Before Kaylee could respond, Adam could see her hair begin to whip around. She put her hands up and quickly stood to the side. He saw Caleb's smile grow as the wind became stronger and stronger. Caleb focused the wind toward a barren wall outside the room. The howling was almost too much to bear, and that was when Adam saw Kaylee put her hand in front of the shield. Her hand jolted back from the force of the wind. She rubbed her arm and shoulder because of it, but she seemed okay. Eva walked up from behind Caleb and whispered in his ear. He nodded, and the wind ceased.

"Wow, that was impressive. It suits you," Kaylee said.

"It's quite powerful," Adam added.

Caleb smiled and stood proudly. "Thanks!"

Eva patted Caleb on his arm and walked up to Kaylee. "All right. So, the plan is that you and I will begin your training tomorrow."

"No offense, but why are you training me? Is it the whole 'I'm a girl' thing?" Kaylee asked.

"It's because I'm the best warrior here," Eva countered. Oliver scoffed, which made Eva whip her head around to look at him. "Do you have something to say?"

Oliver sighed. "Nothing worth saying out loud."

"I feel we should develop a system to keep an eye out for intruders," Adam suggested.

"I agree. We'll take shifts. Until then, let's keep to the manor for now. No excursions unless it is absolutely necessary, and if so, no one goes alone," Eva instructed. Everyone but Oliver nodded in agreement.

"Great, now we are prisoners in our own home. How long will this grand idea last?" Oliver huffed.

"First off, this is not your home. I allow you to dwell here because of Adam. If you don't like my rules, you can leave and not come back. Second, this precaution will continue until I feel it's safe again. Am I clear?" Eva sternly asked.

Oliver's shoulders dropped. "Crystal."

CHAPTER 10

Over a month had passed, and Eva's plan was still in place; however, Adam could feel the group becoming more restless. Besides the weekly trip to a local town to gather food and supplies, no one left the estate. Therefore, they had to find ways to pass the time. Adam spent his time with Kaylee when she wasn't training. She was interested in hearing his stories from his past. This included the places he visited, the people he met, and even the truth behind any lies or half-truths he told her to keep his secret. Their time together was typically in the library at the back of the manor. Most of the time, no one was in there, and it had a comfortable couch.

At first, they would sit on opposite sides of the couch, and it felt awkward to Adam. To him, it felt like an interview the first few times, but after that, the atmosphere lightened. She lay back on the couch more and seemed more relaxed as she put her feet up by him. Her eyes would begin to light up during parts of his story, and they would even laugh together. Kaylee did share bits and pieces of the last ten years for her, but since a lot of it wasn't a fond memory, Adam didn't push.

One day, when Adam was walking from his room, Caleb jogged up to him. "Hey! Do you have a minute?"

"For you, always. What's up?" Adam responded.

"I combed through the magical inventory again, but this time I sectioned off an area for the unknown items. Regarding the items that I know about, I don't see any that are extraordinary. However, I will keep testing the ones I don't know about. At least I discovered what some of the previously unknown items now do," Caleb said.

"Good job!" Adam responded, which made Caleb smile. "Anything in the unknown pile that you feel has the potential to be something powerful?"

"Nothing that stands out. Heck, I'm not even sure if they are all magical," Caleb replied.

Adam slowly nodded as he paused to think. "Either there is a personal connection to the object, or it's something more powerful than any of us realize. What are the unknown items?"

"Let's see. There are a couple of silver rings, a golden Aztec amulet, a copper dagger with a wooden handle, spiked steel knuckles, a bronze goblet, and a few swords crafted out of bronze, iron, and steel...all with leather-wrapped hilts. Oh yeah, there's also a helmet from the Mongolian Empire. I would venture to say around the time of Genghis Khan. All those items have either symbols or some language inscribed on them," Caleb responded.

"That's an interesting collection on its own. I'll let you get back to the fun," Adam said with a half-smile, but as he began to walk away, Caleb grabbed his arm.

"Hey. Any luck with Kaylee?"

Adam shrugged. "Well, she's talking and being nice to me, so there's that."

"Any improvement is better than none," Caleb countered.

"Quite true," Adam said and then walked away.

He continued his way down the corridors. He planned to go outside and enjoy the weather, maybe even go for a leisurely jog.

Halfway there, Adam had to stop short when Oliver stepped in front of him.

"Sorry, mate," Oliver said as he continued to walk.

"No problem," Adam responded, but his eyes narrowed. "Wait, why are you dressed up and in a hurry?"

Oliver sighed as he came to a stop. "I'm headed out. I need to get out of here for a while and have some fun before I go insane."

"You know what Eva said," Adam countered.

"Yeah, I heard what the boss lady said, but I don't care. What is she going to do...despise me more?" Oliver replied with a smirk.

"I can think of worse," Adam commented.

"Are you going to tattle on me? Man, I remember a time when that stick was less up your butt," Oliver said as he took a few steps toward Adam.

"No, I will do what I typically do, cover for you," Adam responded.

Oliver gave him a hearty pat on his arm. "You always have my back. Do you care to join me?"

"Are you leaving already? It's not even noon," Adam commented.

"I can't wait. I'm going stir-crazy. So, are you coming? It would be good for you unless you prefer to mope around the manor, hoping Kaylee will come running to your arms." Oliver said.

"Am I that transparent?" Adam asked.

"You're so transparent that I can see the wall behind you," Oliver teased. Adam's shoulders dropped as he huffed and turned his head.

"What am I supposed to do? I am trying to give her space," Adam retorted.

"Space is a good thing, but too much space creates a distance that can be too far to travel back. Do something before she forgets about the Adam she once knew," Oliver suggested.

"Maybe you're right," Adam replied.

"I know I'm right. So, are you coming with me or not? It will loosen you up before you talk to her," Oliver mentioned.

"I'll take a rain check. Besides, I need to cover for you," Adam responded.

Oliver shrugged. "Suit yourself." He then turned and began to walk away.

"I don't have a stick up my butt," Adam called out.

"That's because it's so far up there that you can't even see it anymore," Oliver loudly said as he vanished into the other room. Adam chuckled at his comment.

Adam resumed walking down the hallway, but he didn't go outside. His new destination was the training room. He needed to think of a way to protect Oliver from Eva's wrath. If it were anyone else, Eva would be mad but understanding. For Oliver, he would be lucky if she only banished him from the manor. However, it was difficult for Adam to think of what to say when his mind wouldn't allow him to forget what Oliver had said.

His thoughts were constantly dueling with each other. Half his thoughts craved to be closer to Kaylee, while the other half was petrified that he would move too quickly and lose her. At the same time, Oliver had a point about too much distance. He struggled to figure out what he would say or even suggest that they do until his mind was derailed by the sound of cold, hard steel clanging together.

He leaned against the doorway and watched as Eva and Kaylee trained. Eva used a single-sided spear while Kaylee had a sleek short sword in each hand. It was the first time he had seen her train, and he was impressed. Her techniques were strong and controlled, and she didn't back down when Eva increased her efforts. Even when Eva managed to cut her. Kaylee's face remained determined as she fought back. He couldn't help but smile at how well she was doing.

It seemed Kaylee was using the sword in her left hand more as a shield while she attacked with the sword in her right hand, but she surprised Eva. When Eva attacked, besides using the sword in her

103

left hand to block, Kaylee ducked under her spear and used that sword to slice Eva's leg.

Eva winced but then smiled. "Congratulations! You finally were able to get past my defenses."

Kaylee smiled from ear to ear. "Thanks! I couldn't have done it without you."

Adam began to clap as he smiled. "You were amazing."

"Really?" Kaylee asked.

"Yes. Any immortal would be a fool to underestimate you," Adam replied. Kaylee smiled.

"I agree, but that doesn't mean you can slack off on your training. However, I feel you are ready to train on your own or with anyone else here." Eva added.

"I won't slack off. I promise," Kaylee responded.

"So, what brings you down here?" Eva inquired.

"There was something I wanted to discuss with you," Adam answered.

"I'll let the two of you be," Kaylee remarked. She then put the swords away.

"You don't have to leave," Adam quickly said.

"It's okay. I need to get something to drink, and I definitely need a shower. I'm all nasty," Kaylee responded.

"I don't think it's possible for you to look nasty," Adam commented. He internally kicked himself for letting that slip.

Kaylee blushed as she smiled and glanced away. "Thanks. Regardless, I need to shower." Adam moved to the side to allow her to leave the room before he entered. He noticed Eva smile as her brow raised.

"Not a word," Adam said.

"What?" Eva was coy with her response.

Adam sighed. "Anyway, I wanted to talk to you about maybe lifting the 'no one leaves the house' rule."

"Oh, really," Eva responded.

"Yes. It's been a month, and there hasn't been any unusual activity. I understand there may be a risk if we relax again, but we can't live in fear forever. Everyone is very mindful, so it's not like we are leaving caution to the wind," Adam explained.

Eva slowly nodded. "You make a valid point, but let me ask you just one question. When did Oliver leave?"

Adam nervously laughed. "What makes you think that Oliver left?" Eva stared at him with her hands on her hips. "Okay, I think he just left, but regardless...I do believe my request is valid."

Eva pressed her lips together and shook her head. "I swear, he thinks only of himself." Adam gazed at her with kind eyes. Eva sighed. "Fine, everything is back to normal."

"And Oliver can continue to stay here...alive?" Adam asked.

Eva rolled her eyes. "Yes."

Adam hugged and kissed her on the cheek. "Thanks! You're the best." He then proceeded to leave the room.

"Wait. I will agree...ouch," Eva winced and looked at her leg. Her brow lowered. "That's odd. The cut from where Kaylee got me hasn't fully healed. It's close, but still."

"Are you sure her weapon wasn't magical?" Adam inquired. His brow lowered as well, for Eva's cut should have been healed almost instantly.

"I'm certain. Caleb and I inspected all these weapons, and I have been here long enough to know what each weapon here looks like. Nothing is magical," Eva replied. Just then, her wound healed.

"Well, at least it healed. Maybe the cut was deeper than you thought?" Adam suggested.

"Maybe, but it healed, so I'm good. Just to be safe, I will also have Caleb triple-check the weapons in here. If you don't hear anything from me, then everything is normal. If he does find something, then you will know because you will hear Oliver screaming as I test out the weapon in question on him," Eva responded.

"You don't think he would have switched out the weapons, do you?" Adam asked.

"I wouldn't put it past him," Eva countered.

Adam shrugged. "So, you were going to say something?" He hoped his question would get her mind away from Oliver.

Eva paused as she looked upward. "Oh yeah, I remember. I will agree to everything you requested under one condition. You take Kaylee out on a date."

"I'm sorry, what?" Adam said, flabbergasted.

"You heard me," Eva said as she grinned.

"I don't know if she is ready for that. We are still taking things slow," Adam countered.

"It sounds like you are making decisions for her again," Eva commented.

"No. I'm just trying to respect her wishes," Adam defended.

"I get it, and that was very honorable of you to do. However, at some point, you must make your move or else you will lose the opportunity to grow your relationship," Eva responded.

Adam paused as he remembered Oliver saying something very similar. Eva continued to talk. "When I say 'take her on a date,' that could be anything. It doesn't have to be a grand gesture."

"You're right, and I've been thinking of how to progress in our relationship, but do you think she even likes me in that capacity anymore?" Adam said as his shoulders dropped while he looked away.

Eva walked up to him and waited until he looked her in the eyes. "Yes, I do, but her guard is up. Heck, her guard has a guard. You must remember that she has been through a lot. Not to add salt to the wound, but you, the closest person in her life, vanished. Also, after she lost you, she dealt with a lot of crap, including accidentally killing someone. Additionally, she discovered that she is immortal, along with the person who abandoned her. Then, when things couldn't get any worse, she learns she can't have children. All of this, while training to survive in a world where people want her dead, possibly including an ancient, evil immortal."

Adam remained speechless as his eyes once again drifted away from Eva. He knew Kaylee had been through a lot, but until Eva explained it, he didn't realize the magnitude. "I feel like I left her all over again. I shouldn't have given her so much space."

"You did the right thing, but only if that stops now. Listen, she is a tough person. She has handled everything that was thrown at her, but underneath all that armor, she's scared," Eva said.

"Of what?" Adam asked.

"You," Eva gently responded. Adam's brow crinkled. "She's afraid of getting her heart broken again by the same person. You need to make her believe, right down to her soul, that you will not purposely break her heart...her trust, again."

Adam frowned as his eyes lowered. Eva's comment pierced him right to his core. He felt disgusted with himself for how he had hurt Kaylee. "I understand, and you are right. Thank you. I will talk to her tomorrow," Adam responded as he hugged Eva again.

"Cheer up. Now you have the opportunity to make things right. To claim the happiness that you threw away all those years ago. Not only for you but for Kaylee. However, you need to talk to her today. Like, as soon as you leave this room," Eva said.

"At least give me a day to think of what to say and where to take her," Adam pleaded.

Eva smiled. "How about we duel? Best two out of three. The winner decides when you will approach Kaylee. Deal?"

Adam shook his head while he smiled. "Deal."

He grabbed the same short sword he used against Paul while Eva kept her spear. The two squared off, motionless...waiting to see who would make the first move. The corner of Eva's mouth curled. Adam smiled, and then Eva attacked. He went on the defense, blocking strikes from multiple angles. She twirled the spear around her effortlessly, and her strikes were strong enough to force Adam to use two hands, or else he would lose his sword. When the timing was right, he lunged forward when she was about to swing her spear. He grabbed the middle of the spear between her hands. Then, he hoisted the spear upwards and jabbed his sword forward. The tip of his blade was a couple of inches from her heart when it came to a stop.

"I thought you were the best warrior among us," Adam teased as he let go of her spear.

"Everyone occasionally gets lucky," Eva countered as she smirked. She then took an offensive stance with the spear resting on her forearm, which was raised to her chest. The blade was aimed at Adam. He gripped his sword with two hands and raised it above his head.

Besides thrusting the spear forward, she flicked the back of the spear forward like an uppercut. Adam swung down hard to deflect her attack. The impact echoed within the room, and he even felt the vibration in his hands. Once their weapons collided, she brought the blade soaring down at him. His eyes grew wide as he ducked and rolled out of the way. Adam stood up and went on the attack to throw her off guard. Their fury of strikes continued until Eva was close enough to Adam to sweep his legs with her foot. His back slammed against the ground, and before he could move, she had the tip of her spear at his throat.

"Still wondering who the best warrior is?" Eva playfully asked. Adam smiled and waited for her to move the spear before he got up.

"Next one wins," Adam commented as the two squared up. He truly hoped it would be him because the thought of asking Kaylee out today made him feel like he had butterflies in his stomach.

"Which will be me," Eva said.

"Don't be so sure," Adam responded.

"I am, and I will tell you why after I win," Eva countered. She then slowly walked toward Adam with the blunt end of the spear pointed at him. His brow crinkled, curious as to what her tactic was.

"I hope you are ready for that date tonight," Eva remarked. Adam's mind began to wander, but was jolted back to reality when Eva swung her spear at him.

He deflected her attack and was quick enough to get the tip of his blade within a handful of inches of her throat. "Do you mean tomorrow night?" Adam said with a smug expression.

Eva smiled. "No, I mean tonight." Her eyes glanced down, so he followed her eyes and noticed she had the blade of her spear right beneath his crotch. "I believe I won. Don't you agree?" Eva asked as she lifted the blade slightly further.

Adam tensed up and withdrew his sword. "I agree, I agree."

"I thought you would see it my way," Eva said and then winked. She then withdrew her blade.

"How did you know you would win? Just that confident?" Adam asked.

"No, because I could tell you forgot one of the basic things I taught you centuries ago. Stay out of your head. If you are in there, you are not in the present. The idea of taking her on a date had you distracted enough for me to slip effortlessly past your guard."

Adam scoffed. "You're right. I'll be more mindful in the future."

"I hope so. Now, your date tonight. You do whatever you feel is best. Remember, it doesn't have to be anything big. Just something that will loosen the two of you up so you'll both become more at ease with each other. Once you get past this date, the rest will fall into place," Eva explained.

Adam put his sword back. "Yep. It's just that simple." He then took a deep breath and shook his hands to rid himself of his nerves.

Eva chuckled. "Wow. Adam, the great immortal. The slayer of Drustan, trembling in fear over asking a girl out."

"I'd rather face a dozen Drustans right now versus chancing something going wrong with Kaylee and me again," Adam commented.

Eva raised one eyebrow. "I know there have been others in your past, but this one is different. I mean, I figured she was, but not to this extent. You really care for her, don't you?"

"More than I ever thought was possible," Adam responded.

"Aww," Eva loudly expressed.

Adam cringed. "Please, don't aww." He could now feel his cheeks becoming flushed.

Eva rested her hand on his shoulder, gazed upon him with sympathetic eyes, and smiled. "I'm happy for you. Just make sure she knows how much you care for her." Adam smiled and nodded.

Eva walked toward the weapons rack. "I will let Paul and Caleb know about the rule change, and you can tell Kaylee and Oliver. Also, when you see Oliver, tell him I want to see him. Make it seem like I am furious."

"I will, but I thought you wouldn't punish him?" Adam inquired.

"I won't, but I can make him scared for a while," Eva responded and then winked.

A devious smile formed on Adam's face. "Maybe Kaylee, you, me, and Oliver can all go on a double date."

Eva pointed the spear at him and glared. She paused before she spoke. "You're lucky you're cute." Adam laughed and left the room.

He didn't go straight to Kaylee's room because he figured she was still getting cleaned up, so he went outside and enjoyed the fresh air while he contemplated what to say to her. He paced back and forth as he thought, but unfortunately, his mind was blank, and he didn't want to ask her for suggestions. He preferred to present her with a few ideas so they could pick one together.

Adam racked his brain trying to think of an idea that wasn't too serious and over the top. Casual was the direction he wished to take. However, it was difficult to think of something that wasn't lame and that she would enjoy. He knew everything she liked during their time together, but he feared that his suggestions would be something she didn't care for anymore. That would make it more evident to her that they drifted apart further than they imagined.

"Hey. Earth to Adam. Are you okay?" Kaylee asked.

CHAPTER 11

Adam almost jumped out of his skin. He didn't hear the door open or her approach him. He felt foolish for his reaction and wished he had been more prepared. Adam quietly stood there for a moment before he finally found any words to say back to her.

He nervously laughed. "You scared me there."

Kaylee partially smiled. "Sorry. I said your name a couple of times before you finally heard me."

Adam fidgeted. "Yeah. Sorry about that. I must have been deeper in thought than I realized."

"I figured that was the case. I remember how you used to pace when you had anything on your mind. What was it that had you so preoccupied?" Kaylee inquired.

"I was trying to think of what I would say to Oliver when I found him," Adam lied.

"Oliver left?" Kaylee loudly asked.

"Yes. That is why I wanted to talk to Eva. I was trying to cover for him," Adam replied.

"Did it work?" Kaylee asked.

"Of course not," Adam replied and then chuckled. "Eva immediately saw right through it."

Kaylee's eyes widened as she smiled. "I bet she was furious."

"She was at first, but we talked, and something good came out of it...well, two things," Adam responded. Kaylee shrugged. "One was that Eva won't banish him from here, but she wanted me to relay a message to him to make him scared...just to mess with him." Kaylee chuckled. "Second, we are now free to leave the estate."

"Really? That's awesome! Nice work," Kaylee said as she patted him on his shoulder.

"Thanks. Eva can be reasonable depending on how you present the idea to her," Adam said.

"The timing couldn't be any better. On one of the outings to get supplies, I noticed a fair was coming to a nearby town. I figured the 'don't leave the house' rule would still be in place, so I didn't say anything. Today is the last day. If I hurry, I can make it there with plenty of time to enjoy it," Kaylee mentioned as she bounced in place, smiling.

Adam held back a smile for two reasons. First, he thought she was cute because of her reaction to being able to go to the fair. Second, she just gave him the idea that he needed. He remembered how much she liked boardwalks and fairs, but he had no idea one was in town.

Adam's palms became partially sweaty. He swallowed hard to overcome the fear that had prevented him from asking her out. "That sounds like fun. Do you care if I join you?"

Kaylee immediately stopped and stuttered. This made Adam nervous, for he thought he had just made a grave mistake. He now wished he could have retracted his comment. Finally, a word escaped her lips. "Sure."

"Are you sure? I don't want to intrude, and it won't hurt my feelings if you'd rather I didn't come," Adam lied.

"No, no...I mean, yes," Kaylee said, flustered. She paused and took a breath. "No, you are not intruding, and yes, I want you to come with me. Sorry. I was going to ask you, but I wasn't sure if you would want to go, and I didn't want you to feel obligated."

"Anything with you is never an obligation," Adam replied as he smiled kindly.

Kaylee smiled as she moved the few strands of hair that dangled before her face. "Really?"

"Really," Adam softly said. Kaylee's smile grew as she began to blush.

"Well, let me quickly change, and I can meet you back here in fifteen minutes?" Kaylee suggested.

"Sounds like a plan," Adam replied. The two then went their separate ways.

It didn't take Adam long to change and return to where they would meet. On his way, it was difficult to erase his smile, even when he was internally debating on how to act during their date. He wondered if it was even technically a date since that word was never mentioned. Adam continued his debate on how to act as he weaved his way around the corners until he arrived at the spot. There was no chance to continue his thoughts because Kaylee was already there. She, like him, was dressed casually.

"Hey. So, are we going to portal there?" Kaylee asked as she cringed.

Adam smiled. "No, and for two reasons. First, since neither of us has a clear picture of the fair, the portal won't work. Or it will, but who knows where we will end up. Second, to save me the embarrassment, I figured I would drive."

"Drive where?" Caleb inquired as he casually walked down the hallway.

"The fair is in town. Kaylee and I were going to check it out," Adam responded.

"Ah. Eva told me about the restrictions being lifted. That sounds like fun. Well, I guess it is. I've never been to one," Caleb remarked.

"Wait. You have never been to a fair before?" Kaylee asked with a raised brow.

"Nope. You guys have fun," Caleb said as he smiled and walked away. Kaylee turned, looked at Adam, and pouted.

Adam shrugged. "You can try."

Kaylee smiled. "Caleb, wait!"

He stopped and walked back to them. "What's up?"

"Why don't you join us?" Kaylee asked.

Caleb cringed. "I really don't do the outside thing anymore. Sorry, but thank you for asking."

"I know. Adam explained it to me, but still. You have never been, and I think everybody should experience it at least once in their lifetime. From what I hear, you have at least two or three lifetimes under your belt." Caleb smiled, but as he was about to respond, Kaylee continued. "I think it's admirable that you don't want to kill anybody. That is why Adam and I will be there to ensure you don't have to break that promise to yourself. Also, it will be in broad daylight with numerous people around. Even if it gets dark, you should be fine because we will be there."

"I don't know," Caleb said as he fidgeted.

"I know you're nervous. Heck, I'm nervous. Look at me, I'm a newbie immortal, and the thought of having to fight other immortals who are hundreds of years older than me is intimidating, to say the least," Kaylee responded.

"It's more my beliefs. The fact that I don't fight doesn't mean I can't," Caleb defended.

"I'm sure you can. Look, Adam and I will stick close to you and make sure that you aren't put into an uncomfortable situation. You can even bring your portal key in case of an emergency," Kaylee said.

"I don't know. Maybe. The thought has crossed my mind lately," Caleb responded.

"The two of us can't hide forever. Please," Kaylee pleaded.

115

"You two will stick by me the entire time?" Caleb asked.

"The entire time," Adam replied.

Caleb paused and looked away. Then, a smile appeared on his face. "I'll go get my portal key."

"Yay! I'm so proud of you. You will have a good time. I promise!" Kaylee exclaimed. Caleb's smile grew before he swiftly walked away.

"You are amazing. For many reasons, but to get Caleb to leave the estate…that's more than amazing. That's 'miracle worker' level," Adam boasted.

"Well, I don't want to brag," Kaylee playfully said as she brushed off her shoulders. Adam scoffed with amusement. "Is it okay that I invited him?" Kaylee nervously asked.

"Of course it is. You got Caleb to leave after decades of being cooped up here. An accomplishment that none of us ever came close to obtaining," Adam responded.

Kaylee let out a sigh of relief. "Okay, good. I was hoping you wouldn't be bummed out."

"It's just another example of how sweet and caring you can be," Adam replied with a gentle smile.

Kaylee smiled. "Thank you for being understanding."

At that point, Caleb rushed back to them. "Ready!" They walked outside, but Kaylee stopped as they reached Adam's car.

"Wait a minute. You said that your grandfather bought this car right off the line back in the sixties. It was you, wasn't it?" Adam shrugged as a guilty smile appeared. Kaylee smiled while she shook her head before they got in the car and left.

Kaylee and Adam engaged Caleb in small talk while Adam drove. It was obvious from his restlessness that Caleb was becoming more nervous the further away they were from the manor. Luckily, it was a short drive to the fairgrounds. Since the fair was located away from the city, it allowed it to take advantage of the open land. Screams mixed with laughter and the sounds of the rides filled the air as they approached the entrance. Adam could already smell the delicious foods that awaited them, and he even caught Kaylee sniffing and smiling. The two of them made sure to stand on either side of Caleb. As soon as they entered, a smile formed on Caleb's face as his eyes bounced between the rides, games, and food.

"Are you ready to experience your first fair?" Adam asked.

"You bet!" Caleb responded while his eyes continued to roam.

"You will love it, but a word to the wise. Rides before food unless you want to see that food again later," Kaylee cautioned.

"Understood," Caleb replied. He nodded as if he took a mental note of Kaylee's suggestion.

"Kaylee, why don't you lead the way," Adam suggested. She smiled, and the group was off.

They first went from ride to ride before they moved on to the games. Adam enjoyed every moment, especially because Kaylee and Caleb were there. It brought him much joy to see her smile and laugh. For Caleb, not only did he enjoy seeing him have the same expressions as Kaylee, but also his "in awe moments" that made his smile grow. There were times that Kaylee and Adam would sneak a peek at each other and smile whenever Caleb's jaw would drop at something else that amazed him. Once again, Adam had to divert his gaze from Kaylee so she wouldn't catch him staring at her. He couldn't help it. She brought him such happiness, and coupled with the memories of their past, it took great restraint for him not to make a move on her.

The afternoon flew by, and their stomachs began to rumble, so they found an empty table to sit at while Adam went to purchase a wide variety of food. The table was big enough for the three of them, plus the stuffed animals they had won. Kaylee had a medium-sized pink rock star bear, and Adam had a small frog. On the other hand, Caleb had four stuffed animals of various sizes since he played some games continuously due to his excitement. Adam had to make a few trips, but he brought over a cheesesteak, hot dog, cheeseburger, fries, a turkey leg, drinks, funnel cake, and various fried items covered in powdered sugar for the entire table to share. Once they finished with their feast, Adam grinned because the best part was coming up…dessert.

"Here you go. I know how much you enjoy these," Adam said as he handed Kaylee some fried Oreos.

"Enjoy…no. Love…yes. Thank you!" Kaylee exclaimed before she popped one in her mouth.

"They can deep fry anything, it seems…even butter," Caleb commented as he sampled everything.

"Yep, deep-fried goodness," Adam mumbled with food in his mouth.

Caleb took a deep breath and paused. "I can see why you said to eat last."

Kaylee smiled. "Did someone finally hit their limit?"

"Yes. I don't feel so fresh," Caleb said as he held his stomach and puffed his cheeks out.

"Even immortals have limits," Adam quietly teased. He then consolidated the remaining desserts onto one plate and threw the rest of the trash out. Then, they moved to a bench to allow others to sit and eat. Caleb sat between Kaylee and Adam.

"Do you regret eating all that food?" Kaylee inquired.

"Not one bit," Caleb said as he smiled and patted his stomach. They chuckled at his comment.

After a few minutes of silence, as they enjoyed the sights and sounds of the fair while they digested their food, Caleb spoke.

"Maybe if I walk around, I will feel better."

"Sure, where would you like to go?" Adam asked as he began to get up.

"No, you guys stay here. I am going to try that game right over there," Caleb said as he stood up. Kaylee and Adam shared a glance.

"Are you sure?" Kaylee asked.

"Yes, I am sure," Caleb said as he confidently smiled.

"Then, go for it," Kaylee responded. She and Adam smiled as Caleb walked away, leaving his winnings in his spot.

"Look at our boy go," Kaylee said.

"They grow up so fast," Adam replied. They both chuckled.

Not too long after, an older couple was looking for a place to sit, so Kaylee offered to move over so they could sit near them. She grabbed some of Caleb's winnings while Adam took the rest, and Kaylee sat beside him. Then, when the couple sat down, they sat a little further toward them, which caused Kaylee to sit shoulder-to-shoulder with Adam. She looked at him with an awkward smile, which he returned. However, it took every ounce of strength for him not to put his arm around her.

"Here, you can have the last one," Adam said as he handed her a fried Oreo.

"I don't know if I have any room left, but I can never say no to them," Kaylee remarked. Adam popped the last bit of funnel cake in his mouth, and as the fried Oreo reached her lips, he quickly tapped her hand. The fried Oreo hit her lips, and the powdered sugar entered her nose, which caused her to sneeze. He laughed because he didn't expect her to sneeze, but his laughter caused him to inhale some of the powdered sugar down his throat. Adam choked and coughed out a cloud of powder. The two began to laugh hysterically at each other while trying to clean themselves up.

"I hope you're happy," Kaylee mentioned as she wiped the tears from her eyes.

Adam took a few deep breaths. "Yep. It was worth it even though I didn't expect it to backfire on me like that." The two laughed some more before they were finally able to control themselves. He looked over and realized the older couple must have left during their laughing fit, yet Kaylee didn't move away. If she was happy where she was, then so was he.

Kaylee turned and looked at Adam. "I'm glad we got to do this today."

"What…almost die from powdered sugar?" Adam teased before he looked at her.

She scoffed with amusement. "You know what I mean. I had a lot of fun today."

"Same here," Adam responded. They gently smiled and stared at each other, lost in the moment.

"Victory is mine!" Caleb announced.

"Impressive. You finally won a prize from that game," Adam said as he and Kaylee smiled at his proud achievement.

"What now? It's starting to get dark, and we have done everything," Caleb said.

"Did you have fun?" Adam inquired.

"I did! Thank you! Both of you…thank you! Not just for this, but for finally getting me out into the world again. It means a lot," Caleb replied.

"You're welcome," Kaylee said. She stood up and gave him a side hug while she held the prizes.

Adam stood up and put his hand on Caleb's shoulder. "I'm proud of you." Caleb's smile grew immensely. "To answer your question, I think it's time for you to take your vast collection of prizes and head back to the manor. I would take you along, but I have a feeling that Oliver may be hanging out somewhere that isn't as 'festive' as this place."

"You have to get Oliver?" Kaylee asked.

"Yeah. I promised Eva I would, or at the very least, convey her message to him," Adam responded.

"Yeah. Better to end on a good note," Caleb said before he surveyed the area. "I think if we head out to the parking lot, we can find a spot to discreetly portal from." Adam nodded, and the group took off.

"Do you want to leave with Caleb or stick with me?" Adam asked Kaylee.

"I'll stick with you. Why should the fun end now, right?" Kaylee responded and then winked.

"Are you sure? Oliver has been cooped up for a long time, so knowing him, he is blowing off some steam, which means…anything can happen," Adam said.

"Well, it's a good thing that we are immortal, isn't it?" Kaylee teased. Adam scoffed with amusement and nodded his head.

"I think this is a good spot," Caleb suggested. They were behind an old van that shielded them from prying eyes. Caleb reached into his pocket and retrieved his portal key, but he struggled to create one while juggling the prizes.

Adam chuckled. "As fun as this is to watch. Let me help you."

"Thanks," Caleb said and then handed over his portal key.

"Can you take our prizes with you, please?" Kaylee asked.

"Sure," Caleb answered. Kaylee handed him both prizes while Adam concentrated on the portal. Not much longer, the portal opened.

"This will put you by the front door. We had fun," Adam said. He then slipped the portal key back into Caleb's pocket. Everyone said goodbye to each other before Caleb entered the portal.

"Should I be alarmed that seeing a person step through a portal feels normal?" Kaylee asked.

"Yes. It shouldn't feel normal. What's wrong with you? Psycho," Adam teased.

Kaylee smiled. "Shut up." They made their way over to his car and left. After driving in silence for a bit, Kaylee spoke.

"It's a big city we are headed to. Do you have any idea where Oliver could be?"

"I know exactly where he is," Adam replied.

"Care to share?" Kaylee asked.

Adam smiled. "There is a bar in the downtown area that he always goes to. The bartenders pour graciously, the crowd is never the same mix of people, and they typically have a live band playing, which he enjoys."

"What about the whole 'Can't stay or go to the same place for too long,' thing?" Kaylee inquired.

Adam tensed up. He felt her comment may have been a jab at him. "He's not a regular. He spaces out his visits enough so that nobody would recognize him. Besides, most people in the bar are drinking, so they either wouldn't remember or believe it was him."

Kaylee nodded. "Makes sense." Suddenly, her eyes grew wide. "I just realized that I don't have a weapon on me. Not even a portal key. I didn't think I needed it, but now that we are going out at night, do I need something now?"

"It sounds like you've got problems," Adam countered with a crooked grin.

Kaylee playfully smacked his arm. "I'm being serious."

"First off, it doesn't matter if it's nighttime. Granted, the chances are heightened, but if an immortal wants to fight you, they won't care about the time of day. With that said, typically, you want to make sure you have a weapon on you. However, when you travel in groups, you can rely on the others if needed, provided they know in advance," Adam explained.

"Can I rely on you?" Kaylee asked with one eyebrow raised and a hint of a smile.

"Yes. A promise I intend to never break with you again," Adam responded. Kaylee smiled right before she looked out the window. A few moments later, she spoke.

"By the way, where is your weapon?"

"Right here," Adam replied as he jokingly flexed his bicep.

Kaylee rolled her eyes. "Great, we're all going to die." Her comment caused them to laugh.

"It's attached to the side of my calf, under my pants," Adam answered.

The corner of Kaylee's mouth curled. "Change of subject. I'm curious, did you almost get sick on the pirate ship ride?"

"Why are you asking me that? You already know the answer!" Adam exclaimed.

"I know, but to see you embarrassed about it is fun to watch. Similar to traveling through portals," Kaylee responded.

Adam sighed. "I should have gone alone." They laughed and spent the rest of the trip reminiscing about the day at the fair.

They finally arrived at the downtown location and found a parking lot a few blocks from the bar. Before they walked toward the bar, Adam scanned the area as they got out of the car. The streets were fairly busy with people, young and old, walking in and out of bars and restaurants. It was noisy, so they continued in silence. As they walked, his mind recapped the day…and it was a good day. So much that he had to mask his smile from Kaylee. They talked and laughed a lot more than he had imagined. He wasn't sure if Caleb's presence assisted with how well the day went, but either way, he was happy. Still, as happy as he was, he wanted to take her on a date, an activity, anything that was just the two of them.

When they walked into the bar, it was packed full of college students, a small group of cowboys and cowgirls in the far back, and a singer with an acoustic guitar playing off to the side. Adam glanced at Kaylee and watched as she smiled while her eyes scanned the cowboy-themed bar. They even had their own mechanical bull in the center of the establishment. The walls were covered in an assortment of bull horns, old boots, lassos, and western pictures. Even the staff was dressed to match the décor of the place.

Adam put his hand on the small of Kaylee's back, which made her quickly look at him. "Follow me." He led her through the bar, and it didn't take long before he located Oliver. Both of his arms were around two different college women while a few stood in front of him. Adam wasn't surprised and had to smile at the defeated handful of guys at the table behind them.

Kaylee's face crinkled. "What do they see in him? Seriously, why haven't they walked away from him yet?"

"One of life's many mysteries," Adam responded.

"Hey! You made it!" Oliver called out. They both waved and smiled while they approached him. Adam knew Kaylee's smile was fake.

"Adam, Kaylee…meet the girls. Girls…Adam and Kaylee," Oliver said, and then took a swig from his beer bottle. After the pleasantries, Oliver spoke.

"I'm so glad you made it. Bartender. Drinks for my two friends here and another round of cocktails for any of these lovely ladies." After the group of girls cheered, some even kissing Oliver on the cheek, Adam and Kaylee ordered a beer each.

One of the drunk girls came up to Kaylee. "Your boyfriend is cute. Does he have a brother?" Oliver almost spat his drink out because of her comment. Once he gained composure and swallowed his drink, he laughed. Adam teased Kaylee by giving her a smug look.

"No, and we're not dating," Kaylee responded.

"Ohhh, so he is available," the girl said as she looked at Adam and bit her lower lip.

"He's not available," Kaylee quickly countered. Her jaw dropped when she realized what she had said. She whipped her head around to see if Adam and Oliver had heard her. She found Oliver with a huge smile and Adam rubbing the back of his neck and looking away. Kaylee sighed. "Where's that beer?"

As soon as she spoke, the bartender dropped off two beers. She quickly grabbed hers and took a few large gulps before she turned away from them, and people watched. Adam wasn't sure what she meant by her comment, but if it was what he thought it meant, then there was hope.

"Ladies, if you would be so kind as to excuse me as I talk to my friends, that would be lovely," Oliver kindly said.

"You're leaving so soon?" One of the girls said while a few others whined.

"Not at all, luv," Oliver replied and then took off his black leather jacket. "How about you hold onto this and I will be back later to claim it, along with any other articles of clothing you would like to hand me." He then draped his jacket over the girl's shoulders, who smiled and then bit her lip.

Adam noticed Kaylee rolling her eyes at Oliver's flirtations. After centuries of being around Oliver, it didn't faze him. It wasn't long before they were lucky enough to find a recently available table and sat down.

"Let me guess. You came out here because of Eva, not to actually enjoy yourself," Oliver commented as he smirked.

"You call taking advantage of women fun?" Kaylee asked while she side-eyed him.

Oliver raised his hands. "Whoa, whoever said I was taking advantage of anybody?"

"Oh, come on. You know alcohol doesn't have the same impact on us as…people who are not like us. You are getting them drunk so you can take advantage of them. I should go up there and tell them you have some horrible, contagious disease or something," Kaylee responded as she glared at Oliver.

"On the contrary, it's the exact opposite. I know you won't believe me, so why don't you ask Adam?" Oliver suggested. The two of them turned and looked at Adam.

"What is he talking about?" Kaylee inquired.

"For the girl, or girls, he is interested in, he asks the bartender to give them less alcohol in their drinks. That way, his conscious is clear if anything happens between them," Adam explained.

"So, you don't try to get them drunk out of their minds?" Kaylee asked when she turned back to Oliver.

"Only the annoying ones I'm not interested in, but only because I want to see them make a fool of themselves. Bonus points if they vomit," Oliver replied.

Kaylee chuckled. "Sorry. I shouldn't have judged you so quickly."

"No worries, luv, I get that a lot. Besides, you think Adam would want anything to do with me if I were the monster you claimed I was?" Oliver said.

"No, I guess not," Kaylee responded.

"Although I do feel the judgment coming from him at times," Oliver said with a crooked smile.

Adam's brow lowered as he took a sip. "Well, that's because you tend to do questionable things, but to be fair, I don't think I have given you that look in a long time."

Oliver laughed loudly. "Long time! Your perception of time is skewed, mate." Adam's brow crinkled. "Don't you remember during the drive to Eva's place over a month ago? You know…about the motorcycle I stole?"

"You stole a bike?" Kaylee asked with a raised brow.

"Before you start, like I told Adam, the guy had it coming to him," Oliver countered.

Adam shook his head. "I can only imagine what the man did for you to steal his bike."

Oliver smiled and turned to Kaylee. "You know, he didn't always have that stick up his butt." Adam put his hand over his face and shook his head.

Kaylee smiled. "Adam is fun. We went to the fair today, and in the past, we did many fun things together. Some low-key, some…not so much."

"There was a time he was as fun and wild as me," Oliver mentioned as he smirked and glanced at Adam.

"Seriously?" Kaylee said as she smiled and looked at Adam.

Adam grinned. "We all go through our phases in life. Besides, it was during a time that there was no photographic evidence to be obtained, and if one wanted to disappear, they just had to move to the town on the other side of the mountain."

"I see more storytelling in our future," Kaylee said as she nudged Adam's arm.

"When you do, make sure you tell her about the tavern in Ireland almost three hundred years ago," Oliver commented while he leaned toward Kaylee. Oliver's eyes remained on Adam as he did.

He stared back at Oliver, his mind absent of what he was referring to. "What are you talking…" Adam began to ask until it dawned on him. He tightly closed his eyes, and his face crinkled from embarrassment.

"What happened in the tavern?" Kaylee excitedly asked.

CHAPTER 12

Oliver looked at Adam before a devious smile formed. He then looked back at Kaylee. "I will answer your question with a question of my own. Have you ever seen Adam naked?"

Kaylee spit out her beer and choked a little as she began to smile. "What? No. Wait, Adam was naked? Like full-blown naked?"

"I wasn't fully naked," Adam defended.

"He was wild and free," Oliver replied.

Kaylee began to laugh as she put her hand on Adam's arm. "You have to tell me this story."

Adam sighed as he squeezed the bridge of his nose. He was reluctant to tell her because he was afraid she would see him in a different light. However, when he saw how her face lit up with curiosity, he couldn't resist and even smiled.

Adam took a large swig from his bottle before he began. "You see, what happened was, Oliver and I were in that tavern, just minding our business, until these two large men entered. They challenged people to drinking games, which sometimes could be quite amusing. Of course, people wagered on it and lost, as no one could out-drink them. We even politely declined when they asked us to be next. Everything was fine until they had too much to drink.

They began to threaten people, and when one of them pushed a woman aside, we had witnessed enough."

"So, your solution was to strip?" Kaylee remarked.

Oliver and Adam smiled before he continued with his story. "No, it was Oliver's idea for me to challenge them in a winner-takes-all drinking contest. I didn't think much about it because they have already been drinking and well...I'm immortal."

"Apparently, I made a slight miscalculation as to how much alcohol they could consume," Oliver commented with a crooked grin.

"It also slipped your mind to inform me that you have seen these people drink in the past, and they were impressive, to say the least," Adam said.

"How impressive were their drinking skills?" Kaylee asked.

"Like, immortal level," Oliver replied.

"They were immortal?" Kaylee loudly whispered.

"No, but they could drink like one," Adam said and then side-eyed Oliver, who shrugged as Kaylee's smile grew. "Anyway, we began our contest, and I won. Unfortunately, Oliver must tell you the rest because it was all a blur for me."

Oliver leaned forward. "No worries, mate. I would be honored to help you out." Adam shook his head, yet grinned. "So, after an obscene amount of alcohol, the two men collapsed. Victory was ours, but as we collected our winnings, Adam wanted to stay and fraternize with the locals. Now, don't get me wrong, I love to socialize, but when he stumbled around announcing to everyone, loudly, that he was 'immortal,' I felt it was time for me to intervene."

Kaylee's eyes and smile widened as she turned to Adam. "You didn't."

Adam slowly nodded and squinched his face. "That part does seem vaguely familiar."

Kaylee laughed. "When did he strip?"

"Right when someone asked him to prove it. Luckily, I had already hidden all the sharp objects and confiscated his spectral sword. He tried to show his markings, but of course, no one else could see them. They laughed and thought he was just being a drunken fool. In all his 'wisdom,' he figured the only way he could prove it was to strip and reveal that he had no scars," Oliver responded. Kaylee and Oliver burst into laughter. Adam tried to hold back a smile, but eventually, a smile broke through, and he began to laugh along with them.

"What happened after that?" Kaylee said as she wiped the tears of laughter from her eyes.

"Oliver eventually convinced me to put my clothes back on, and we left. I have never been back to Ireland since," Adam replied.

"Too bad cameras weren't invented yet to capture that golden moment," Kaylee remarked as she briefly leaned her shoulder into his and smiled.

"Yeah, but I always wondered if someone sketched that glorious night," Oliver teased.

As entertaining as the moment was, Adam was distracted by Kaylee. Her smile lit up the room and, as always, made him smile. He would tell thousands of embarrassing stories about himself if it meant he could see her smile over and over again. He hadn't heard Kaylee laugh and smile so much in a long time, and today, he witnessed both. Even her laugh filled him with joy. She deserved happiness, and he would do anything to ensure she achieved it. He wouldn't settle for anything short of that.

Kaylee took another sip of her beer, glanced at Adam, and caught him gently smiling at her. Normally, he would have quickly looked the other way, but not this time. She smiled in return as she stared back at him.

Oliver cleared his throat, which got their attention. "Well, as much fun as this is, I do have a lady…or ladies, waiting on me."

"Thank you for the drinks and that story," Kaylee said.

"You're welcome, luv. I got plenty more where that came from if you ever get bored," Oliver responded.

Adam smirked. "Stories that he will keep to himself unless he wants me to stop smoothing things over with Eva."

Oliver smiled, and then his brow lowered. "Didn't you have a message from her?"

"Yeah, long story short, she wasn't happy that you left, but after I convinced her to lift the ban, she was less irritated. However, she still wants to talk to you. You know, instill fear in you and whatnot," Adam explained.

"Talk and not kill. I call that progress," Oliver said and then winked. Adam smiled. "Now, if you'll excuse me. I am going to reclaim my jacket and hopefully some other articles of clothing."

"You're a pig," Kaylee said with a disgusted look.

"I know," Oliver whispered with a cocky smile. He then left and joined the ladies he was with earlier. It took effort, but Adam held back his smile from Oliver's comment.

"I have a question. If you and Eva are so close, why haven't you warned her that Oliver is interested in her?" Kaylee inquired.

"To do so would be an insult to her. You have to remember that she is over six hundred years old. She has seen every attempt known to man when it comes to men's advances toward her. She is smart and doesn't fall for tricks and smooth-talking. Besides, it's not like Oliver is being shy about his intentions," Adam explained.

Kaylee rolled her eyes. "That much is true."

"If anything, I am more worried for Oliver than Eva. It's humorous to me to watch as he constantly gets rejected, but if he pushes it too far, she may cut off something that may not grow back," Adam joked. Kaylee partially choked on her drink before she laughed.

They didn't talk much after that since the entertainer's break was over, and she was back on stage, ready to sing. At one point, he saw Oliver leave with the girl he was interested in while the other girls pouted. Kaylee and Adam finished their drinks and listened to the talented lady on stage.

A few songs in, there was a commotion at the back of the bar. They turned their heads and saw a group of college men standing toe-to-toe with a handful of cowboys. The singer tried to continue, but they were getting louder, and eventually, she stopped. Now, all eyes were focused on the back of the bar.

"I really wish those drunk college jerks would just leave and not come back. They have been coming around lately, and it feels as if they aren't picking a fight, then they are just being a nuisance," the waitress commented as she grabbed their empty bottles.

"Maybe we need to do something about it," Kaylee suggested to Adam. He didn't respond. Instead, he surveyed the area.

"Honey, I appreciate it, but don't get yourself injured because of them. Besides, there are way too many of them," the waitress responded before she left.

"Are you really just going to sit there?" Kaylee asked, but again, Adam said nothing as he continued to look around. "Is it because I am here? I have been training with Eva for a while now, and I think we can do something about it. I mean, why have these powers if we don't put them to good use?" Kaylee's brow furrowed. "What are you looking at?"

"I'm surveying the room. I agree with you, but we can't just jump into any situation without being smart about it. We are not superheroes with secret identities. If something happens…let's say a cut that magically heals in front of everyone, then we expose not just ourselves but all immortals. Our life is not meant to be in a petri dish to be studied or harnessed." Kaylee fell silent as her eyes glanced around the room, so Adam continued. "I don't see any bouncers. I also don't see any security cameras in the area where they are located. Also, it seems no one else will intervene; however, you can bet people's phones will be out and videoing. Our best bet is to try to diffuse the situation, but if we can't, the further back in the bar we can take the fight, the better. Between the obscurity and the large group of people, there is a lesser chance that anyone will get a good view of us."

"Got it," Kaylee said. She immediately left her chair and headed over to the two groups standing within inches of each other. Adam sighed and followed her.

He was a few steps behind Kaylee as she marched toward the crowd. He could see that the cowboys were outnumbered three-to-one, but that didn't stop them. The college men's physiques ranged from lanky to muscular, whereas the cowboys all seemed in good shape. They threaded their way through the spectators until they reached the side of the opposing groups.

"Okay, knock it off! People are trying to have a good time, and you drunk idiots are ruining it!" Kaylee exclaimed.

"You need to mind your business, blondie, and shut up," one of the college men yelled.

"Or what?" Kaylee said as she stared him down. As she was about to approach him, Adam gently grabbed her arm and stood to the side of her.

"You need to keep your girl in check," a different college man demanded.

Adam's brow raised, but he remained calm and took a few steps further. "She is the least of your worries."

"Oh really? What are you going to do about it?" A few college men stepped up to Adam with their fists clenched, but it didn't faze him.

He turned his head and addressed the cowboys. "What happened?"

"These little boys thought it would be cute to catcall our ladies, so we demanded an apology," one of the cowboys responded. The cowboy's eyes continued to burn holes into the college men.

"Is that true?" Adam asked.

"Yeah, but it was all in good fun," one of the college men responded.

"Well, they didn't think it was fun. It was rude, and you should apologize," Adam calmly said.

"And if we don't," the college man taunted.

"Then, I will step aside and let my friend here continue her thought," Adam said as his eyes drifted to Kaylee. At first, her brow crinkled, but then it lightened up, and the corner of her mouth raised.

"Tough man, letting a girl fight his battles. We aren't apologizing to this Southern trash. Besides, what's she going to do? If anything, I bet she's the kind of girl that would like guys to cat-call her," the college man boasted as he pushed Adam. The push barely moved him.

Adam smiled and shrugged before he stepped aside. As soon as he did, Kaylee sent her foot crashing into the guy's groin. A high-pitched scream came from him as he grabbed his crotch and bent over. Kaylee followed up with an uppercut that sent him crashing to the floor. Adam's fist smashed into the man who was standing in front of the closest cowboy. The impact sent him flying back into his friends. While the college men stood in shock, the cowboys swung next, leveling the ones they hit. At that point, some college men retreated while the others charged.

During the brawl, Adam directed Kaylee to bring the fight further back into the room, which she did. At first, he stood by her as they fought, but once again, he was impressed by how well Eva taught her. She handled herself well, and she showed a lot of skill. At first, the men wouldn't hit her, but as she became more aggressive, they started to swing, but she blocked their attacks. He even saw her get punched, but she regained composure quickly and retaliated. Once he knew she could handle herself, he moved away.

Each punch Adam landed, either to their face or stomach, dropped each college man that he came across. He even sent some men flying backward with an occasional front kick to their chests.

The ones that were lucky to get a punch in didn't faze him as his adrenaline pumped while he continued to fight. As the brawl continued, he grabbed some by the back of their shirts and flung them over tables. For others, he sent an elbow crashing into the bridge of their nose when they tried to grab him from behind. A few more retreated when they noticed how quickly and brutally their side was losing. Finally, the cowboys, Adam, and Kaylee stood above the fallen college men. Of course, Adam and Kaylee were not hurt, and he hoped nobody noticed their lack of bruises and cuts. The cowboys had some minor cuts and bruises, but nothing serious.

The college man who started it all slowly stood up with an empty beer bottle. He swung it at the head of the cowboy who had stood up to him earlier. Adam noticed the cowboy didn't see it coming, so he rushed over and stuck his arm out. The beer bottle smashed into his forearm and shattered. The cowboy jerked around and saw the aftermath. Adam grimaced at the pain, but it was fleeting. He quickly grabbed the man's arm and yanked the broken beer bottle from his hand. With one hand gripping the top of the guy's shirt, he shoved him into a wooden beam. He then moved his hand to his throat and raised the broken bottle to his face.

"Please...please don't kill me," the college man whimpered.

Adam's jaw clenched and his brow furrowed while he slowly put the broken bottle within an inch of the man's eye. He held it there while the man trembled. "If you or your friends ever return to this bar, next time, I won't stop! Do I make myself clear?"

"Yes...yes," the man said through his tears.

"Do I?" Adam turned his head and yelled to the rest of them.

"Yes," they all responded. He could see the fear in their eyes.

"Good. Tell your friends who cowardly ran away the same message," Adam demanded. Then, he turned his attention back to the man trembling before him. "Now, I believe you still owe this man, their ladies, and everyone else here an apology."

"I'm sorry! I'm sorry!" The man called out as he trembled.

Adam turned his attention to the cowboy and his group. "Do you accept his apology?"

They all shook their heads and smiled. Then, the cowboy closest to him spoke. "We sure do. Heck, we were already good once we saw him pee himself." Adam's brow lowered, and he looked, and sure enough, the man's jeans were soaked around his crotch. He scoffed with amusement.

"However, I would like to say one more thing to him," the cowboy requested. Adam nodded and tossed the beer bottle aside before he pushed the man toward the cowboy.

The cowboy squared up to the college man and decked him. The man fell backward and was out cold. Adam looked at the cowboy. "Well said." He turned and looked at Kaylee, who smiled from ear to ear. He also smiled, but it was short-lived when they heard sirens outside.

"I believe that is your cue to exit," the cowboy remarked.

Adam nodded. "I believe so."

"Thank you," the cowboy said. The two of them firmly shook hands.

"Anytime," Adam said and then nodded to the rest of the cowboys. They returned a similar nod of respect.

"I presume it's a bad thing if we get sent to jail," Kaylee said rhetorically.

"It's definitely not a good thing. However, even if we manage to leave, we are parked far enough away that one of his college buddies could identify us as we make our way to my car. We need a quick exit," Adam responded as he glanced around.

"Here," the cowboy said as he reached down and grabbed the keys from the college man's pocket. Adam's brow creased as he stared at the keys. "Come on. Just take them. They're dry, and you need a quick exit. I heard him bragging about his new 'hog' that I'm sure his daddy bought him. They arrived when happy hour started, so I'm sure he is parked nearby. We'll cover for you here."

At that point, Kaylee stood next to him, speechless, as her eyes bounced between Adam and the keys. He didn't want to steal the person's motorcycle, but couldn't think of another alternative. Then, Oliver's logic entered his mind, which made him sigh. Adam took the keys. "Thank you." He grabbed Kaylee's hand and went to leave, but noticed her eyes were scanning the area around the bar.

"What is it?" Adam asked.

"I could have sworn I saw some woman staring at us," Kaylee responded.

"Everyone is staring at us," Adam countered.

"This was different. She was calm, and her eyes were focused just on us, but she vanished," Kaylee replied.

"Okay. One problem at a time. We'll discuss her later, but now, we need to go," Adam said. She nodded, and they slipped out the back door.

They rushed around the side of the building and stopped at the corner. Adam peeked around the corner and saw two police vehicles. He noticed that the officers were making their way to the front entrance.

Adam turned to Kaylee. "Okay. Just follow my lead and act natural." She nodded. Adam peeked around the corner again and noticed all but one had made it inside. The last officer seemed to be talking to people outside and not allowing anyone else in or out of the building. They straightened their clothes and quickly fixed their hair. "All right, let's go."

They walked casually down the sidewalk. As they did, Adam's eyes searched the street for the motorcycle. Since they had no bruises or cuts, they didn't stick out in the crowd. However, it only took one of the college men to identify them, and they would be busted. They had to move quickly.

"I can't believe we are about to steal someone's motorcycle," Kaylee loudly whispered.

"You aren't the only one," Adam loudly whispered back. Finally, he noticed a Harley-Davidson parked on the same side of the street as them, just past the bar.

Adam took Kaylee's hand. "I see his bike. It's just past the crowd of people up ahead. The officer is dispersing the crowd, so we can just walk right by. The problem is that the bike is close enough to the bar that it may bring suspicion if we try to leave."

"Then we must be swift about it. Tell me, have you ever ridden a motorcycle before?" Kaylee inquired.

"Briefly. It was a few decades ago. I'm hoping the phrase 'it's just like riding a bike' applies here," Adam responded. He smiled to ease any tension she may have had, but also to cover up his nervousness. Unlike Oliver, this wasn't like him, so it didn't feel natural. He imagined how much more confident and sly Oliver would have been about this versus himself.

They reached the bike, and as much as he despised its owner, he couldn't help but admire the craftsmanship. Adam glanced around and noticed the officer wasn't looking in their direction, so he got onto the bike, followed by Kaylee behind him. Adam knew that once he started the motorcycle, the roar of the engine would gather unwanted attention.

"Hold on tight," Adam said over his shoulder. He could feel Kaylee's arms around his stomach tighten. He took a deep breath, and as he was about to start the engine, he heard a loud noise behind them.

They looked over their shoulders and discovered the noise was coming from a car down the street, showing off. With the crowd's attention now drawn to the other vehicle, he knew it was now or never. His heart raced, and his breath quickened as he was about to start the engine.

Kaylee repeatedly tapped Adam on his shoulder. "I see that lady again."

CHAPTER 13

Adam glanced over his shoulder but couldn't get a clear view of the person Kaylee referred to. "We'll deal with her later. For now, hold on tight." He felt her grip tighten right before he started the engine and sped off. The bike wobbled slightly until he regained control. After that, he kept it around the speed limit so he wouldn't draw any unwanted attention and, most of all, not crash the bike.

They stopped at a traffic light about a mile away. Kaylee leaned forward so she was close to his ear. "You're doing great. Too bad we aren't on the open road so we can really have some fun," Kaylee loudly commented. Adam turned his head and smirked. Kaylee gulped. "Why do you have that look on your face?"

It was a two-lane road, and the traffic lightened as they drove from the downtown area. He was behind one car at the light, so when it turned green, he jolted forward and around the car in front of him, just narrowly missing the oncoming vehicle. He heard someone honk the horn at him, but he didn't care. His confidence regarding riding a motorcycle came back to him as he flew down the road, swerving around any cars in his way.

As he drove, he could hear Kaylee's screams convert from fear to excitement. That, and just the ride itself, put a huge smile on his face. It's been a long time since he let loose, and it felt good. If he was being truthful with himself, he was also trying to impress Kaylee. After a few miles, Adam stopped at a local late-night coffee shop.

"Whoa! Now, that was fun. I never rode on a motorcycle before," Kaylee said as she got off the bike.

"Glad I could help. I will admit, it did feel good to ride again," Adam responded as he got off the bike.

"I also can't believe you stole that bike. You...of all people," Kaylee said as she smiled and poked Adam in his stomach.

"First off, we stole it, not just me. Second, don't tell Oliver. I will never hear the end of it," Adam replied as he smiled and stood closer to Kaylee.

"My lips are sealed," Kaylee said. She then moved slightly closer to him as she continued to smile. "This night has been interesting, to say the least. We went from a fun, wholesome day at the fair to racking up criminal charges, including a felony."

"Well, I didn't want you to get bored," Adam playfully said.

"Thanks," Kaylee responded, and then her smile slowly dissipated. "Back at the bar, you left me alone soon after the fight started. Why?"

"Because it didn't take me long to see that you could handle yourself. You are a strong, fierce woman. No matter what life throws at you, you never back down. You keep pushing forward. You proved that again tonight. You are an amazing woman," Adam said as he smiled kindly at her.

Kaylee blushed. "Thank you. That means a lot. Is that all?" Kaylee's brow raised as she smiled.

"You managed to look sexy during the brawl," Adam teased. It just came out, and he was worried about her reaction until she burst into laughter.

"I'm glad I didn't look like some hideous monster out there."

"Did I look sexy back at the bar?" Adam asked with a crooked grin.

"Yeah...not so much," Kaylee responded and then winked.

Adam laughed. "I'll try to work on that."

Kaylee moved even closer to Adam and put her hands on his arms. "Thank you. I really enjoyed myself today, and it's because of you."

Adam gently placed his hands on her hips. "I enjoyed myself today as well. It always makes me happy to spend time with you, but today was fun. Especially, seeing you smile so much. I'll admit, that's something I've missed." Kaylee smiled but then turned her head away. "So, what does she do...she turns her head so I can't see her smile."

Kaylee giggled. "Because you are making me blush...it's embarrassing."

"Not to me," Adam gently said.

The two of them stared into each other's eyes. He felt as if time had stopped as he became lost in her eyes. Then, without thinking, he felt himself beginning to lean toward her, and to his surprise and glee, she began to lean toward him.

"Excuse me. Sorry to interrupt, but this parking area is for customers only. Are you here to order anything?" The waitress's face cringed as she politely asked.

They were both jolted back to reality and quickly took a few steps back. Adam cleared his throat and stammered briefly before he could speak. "Yes, sorry." He then ordered two coffees.

The waitress went back inside to get their order. Adam didn't know how to act since the moment had passed, and he wasn't sure how Kaylee felt about what had almost happened. As much as he wanted to continue where they had left off, he proceeded with small talk, just to be safe. They talked about random things, including which route to take back to his car. It didn't take too long for their coffees to come out. They continued their small talk at a nearby table while they drank. Once they were done, they hopped on the bike and drove back. Adam pulled off the main road and found a quiet side street a few blocks from the bar. They got off the bike and scanned the area. No one else was around.

"All right. We can return to the sidewalk by the main road and head back to the car. The officers would have cleared the college men and cowboys out of the bar by now," Adam said as he began to walk.

"You're just going to leave the bike here?" Kaylee inquired.

"Yep. Hopefully, no one will steal it," Adam responded. A devious smile appeared on his face as he tossed the keys over his shoulder.

Kaylee laughed. "You're bad." Adam shrugged.

The two strolled down the street while they kept a watchful eye on their surroundings. They passed the bar, and it seemed quiet. It was close to midnight, so fewer people were around compared to hours ago. Not too long after, they made it back to Adam's car. As they were about to get in, he saw Kaylee's eyes widen as she stared over his shoulder.

He turned his head and saw a pale woman who stood at the edge of the alleyway across the street. There was a nearby lamppost that cast some light on her. She wore black leggings and a dark green hooded cloak that came down to her thighs. Even though the hood was over her head, he could see her short bleach-blonde chin-length hair poking out the sides of the hood.

"Stay here," Adam said without looking behind him. He then started to walk toward the woman.

"Yeah, I don't think so," Kaylee countered. He could hear her quickly go around the car and walk beside him. He held his hand out so she wouldn't go past him.

They reached the edge of the parking lot and stopped. The woman didn't move. She continued to stand while her ice-blue eyes stared back at them. He scanned her over, but her clothes covered most of her body, so it was difficult to see if she was immortal. However, it didn't take centuries of experience to know that she was.

"Her neck," Kaylee whispered. Adam squinted, and sure enough, he could see a partial immortal marking on the side of her neck.

"Hello. What brings you out at this time of night?" Adam asked. The woman slowly smiled and then bit her lower lip. She then slightly lowered her head and looked at him through her eyelids. Her smile never faded as she slowly walked backward until she disappeared into the dark alleyway.

"Um…yeah. That wasn't creepy at all," Kaylee commented.

Adam sighed. "Let's go." He then turned around and headed back to his car.

"Wait. Aren't we going after her?" Kaylee asked as she followed him.

"No," Adam replied.

"Why not? It's two against one. Besides, she may have some answers for us," Kaylee questioned as she reached out and grabbed Adam's arm to stop him.

Adam stopped and turned around before he breathed heavily through his nostrils. "She's baiting us." Kaylee's brow crinkled. "Nothing ever good happens down a dark alley. Think about it. She's outnumbered and doesn't know you are weaponless, so why would she want us to follow her?"

Kaylee's eyes wandered for a moment before they returned to Adam. "It's a trap."

"Most likely, and I'd rather not spring it. We need to be smart about this. We'll deal with her, just not now," Adam explained. Kaylee nodded, so they got into Adam's car and left.

The drive back to the manor was quiet, minus the occasional small talk. Adam purposely took the longer route, with extra turns to make sure they were not being followed. As he drove, Kaylee also kept an eye out for anything that looked suspicious. It was the middle of the night before they arrived back at the manor, but luckily, they were not followed. He felt relieved.

They crept into the manor so they wouldn't wake anyone up. When they were further inside, Adam could hear the faint noise of Caleb playing online games in his room, which made him smile. He was grateful the mysterious woman didn't show up at the fair and ruin his outing. At least, they didn't notice her at the fair.

"What now?" Kaylee whispered.

"There is no need to disturb the entire household, and I am not even sure if Oliver is back, so I say we get some sleep. In the morning, we can tell everyone what we witnessed," Adam suggested.

Kaylee nodded. "Sounds good. Well, I'm off to bed. Despite the appearance of that strange woman, I still had a good day."

"Yeah, I enjoyed our date…" Adam froze, and his face felt like it was on fire. "Day, I meant day," he stuttered. He was mad at himself for allowing that word to slip through his lips. "Sorry. Have a good night." He gave her a fake smile before quickly turning around and walking away.

"Adam," Kaylee loudly whispered. He turned around and hoped she couldn't see how red he imagined his face was. "I look forward to our next date." She smiled, tucked her hair behind her ear, and walked away.

The only reason why Adam was glad she had left was that she wouldn't see the ridiculously cheesy smile he had. He was fearful and nervous before they left for the fair, and now, his heart was filled with happiness and hope. "Don't screw it up," Adam whispered to himself before he went to his bedroom and retired for the night.

By the time Adam woke up, got ready, and headed to the kitchen for coffee, it was late morning. On the way there, he saw Kaylee pacing the hallway. He smiled when he saw her smile and walk over to him.

"Good morning," Adam said.

"Good morning. How did you sleep?" Kaylee asked.

"Good…once I finally fell asleep," Adam responded.

"Same here," Kaylee said.

"So why are you imitating me by burning a hole in the floor with all your pacing?" Adam inquired.

"I guess I'm just anxious about how Eva will react when she hears the news. That, and just knowing they are still out there, is nerve-racking, but I guess it's just a normal day in the life of an immortal," Kaylee commented.

"Sometimes, but even after centuries, it still can make you nervous. The key is to rely on your skills and the ones around you. To be prepared, but not to dwell on it and let it consume you," Adam responded.

Kaylee scoffed. "Easier said than done."

Adam grinned. "Come on, let's go get some coffee." The two headed toward the kitchen, and when they entered, Paul and Eva were already at the table, talking while they sipped their coffee.

"Hey, sleepy heads. Nice of you to finally join us," Eva cheerfully said. Adam nodded and smiled as he went straight for the coffee.

"It looks like someone is in desperate need of coffee," Paul remarked.

"Must be. I heard Adam's car pull up late last night. Any later, and the sun would have begun to rise," Eva said. She rested her chin on her fist, raised an eyebrow, and smiled.

"Well, I know Caleb had a wonderful time. He talked about the fair for what seemed like forever, and for us, that is a long time," Paul jested.

"By the way, thank you," Eva said as she stood up, approached Kaylee, and hugged her. "I was beginning to wonder if he would ever leave, and you accomplished the impossible yesterday."

"I'm glad I could help and that he had a great time," Kaylee replied.

Eva's brow lowered, and her head tilted slightly. "There's something else. I can tell by your tone. What happened?"

"Well, Adam and I found Oliver, and he relayed your message. Then we stayed at the bar afterward and had some drinks," Kaylee responded. She went to continue, but it was as if the words didn't want to leave her mouth.

Adam figured she was debating how much to tell her and how to bring it up, so he jumped in. "We spotted another immortal."

"You what?" Eva exclaimed. Adam went to continue, but she held her hand up, walked to the kitchen doorway, and called for Caleb. It didn't take long for him to arrive.

"Is everything okay?" Caleb asked, slightly winded.

"I'm not sure yet. Can you please find Oliver and bring him here? Tell him it's urgent," Eva responded. Caleb nodded and ran off.

While they waited, Adam and Kaylee made their coffees and sipped in silence as they watched Eva stand in the middle of the kitchen, deep in thought. Paul didn't seem bothered by the news as he began to read a magazine.

"Everybody can relax, I'm here," Oliver announced as he and Caleb entered the kitchen. Oliver glanced around the room before his eyes returned to Eva. "So, you wanted an audience for when you scold me?" He smiled as he put his hands into his pockets.

"I'll deal with your defiance later. Right now, we have bigger issues at hand," Eva said, then looked at Adam.

"Kaylee and I were headed back to my car last night, and we saw a bleach blonde woman with ice-blue eyes standing across the street near an alleyway. She wore a hooded cloak, but we did see an immortal mark on her neck," Adam said.

"What did she want?" Paul inquired.

"I don't know. She only smiled at us and then went into the alleyway. We left right after she did," Adam responded.

"You didn't go after her?" Oliver asked with his hands raised to either side.

"Of course, he didn't. It was obviously a trap," Eva interjected.

146

"Did you see her at any other times?" Caleb asked.

"Nope. Just that time," Adam lied.

"Well, that confirmed that Cassian's followers are still in the area," Paul remarked.

"Do you think you were followed?" Oliver inquired.

"No. We watched the entire way and took various back roads just to be safe," Adam replied.

"Does that mean we are back on lockdown?" Caleb shyly asked.

Eva stood still while she was deep in thought before she spoke. "No." Adam, along with everyone else, smiled. "We tried that, and it didn't work. I will not be a prisoner in my own home any longer. Everyone is still free to come and go as they wish. However, I do want everyone to carry their weapon with them. I also don't want anyone traveling alone, so if you leave, grab at least one other person to accompany you. They have proven they don't mind teaming up to fight and seem determined to get whatever the mystery object is. As for nighttime, no one needs to stand guard, but I will add some extra precautions around the house and the gate to strengthen the security around here. Does everyone agree?"

Everybody nodded their heads. Eva then turned her attention to Oliver. She gave him a stern look. "Do you agree?"

"Yes, I agree," Oliver responded.

Eva stood closer to him. "I hope so, because if something happens to any of us because you go rogue again, I don't care how close I am with Adam, you will have me to deal with. Do I make myself clear?"

"Crystal," Oliver replied with a deadpan expression.

Kaylee cleared her throat. "Um...I don't have a weapon yet."

Eva turned around and smiled. "Well then. I guess it's time to remedy that." She then turned to Caleb, but before she could say anything, Caleb spoke.

"I already have something planned for this moment. I was just waiting for you to give me the word. Kaylee, just give me like ten minutes, and I will be ready."

"That sounds good. Thank you," Kaylee responded as she grinned.

"Awesome," Caleb said with excitement before he scurried off.

Eva smiled at his reaction. "I can only imagine what he has planned for you."

"What girl doesn't like shopping for weapons?" Kaylee jokingly responded.

"Accessories," Eva said as she winked. "Okay, everyone. Be safe, be smart." She then strolled over to Adam and put her hand on his shoulder. "Don't think I won't find out the details behind your fun night." Adam scoffed with amusement as she smiled and walked away.

"Are you ready to see what Caleb has in store for you?" Adam asked.

"As ready as I'll ever be," Kaylee responded. The two gulped down the rest of their coffees and slowly walked to the training room.

When they entered the room, Caleb had various weapons on display. Adam recognized them from the larger assortment of identified weapons Caleb had handled over the years. He knew how important the decision was, so he let Kaylee stroll in first so she could pick out her weapon without any distractions. So, instead of following her in, Adam leaned against the doorway. He smiled when he saw Caleb become giddy when Kaylee approached the table.

"Okay, I think you will be impressed with what I have laid out for you. I talked with Eva, and she told me what fighting styles and weapons seemed more of your strong suit, so I took the liberty and picked out the top five weapons to mirror what Eva told me. I hope you don't mind," Caleb said.

"Not at all. Thank you," Kaylee responded. Caleb smiled, rubbed his hands together, and took a step back. She turned her head to look at Adam. "How do I choose?"

"Whatever you feel drawn to the most. When you hold it, you will know if you made the right choice," Adam replied. He pointed his eyes toward the table and slightly smiled. Kaylee nodded, took a deep breath, and directed her eyes toward the weapons.

Adam watched as her fingers lightly touched each weapon as she slowly walked down the side of the table. There were two types of swords, a pair of daggers, a mace, and a small axe. After she touched each one, she repeated the process but stopped at the twin daggers. Adam watched as she picked them up and examined them.

They had long, black, shiny blades that had to be around one and a half feet long. Each blade had a small, golden tree-like design near where the blade met the handle. There was no guard, just a handle wrapped in black leather with gold protruding from the bottom and top of the handle. The blade seemed sharp on one side and was straight until a few inches from the tip of the blade, where it began to curve slightly.

"I choose these," Kaylee whispered as she continued to examine them. Adam smiled because even though she didn't realize it, she had made a huge step in her immortality journey.

"I knew it!" Caleb exclaimed as his arms shot up into the air. It was so loud that Adam chuckled to himself when Kaylee almost jumped out of her skin. "Sorry, I didn't mean to scare you. I just had a feeling that you were going to pick them."

At this point, Adam walked into the room and to the side of Kaylee. "Good job and definitely a good choice."

"Really? What's magical about them?" Kaylee asked Adam. He knew, but decided to let Caleb respond, so he gestured toward him. Kaylee turned her attention to Caleb.

Caleb's eyes gleamed. "Legend has it that during the medieval times, a secret society of assassins needed a weapon far more powerful than anything they had, so they went on a voyage to Iceland. There, with the assistance of a sorceress, they formed these daggers at the foot of a volcano. The blades are made of pure obsidian, which makes them extremely sharp. Now, everyone knows how brittle obsidian can be, but the magic that created these weapons makes the blades as durable as steel."

"So, very sharp and durable blades. Leave it to me to pick the bland magical ones out of the group," Kaylee said, disheartened. Adam and Caleb glanced at each other and smirked.

"Do you really think I would give you something boring like that?" Caleb commented with a crooked grin.

"There's more?" Kaylee asked. Her brow lifted with curiosity.

"Oh, there's more. It will take practice, but everything else I am about to describe can be done through your mind," Caleb responded.

Kaylee smiled. "Like what?"

Caleb came around the table to stand next to her. "Normally, Eva doesn't like us using our magical weapons here, but I think she will let it slide. There are three other things these weapons can do. First, the blades are meant to be carried stealthily, so picture the length of the blades reduced in size. Will it to be so."

Kaylee stared at the blades. Adam saw her forehead crinkle as her lips pressed together. A few moments later, the blades shortened to around four inches in length within the blink of an eye. She smiled, and as Caleb was about to speak, Kaylee stared at the blades, and they converted back to their original length.

"Wow, you seemed to get the knack of that quickly," Caleb commented, which made Kaylee's smile grow.

"I agree. Controlling weapons through your mind is not easy. Very impressive," Adam remarked.

"Second, place your hand high on one handle and low on the other handle. It doesn't matter which dagger you do that with. Once you've done that, bring them together. Pretend like you are holding a sword and will them to be one," Caleb directed.

Kaylee did as instructed, but the daggers would not combine. She huffed, and her brow furrowed. "Why can't I do …" Before Kaylee could finish, the twin daggers became a sword. "Whoa!" Adam couldn't help but chuckle at her being caught off guard by the transformation. Kaylee examined the sword. The blade was double the length of the daggers and mirrored their appearance.

"The assassins liked the option of killing with either the daggers or the sword, depending on what the situation called for. It also made it a versatile weapon to carry. You can convert them back to dagger form by reversing what you just did, but before you do that, let me show you the last thing it can do," Caleb said. Adam knew what was next, so he and Caleb took a step back.

"Okay, you two are making me nervous," Kaylee mentioned.

"Sorry. If you will notice, there is now a one-inch obsidian pyramid at the bottom of the handle," Caleb mentioned as he pointed. Kaylee looked over the new addition.

"For the last thing, I want you to point that pyramid at the iron shield in the corner of the room. The one with the dents in it that we use for practice," Caleb instructed.

"You mean like this?" Kaylee lifted the handle, but it was pointed at them. Before she could turn around, their eyes grew wide as they scurried out of the way. "What?" Kaylee asked.

"You'll see. Just carefully point the pyramid at the shield," Adam responded. Kaylee shrugged before she turned around and did what they asked.

"Okay, now attack it, but without moving. Keep the handle pointed at it and visualize striking it from a distance. In a way, in your mind, imagine reaching out and striking it with the pyramid," Caleb said.

Kaylee did what he asked, but after a few minutes, nothing happened. "Guys, I don't know if I am doing this right."

"Try harder. Concentrate. Imagine that your life depended on it. Make your weapon feel what you are feeling," Adam calmly said.

Kaylee nodded and took a deep breath. Her face strained as she concentrated. Not long after her next attempt, a jagged black light shot from where the pyramid was. There was a loud clang, and Adam could see a dent with a little smoke around it from where the light had hit the shield.

Kaylee cheered. "That's so cool. No wonder you guys were so scared."

"Not scared. More like cautious," Caleb stuttered.

"Yeah, cautious," Adam repeated.

"Yeah, right. You two were scared," Kaylee teased. Before Adam and Caleb could respond, Kaylee noticed the pyramid was missing. "Where did it go? Do I have to reload it or something?"

"It will reappear on its own. You can only use that special attack once per day. It was intended as a last-resort tactic in case the assassin was in trouble," Caleb explained.

"Understood," Kaylee replied. She then pulled on the handle to convert the sword back into the twin daggers. "This weapon is freaking awesome! Thank you so much!"

"No problem. Any time. Here, you will need these as well," Caleb responded. He handed her sheaths for the daggers and the sword. "They are specially made to withstand the sharpness of the blades, and the straps can be configured to be worn on various locations on your body." Kaylee smiled and gave Caleb a side hug.

"Remember, practice with them as much as possible since this will be your primary weapon. The more you practice with a magical weapon, especially one that activates using your mind, the more in tune you will be with your weapon. In return, your weapon will become an extension of yourself. Eventually, activating your daggers' abilities will be as easy as breathing."

"Yes, sensei," Kaylee teased. Adam sighed. "I get it." A playful smile then appeared on her face. "Care to help me train?"

"I would be honored," Adam mocked and then bowed.

"As you should be," Kaylee responded.

"What are your plans for today, Caleb?" Adam inquired.

"Eva is taking me to a vintage arcade place. I've always wanted to try those types of games. I don't think they will be any harder than the online games I play now, but she feels otherwise," Caleb replied.

Adam smiled at his excitement and eagerness. "Have fun."

Kaylee and Adam left the room and went outside.

"We like to practice out here. It's spacious and secluded by the trees. Just up ahead is the range area where Paul likes to practice with his weapon," Adam explained.

"So, we can use our magical weapons outside but not inside. Why is that?" Kaylee asked.

"Eva considers it bad luck," Adam responded while they continued to walk.

"When did that become bad luck?" Kaylee inquired.

"Ever since the day Eva almost killed me," Adam replied.

CHAPTER 14

Kaylee stopped. "Whoa! You're just going to drop some insane information like that and casually walk away. Immortal world or not, this girl is going to need details, so spill it."

Adam shrugged. "It happens." He then winked and continued to walk.

"Seriously!" Kaylee exclaimed and then jogged to catch up.

Adam smiled. "It was about a century and a half ago in that very training room we were just in. We were practicing, and she caught me off guard with a new move she decided to try."

"And?" Kaylee asked.

"And her blade pierced my chest and just barely missed my heart," Adam responded.

Kaylee's jaw dropped. "Oh my gosh! I can only imagine how horrible she must have felt."

"She did. Regardless of how many times I explained to her that it wasn't her fault and that it was an accident, she wouldn't leave my bedside for that entire week," Adam recollected.

"Wait. A week? I thought we healed rapidly. I understand wounds from magical weapons take longer, but still. Why so long?"

Adam stopped when they reached the training area and turned to Kaylee. "Think of it as a scale. Damage from non-magical weapons heals rapidly. However, some may not heal as quickly if the damage is severe enough. As for a fatal wound, like a sword through the heart, the immortal would die, but only temporarily. It could range from a few minutes to hours before the immortal would come back to life. Now, damage from magical weapons takes longer. How long would depend on how bad the wound is. However, if the damage from a magical weapon does enough damage to the immortal or is a near-fatal wound, it takes significantly longer to heal. It could be a day, a week, a month, or however long for the immortal to heal, and even then, there is no guarantee the immortal would live. Of course, a fatal wound from a magical weapon means death."

Kaylee was silent for a moment as she processed what Adam had said. "That's…good to know, I guess. Still, after all that, I'm surprised she lets anyone practice with magical weapons on the property. I would be worried sick that it could happen again, or worse…someone died."

"For some time afterward, she didn't allow anyone to practice with magical weapons on her property. I recall how Eva didn't use her weapon for a year and wouldn't even raise a non-magical weapon at me for about twenty years. Regardless of how many times I told her it was safe to practice with non-magical weapons, she couldn't do it. The memories were too much for her. Ever since that day, she has never practiced using a magical weapon with me. It was probably around fifty years ago that she finally allowed magical weapons to be used as practice, but not in the manor," Adam responded.

"I guess it's like you said before, the more you practice with your weapon, the more in tune you are with it," Kaylee mentioned.

"Exactly, and Eva knew it, too. Don't get me wrong; practicing with non-magical weapons against others is good. Heck, even practicing with your magical weapon against an imaginary opponent is helpful. However, at the end of the day, you must practice with your magical weapon against a live target. Only then will you get a true feel for your weapon," Adam explained.

"Well, this practice session went from fun to terrifying," Kaylee remarked.

Adam smiled. "You'll be fine."

"It's not me I'm worried about," Kaylee countered.

"From what I hear, you seem to be a natural. You picked up the techniques quickly, and just from the little I saw, your movements while you fight flow effortlessly. Yeah, you still need to practice and sharpen your skills, but if I didn't know any better, I'd say you've been practicing for quite longer than you have been," Adam commented.

Kaylee grinned. "Really?"

"Absolutely. Even now, when learning about your daggers, you picked up on it faster than anticipated. Even more remarkable is that those daggers take more concentration than you realize. Don't tell Oliver this, but he couldn't figure them out," Adam mentioned.

"Seriously?" Kaylee's smile grew.

"Seriously. He couldn't get past the part of combining the daggers to form the sword. He just stood there, clanking them together until he finally gave up," Adam responded as he smiled.

"I wish I could have seen that," Kaylee remarked. The two laughed at Oliver's expense.

"Okay. You can do this. Just remember, with practice comes control. Until then, try not to kill me," Adam teased.

"That's the fear that keeps racing through my mind," Kaylee said as she lowered her daggers.

Adam smirked and then activated his sword. Kaylee stared at the greenish blade as Adam slowly raised it. "You think too much, and that's coming from a guy like me."

He did an overhead swing toward Kaylee's head. She raised both blades above her head and crossed them. His blade slammed into the crook of the two daggers. He kept the pressure on, but Kaylee's arms didn't bend much. She smirked right before she pushed his blade away and began to slash at him at different angles while alternating hands. Adam successfully blocked each one and was impressed with how quickly she became proficient in using both hands. During her assault, he ducked under a slash that was aimed higher than the other attacks. While crouched, he moved his sword forward, which caused her to stop short to avoid being impaled. Adam held his position while he had a smug expression.

Kaylee grinned. "Don't give me that look. You got lucky."

Adam stood up. "That may be the case. Just remember that defense is just as important as offense." As soon as Kaylee nodded, Adam thrust his sword forward.

She deflected it and moved closer as she thrust her dagger forward. Adam dodged the attack, and then their melee began. He noticed her technique improved with each move she made, but as she blocked one of his attacks, her counterattack sliced him across his left bicep.

"Oh my gosh! I'm so sorry," Kaylee said as she sheathed her daggers and grabbed his arm. Adam winced. "Sorry...again," Kaylee said as she cringed.

Adam scoffed with amusement. "I didn't realize you still had all this pent-up hatred for me."

"Shut up! I don't have any pent-up hatred for you," Kaylee defended.

"So, it's all gone now?" Adam asked.

"Yes. I mean, no," Kaylee huffed. "I never hated you." She then noticed that Adam was holding back a smile. "Are you just trying to rile me up?"

Adam shrugged. "Well, you are cute when you're angry." He then followed up with a wink.

Kaylee's face lit up. "You keep that up, and I will hate you." Adam chuckled. "Seriously, though, I'm sorry."

"It's okay. Believe it or not, it will heal," Adam responded.

"I guess I need to work on my control," Kaylee gently said as her fingers slowly glided across his arm. She watched as the superficial cut began to slowly heal.

Adam didn't realize how close she was to him until her eyes drifted up from his arm to meet his. Her hand remained on his arm while she stared into his eyes. He felt himself lost in her gaze as she gently smiled at him. She was as beautiful on the inside as she was on the outside.

"You know I could never hate you. Annoyed, yes, but never hate," Kaylee said with a crooked grin.

"You remember that sentiment after I win the next few rounds," Adam playfully said as he backed up.

"Oh, really? Well, come on then. Time for you to be humbled," Kaylee responded as she smiled and unsheathed her daggers.

Adam smirked before he did the same overhead strike that he did when they first started. She blocked it the same way, but as she went to push his sword away, Adam deactivated his sword. Kaylee's hands were above her head, and she was off-balance. Her eyes and mouth grew wide from the shock. Before she could react, Adam had the hilt of his sword pointed at her head. Kaylee kept her arms up in surrender. He knew that she realized that if it was a real fight, all he had to do was re-activate his sword, and she would have been dead.

"You were saying?" Adam teased.

"That was a cheap move," Kaylee responded as she lowered her arms.

"In battle, you must take advantage of your weapon's special abilities as much as possible. That move there saved my life a few times in the past," Adam explained as the two took a few steps away from each other.

"I'll keep that in mind," Kaylee responded. She then attacked.

This time, Adam used his agility and dodged her attacks by leaning backward or to the side. He only used his blade occasionally to block an attack that was impossible to dodge. He noticed her attacks became wilder as she gritted her teeth and her brow furrowed. Then, she yelled as she took a long swipe at his head, which he ducked, and as her momentum brought her forward, he swiftly walked right behind her. She turned around, and her breath left her as she bumped into his body.

Kaylee looked up at him as the two of them breathed hard. Their bodies were still pressed together as her face eased and matched his gentle smile. They were frozen in time for what seemed to be an eternity, but actually only a few moments before she cleared her throat and slowly backed away.

"I know. Control my emotions. Eva has told me that as well, and no, it's not cute," Kaylee said over her shoulder. Adam laughed before they took their positions.

They began fighting again, each taking turns with offensive and defensive maneuvers. At times, it was difficult for him to concentrate. He found his mind wandering back to when their bodies were pressed together. This round seemed to go on longer as the clang of their weapons echoed throughout the area. It was a dance of give and take as they moved about. During their battle, she tucked and rolled past him, and as he turned around, her blade was inches from his stomach. It seemed the fleeting moment she was out of his sight; she combined her daggers into a sword, which he didn't anticipate, so the additional length of the blade caught him off guard.

"Utilize your weapon's special abilities," Kaylee said. She then winked before she stood up.

"You're a quick learner," Adam responded as he grinned.

"Thanks. I just hope it's enough for whenever the time comes that another immortal challenges me," Kaylee commented.

"It will be. Your skills have increased immensely over a short period of time, and now you have an exceptional weapon. So those things, accompanied by your inner strength, will make you a force to be reckoned with," Adam replied.

Kaylee smiled, but it was fleeting. "I hope so. It's just that most immortals are way older than me and have been fighting and killing for centuries. Then there is me."

"I could echo what I just said, but if you don't believe in yourself, you will lose," Adam responded.

Kaylee nodded, and soon after, their training commenced. This time, their fight was more about technique than trying to best each other. The pace was slow but consistent as they moved around each other. Once again, he was impressed by how she adapted to different scenarios without being flustered. Her weapon remained in the form of a sword so she could get extra practice. Adam tried his overhead attack again. She turned her blade sideways and raised it over her head to block it. As he pushed down, he waited to see how she would counter. Instead, she leaned her head closer to his.

"So, what are we doing for our second date?" Kaylee asked.

He blinked multiple times as he shook his head. That was the last thing he expected to hear during their training. While his mind was briefly preoccupied, she pivoted her body and hip-tossed him to the ground. Adam remained sprawled out as he looked up at her blade pointed at his face.

"Eva mentioned that if I wanted to win against you, I just had to distract you," Kaylee said with a smug expression.

Adam smirked. "Is that so?"

"Yep, and it seems like it's an area you still need to work on," Kaylee responded before she extended her hand.

Adam grabbed her hand, but instead of letting her hoist him up, he yanked her down to the ground. She rolled onto her back, but before she could do anything else, Adam straddled her. He leaned down and had one hand on the ground, near her head, and the other had his sword pointed at her face.

"Never presume a battle is over," Adam said with a crooked grin.

"It was over. You're just a sore loser," Kaylee teased.

160

Adam moved his sword away from her face. "What you call a sore loser, I call an opportunity for enlightenment."

"Translation, sore loser," Kaylee responded. The two laughed and then became silent as they stared into each other's eyes while Kaylee ran her fingers up and down his arm.

"Bloody hell! This is a training area, not an area for frolicking," Oliver shouted as he approached. Adam sighed as his eyes closed, and he slowly shook his head.

"And you still choose to be friends with him," Kaylee sarcastically commented.

"Sometimes I question that decision," Adam remarked. He then deactivated his sword and helped Kaylee up.

"I'm going to head inside and get cleaned up. Thanks for the lessons," Kaylee said as she grinned and turned around.

"Any time," Adam said. Kaylee walked away but kept eye contact with him for a few seconds longer before she turned her head.

"Should I slip her a note that says 'Do you like Adam? Check yes or no.' Then, we can get together and giggle as we read her response," Oliver teased as he stood right behind him.

Adam turned around and placed the hilt of his dagger against Oliver's chest. "Why am I friends with you?" Adam's eyes narrowed while he stood there.

Oliver didn't react to Adam's reaction and remained nonchalant. "I always figured it was for my charm, counsel, and dashing good looks."

Adam lowered his hand and scoffed with amusement. His eyes were then drawn to what was strapped on Oliver's back. "Why are you carrying Drustan's axe?"

"You mean my axe? It's because I wanted to test out its flame-throwing ability. I figured if Cassian is as big of a deal as Caleb makes him out to be, I may need more firepower. No pun intended," Oliver explained.

161

"True, but be careful. You must envision burning your target. The ability draws from the darkness within you," Adam commented.

"Ooh, spooky," Oliver mocked. Adam sighed. "Relax. I'm proficient in that area. I control my darkness every day, so I'm not worried about this axe trying to exploit it." Adam nodded and patted Oliver on the shoulder. As he turned around, Oliver spoke.

"I was thinking about going back to that bar later. Do you want to tag along?"

Adam already knew he couldn't return to that bar for a long time, but another reason entered his mind. One that he had to hold back a smile. "I can't. I have a date tonight."

Oliver shrugged. "Suit yourself." Adam continued to walk but stopped when he heard Oliver call his name. "Good luck, mate. She seems like a good person."

Adam grinned. "She is. Thank you." He then continued back to the manor.

He needed to catch Kaylee in time before she made any other plans, but most importantly, he needed an idea for the second date. He racked his brain as he tried to think of something that would top their first date. Adam debated taking her to a fancy restaurant or doing something like putt-putt, but everything seemed generic. He knew she would enjoy them or anything because he knew she was more about the person than the activity, but still.

Then it dawned on him. A huge smile appeared when the perfect date idea formed in his mind. Adam decided to shower first since he preferred not to smell like sweat and the outdoors when he asked her out again. Once he was done, he began to roam the hallways in search of Kaylee. He quickly turned one of the corners and almost ran into her. They both gasped.

"Sorry. I didn't mean to frighten you," Adam quickly said.

Kaylee chuckled. "It's okay. Why are you in such a rush?"

"Honestly, trying to find you," Adam replied.

The corner of Kaylee's mouth rose. "Really? Why's that?"

Adam took a breath. "To ask if you would like to go on our second date tonight."

Kaylee smiled and brushed the hair away from her face as she briefly looked away. "Sure, that would be wonderful. What did you have in mind?" Before he could speak, he heard someone shout Caleb's name. He turned around and saw Paul enter the room while he carried a medium-sized cardboard box.

"Caleb!" Paul shouted again.

"What is it?" Adam asked.

"I got something that may be useful," Paul replied.

"What's up?" Caleb asked as he entered the room.

Paul put the box on the ground in front of Caleb and grinned. "I got a present for you." A small smile appeared as Caleb arched his brow. He then eyeballed the box. "The only way you'll know is if you open it."

Caleb shrugged and opened the box as Adam and Kaylee moved behind him to get a better view of its contents. Adam noticed several old, thick books. "Whoa," Caleb said as his eyes grew larger when he pulled one out, blew off the dust, and opened it. From what Adam could see, they appeared to be journals. This particular one was in Latin, but it seemed not all the journals were in Latin, since another random journal he pulled out was in Sanskrit. He also noticed sketches of objects and people on some of the pages.

"I got in touch with one of my contacts who works at a library in New York, who owed me a favor. I had him send me anything old that referenced the name 'Cassian and immortal' in the same text from the library's private collection. This box contains everything he could find," Paul explained.

"This is awesome. I can only imagine what information lies within these pages," Caleb commented.

"You can read those languages?" Kaylee inquired.

"When you have lived long enough, you tend to pick up a few languages. However, Caleb's thirst for knowledge has led him to learn several languages," Adam responded.

"Especially the older ones. That's where all the juicy information lies," Caleb mentioned. Kaylee giggled.

Paul sighed. "There's more. I talked to my contact, and apparently, if the legends are true, Cassian is far more dangerous than we anticipated."

"How so?" Adam inquired.

CHAPTER 15

Paul's eyes drifted to each of them as his face became sullen. "Legends have it that no immortal has come remotely close to defeating him, except for the original people who were turned immortal. Even then, he has been mentioned to be unstoppable multiple times within the books." Paul went to speak but stopped.

"What? What else is there?" Adam asked.

Paul took a long breath. "The books also discuss how evil he is and how he possesses magical powers. Not only that, they mentioned that he was the one who had purposely unleashed the Black Death almost seven hundred years ago. He seems to be in the background of multiple wars throughout the centuries, pulling the strings."

"So...super bad guy. Got it. Good to know," Kaylee sarcastically said.

Adam remained silent. It wasn't uncommon for an immortal to be a part of history and even influence it, but not to this extent. But why, he wondered. An immortal typically didn't get involved unless there was a reason. Whether it be personal, financial, pleasure, or something else...there was always a reason. They needed to know more, and he hoped Caleb could discover more about Cassian within the books and journals. Even more...how to stop the unstoppable.

"I'll start looking at these right away," Caleb said. He picked up the box and was about to leave, but stopped. The joy vanished from his face. "Oh, I had plans with Eva to go to an arcade. I need to tell her I can't now."

Adam shared a quick look with Kaylee and then Paul before he spoke. "Just start your research tomorrow."

"Really? Are you sure? End of the world seems more important than games," Caleb replied.

"One day shouldn't make a difference. Besides, if the box came later today, then you would have been gone, and it would have waited until tomorrow anyway," Paul said.

"Yeah, and besides, you don't want to break plans with Eva," Kaylee added.

Caleb looked back and forth between Kaylee and Paul. Adam could see the struggle in his eyes. "You deserve it. The books can wait one day. Go ahead. Paul won't tell anyone else until you are back and our lips are sealed," Adam said. Paul and Kaylee both nodded.

A large smile appeared on Caleb's face. "Okay. Great. I'll go. Thanks, everyone! I'll put these in my room to look at later." Adam smiled as he watched Caleb scurry off.

"It's good to see him having fun," Paul commented.

"It is," Adam replied.

"Well, I'm off to the outside training area. If any of the legends are true, I will need to make sure my shot is as accurate as ever," Paul said before he proceeded down the hallway.

"Be careful not to get burned. Oliver is practicing with Drustan's axe," Adam called out. Paul didn't turn around. He just waved his hand in acknowledgment and continued to walk away.

Kaylee stepped in front of Adam and placed her hands on his arms. "What you did for Caleb was very sweet of you."

Adam smiled. "The kid hasn't truly lived in a while and is such a good person. He deserves it."

"And what about us?" Kaylee asked.

Adam stammered. "Um…we deserve to be happy too."

Kaylee chuckled. "I meant our date."

"Oh!" Adam said. He could feel his face turn red and hoped it wasn't too noticeable. "Yes, our date." Adam took a breath to compose himself. "I was thinking we could have our date in my room tonight."

Kaylee's face turned red as she looked around and stammered. "Um…um, I don't know if we are at that point yet. You know I want to take it slow and…wait, are you trying not to laugh right now?"

Adam laughed and enjoyed how cute she acted as she squirmed. "Yes, because I meant a movie night. Like how we used to do. Get your mind out of the gutter."

"Shut up," Kaylee said. She briefly looked away as she tucked her hair behind her ear and grinned.

"Well?" Adam asked while he continued to smile.

"Yes, that sounds wonderful," Kaylee responded.

"Good. Eight o'clock, my room, and dress as comfortably as you want," Adam said. Kaylee nodded.

Adam smiled and rushed to his room to sort out the details of their date. He wanted to do his best to recreate how they used to have movie nights. He first gathered a handful of DVDs from the common area that he knew she would enjoy, which were typically action and romantic comedies. He preferred DVDs over streaming so he could have them laid out for her to see. That way, it would demonstrate he still remembered what she liked and would better set the tone for the movie night.

He then pillaged the manor for other items to put into his room, starting with the blankets and extra-large pillows. Adam placed those on the floor near the foot of his king-size bed. He then ventured to the kitchen and grabbed candy, chips, soda, and popcorn to make later. As he situated his room for tonight, he stopped and double-checked to ensure he had everything.

Adam smiled at what he had created and hoped that she would enjoy it; however, there was one detail he wasn't sure about…the placement of the pillows. They seemed too close together, and he didn't want to make her feel uncomfortable. So, he spaced out the pillows and placed the snacks and DVDs between them. He then changed into a plain heathered gray t-shirt and a black pair of mesh basketball shorts. A deep breath followed after he looked at himself in the mirror and hoped she would be dressed as casually as him.

As the sky darkened, he could hear Oliver and Paul leave for what he presumed would be the bar. Caleb and Eva had already left an hour before them, so now it was just him and Kaylee. The closer it got to eight o'clock, the more nervous he became, and he wasn't sure why. These kinds of nights were common for them in the past, but now, there was more meaning behind them. He paced the room, trying to plan out how their date would go. Then, he heard movement in the hallway, so he stopped, took a deep breath, and hoped she didn't catch on to how he spent the last thirty minutes pacing his room. Kaylee entered, and her brow rose as she scanned what Adam did.

Adam felt his heart drop to his stomach. "What? Is everything okay? Too much?"

Kaylee smiled. "No, it's perfect." Adam felt a weight lift from his chest. Then, they both looked at what they were wearing. Kaylee wore a pair of short black running shorts and a heathered gray t-shirt that barely came down to her waist. "Apparently, we're twinning."

Adam smiled. "It appears that way." He had an internal sigh of relief that she was dressed as casually as him.

Kaylee slowly walked further into his room and glanced around. "You know. All this time here, and I've never been in your room. I mean, I have seen it as I walked by, but never actually came in." Adam shrugged and gestured for her to walk around and look. Kaylee strolled around and viewed the different pictures, trinkets, and paintings throughout the room. Her brow crinkled when she

168

looked closer at a particular picture. "Wait a second. Is that you in that picture?"

"That would be correct. Some of my friends insisted we take a picture before I left. The town marshal was having trouble with a rowdy set of individuals. So, he deputized me long enough to assist him with that issue," Adam replied.

"That looks like the Wild West. Wasn't that like the late eighteen-hundreds?" Kaylee asked.

"It seems someone didn't sleep through their history class," Adam joked.

Kaylee smiled. "Aren't you afraid someone might discover you are immortal?"

"In this case, no. Whenever something like this arises, I tell them either that was a photo taken at a carnival or it's my great, great-grandfather. That typically shuts down any further questions. Besides, it's funny to have evidence like that right in front of someone, and they don't even realize it."

Kaylee scoffed with amusement. "I bet. Wait a moment. Is that you...and Paul at the peak of Mount Everest?"

"Yep. That was about fifty years ago," Adam responded.

"I can't believe you did that. It's such an amazing accomplishment," Kaylee commented.

"Thank you, but to be fair, I died like five times while doing that," Adam said as he cringed.

Kaylee burst into laughter. "Oh really."

"Yep. Paul died only three times, so he likes to rub that in my face from time to time," Adam added.

Kaylee laughed some more. Then her eyes met a marble sculpture in the corner of his room. "I presume that sculpture of that bust is supposed to be you. Probably done by Michelangelo himself," Kaylee mocked. When Adam shrugged, her jaw dropped. "You're kidding."

"It was his way of rewarding me when I helped him move some of his larger sculptures around, as well as my words of encouragement. I wouldn't accept payment, and he knew I traveled, so he gifted me this smaller version of what he wanted to do. His signature is on the bottom of it," Adam responded. He motioned with his eyes to the sculpture.

"No way!" Kaylee said as she rushed over and tilted it to see underneath.

"His signature has faded, but luckily, he also carved his signature in it. He wanted that gift to immortalize the goodness in humanity, and his signature to be immortal too. Ironic, I know," Adam commented.

Kaylee's eyes squinted. "It's faded, but I also see the name 'Adamo' near his name. Who is that?"

"That's me," Adam responded. He grinned when Kaylee looked at him with a crinkled face. "It's my birth name. I switched it to Adam when I moved to the States to help blend in. Afterward, that name stuck with me, so I adopted it. I haven't heard 'Adamo' in ages."

"You're full of surprises, aren't you?" Kaylee commented.

Adam smiled and shrugged. "It's part of my charm."

Kaylee scoffed with amusement. "Oh really. Anyway, I know you told me stories involving famous people you've met, but you kind of left him out."

"To be fair, most people I met were not famous then. Also, I lived a long time; therefore, I have many untold stories," Adam politely countered.

"Well, I guess you will have to catch me up on these stories someday," Kaylee said as she approached him and smiled.

Adam smiled. "I guess so." Once again, they stood very close to each other, gazing into their eyes.

170

Kaylee lightly cleared her throat, and as she turned her head, he noticed her eyes narrowed on something. "What's that?" She then proceeded to walk around his bed to his nightstand.

"The small chest?" Adam asked rhetorically. He kicked himself because, with all the preparation and planning he did, he forgot to hide it.

"Yeah. I don't know why, but it just seems out of place," Kaylee responded while she looked it over.

"It's, um...nothing. Just some random decoration," Adam stuttered.

Kaylee turned her head with a raised brow. "You're lying."

Adam scratched the back of his head as he looked around. "No, I'm not."

Kaylee smiled. "Yes, you are. I know you too well to know when you are lying."

"Like all those years we were friends, and you had no idea I was immortal," Adam playfully countered as he walked around the bed to stand beside her.

Kaylee chuckled. "Fair enough, but I know you are lying now. So...what is it? A gift from an ex-girlfriend or something?" She asked as she lightly poked him in his ribs.

"Not exactly," Adam said.

"Then what is it, or do I need to open it up to find out?" Kaylee asked. The corner of her mouth curled as she placed her hand on the chest.

Adam sighed. "It's a memory chest." Kaylee's brow slightly lowered. "You see, we may be immortal, but our memories are not. You know how much trouble you have trying to remember something from years ago; well, imagine centuries ago. Yes, there are items and pictures I have saved over the years. I've brought these things over from storage just to have them here to make it feel more like home. However, that chest there contains my most precious memories. Memories that have touched my heart, and I never want to

171

lose them. For a while, I had them stored in a safe deposit box, but over time, I felt lost without them, so now they stay with me. I always kept them with me as I traveled, but I feared something would happen to them, so I left them here under Eva's protection. This past decade was the longest I have ever been without them."

"Why is that?" Kaylee softly asked.

"Because I was with you, and that was all I needed. Then, when I left, I was so hurt and lost that I needed time to be alone to deal with the pain," Adam replied. Kaylee was speechless as her eyes welled up while she pressed her lips firmly together. "And this is why I lied. I didn't want to ruin our date."

She didn't say a word. Instead, she buried her head into his chest and hugged him. He hugged her back while resting his chin on top of her head. The two remained like that for a little while, which he didn't mind. He could have held her forever.

Kaylee backed away, followed by a sniffle as she wiped her eyes. "Sorry," she said as she tried to wipe her tear stains off his shirt.

Adam smiled. "It's all right. I understand if you want to do this another time…"

"No," Kaylee quickly interrupted and then walked over to view his movie selections. It didn't take long for her to pick out an action and romantic comedy movie. "I believe we should start with the romantic comedy first." Her smile reappeared.

He smiled and nodded his head slightly. "Sounds good to me. I'll make the popcorn and get some ice for the drinks."

"Good idea! You can't watch movies without some junk food," Kaylee replied.

Adam scooped up the bowl and cups and went to the kitchen. Once he was done, he returned, and Kaylee was sitting on the pillows at the foot of the bed. He noticed she had the two movies lying on her lap and was surrounded by bags of candy. He then noticed that the gap between their two spots had vanished.

172

"Yay! I could smell the popcorn from here," Kaylee cheerfully said. She raised her hand for the bowl and swapped the movies for the popcorn and drinks. By the time he got to the TV, Kaylee was already munching away on the popcorn.

"It's a good thing I made extra," Adam teased.

"Shut up," Kaylee mumbled.

He turned the romantic comedy on, flipped the lights off, and sat beside Kaylee. He was surprised at how comfortable the pillow layout was. However, he was unsure how to act since he was now shoulder-to-shoulder with Kaylee. His body was stiff, and he felt awkward. Then, Kaylee nudged him. He looked over, and she smiled and winked at him as she presented him with the popcorn bowl. That look from her made him instantly relax as he smiled and grabbed a handful of popcorn. She then leaned more on him as they began to watch the movie.

Hours passed as they remained side-by-side, surrounded by empty cups, bowls, and wrappers, while they enjoyed both movies. Even with the immense threat that loomed over them, this was their time, and nothing could ruin it. Once the movies were over, they didn't move.

Instead, Kaylee snuggled up to Adam, and he had his arm around her. She lay her head on his chest and rested her arm across his stomach while they chatted about random subjects. Her head was slightly tilted toward his face, so the longer they talked, the more he noticed her eyelids becoming heavy. Also, her words became slower and more spaced out. He then found himself continuously lightly running his fingers through her hair.

"If you keep that up, I'm going to fall asleep," Kaylee mentioned.

Adam scoffed with amusement and then stopped. "Sorry."

"I didn't say you had to stop doing it," Kaylee said. He continued, and her relaxed smile returned. After some silence, he thought she had fallen asleep until she spoke again. "Did you ever go on our trip?"

"Our trip?" Adam asked.

"Yeah. You know. Where we planned to go after I graduated," Kaylee responded. He could hear the tiredness in her voice.

Adam instantly knew what she was referring to. "Alaska, to see the northern lights."

"Yeah. Did you go? Have you ever been? I know you said you had never been before, but maybe you did like two hundred years ago and didn't know how to tell me," Kaylee replied.

"I've been to many places, but never there. After I left you, I thought about going. In some weird way, I thought of it as a tribute to you, but I couldn't do it. I felt too guilty to book the trip, so I never went. How about you?" He continued to run his fingers through her hair while he waited for her response.

"No. I thought about going out of spite, but I couldn't," Kaylee responded. She never looked up at him the entire time. Instead, she kept her head on his chest.

"How about I take you to Alaska once we are past this Cassian ordeal?" Adam asked.

"I would love that," Kaylee said. He felt her arm that was laid across him tighten briefly before she snuggled closer to him.

They remained silent again, and he could feel her body loosen and her breathing change. He thought about scooping her up and bringing her to her bed, but he was afraid that would fully wake her up. There was also the selfish side of him that truly enjoyed the moment. Adam felt so much at peace that it relaxed him to the point where he was now tired. He had to stretch, but he was able to lean over enough to grab the remote and turn off the television. It was already muted, so it was more to turn the remaining light off in the room.

"Goodnight," he whispered before gently kissing the top of her head.

Kaylee slightly stirred and briefly held him tighter. "Goodnight," she whispered. He didn't know she was still awake. Maybe he woke her up when he reached for the remote, but he was relieved and glad that she was fine with his innocent gesture. He fell asleep not too long after that.

CHAPTER 16

Adam awoke the next morning in the same position he had fallen asleep, but further down the pillows. Kaylee was still sleeping, but her head was now on a pillow on his arm, near his shoulder. Her arm was still draped over him. He smiled at how peaceful and beautiful she looked. He needed to get up, so he carefully slid his arm from under her as he shifted his body away. As soon as he stood up, he realized that his arm that Kaylee was on was asleep. He rubbed and shook his arm as he headed to the kitchen for coffee. The pins and needles stayed with him until shortly after he entered the kitchen. He leaned against the counter and reminisced about the previous night while he waited for the coffee to brew.

"Rough night?" Eva said with a smirk as she leaned against the doorway.

Adam's brow lowered for a moment as he stared at her. Then, he sighed. "You saw Kaylee and me asleep, didn't you?"

"I sure did," Eva responded as she smiled and approached him.

"Someday, I will remember to close my door," Adam commented.

Eva giggled. "It's nothing to be ashamed about."

"Nothing happened. We watched movies and talked before we fell asleep," Adam defended.

"Regardless, you two are adorable. Even more adorable than your face, which is a few shades of red now," Eva said with a devious smile as she reached for a mug.

"Thanks," Adam sarcastically said as he poured the freshly brewed coffee into Eva's mug, followed by Kaylee's, and then his own.

"Before your face turns the color of a tomato, I'll change the subject. Paul came and talked to me about the box that was sent here. I told him to relay what he told me to Oliver before he left," Eva commented. She then proceeded to get the creamer from the fridge and add it to her coffee.

"I figured he would. Did you tell Caleb that you knew?" Adam asked.

"No. I wanted him to enjoy the arcade. I'll act like I found out today," Eva responded.

"Oh yeah. How did he like the arcade?" Adam inquired.

"He enjoyed it once he got used to it. Apparently, it's totally different from playing online games. It was quite comical watching him trying to get the handle on it," Eva said as she smiled.

"That bad?" Adam said as he cringed. He then added creamer to his coffee.

"There was a point that he almost fell off the motorcycle for the arcade game," Eva responded right before they both laughed.

"I'm glad he had a good time," Adam commented.

"Me too. I'm sure his nose will be buried in those books for a while now," Eva mentioned.

"Any sign of being watched last night?" Adam inquired as he began to add the creamer to Kaylee's coffee.

"None," Eva replied. She then stared at Adam as he continued to pour the creamer into Kaylee's cup. "Um...would you like some coffee with that creamer?"

Adam grinned and finally stopped. "She likes a lot of creamer."

Eva's brow rose. "I guess so."

177

Adam then noticed her demeanor shift as she became distant. "This Cassian business has you worried, doesn't it?"

"It does. You and I have faced many immortals in our time. Some were powerful and dangerous, but Cassian seems to be at an entirely different level. Part of me feels I should invite him into my home and let him get whatever object he is searching for, just to avoid the conflict," Eva responded.

"You could, but what's to say he wouldn't still try to kill us after he obtained the item? Also, you and I have enough experience to know that whatever he wants with it can't be good," Adam replied.

Eva sighed. "I guess you're right."

Adam hugged Eva. "Wow, you must be worried to admit I was right."

Eva chuckled before she took a step back. "Don't get used to it. Now go bring your girl her creamer with a splash of coffee."

Adam smiled and grabbed both mugs, but right before he left the kitchen, he stopped and turned around. Eva noticed and looked in his direction. "Don't worry, Eva. Whatever it takes, I'll do my best to protect your home and keep everyone safe."

Eva smiled. "I know you will."

Adam returned to his room to find Kaylee still asleep, so he sat down beside her. He then hovered her mug near her face. It didn't take long for her to wake up.

She sat up and stretched before she turned to Adam and smiled. "Good morning. Have you been up long?"

"Good morning. Just long enough to make you this," Adam replied as he handed her the coffee mug.

She smiled. "It smells good. Thank you." They sipped on their coffees while making small talk for the next few minutes before she stood up.

"I'm going for a run before I get cleaned up, but before I go, I just wanted to say that I really enjoyed our date last night. To be honest, it was perfect," Kaylee said.

"Well, I'm glad at least one of us did," Adam teased.

Kaylee's smile grew. "Seriously!"

Adam smiled as he approached her and placed his hands on her hips. As he did, she placed her hands on his biceps. "It makes me happy to know that you enjoyed the night. It was wonderful for me, too." The two stared into each other's eyes, and as he was once again lost in her gaze, she took a deep breath as she smiled and backed up.

"I'm trying my best to take this slow, but it's difficult between our history and where we are now. Emotionally, the second date might as well have been the hundredth date, but I'm still trying to take this slow. Why? Because I'm crazy, and I need to work past some things in my mind. Trust me when I say that it is taking substantial effort not to kiss you right now," Kaylee admitted while she fidgeted.

Adam smiled. "I appreciate your honesty. Take it from somebody who used to hang out with Sigmund Freud, you're not crazy for wanting to sort things out first."

"You were friends with Freud?" Kaylee asked with a raised brow.

"He was a brilliant and good man, but his cigar habit was disgusting," Adam remarked. Kaylee scoffed with amusement. "As much as I want that kiss to happen, I will honor your wish."

Kaylee smiled. "I know. That is why I feel so safe with you."

Adam leaned in, close enough for her to feel his hot breath against her skin, and whispered in her ear, "But I may have to tease you about it, occasionally." He could hear her breath tremble as goosebumps appeared on her skin.

Kaylee stepped away. "You're mean but okay. Just remember." She bit her lower lip as she walked up to him. With her body slightly touching his, she reached up, cupped the back of his head, and gently pulled him toward her as she stood up on her toes. Her cheek lightly touched his before she whispered in his ear, "Two can play that game, and I don't think you'll win." Her breath sent shivers throughout his body. Then her fingers lightly slid across his face and down his chest. He quickly took a step back and suppressed any urges that were trying to surface.

"I think you're right," Adam said. Kaylee winked before she left the room.

The following week seemed to fly by for Adam. If he wasn't training or meditating, he was spending time with Kaylee. They went on a couple of dates outside the manor to a nice restaurant, followed by a stroll through town. The nights they stayed inside were spent doing random things. They even found laughter and fun in something as simple as a board game. They enjoyed each other's company. He chose not to flirt too heavily with her because even though it was harmless, he didn't want to indirectly make her feel pressured. As for the rest of the household, everybody came and went as normal while Caleb read and studied the books.

About halfway through that week, in the middle of the night, Adam screamed as he jolted up in his bed from a nightmare. He wiped the sweat from his forehead and took a few deep breaths to control his breathing and erase the vivid, bloody images from his dream. Just as he was done doing that, Kaylee rushed in.

"Are you okay?" Kaylee asked as she walked to the side of his bed.

"Yeah, why?" Adam inquired.

"Because I heard you scream a few rooms over. I'm surprised you didn't wake the entire house. Did you have a nightmare or something?" Kaylee asked as her eyes scanned him over.

Adam scratched his head. "Yeah. Sorry about that. I didn't mean to startle you. Why are you up at this time?"

"I woke up and was thirsty, so I went to get something to drink. That is when I heard you yell. It must have been one terrible nightmare to make you scream like that. I don't think I ever heard your voice like that before. Full of pain and fear," Kaylee remarked as she sat at the edge of his bed.

"When you are as old as I am, you tend to experience a vast number of unnerving events, to say the least. One of the benefits of the curse," Adam sarcastically replied.

"Do you want to talk about it?" Kaylee asked as she put her hand on his knee.

Adam shrugged. "There's not much to say. I was reliving a war I was in, but I can't place which one it was. I think it was a few mashed together."

"I'm sorry. You know…I've noticed you only told me about the good stories in your life, minus the one about your parents. Why is that?" Kaylee inquired.

"I didn't want to burden you with the unpleasant events of my past," Adam replied.

"Your burdens are my burdens. I have unloaded all kinds of bad stuff on you, and you were there for me every step of the way. Let me be there for you," Kaylee said as she rubbed his knee.

"I am immortal," Adam said in a stern tone.

Kaylee's brow crinkled. "What is that supposed to mean?"

"The curse of immortality is unforgiving and relentless. To survive, I must bury those horrible memories away or else they will consume me," Adam responded with a deadpan expression.

"Yeah, because the screaming nightmares are a good indicator that it is working," Kaylee countered.

Adam's face lightened. "No one said it was foolproof."

"So, you want me to not talk about the things that are bothering me?" Kaylee said as she crossed her arms.

"Of course not," Adam quickly said.

"Fine. I will open up to you if you do the same with me. That is fair, especially if we are trying to move forward in our relationship," Kaylee replied.

Adam sighed. "You're right. I'll be more open with the not-so-good things in my life."

Kaylee smiled and placed her hand back on his knee. "That's better. So, tell me something. A story that isn't a good one."

Adam shrugged. "I don't know. It's hard to select the best of the worst with over five hundred years of memories. You already know about my parents."

"Okay, then just pick one. The first one that comes to mind," Kaylee suggested.

"Well, there is this girl I'm fond of who won't kiss me," Adam teased.

"Come on. I'm being serious," Kaylee whined.

Adam briefly paused to think of something. "You want a story, here's one. My parents not only abandoned me, but also banished me from our village. I've had to kill to survive. You've seen my immortal markings. They cover about half of my torso and arms, so that shows I've had to kill a lot of immortals to survive. I remember every wound they inflicted on me. I may not remember their faces, but I remember the pain. I remember the fear of wondering if I would live or die. I have also been in a handful of wars, and as brave as that sounds, it's not. I knew I was going to survive. I was there just to help the cause I felt was just, but during that time, I experienced so many men…good men…friends, killed for that same cause. I have seen horrific crimes of war. Elderly people, women, and children slaughtered and burned…which, by the way, is a smell you don't forget." Adam paused and cleared his throat as his eyes welled up.

"I've had immortal friends, whom I have known for decades, even centuries, die. There were times when the loneliness was suffocating. Billions of people roam this Earth, and I felt like I was all alone, locked in solitude. I try my hardest to push past that by making connections with people, but immortality has a way of making that difficult. So, now you have a better understanding of the pain I've lived with for centuries." A tear escaped his eye, which he quickly wiped off his cheek. He looked at Kaylee, and she had tears rolling down her cheeks.

"I'm so sorry," Kaylee said with a cracked voice before she hugged him.

"I'll live. I just hope the curse doesn't harm you as much as it did me," Adam said.

Kaylee let go and sat close to him. "I know you will, but no one should have to go through what you did, especially someone who's as good as you. I'm sorry. Not only for the fact that you had to experience that, but also because I could have been there for you all this time, but I wasn't."

"You shouldn't beat yourself up over things you didn't know about. I never told you," Adam said.

"You can say that all you want, but I still feel I should have known. Some way, somehow…I should have known," Kaylee responded and then wiped her eyes. "Lie down."

"What?" Adam said with a crinkled brow.

"You heard me. Lay down and get comfortable," Kaylee directed.

"Okay," Adam slowly said as he lay back down. Kaylee then snuggled up to him.

"What are you doing?" Adam asked.

"I'm sleeping here tonight," Kaylee responded.

"As much as I would love that, I would hate for the first time you're sleeping in my bed to be out of pity. I'll be fine. I'm over five hundred years old and have dealt with this for just as long. What's next, a nightlight?" Adam teased.

"Do you need a nightlight?" Kaylee countered. Adam scoffed with amusement. "I'm not doing this out of pity or because I don't think you can handle this. I'm doing this because I want to be there for you. You have been there for me so much that now it's my turn."

Adam let out a long breath. It wasn't out of frustration but out of relief. As much as he hated to admit it, she was right. It did feel good to talk about it, and it also made him feel closer to Kaylee. Her comfort was welcomed. "Thank you." He then put his arm around her and kissed the top of her head. She smiled as she held him tighter. "With any nightmare, you can't just go right back to sleep. You need good thoughts in your head first."

"Fair enough. Tell me another good story from your past," Kaylee responded.

"Okay. That horrible story did have glimpses of moments that showed the good within people. I have seen people come together to help the sick and wounded and to honor the ones who have fallen. I've witnessed a farmer defending his wounded dog against a handful of armed soldiers and won. Men who triumphed in battle in the face of certain death. Unlikely heroes who rose to the occasion on their own accord when needed. The compassion of the people of one nation to help strangers in another nation. As for the ones that I have lost, as horrible as it was, I still cherish the memories and the things they have taught me. Focusing on the good memories is one of the ways that helps me survive this curse."

Kaylee leaned up and kissed him on his cheek. "Thank you for sharing the good and the bad, and thank you for letting me be there for you." With a weight lifted off his chest and the warmth of Kaylee's affection, it didn't take long for Adam to fall back asleep.

Later that week, Adam and Kaylee were laughing as they left the billiard room one night when Caleb rushed over to them.

"There you guys are. I have everyone else gathered in the library. I am finally done with those books and must share what I've found."

"I presume it won't make any of us feel better," Adam commented.

"No…not really," Caleb responded.

"I figured that would be the case. Okay, lead the way," Adam said.

As they entered the library, he saw Eva's fingers scrolling through the books while Paul sat on the couch. Oliver was in a chair on the other side of the room, rolling his coin between his fingers.

Adam and Kaylee sat together on the adjacent couch while Caleb walked over to Eva.

"Now that everyone is here, please tell us what you've found," Eva said. She then went and leaned against the couch that Adam and Kaylee were sitting on.

"Okay, but just to warn you, my research uncovered more bad than good," Caleb commented.

CHAPTER 17

Oliver sighed as he continued to roll his coin between his fingers. "We're all big boys and girls here. Go ahead, purge…but don't bore us with all the gritty details. Just summarize how unpleasant Cassian will make our lives."

Caleb took a deep breath before he continued. "The books were cryptic, but they confirmed the legends we discussed. That includes Cassian being one of the six original people who were cursed. The warlock needed six people because the spell required a pentagram with a person at each point and one other in the middle. It even mentioned the other five people's names, but I already knew that and have information on them. It didn't have much information about the ritual outside of what I already told you. Obviously, I'm sure there was more to it. I guess you had to be there."

"I guess so. How about we skip to the 'fun' part," Oliver commented.

"Of course. Anyway, the texts go on for pages about how evil he became over the millennia, but there was no reference to the exact reason why. 'The World Ender' and 'Death' are just some of his nicknames referenced in the materials. Also, it is said that to face him is to face a legion of immortals. It further stated that he has magical powers beyond any other immortal. One power that was mentioned numerous times was necromancy. More than once, it made a point about how he can't be killed. I thought that was odd. You know…being immortal and all."

"Brilliant. Where's the good news, Caleb?" Oliver blurted out.

Caleb smiled. "I figured out what he is looking for."

Silence filled the room while everyone shared a look. Adam felt a much-needed glimmer of hope that sliced through the despair of what Caleb conveyed about Cassian. He felt Eva grab his shoulder, and when he looked up, he saw that same glimmer in her eyes. Adam also felt Kaylee's hand on his back, so he turned his head and saw her smiling.

"Bloody hell, mate. Lead with that next time. What is it?" Oliver asked. All eyes moved back to Caleb.

He reached over to something wrapped in leather and brought it to the center of the table. Caleb unraveled it, gently laid it in his hands, and presented it to the group. "It's that old copper dagger from my unidentified magical weapons pile. There are only a few drawings of it, but no words. However, I found those obscure drawings beside the references to the ceremony where the curse took place."

"You're telling me that we possess the dagger that started immortality? The same knife that the most powerful immortal in the world wants. Yeah, this story will have a happy ending," Oliver sarcastically commented as he pocketed his coin.

"What significance would it have to him now? Is he trying to find a way to reverse the curse?" Kaylee suggested.

"It's possible, but if he is as evil as it seems, then unlikely. Besides, why not use the chance to be mortal again as a tactic to persuade us to give him the knife?" Eva responded.

"That knife was used to kill those six people to trigger the curse. It must be filled with dark magic. We need to destroy it," Adam suggested. Everyone agreed, except one.

Caleb raised his hand to get everyone's attention. "I already tried it. It started as an accident. While moving weapons around to gain access to this dagger, the blade of another weapon fell and hit the wooden handle. The blade of that sword was definitely sharp enough to have cut the handle, but I didn't find a mark. When I examined the dagger, I couldn't find a single blemish on the blade or the handle. So, I experimented with it. I started small and increased the intensity, and nothing, I mean nothing, left a mark on it. I'm talking about smashing and cutting it with other powerful magical weapons, attempting to melt it in a crucible furnace, freezing it, and various other methods. Nothing worked."

"The blade is immortal," Paul commented.

"It seems that way," Caleb replied.

"If that is the case, can't you open a portal and dump it somewhere remote so it will never be found? In the middle of the Amazon, a remote area on Mount Everest, in the deepest part of the ocean, in an active volcano, or somewhere? Heck, stick it in the middle of some concrete, bury it, and then build a house on top of it," Kaylee suggested.

"I second that," Oliver voiced.

"It won't work," Adam mumbled.

"Adam's right," Eva confirmed. "One way or another, Cassian will find it. The dagger will wash up on some shore, or that volcano will erupt and spew the dagger out. One way or another, the dagger will be revealed. He seems determined enough to continue to search the ends of the Earth to find this dagger. One year, a thousand years, he will find it. It wouldn't surprise me if he had a magical means to track it down. All we would be doing is delaying the inevitable, and I, for one, will not be responsible for the end of the world or any innocent blood spilled that we could've prevented."

"What about our blood?" Oliver firmly asked. Eva turned to him but didn't speak. "Are you willing to spill our blood, to lose people close to you over this dagger, because that is exactly what will happen? A 'World Ender' isn't going to waltz through here just for the dagger and a spot of tea. Lives will be lost. I know I'm expendable, but what about the others in this room?" Oliver stood up and walked over to Eva. "You may be willing to die over this, but are you willing to sacrifice Adam, Paul, and Caleb? People you have known for many years. Even Kaylee, whom you've grown fond of over her brief time here. Do you want their ghosts haunting you for eternity?" Oliver calmly asked, yet his eyes were stern.

Eva remained quiet as she turned and walked a few steps away from him. "I have enough ghosts haunting me to last a hundred lifetimes," she softly said as her eyes drifted downward. Adam could hear the sadness in her voice and, unfortunately, shared her sentiment. She turned around and addressed the group. "I believe this dagger came into my possession for a reason, but it doesn't mean you must share that belief. Therefore, no one here is obligated to help. You may leave with no dishonor or judgment from me, and once this matter has been settled, you are welcome back to my home. I'll confess, part of me wants everyone to leave because I don't want to add anyone to my cemetery."

Adam glanced around the room and watched as people's eyes diverted from Eva as they thought about her words. He stood up, for Adam already knew his answer. "You've been there for me over the centuries. You were the first person to teach me what it meant to be an immortal and how to deal with my demons. You also accepted me into your home. It would be a shame if I abandoned you now." He noticed a smile appear on Eva's face.

"I don't know how much I can help, and I will admit, I'm scared. Even though I've trained every day since I have been here, I have never been in battle before or had any experience fighting. No, I don't count what happened at the club as experience. However, you have taken me in and trained me, given me counsel, and most of all, a place to call home. If it wasn't for you, I know I would have eventually died once my path crossed with an evil immortal. You saved me. Therefore, I will stay and fight alongside you as well," Kaylee announced as she stood beside Adam. Eva's smile grew.

189

"I will also stand and fight with you," Paul announced as he stood up. "This is my home too, and you've done far too much for me to just walk away." Eva's smile continued as she nodded.

"I want to stay and help. You have provided me with something more than just a home. You provided me with a place where I didn't have to feel afraid anymore…a sanctuary. Then, in recent weeks, everyone here has shown me additional kindness and support by helping me to push past my fears and live again. I'm not sure how much my shield and I can help, but I will do what I can," Caleb stated.

"You're stronger and braver than you realize," Eva said before she hugged Caleb. After that, all eyes turned to Oliver.

"Bloody freaking hell, the lot of you are insane," Oliver huffed as he turned around and put his hands on his hips. A few moments later, he turned back around. "I guess I'm the only sane person here because I know I will survive this," Oliver added as he patted his pocket that contained his coin.

"So, you'll stay and fight with us?" Adam asked.

"If a pacifist is going to stay and fight, then yes. If anything, to save my dignity," Oliver responded.

"I didn't know you had much left to defend," Adam teased.

"There isn't much, but that small amount is worth keeping intact," Oliver responded.

"Thank you, everyone. You standing by my side means more to me than you'll ever know, and yes, that statement includes Oliver," Eva said. She glanced at him and gave him a swift nod of approval.

Adam looked at Oliver, and when Eva wasn't looking, he turned his head toward Adam. "Progress," Oliver mouthed. Adam pressed his lips together and looked away to keep himself from laughing. He and the rest of the group joined Caleb around the table with the books sprawled across it.

"What else were you able to decipher?" Adam asked.

"That was mainly it. I was basically reading the same thing over and over, but in different languages," Caleb responded while he carefully flipped through the pages.

"In a way, that confirms the stories," Paul added.

"True, but how much is story versus how much is fact?" Eva countered.

"Exactly. We aren't sure what is real or what may have been real, but then twisted over the years, and that final version is what made it to these books. Also, keep in mind that some of the translations I did were not word-for-word since there was no English counterpart for it. That means that I had to make my own interpretations, and those may or may not have been correct," Caleb added.

"I have a feeling we will find out how accurate these books are sooner rather than later," Adam commented.

"As for your translations, I would trust them over the best scholars in the world," Paul added. Caleb smiled while everyone else agreed with Paul's comment.

"Well, I just saw our immortal mark, so we must presume that it is more fact than fiction," Kaylee mentioned as she watched Caleb flip through the pages.

"What do you mean, 'our' immortal mark?" Adam asked as his brow crinkled. The room fell silent as everyone looked at Kaylee with the same expression as Adam.

"You know...the immortal mark we all received in the same spot, over our hearts. I just saw it a few pages back," Kaylee responded. Caleb's brow crinkled before he began to go back a few pages.

"Hey Eva, I thought you said you trained her," Oliver said with a crooked grin. Eva side-eyed him.

"But I just saw it. Caleb will find it soon, and you will see what I am talking about," Kaylee huffed.

"That's impossible," Paul commented.

191

"You are all freaking me out. What am I missing?" Kaylee asked as she grabbed Adam's hand. Her eyes bounced from person to person.

"Kaylee, our initial marks may be in the same location, but they are like fingerprints. They look similar, but no immortal mark is the same," Adam responded.

CHAPTER 18

Kaylee's brow raised. "What do you mean, they're not the same? Are you sure? They must be the same. If not, that means my mark is in some ancient book about rituals, immortals, and Cassian." Adam could hear her voice tremble, and that fear was mirrored in her eyes.

"I'm sorry," Adam said.

"It's true," Eva confirmed.

"Great. That's just great. Caleb, any idea how I am linked to this?" Kaylee asked.

"I just found the mark. Actually, there is this mark, and then the same one a few pages later, but it is inverted. These are the only marks in this book," Caleb said.

"Let's compare Kaylee's mark to the ones in the book to make sure they are identical," Eva suggested as she moved to the side of Kaylee. Kaylee touched the top of her shirt, looked around, and cringed. "This is not a show. Women only. Turn around," Eva sternly directed. The men in the room quickly turned around to give them privacy. A couple of minutes later, Kaylee spoke.

"It's safe to turn back around."

"So, what's the word? Are they identical?" Paul inquired. Adam didn't need to hear her say it, her sullen face revealed everything.

"Yes. The marks are identical. Right down to the tiniest of details," Eva answered. She briefly rubbed the top of Kaylee's back.

Adam put his arm around her. "We'll find out what it means, somehow…someway, we will find out the significance of your mark." Kaylee nodded.

"In the interim, I wouldn't let Cassian or his goons see you in a low-cut shirt any time soon," Oliver casually commented as he smirked.

"What's the plan?" Paul asked.

"For now, I will hide that dagger somewhere in the manor. I want it in an obscure location, away from the other magical weapons. After that, I say we go into town and force their hand. Teams of three. One team goes out while the other stays here to guard the manor. Since they are lurking around, maybe we can get an audience with Cassian. Better yet, eliminate some of his followers to force him to reveal himself," Eva suggested.

"I like where your mind is, but are you sure you want to rattle that cage?" Oliver asked.

"It's better than sitting here and waiting for them to randomly appear on our doorstep someday," Eva countered. Oliver nodded with approval.

"Rattle the cage, it is," Adam commented.

"We will start tomorrow," Eva directed. Shortly after, everyone dispersed. Adam and Kaylee silently strolled down the hallway until they were away from everyone.

"What are you thinking?" Adam asked.

"I'm racking my brain, trying to figure out how I fit into this. All I can think of is that I am a descendant of his. Even worse, I'm the key he needs to end the world. I'm wondering if I need to be locked up or if I need to disappear. I might be as valuable to Cassian as the dagger," Kaylee responded as she crossed her arms over her stomach and stopped walking.

Adam put his hands on her shoulders. "I doubt it has anything to do with you being his descendant. In theory, there have been thousands of them over the years, so even if you were, it doesn't make you special." Kaylee's brow raised. Adam smiled. "You know what I mean."

A smile broke on her face. "I know."

His smile grew. "Even in desperate times, you still find humor." Kaylee shrugged and smirked. "Anyway, as for your other thought, you may be part of his diabolical plan, but at the same time, maybe not. All we can do now is to stick to Eva's plan. Our group is the only one that knows about your mark, so your secret is safe with us."

"Thank you, and I get it, but seeing my mark on that page still haunts me," Kaylee said.

"Do you want to go do something? It may take your mind off it," Adam suggested.

"Not today. Maybe tomorrow. I think I just need time to process," Kaylee replied.

"Take all the time you need. You know where to find me," Adam softly said with a reassuring smile. Kaylee smiled and hugged him. She held on to him tightly for a while before she let go and walked away.

When she left, he allowed his guard to drop, so his fear and anxiety surfaced as he walked back to his room. He knew there had to be a reason why her mark was in a book created long before she or any of them were alive. He wondered if Cassian and Kaylee were linked or if she was right about being the key to everything once he found the dagger. He tried to entertain hopeful ideas as to what the mark could mean, but only the fearful ones remained in his mind.

He desperately wanted to be with her because he knew how worried she was, but he also wanted to respect her wishes even more.

All he could do now was hope she would come back to him soon. Even more, he hoped she would be okay.

The next day, he kept to himself and didn't hear much from anyone else. He did some light training to pass the time and to help with his focus. Even then, it only took up so much time in the day, so he decided to go to bed earlier than usual. Adam also knew he wouldn't be able to sleep with the thoughts of everything dancing around in his head, so he meditated before he headed to bed. Even with meditation, he still had trouble sleeping, so he pulled out a book and began to read. He could feel his eyelids becoming heavy, and that was when he heard a tap at his door.

"May I come in?" Kaylee asked.

"Of course," Adam replied as he put his book down and sat up. "What's wrong?"

"I can't sleep, and I know this is going to sound silly and childish, but I was wondering if I could sleep with you tonight," Kaylee asked. Adam's brow rose. "I mean, sleep next to you. Not sleep with you," Kaylee stammered while blushing.

Adam smiled. "I knew what you meant. I just wanted to tease you."

Kaylee smiled and briefly looked away. "Very funny, but seriously. It's not that I'm scared. It's just…I think I would feel more relaxed if I were with you. Maybe then, I could actually fall asleep."

"Hop on in. Maybe we'll both manage to get some sleep," Adam said as he patted the open area on the bed.

"Thanks," Kaylee said. She walked around the bed, got under the covers, and situated herself close to Adam. He turned off the lamp, lay down, and put his arm up so Kaylee could snuggle with him. He wanted to ask if she had sorted out what she was dealing with yesterday and most of today, but he was afraid he would get her mind going again. Therefore, he chose to be silent about it. Besides, he figured she wouldn't have come to him if she were still working things out.

"How can your heart sound so calm and steady?" Kaylee asked while her head was on his chest.

"I eat healthy and exercise," Adam joked.

Kaylee giggled and then moved her head so she could see him. "Seriously, how are you not anxious? Especially with everything that is going on. Don't take this the wrong way, but I presumed you would be in your head, worried."

Adam smiled. "Well, you are not wrong. I am worried. Worried about the outcome of the events to come," he said as his smile left him. "I don't want to lose anyone, especially you, but in my centuries of experience, I'm afraid Oliver is right."

"Right about what?" Kaylee inquired.

"Lives will be lost," Adam responded.

Kaylee's brow lowered. "Yet, your heart is not unsettled by this?"

"Far from it, and I hope I am wrong, but I can't let it get to me. If I do, I will lose focus, and if that happens, people could die. I will admit, it has taken a lot of effort for me not to open a portal to somewhere far away and shove you through it."

"What's stopped you?" Kaylee softly asked.

"I fear your wrath more than Cassian's blade," Adam teased.

"Seriously," Kaylee responded as she smiled and lightly smacked his chest.

Adam smiled. "There are many reasons. Mainly, I didn't want you to resent me, or yourself, if something went wrong and you felt you could've prevented it. Also, if you are the key to whatever Cassian is trying to do, I want to be there to help protect you. Lastly, we are stronger together than apart."

Kaylee smiled, leaned up, and kissed him on his cheek. "Thank you," she whispered. The kiss and her hot breath against his cheek and ear sent a tingling sensation throughout his body.

As she slowly pulled away, her face was still close to his. Close enough for her nose to brush against his cheek as she did. She hovered in front of his face as they stared into each other's eyes. They stayed like that for a few seconds before she lay her head back on his chest. He desperately wanted to kiss her, but he still didn't want to move too fast. Adam felt she wouldn't have stopped him, and he didn't know if she was waiting for him to initiate the kiss or was debating whether she wanted to, but he decided to play it safe again. They were making such beautiful progress that he didn't want to ruin it.

Adam kissed her on the top of her head, and when he did, he felt her hold him tighter. "You're welcome. Anything for you." The two lay in silence, and eventually, he felt her body relax. Once again, with her there, he felt at peace and fell asleep soon after.

The next few days were business as usual, to an extent. Everyone was training extra and finding reasons to leave the house to see if they could spot anyone. Of course, in groups of three. Adam increased his meditation to keep his mind focused. He had to ensure he was at the top of his mental and physical game because the lives of the people he cared about were in jeopardy.

"Okay, I am going to the diner. They serve turkey and stuffing on Thursdays, and I haven't been in a while. I swear I could eat that every day," Eva announced as she entered the study.

"You better be careful. Around these parts, it's dressing, not stuffing," Adam teased.

"Whatever you want to call it, it's delicious," Eva countered.

"It does sound good, so I'll go with you, but who do you want to take as our plus one?" Adam asked.

"Well, Kaylee and Caleb are reading, and I think Caleb planned on showing her some of his online games. I want someone with a few hundred years of experience to stay with them, and I trust Paul far more than Oliver, so…I guess Oliver," Eva replied as her shoulders dropped.

"So, you want to invite Oliver to come with us. Wow, that had to be hard to say," Adam said while laughing.

Eva rolled her eyes. "You have no idea. So, if you can please tell him our plan, I would appreciate it."

"I'll get right on it," Adam said as he closed one of Caleb's books.

"Anything of interest?" Eva inquired.

Adam sighed. "I was trying to make sense of that mark to see if we could narrow down what it meant, but nothing."

Eva sat on the arm of the chair he was sitting in and placed her arm around his shoulders. "Don't get discouraged. We will find the answers. They are out there, somewhere. Until then, stay focused on the present and know I will do what I can to protect Kaylee. Or, should I say...your girlfriend."

Adam felt his cheeks flush as he tried to respond quickly, but all that came out was mumbled nonsense until finally, he was able to speak coherently. "We haven't put a label on our relationship."

A playful smile appeared on her face. "Regardless, to see your adorable reaction to my comment makes me think otherwise. It may not have been mentioned, but you both feel that way. Now, if you will excuse me, I need to get ready. We'll leave in an hour. Also, to ensure that you will have an appetite, you can drive. No portals for you, and I prefer not to use the car service. I don't want an innocent bystander caught up in this."

"That makes sense, and thank you. Food tends to sound more appetizing if I haven't hurled moments before," Adam responded.

"Anytime," Eva said. She then gave him a quick kiss on his cheek before she left the room.

Adam glanced at Caleb's book and hoped Eva was right about finding the answers. He then proceeded to the guest house, where he figured Oliver would be. He reached the door and knocked, slowly opening the door and peering in as he did.

"What are you doing? Just come on in," Oliver called out as he walked toward Adam.

"I didn't want to barge in unannounced. Besides, I wasn't sure what you were up to. I didn't want to see anything that I couldn't scrub from my mind later," Adam jested.

Oliver smiled. "Smart move, mate, but if that were the case, then the door would have been locked. So, what brings you to the 'Outcast's lair' this fine day?"

"To deliver news that I thought I would never have to deliver," Adam replied. Oliver's brow crinkled. "Eva wanted me to invite you to eat with us. It's nowhere fancy. It's just a diner in a local town nearby, but the food is good."

Oliver smiled from ear to ear. "Oh, now did she."

"Yes, and before you say 'progress,' it's because she trusts Paul to stay behind to watch over the others rather than you," Adam added.

"Rubbish. It's all an act. She wants me there because she enjoys my presence," Oliver said with a smug expression.

Adam sighed but smiled. "Don't push it. Meet us at my car in about forty-five minutes."

"I wouldn't miss it," Oliver said as he patted Adam on his shoulder and walked into his bedroom.

Adam walked back inside the manor. He was already dressed for the occasion, so all he had to do was grab his sword and tuck it away under his clothing. After that, he strolled down the halls until he reached the library. He saw Kaylee and Caleb sitting on a couch, peacefully reading. Adam smiled and was thankful their minds were whisked away by whatever stories they were reading. A welcome break from reality, for sure. He was about to leave when Kaylee looked up and smiled. He returned the smile before he left. While on his way to the front of the manor, he bumped into Paul.

"Hey there. Did Eva tell you about her plans tonight?" Adam inquired.

"She sure did. I don't mind. Whatever she needs me to do…I'm happy to help," Paul responded.

"I appreciate it. Keep them safe," Adam said as he shook Paul's hand.

"Will do," Paul replied.

"Hey, Paul. Curious, do you have any idea where Eva hid the dagger?" Adam asked while Paul was walking away.

He stopped and turned around. "No idea, and she isn't telling anyone either. I patrolled this house multiple times and have yet to find its location."

"She's clever. I'm going to head out. Hold the line while I'm gone," Adam said.

Paul lifted his arm to flash his wrist crossbow. "Hold the line." Adam grinned and walked away. He was glad Paul still remembered when they had to hold the line to save a squadron of troops escorting civilians out of a war zone during the American Revolution.

Adam approached his car and saw Oliver leaning against it with a crooked smile. He didn't see Eva yet, which explained why Oliver was still smiling. "Someone's early."

"I hate to keep a lady waiting," Oliver responded. Just then, the door opened behind Adam.

"Okay, boys, let's go. I'm starving," Eva said as she walked toward the car. Adam was going to open the door for Eva, but he noticed Oliver already had his hand on it. Therefore, he went around his car to get in and start it up.

"Eva," Oliver said as he smiled and opened the door for her.

"Thank you," Eva cordially said as she got into the car. Oliver closed the door and loudly whispered, "Progress," before he got into the backseat. Adam smiled and shook his head as he reached the other side of his car. Shortly after, they drove off.

They arrived at the diner, which was large in scale for a small town. The establishment was busy but not packed, so they were able to find a booth. Eva sat next to Adam, and Oliver sat across from them. Not too much longer, a waitress came over and took their orders. Each of them ordered the same thing, which was the turkey special. Adam smiled as he watched Eva devour her meal as if she hadn't eaten for weeks. To her credit, the food was good. Once they finished, they engaged in small talk while they sipped on their drinks.

"I'm going to the restroom. Afterward, we can discuss if we will hang out around the town to see if anyone approaches us or just head home," Eva said as she stood up. Adam and Oliver nodded in agreement before she left.

"I doubt anyone of interest will be in this town. Heck, I'm surprised you were able to find the one road this town has," Oliver commented.

Adam went to speak, but his attention was directed elsewhere. "You were saying," he said as his eyes remained on the person walking toward them. Oliver's brow crinkled, and as he was about to turn around, their new guest sat down next to him.

Oliver sighed as he pinched the bridge of his nose. "Blondie from the other night, I presume."

"Hello boys," the woman exclaimed. She wore an outfit similar to the first time he saw her, but her hood was down. The lady smiled as if she had just run into her old friends. "Scootch over," she said with a stern face as she bumped Oliver. His brow remained creased as he looked at Adam. He then moved over. As soon as he did, her smile returned.

"Nice to see you again," Adam sarcastically said. The girl didn't say anything. Instead, her eyes roamed all over the diner. Adam's brow lowered before he shot Oliver a quick look. He then cleared his throat.

"What? Sorry. I didn't hear you. The voices," the woman casually mentioned as she pointed to her head.

Oliver's face crinkled as he looked back and forth between the woman and Adam. "And what are those voices saying?"

"It's a secret," the woman said as she playfully smiled and put her finger to her mouth. "Don't ask me again," she said louder as she whisked a knife from within her sleeve and held it to Oliver's ribs.

Oliver raised his hands as both Adam's and his eyes grew larger. "Not a word."

The woman smiled and retracted her knife. "Good. You're cute," she said as she smiled and stared at him.

"Thank you," Oliver responded with a shrug and a fake smile. He then turned to Adam. "Jump in at any time, mate."

"Why are you here?" Adam asked.

"For the same reason as the first time we met…to talk. I hope you are not rude again." Her eyes narrowed as her smile vanished.

"I apologize for my rudeness. I would be more than happy to talk to you," Adam smiled politely. She seemed unstable, so he didn't want to provoke her. He also wanted to try to get as much information out of her as possible.

"Not with me, silly. Cassian," the woman replied.

"He's here?" Oliver asked.

She giggled. "Yes. Follow me." Adam and Oliver shared a look before everyone got out of the booth, but they didn't go far.

"Edith," Eva said before her jaw dropped.

"Well, well, well…it's my bestie, Eva. Still caring for the needy?" Edith asked with a devious smile. Eva's brow furrowed as she sneered and walked quickly toward her. Adam noticed she had already removed the bar from her bracelet. He stepped in front of her and caught Eva in his arms. Her momentum almost knocked him over.

Eva never took her eyes off Edith. "It's you. Yeah, the hair is different and the clothes, but you're still the same monster from all those years ago."

Edith giggled. "So, I see you made new friends. I'm so glad I've met them. I wonder how your last set of friends are doing," Edith said. She bit her lower lip as she took a few steps toward Eva.

Adam felt Eva's muscles tighten and noticed the bar from her bracelet was just big enough to hold in her hand. "Be mindful, we are not alone," Adam whispered into her ear. Eva breathed heavily as her eyes glanced around at the people in the vicinity who were now watching them. She huffed. "Fine, then let's take this somewhere more private," she said through her teeth as her eyes bore down on Edith. He had never seen Eva like this and could only imagine what Edith had done to her.

"All in due time, but for now, Cassian demands an audience with you. Come along," Edith said, carefree, before she turned and strolled away.

"Focus. I'm sure you have a valid reason for your hatred toward her, but this is what we've been trying to accomplish for a while now," Adam added.

"You have no idea what she did to me…to my friends," Eva commented as her eyes stayed with Edith.

"I don't, and I will have your back if you decide to pursue Edith later, but for now, we need to stay on the task at hand," Adam responded as he gently moved her face so she would look at him.

Eva looked into Adam's gentle eyes and let out a deep breath. "Fine." She then proceeded to follow Edith, but Adam stepped in front of her.

"Maybe I should take the lead this time," Adam commented. Eva sighed and gestured for him to walk ahead of her. Adam gently smiled and nodded before he turned around, but as he did, he glanced at Oliver and motioned, with his eyes, for him to keep an eye on Eva. Oliver caught the look and did a quick nod.

Adam dropped some cash on their table and then followed Edith. As they followed her to the opposite side of the diner, he felt the anticipation brewing inside of him. He had no idea what to expect, but he hoped that since they were in public, there would not be any altercations. Adam surveyed the diner for anything unusual in case it was a trap, but everything looked normal. This was one of the few times he was thankful that Kaylee and Caleb weren't with him.

As they turned the corner, he saw a man in a black trench coat, maroon shirt, and black suit pants and shoes. His dirty blond hair was styled as a buzz cut. He sat at the back corner of the diner with no one around him and paid them no attention as he ate his cheeseburger and fries. It was hard to tell between the man's clothes and the booth, but he seemed to be of an average build.

"As you requested," Edith said as she stood near him. While chewing, he motioned her away and then waved Adam and his group to come forward. Edith walked away, sat down at a nearby booth, and observed them while the rest walked over and stood by Cassian's booth. Adam anxiously waited for what was to happen next.

CHAPTER 19

Cassian swallowed his food, politely wiped his mouth with a napkin, and sipped his soda. "Please, sit, but I don't see the need for the entire collective to be present."

"I'm guessing that sitting next to you isn't an option," Oliver remarked as he smirked. Cassian cut his eyes toward him. "Yeah, I'll just go sit with Blondie." Eva and Adam slid into the booth while Oliver sat with Edith.

"Cassian, I presume," Adam said matter-of-factly.

"Yes, and you are?" Cassian asked.

"I'm Adam, and this is…"

"Eva," Cassian interrupted. Adam's brow creased.

"How did you know my name?" Eva inquired.

"Because you are the owner of the manor that houses what I desire," Cassian responded, deadpan.

"You mean the dagger," Eva countered.

"Precisely," Cassian replied, unfazed.

"If you know where it is, then why haven't you come to retrieve it?" Eva asked.

"Oh, I will unless you hand it over to me tomorrow at noon at this very same diner. If not, I will visit your home the next day…and I won't be alone," Cassian said before he ate another fry.

"We'll stop you," Adam countered.

Cassian stopped eating and straightened his posture. He still was expressionless, yet his blue eyes seemed cold, almost dead to Adam. "You have an abundance of hubris, yet your confidence in your skills is overinflated. I can't be stopped. You see, I'm old…over six thousand years old. Not only that, I'm an original immortal, and most of my torso, arms, and legs are covered in markings. I could easily kill you, your two friends, and even Edith right now, and your combined essence wouldn't even prevent me from enjoying my milkshake." He then reached over and took a sip from his chocolate milkshake. Adam remained unfazed on the outside but felt fear creep into him after Cassian's comment.

"Why do you want the dagger?" Eva inquired.

"Why do you defend it so?" Cassian replied.

"Because your reputation isn't one filled with unicorns and sparkles," Oliver commented from the other table.

Edith giggled. "That's why you should give him what he desires."

Cassian kept his eyes forward. "History may view me as the villain, but in time, the world will see me as their savior."

"Said no tyrant ever," Oliver mocked. Cassian glanced at Oliver without moving his head.

"Please forgive my friend. He tends to speak without tailoring his response first," Adam said before he side-eyed Oliver. Oliver shrugged. "The message he was attempting to convey was that maybe we would feel more at ease if we knew your intentions with the dagger."

"My plans are beyond your comprehension, so I will keep this simple. Hand over the dagger tomorrow, or else I will slaughter anyone who stands in my way of what is rightfully mine," Cassian said as his eyes narrowed and his face became stern. It was the first time Adam noticed any emotion from him.

"I have a counteroffer," Eva said. She then quickly pulled out her weapon and extended it, but not fully. She stopped it right before it reached his heart. "Leave now and never bother us again, or else I will kill you right here, right now. I don't care who is around. Not when it comes to my home...my family," Eva said through her teeth as her eyes flared. Cassian did not react.

Edith quickly stood up and reached for something under her sleeve, but Oliver already had his dagger to her throat. She stopped, but her eyes remained on Cassian, who raised his hand for Edith to stand down. Adam was thankful that no one was around to notice what was going on.

A sinister smile formed on Cassian's face right before he unbuttoned his shirt and leaned forward just enough for the tip of her spear to pierce his chest. Adam saw nothing but markings where his shirt was unbuttoned. "Go ahead. You can't kill me, but feel free to try." Eva's brow crinkled at his response. Cassian then took the spear and pulled it toward him so that the tip of the blade went further into his chest. His smile grew, and he showed no ounce of pain. "Come on, take your shot. Maybe I'm not being truthful about your inability to kill me. You don't want to regret not taking this opportunity, especially after I've killed your loved ones."

Eva's brow furrowed, and she pushed the blade slightly deeper into his chest. Cassian's sinister smile grew as he stared into her eyes. Adam didn't know what to do and wasn't sure if Eva would kill him in such a crowded place. Once again, he had never seen her act this way. He also wondered if Eva was testing Cassian to see if he was bluffing.

"Mmm. Feels good, doesn't it?" Cassian remarked. His smile was unnerving.

Eva clenched her jaw but then sighed before she retracted her spear. Cassian scoffed, grabbed a napkin, and wiped away the blood that trickled down his chest. To Adam's surprise, the wound was already healed.

"I believe our meeting is at an end. I will be here tomorrow at noon. If the dagger is not in my possession at that time, I will take it by force the following day. You may go," Cassian said without emotion as he buttoned his shirt. He reached over and took another sip of his milkshake before continuing his meal.

"You heard him. Time to go," Edith said sternly as she moved Oliver's blade away from her.

Adam nodded at Oliver and took Eva's hand as he left the booth. He did so because he was afraid of what she would attempt next. At first, Eva didn't budge as her eyes darted between Cassian and Edith. Then, her shoulders dropped, and she followed Adam and Oliver out of the diner. As they arrived at Adam's car, he noticed James walking from another direction toward the diner. James tipped his hat at Adam and smirked while he continued on his path.

"Friend of yours?" Oliver asked.

"That's James, the other guy at the club who had the lightning axes," Adam responded as everyone got into his car.

"I don't want to talk about it," Eva announced as she turned her head and looked out the window. Adam knew not to push it, especially with it still fresh on her mind. He remained silent and drove off. Even Oliver knew better and remained quiet.

They rode in silence the entire trip. Eva never looked away from the window as he drove. His mind kept replaying the events at the diner. Between Cassian's calm yet confident demeanor and his age, he made Adam nervous. He never met anyone close to his immortal age, and the fact that Eva's spear in his chest didn't remotely faze him made his mind race with the possibilities of what Cassian could do. Adam even wondered if the stories Caleb mentioned were more fact than myth. His mind then wandered to Eva. As much as it would annoy and possibly hurt her, he needed to know what Edith did to make her unhinged. He understood her anger toward Cassian once he made his threat, but Edith was a different type of anger… on a personal level.

Adam pulled into the driveway, and as they got out, Eva stormed toward the manor. Adam and Oliver had to walk quickly just to keep up with her. She flung the door open and marched her way toward the study. Adam and Oliver trailed behind her.

"Eva…Eva, slow down. We need to talk about this," Adam called out, but she didn't listen.

Paul began to walk into the hallway but quickly stepped back so Eva wouldn't plow through him. His brow crinkled as he raised his hands and looked at Adam.

"We got a problem. Gather the others. We'll be in the study," Adam said as he passed him.

"I'm on it," Paul responded.

"Eva," Adam called out as they entered the study. Eva held up her hand to silence him.

"We need to talk about it," Adam demanded as the rest of the group entered the study. He only got a glimpse, but he could see the worried and confused faces plastered on everyone.

Eva poured herself a full glass of bourbon and downed a large portion of it. "I don't want to talk about it," Eva said with her back to Adam.

"I'm sorry, but you must. I've never seen you like this, and in a couple of days, you need to be focused because lives will be at stake. Let me help you unload whatever pain you have bottled up," Adam pleaded, and as his hand touched her shoulder, Eva reacted.

She flung around and swatted his hand away from her. "Just leave me alone!" Eva screamed, inches from his face. She then threw the partially filled glass into the dormant fireplace. It shattered as Eva stared at the fireplace and wept.

Adam stayed calm. "Please."

Eva turned around. She had tears running down her cheeks. "Edith took everything from me," Eva yelled. She then took a deep breath and continued. "Over two centuries ago, I lived in a small town in Sweden. It was so peaceful there. I helped manage an orphanage, and I grew close to the kids. So much, that I found ways to make myself appear older over the years so that I could stay longer. I grew attached to the kids. Some even called me Mom. It was the first time I ever felt like a mother," Eva said as her voice cracked and a few more tears fell. "It was then that I met Edith."

Adam could see out of the corner of his eye that Oliver was filling in the blanks to the others when needed. His heart felt heavy for Eva. He desperately wanted to stop her from talking and hug her, but he stayed put. She needed to unpack this burden.

"I could tell her mind wasn't right, but she seemed innocent. I befriended her. She helped at the orphanage, and we would hang out and talk afterward. For the next year, everything was good until she wanted to leave. I told her it was fine and I would miss her, but I was going to stay longer. My choice did not sit well with her. She felt betrayed and couldn't understand why I wasted my time with mortals since they would die anyway. I tried to explain myself and even mentioned we could pick a location to meet in another five to ten years, but she didn't like it. Finally, she left, and I didn't see her for a few days until she appeared at the orphanage." Eva steadied her emotions the best she could with a deep breath before she continued.

"She stood there and looked around the room, which was filled with kids and my fellow caregivers. She then began to scream and wouldn't stop. She was scaring everyone, and I wanted to calm her down, so I rushed over to her. As soon as I reached her, she stopped screaming. She smiled and looked me dead in the eyes before she ran her dagger into my stomach. I tried to leave, but she held my arm tight and rammed the blade a few more times into my abdomen. I crumbled to the ground, but she wasn't done yet. She announced that everyone would be spared if they watched her kill me, and out of fear, that is what they did. She then repeatedly stabbed me in my chest before finally burying the blade into my heart."

Tears filled Eva's eyes. Adam felt horrible for her, for he had a strong suspicion of why Edith did it. Judging by everyone else hanging their heads, except for Kaylee, they shared his thoughts.

"I don't get it. Edith must have thought the blade was magical, and it obviously wasn't. What am I missing?" Kaylee asked.

Adam looked over his shoulder. "Edith killed Eva in front of everyone, including the kids. She purposely used a non-magical blade." His eyes remained on Kaylee for a few seconds until he saw her eyes widen and her jaw drop.

"Oh, Eva. I'm so sorry," Kaylee said. She frowned and placed her hands over her heart. Eva didn't react to Kaylee and continued her story.

"I woke up in what we call today a 'morgue' and I wanted to run back to that orphanage, but I knew I couldn't. They saw me brutally slain, and it would have scared the kids, who were probably already traumatized after they witnessed me die. Of course, it would have raised too many questions. I can't remember how long it took me to stop crying and move on, but I can never forgive Edith. I hate her! She took my kids away from me!" She then screamed, but when Adam went to comfort her, she pulled away. "There's no time for pity. It's time for action!"

Adam respected her space and slowly walked backward. His heart ached for her, and he could only imagine the various levels of pain and anger she felt. He felt worse because he thought he knew everything about Eva, but apparently not. He wasn't mad at her for keeping this a secret, but more at himself for not knowing about it sooner. Eva began to pace the room.

"If that wasn't enough, I presume there's more," Paul commented.

"Plenty more," Oliver remarked. Paul's eyes scanned the room to see who would explain.

"We ran into Cassian, and he said we had until noon tomorrow to hand over the dagger or he would come for it the following day.

He also mentioned he wouldn't be alone," Adam explained. The room went quiet with the weight of the news.

"Wait, he knows where we live?" Caleb asked.

"It appears so, mate," Oliver answered.

"Any idea of how many more?" Paul inquired.

"Not sure. We saw James there along with Edith, so it could be just them. Maybe more? I have a hunch that he could come by himself, and that would be plenty," Adam responded.

"Why's that?" Kaylee asked.

"Oh, I don't know. Maybe because he is over six thousand years old. Also, let's not forget that he invited Eva to kill him, and the man didn't even flinch when her spear was partially in his chest," Oliver replied.

"There's that, but there was a calm confidence about him. That's something you can't fake," Adam added.

"I presume we still aren't giving him the dagger or making a run for it," Caleb commented.

Eva stopped pacing. "That's right. We will make our stand here. I don't care how old he is. All immortals die the same way. We have a strong group here, and this is our home. His confidence will lead to his end." Adam could see the determination etched into her eyes.

"Then we need a plan," Kaylee fearlessly said.

CHAPTER 20

Everyone looked at Kaylee, but no one spoke, so she moved to the center of the room. "Well, let's hear some ideas. We have an ancient immortal about to visit us, so I presume it will take some planning for us to survive."

"You're right, but not now. Right now, I want everyone to think of ways to make a stand, and we will meet back here tomorrow, around mid-morning. Fresh minds will generate the best ideas. Sound good?" Eva addressed the group. Everyone agreed to her proposal and left the room.

As Adam left, he overheard Oliver describing Cassian to the others. As they reached the end of the hallway, everyone broke off into separate directions except for Kaylee, who waited for Adam.

"How are you holding up?" Adam asked.

"I'm fine. If I had a nickel for every time an ancient immortal threatened me, I'd be rich," Kaylee joked.

Adam scoffed with amusement. "Is that so? In that case, we have nothing to fear."

"Exactly," Kaylee responded, but then her smile faded. "It's going to be horrible in a couple of days, isn't it?"

"Battles are always horrible. All we can do now is prepare and hope things don't end as terribly as they could," Adam replied. The two silently walked the rest of the way to Adam's room.

"I hope I can sleep tonight," Kaylee commented.

"Regardless of how active your mind is, you will," Adam replied.

"How can you be so confident? Unlike you, I can't just fall asleep in two seconds," Kaylee remarked.

"Because tonight will be uneventful. There is no immediate threat, so we might as well take advantage of it. After today, sleep may become more elusive," Adam responded.

They lay down, and Adam played with her hair until she fell asleep. His mind was preoccupied with his strong feelings for Kaylee, but once she fell asleep, he contemplated tactics for when Cassian arrived. Of all the ideas, each one involved protecting Kaylee at all costs.

The morning arrived, and after a trip to the kitchen to grab coffee, Adam and Kaylee made their way to the study. Once everyone trickled in, the meeting began. At first, each person gave suggestions as to what should be done. Eva listened carefully to everybody's input and never gave her opinion. She just sat quietly and listened.

"Well, everyone has voiced how they feel tomorrow should be handled. I guess it's your turn," Caleb mentioned to Eva.

"I plan to take the best parts of everyone's ideas, including my own, and piece them together. Not one person should decide tomorrow's fate. Once I am done, we can all decide if it's the right course of action. Agreed?" Everyone agreed with her suggestion, and in Adam's mind, it was a smart move on her part.

"What do you propose?" Adam asked.

Eva took a moment to compose her thoughts. "First off, let's look at who we are up against. We know what James is capable of, so that is useful. As for Edith, she is a skilled warrior, but nothing any

215

one of us couldn't handle. Her strength lies in her weapons. She has always been obsessed with acquiring the most unique and deadliest magical weapons. We must be careful with whatever she is using these days, but if you can conquer her weapons, she will be easily defeated. Now, we must presume Cassian is as powerful as the books mention, so only engage him if you must. If you do, try not to do it alone."

"Sounds easy so far," Oliver sarcastically commented.

Eva paid him no attention and continued. "We can't keep the dagger in one central location. We also would be limiting ourselves if we barricaded ourselves into a room or one of the small structures outside. Besides, I have a feeling that Cassian would be able to break through any fortifications we place in front of him. Therefore, we will patrol outside the manor while one of us conceals the dagger on their person. However, we will act as if the dagger is in the manor. The only possible visibility of the property would be from the gate, so logically, their attack would come from the front of the manor. Therefore, we will focus our patrol there and stick together. Caleb and Paul will stand behind the four of us and provide long-range attack and defense, while the rest will attack them head-on. I suggest that Paul open fire at Cassian while we take out his support. Caleb will be there to send anyone who gets past us or has the upper hand tumbling away. Make sure to have each other's backs. Once we eliminate his support, if Cassian isn't already dead, we will target him next."

"That sounds great, but who is the lucky one who gets the honor to carry the dagger?" Oliver sarcastically asked.

"I will hold it," Caleb blurted out.

"That's brave of you, but if they figure out you have the dagger, they will come after you. This means you will have to defend yourself, and I know how you feel when it comes to taking another person's life. I offer myself. It was my idea to keep the dagger here and guard it. I accept responsibility," Eva proposed.

"That's honorable, but you can't have it any more than me, Kaylee, or Oliver, because we will be too close to Cassian. What if something happens during the fight and the dagger becomes exposed?" Adam responded.

"To be clear, I had no intentions of holding that bloody thing," Oliver commented. Eva rolled her eyes and then paused to think about Adam's comment.

"I can see your point, but if that is the case, then that leaves Paul," Eva said before she turned to Paul. "Is that a responsibility you are ready to take on?"

"I am. Whatever needs to happen to protect everyone here and rid ourselves of Cassian, I'm game," Paul replied without hesitation.

"Thank you. I will entrust the dagger's protection to you," Eva said as she placed her hand on his shoulder.

"Now we need contingency plans in case our current one fails," Adam commented.

Eva walked forward. "I'm already ahead of you. If something goes awry, then we will fall back to the forge. It's our most secure area, besides the vault in the training room. I chose the forge instead of the training room because we won't be as confined, yet it is still secure. Also, it's like a mini fortress. I know that goes against my previous comment about confinement, but if we need to fall back and regroup, that would be the best place. When this meeting is over, I will have Caleb move the more powerful weapons to the forge in case we need them."

"That's a good plan, but I am going to add one more contingency plan if all else fails. We portal out of here. No set destination. Just go through the portal, and we will find each other later," Adam suggested.

"I agree, but only if it looks grim," Eva added.

"Of course, but there can't be any hesitation. No matter what is going on, if it is time to portal out of here, then do it," Paul said.

"I agree," Adam added. Everyone else nodded in agreement. He felt Kaylee's hand gently grasp his. Adam's eyes drifted to hers, and he could tell she was putting on a brave front as her eyes remained forward.

"Then it's settled. We will have dinner here, together. After that, we are on high alert until this is over," Eva directed.

"Where's the dagger?" Paul asked.

"In the kitchen drawer where I keep the other utensils," Eva casually responded.

"You kept the most important weapon, possibly in all of history, in the same drawer that I get my spoon out of to eat my cereal," Oliver said as he rubbed his face.

"Yep, and you never noticed, did you?" Eva asked as she smirked.

Oliver sighed. "Apparently not." Adam glanced at Oliver and grinned while he slowly shook his head in judgment. "What? It's a huge drawer, and the lighting in the kitchen is terrible." Everybody laughed at Oliver's expense, but truth be told, Adam used utensils out of that same drawer and never noticed it as well.

"I'll retrieve the dagger and keep it on me from here on out," Paul said before he left the room. Once he left, everyone else dispersed.

"So, what do we do until dinner?" Kaylee asked.

"It's whatever you would like to do," Adam responded. He realized he was still holding her hand.

"There are a lot of things, but I honestly don't think my mind will be into any of them. My brain is cluttered with everything that could happen tomorrow," Kaylee responded.

"Here. Sit down in the middle of this couch," Adam said as he gestured.

Kaylee's brow lowered, but she followed his suggestion. "Okay, now what?"

Adam sat beside her and gently turned her shoulders so her back was facing him. He then began to massage her neck and shoulders. "Nothing, just relax. Empty your mind and focus on the massage."

"Mmm. That feels good. You don't have to do this," Kaylee said.

"I could stop if you want me to," Adam responded.

"No, no…keep going. I was just saying you don't have to," Kaylee quickly replied.

Adam smiled. "I know I don't have to; I want to. Since you haven't learned how to meditate yet, this was the next best thing I could think of."

"You should have more good ideas like this," Kaylee commented. He could feel her body become less tense the more he rubbed.

As he rubbed her neck and shoulders, her hair started to get in the way, so he gently moved it aside, but as he did, his fingers grazed her neck. A shiver ran through her body, and a few goosebumps appeared. "Sorry," Kaylee said. She quickly put her hair in a ponytail.

"No, I'm sorry. It was an accident. I didn't mean for my fingers to touch your neck like this," Adam said as his fingers lightly touched her neck again.

"Yeah, an accident," Kaylee playfully said as she squirmed.

Adam smiled and continued to massage Kaylee, with only "accidentally" grazing her neck occasionally. During this time, his mind stayed focused on Kaylee. Her relaxed state was all he needed for his mind to rest. After an hour of massaging her shoulders, neck, and upper back, he finally stopped. Once he did, she leaned back on him. He put his arm around her so she could be more comfortable.

"Thank you," she whispered. She then began to rub his hand and arm lightly. They remained on the couch, which had a beautiful view of the trees. Over half of the leaves had fallen, but the sight was still tranquil, so they sat there and enjoyed each other's company as they admired the scenery. To Adam's amusement and delight, he caught Kaylee staring at him. She tried to mask it by quickly turning her head, but he caught a glimpse of her grinning as she tucked her hair behind her ear.

Adam lost track of time and even dozed off a time or two until he was startled back into reality. Both he and Kaylee jumped up when they heard Caleb calling for assistance. They bolted toward the front door and were the first to arrive, with Oliver a few seconds behind them. They found Caleb standing on the porch. He was staring at Edith, who was on the grass, about ten feet away from him.

"Well, no need to rush out here on my account. I was just taking a leisurely stroll around the property. It was so beautiful that I even took pictures," Edith said. A sinister smile formed as she waved a camera at them before she put it in her pocket.

"Why are you here?" Adam firmly asked. He masked his fear over the implications of the pictures that she mentioned.

"Somebody was naughty and didn't bring Cassian his dagger," Edith replied as she strolled parallel to them. Her smile changed to a fake pout.

"I thought he wouldn't come for it until tomorrow," Adam responded.

"That is still the case. He is a man of his word. I am here to inform you that he will be here at dawn to claim what is rightfully his," Edith replied.

At that point, Adam could hear people running along the side of the manor. Edith created a portal. Just then, he heard Eva scream Edith's name. He quickly turned to see Eva sprinting with her spear in her hand, with Paul right behind her. Paul then stopped and aimed his crossbow at Edith.

"Until next time," Edith said. A playful smile appeared as she looked at Eva while she walked backward into the portal. The portal closed as an arrow sailed through the area where it once was.

Eva yelled in frustration. "What happened? What did she say?"

"She informed us that Cassian will be here tomorrow, at dawn," Kaylee responded.

Eva and Paul approached the rest of them as she retracted her spear. "Good. We will be waiting for them. Finally, we have a chance to end this."

"There's more, luv," Oliver commented. Eva initially looked at him before her eyes drifted to Adam.

"She has pictures of the property," Adam solemnly added.

Eva's eyes widen. "No…it can't be." Adam stared back sympathetically. She then turned around and screamed.

"Why is that such a bad thing?" Kaylee inquired.

"Because Cassian can now portal to any location where she took a picture. They basically have full access to the property," Oliver explained.

"Which means they can show up anywhere tomorrow," Caleb added.

CHAPTER 21

Adam took a few steps toward Eva. "This also means we must alter our plan since we don't know where they will pop up. They could show up in one or multiple locations. It's something we must be prepared for."

"We'll need to split up to cover the grounds," Paul suggested.

"As tall as this manor is, can we not just view it from a window and then portal to wherever they appear?" Kaylee suggested

"There isn't a location that gives us an entire view of the property," Paul answered.

"Eva, what do you think?" Adam asked. He didn't like the idea of splitting up, but unfortunately, he couldn't think of another alternative.

Eva had her back to them and her hands on her hips. After a moment, she let out a large sigh and walked toward them. "We have no other choice. We will split into pairs, and each group will take a section of the property."

"I'll pair up with Kaylee," Adam quickly mentioned.

"No," Eva countered, and before Adam could rebut, she raised her hand and continued to talk. "I get why you want to be with her, but we must think strategically. She will be with me since I spent the most time with her during her training; therefore, I know her strengths and weaknesses better than anyone else. You will pair up with Oliver since you two have previously fought together. Paul and Caleb will be the last pair since they have long-distance weapons. They could keep Cassian and his followers away long enough for us to arrive. They will be at the highest point of the manor...the observation room. Hopefully, the opposition will think they took the position in the observation room as a strategic vantage point, rather than keeping the dagger far from them. Kaylee and I will stake out the back of the manor while you and Oliver take the front. I will give each team a walkie-talkie, and once we know where they are, we can act. Either separately, if they are spread out, or we can portal to the location if they are together. How does that sound?"

"Sounds like it will work," Paul answered.

"I'm in," Caleb added.

"A chance for Adam and Oliver to be back in action again. You know I'm in," Oliver responded confidently. He then slapped Adam on his shoulder.

Adam wanted to respond, but he couldn't. Yes, Eva's plan was smart, but his heart didn't care about logic. He felt confident in Kaylee's skills, but Cassian was on an entirely different level. He wanted to be there so that he could protect her, even if that meant he had to lay down his life for her.

"Adam, I'll be okay. Trust me," Kaylee softly said as she held his hand.

Adam sighed. "I do believe in you, and I know Eva is the best of us...it's just Cassian that makes me nervous. Call it a hunch, but I fear the books may have underestimated how truly powerful and terrifying he is."

"Remember, if any team doesn't have anyone to fend off, they can help out whoever needs it," Eva added.

"Which most likely will be wherever Cassian is," Paul commented.

"And what happens if we have to portal to another team's location? What's Adam going to do, puke on them?" Oliver said. He shrugged when Adam cut his eyes at him.

"I'll push past it. It's only temporary, and I won't let something like that prevent me from doing what needs to be done," Adam responded.

"Then it's settled. We are still having dinner soon, so don't be late," Eva announced.

Everyone left but Adam and Kaylee. He gazed into the distance, playing out multiple versions of how the battle could go tomorrow. He didn't snap back to reality until Kaylee gently touched his shoulder.

"Whose mind needs to be distracted now?" Kaylee remarked with a gentle smile.

"Sorry, I'm just imagining how this will turn out tomorrow," Adam replied.

"And?" Kaylee asked.

"And...I wish I knew," Adam responded, defeated.

"Come on. Let's go eat," Kaylee said as she took his hand. He smiled, and they walked inside.

Eva had a large spread of food delivered, and not to his surprise, there was turkey and stuffing within that spread. There was also prime rib, salads, macaroni and cheese, baked potatoes, deviled eggs, applesauce, and many other sides. There was also a pile of chocolate chip cookies. Of course, there was wine.

They feasted and shared stories as they ate. The meal was intended to distract everyone from dwelling on the upcoming event, which it did. It also had a secondary purpose, which was to have one last fun night together in case someone didn't survive tomorrow. It was Eva's style, and as morbid as the idea behind the dinner was, he did enjoy it. He smiled while the stories were shared, and the food was delicious. It brought Adam joy to watch as Kaylee smiled and laughed at the comical stories shared at the table, usually at the expense of one of them that happened over the years. Hours passed, and dinner, to Adam's dismay, eventually came to an end.

Eva cleared her throat. "Okay, everyone, it's time."

"Time for what?" Oliver asked Adam. Kaylee turned to him as well, curious about his response.

"Time for us to say our goodbyes," Adam responded.

Eva nodded at Paul and hugged him for a long time before she moved on to Caleb.

"Not much of a goodbye. She didn't even say anything," Kaylee commented.

"That's because between Eva, Paul, Caleb, and me...we have already said our farewells and expressed how we feel toward each other. We did that because if someone leaves, you never know if you'll ever see them again. So now, this heartfelt gesture speaks to what we already know. For the two of you, I'm sure everyone will speak since no one has expressed their feelings yet. At least, not to that level," Adam explained.

"Yeah, you guys have fun with that," Oliver said as he patted Adam and Kaylee on their backs. "Good luck, everybody," Oliver addressed the room before he left.

"He's not big on emotions, is he?" Kaylee commented.

"No, but he did wish everyone 'good luck' so that's something," Adam jested. Kaylee smiled.

Adam approached Paul and Caleb separately, nodded, and gave them a hearty handshake. With Paul, he leaned, while still holding his hand, and gave him a quick hug, followed by a few firm pats on his back. As for Caleb, he let go of his hand and hugged him as he patted his back a couple of times.

Eva approached Adam and kissed him on his cheek before she hugged him, one that he wasn't sure if she would ever release him from. With their type of relationship, he didn't mind at all. "I'll keep her safe," she whispered into his ear before she let go. Adam smiled and mouthed the words "thank you" before she moved on to Kaylee.

Eva talked to Kaylee for a while, and he didn't want to stand there awkwardly, so he left and headed back to his room. He knew Kaylee would eventually be there, so when he arrived at his room, he thought about what he would say to her. He wanted to share his feelings with her, but he wasn't sure what he could convey without crossing any boundaries. Unfortunately, his mind was cluttered with Cassian's invasion tomorrow for him to think clearly. He sat on his bed and wondered how strong Cassian truly was and if he had any additional followers from the ones he saw. Kaylee startled Adam when she sat next to him.

"Sorry, I didn't mean to frighten you," Kaylee said as she laughed.

"It's okay. I was just thinking about Cassian," Adam replied.

"I'm sure those were fun thoughts," Kaylee said sarcastically.

"Loads of fun. So, I take it your talks with everyone…well, everyone except Oliver, went well?" Adam asked.

"Yep, especially Eva. Everyone got me teary-eyed, but my talk with her was very heartwarming," Kaylee responded.

"I'm glad it went well," Adam said. He didn't know what to say or how to start their talk.

"So, anything that you want to say to me?" Kaylee asked as she nudged his arm. She had a cute hint of a smile as she did.

Adam abruptly stood up and walked a few steps away. "That's my dilemma. I have so much to convey, but don't know what I can say." His back was still toward her, but he could hear her stand up.

"Just say it. Whatever is on your mind…whatever is in your heart, just say it. Don't get me wrong. I appreciate you taking it slow with me. It means a lot, but at some point, we'll stall out if we continue at this pace. For a moment, just forget that I told you to move slowly with me and just speak your mind. Please!" Kaylee pleaded.

Adam quickly turned around. "Fine! Do you want to know how I feel? Well, here it is. For the first time in my life, I know what true

226

fear is. Yes, I've been scared and nervous before, but this fear…the fear of losing you, is suffocating. I don't know how I would survive. You make me weak yet strong at the same time. When I am around you, it's as if it's just you and me, and all the problems in the world fade away. Even just your smile lights up my soul. It's been hard to keep my feelings bottled up." At this point, Kaylee's eyes were watery, but the floodgates were open, and there was no going back now.

He approached her, put his hands on her hips, and gently pulled her closer so her body was touching his. She responded by putting her hands on his arms. "It took all my strength not to tell you how beautiful and amazing a person you are, inside and out. In all my years on this Earth, I have never met anyone remotely close to how perfect you are, nor have I been as connected to someone as I am with you. As cheesy as it sounds, even though I was born over five hundred years ago, I never felt alive until I met you."

Kaylee sniffled and smiled. "It's not cheesy."

Adam slightly leaned toward her. "I thought battling immortals to the death was hard, but it is nowhere as difficult as it was not to kiss you every time that you were near me. Even now, the temptation is unbearable." His face was now inches from hers as he gently ran his fingers down her cheek.

"So unbearable that…" Before he could finish his sentence, she flung her arms around his neck, lifted herself onto her toes, and kissed him. It caught him off guard. She stopped and looked at him as she bit her lip. His hands cradled her head as he kissed her gently; however, the gentleness didn't last long as everything he had kept bottled up rose to the surface. His kiss became more passionate and intense, which she reciprocated. Their tongues clashed as their hands explored their bodies.

"Hey guys, guess what? Paul and I…oh my gosh, I'm so sorry!" Caleb exclaimed. Adam and Kaylee were jolted out of their world to see Caleb standing in the doorway with his hand over his eyes.

"I really need to start closing that door," Adam quietly remarked as he and Kaylee breathed heavily, still wrapped in each other's arms.

Kaylee giggled. "Probably for the best before things went too far, too quickly."

"I'm sorry. I didn't know you two were an item, and the door was open. I'm going to go now," Caleb frantically said. He turned around and tried to leave, but bumped into the wall because his eyes were still covered.

Adam smiled. "It's okay. Come on in." He took a deep breath to calm himself and backed away from Kaylee. She also took a couple of deep breaths to gain control over her breathing.

Caleb lifted his finger and peeked through before lowering his hand. "Sorry. I just came in here to tell you that Paul and I are going to set up fake archers in the windows throughout the top floor. It was a technique he used to defend a castle centuries ago when they were few in number. It kept the bandits away long enough for them to execute their plan."

"Smart. We need to utilize every trick in the book," Adam responded.

"Great. If you hear a bunch of noise, that is what we are doing. After that, I will move a select group of weapons to the forge," Caleb added.

"Thanks for the heads up," Kaylee said. Caleb smiled before he left.

"So…I guess we are officially a couple now that Caleb saw us," Kaylee playfully commented.

"Yeah, that's the reason. Nothing else," Adam joked.

"If I didn't make it clear about how I felt when we kissed, just know that I feel the same way as you," Kaylee said.

Adam smiled. "That's taking the easy way out. 'Oh, what you said…I feel the same way, too.' So out of all the centuries you have lived, you never met someone like me?" Adam teased.

"Shut up," Kaylee laughed as she playfully slapped his arm. "Maybe besides that part, the rest is true. I never met someone as handsome as you; that also gets me. I can truly be myself, and you embrace everything. The good and the bad. Your personality could not be any more perfect for me. I feel so at ease with you, and I can't imagine a day without you in it. I've been down that road, and it was horrible. Now that you are in my life, I don't ever want you to leave. My heart is yours." She leaned up and gently put her hand on the side of his neck as she kissed him.

The kissing started to become more intense, so she pulled back. "As much as I want more to happen, I still want to take things slow. I don't want to rush into anything too quickly, even with what will happen tomorrow. Right now, I feel I am in the perfect place with you, and I don't want to ruin it. I hope you understand."

"So, the 'I'm going off to war, let's do it.' response won't work," Adam joked.

"Seriously?" Kaylee laughed.

Adam looked at her and gently smiled. "I understand, and if we move slow or fast from here forward, I'm happy. Being at the point where we are in our relationship means more to me than you'll ever know. I feel at peace and excited for us to grow even closer."

Kaylee gave Adam a quick kiss and smiled. "Thank you. That means the world to me. Now, what do we do with the rest of the hours? I don't know about you, but I don't think I can sleep knowing what is about to go down."

"I say we enjoy each other's company. We can lie down and rest our eyes for a while before we dive into a large mug of coffee. Eva wants us all up and at our stations an hour before sunrise," Adam responded.

Kaylee smiled and nodded before they got into bed and cuddled for a few hours. To his surprise, he actually dozed off for most of that time. From her steady breathing, he wondered if she had fallen asleep. When they were awake, they reminisced about their time together. Both at the manor and back at college. Even with the upcoming battle just a few hours away, his mind wasn't focused on that. There was time for that later. For now, he embraced Kaylee and let his mind be filled with the joy of the new milestone they reached in their relationship. They were happy, and he wouldn't let Cassian or anyone take that from Kaylee and him.

CHAPTER 22

It was the wee hours of the morning when Kaylee and Adam rolled out of bed. She left to go to her room to get ready, and they planned to meet in the kitchen with everyone else soon after. He wore blue jeans, a white T-shirt, dark brown combat boots that he wore his pant legs over, and he grabbed his spectral sword. He wanted to keep his wardrobe and weapon choice the same in any fight he would have with an immortal. This way, he would feel the most comfortable when the fight started.

Adam felt the need to go to the kitchen sooner, rather than later, so he could be around people. If not, his mind would wander to the unpleasant outcomes that could happen today. He left his room, and Eva handed him a cup of coffee when he arrived at the kitchen. It appeared that everyone else was already there with their coffee. The room was quiet since everyone was still waking up.

Each person was ready for battle, and sure enough, Oliver had both his dagger and Drustan's axe. The axe was strapped to his back, and when he looked at Caleb, his shield was strapped to his back as well. Even Kaylee had her weapons crisscrossed on her back. As he moved about the kitchen, he noticed Paul had a secondary weapon sheathed and strapped to his waist. Adam recognized the short sword from the ruby-encrusted handle, which, ironically, was soft to the grip. The sword's magical power was its sharpness. It made Kaylee's sword seem dull. He presumed Paul chose that weapon as his backup since it was like the non-magical sword he had trained with.

"It's about that time. We should take our positions," Eva suggested. She handed Paul and Adam a walkie-talkie and kept the third one.

Adam went up to Caleb when he noticed him trying to control his breathing as he fidgeted. "I know you are in a situation that goes against your nature. It's okay to be nervous. Just don't let it dominate you."

"I know, and it's okay. Whatever I need to do to protect my family," Caleb replied.

"That's honorable of you, and as you already know, I'm proud of you, little brother," Adam responded as he patted him on the shoulder.

"Thank you," Caleb said as he smiled.

As Caleb talked to the others, Adam turned to Paul. "Keep him safe."

"Will do," Paul replied.

"Good luck," Adam said.

"Good luck," Paul responded before they shook hands. Paul then followed Caleb out of the room, but not before he acknowledged the rest of the group.

Adam turned and looked at Kaylee. He sighed because he desperately wanted to stand by her side, and he hoped he would see her again, alive. Eva took a step closer to him. While his eyes stayed focused on Kaylee, she spoke.

"Don't worry. I'll keep your girlfriend safe."

Adam shook his head. "Wait, what? How did you know?" He looked at Kaylee, but she was as surprised as he was.

"You know Caleb can't keep big news to himself," Eva said as she winked and kissed him on his cheek. "Stay safe."

Adam smiled and slowly shook his head. He found Eva's comment comical. "You too," he replied as he rubbed her shoulder. He then walked up to Kaylee and kissed her, gently and slowly, on the lips. As their lips parted, their faces remained close.

"Come back to me," Kaylee whispered as she looked into his eyes.

"Always," Adam whispered. He tore himself away and walked toward Oliver, who finally got out of his chair.

"It's about bloody time. For a moment, I thought the lot of us were going to sit around in a circle and braid each other's hair. Come on, mate. We got an ancient immortal to bag," Oliver said with a smirk as he left the room. Adam grinned and followed his lead.

They walked out front, and the brisk morning air welcomed him. As they passed the driveway, Adam noticed something was off. "Um...where's my car?"

"Relax. I took the liberty and moved it far from the manor, but still on the property. It's away from the action because I know you wouldn't want your precious baby scratched," Oliver replied.

"Thanks. I totally forgot about it," Adam responded.

"Probably because you were too busy playing doctor with Kaylee," Oliver said with a crooked grin.

Adam sighed. "Oliver..."

"Oh, calm down. I know. 'Oliver, it's not like that. I care about her,' blah, blah, blah. Don't get me wrong. I'm happy for you, but now we need to focus on the present," Oliver said.

"You're right," Adam responded.

"I know I am, but now look at us. Adam and Oliver...back together again. We need a theme song or something," Oliver commented.

"It has been a while since we fought side-by-side, and we do make a good team," Adam remarked.

"There you go! That's what I'm talking about," Oliver said with enthusiasm.

The two walked about fifty feet past the circular driveway before they stopped. Adam pulled out his walkie-talkie. "We are in position. Paul, are we good?"

"We are in position, too, and yeah, my arrows won't reach you out there. You have about twenty feet of a safety cushion before my arrows will hit their target accurately. If someone slips by you, I can take him out from here without having to portal down. If I miss, Caleb's shield should stop them as they reach the circular driveway," Paul explained.

"Good," Adam responded.

"We are in position now," Eva responded.

Silence filled the air until Oliver spoke. "I don't have many friends. Not many at all, but I consider you to be one...one of the best of them."

"I value our friendship as well, but be careful...you're letting your emotions show," Adam jested.

"Sunrises tend to do that to me," Oliver joked. Adam scoffed with amusement.

The sun had not broken the horizon yet, but the sky was now filled with orange and purplish light. A thin layer of fog surrounded them, but it wasn't too thick. It was quiet, eerily quiet as the anticipation built. Adam and Oliver glanced around but saw nothing. Then, the sun broke the horizon, but Adam remained unnerved. There was so much at stake. He was ready for battle and to do whatever it took to win and keep everyone safe. Moments later, Adam saw a portal open in front of him.

It was about thirty feet away from them, and with the fog, he knew Paul and Caleb didn't have a clear view yet. Then, Cassian slowly walked through the portal, expressionless, as he glanced around. His outfit was similar to the other day, but strapped to his back was a great sword. If he had to guess, it was just a foot or so smaller than Cassian himself, but that wasn't what grabbed his attention.

Cassian also wielded a scythe that looked like he had taken it from Death itself. The staff was made of old, twisted roots with a human skull at the top of it. From the back of the skull was a long, curved blade. Black smoke, almost flame-like, came out of the skull's eyes. If the smoke were green, it would have looked like his sword. Then, to Cassian's right, about ten feet away, another portal opened to reveal James walking through it. He was already holding both axes and was dressed in his usual attire. He smiled and nodded at Adam and Oliver.

"I don't see Blondie," Oliver commented.

"She may have appeared somewhere else," Adam responded as he looked around.

"Only two of them. Not so bad," Oliver said as he readied his axe.

Adam reached for his walkie-talkie, but before he could respond, he saw the same blackish flames from the skull now appear in Cassian's eyes. He then noticed James's portal closed, but Cassian's remained open. Then, one by one, six fully armored knights appeared from Cassian's portal and spread out behind him, three on either side of him. The flames vanished from his eyes once the knights were in position.

"You were saying," Adam remarked. He activated his sword while Oliver ignited his axe. Cassian seemed unfazed by their weapons.

"He's controlling them, but how?" Oliver asked as they both stared at the knights.

Adam noticed that the same blackish flames were coming through the slit in their helmets. They also stood abnormally still. The fog lifted enough for them to get a better look, and that is when they noticed the armor seemed deteriorated. The few spots that were exposed revealed a terrifying revelation...decayed flesh. Adam's jaw dropped.

"Bloody hell. They're walking corpses," Oliver said.

Then, another portal appeared about ten feet to Cassian's left. Edith walked through holding a cutlass and dressed in tight, black nylon clothes. The blade of her cutlass was polished enough that it almost appeared to be a mirror. "I guess she decided to join the party," Oliver commented.

Adam's eyes narrowed. "Her belt."

There was an ivory blowgun attached to her belt. He wasn't sure why, but that type of weapon brought to this kind of battle didn't seem practical and, therefore, dangerous.

"Got it, but I'm more worried about the undead knights," Oliver responded.

"Edith," Cassian said without looking at her. At this time, his portal closed, and only her portal remained open. She smiled and removed a pouch from her belt. She poured some sand-like substance on her palm, turned around, and blew it into the portal. The portal flickered and kept flickering as she turned around to face them. Cassian's eyes turned black once again as his entire group slowly began to advance.

"What's going on down there? We can't fully make it out yet," Paul said.

"It's Cassian, Edith, James, and a group of undead knights," Adam responded.

"Undead?" Eva inquired.

"Exactly. We are way outnumbered over here," Adam replied.

"On our way," Paul said.

"We are on our way, too," Eva added. Adam looked around, but no portals appeared.

"Something's wrong. I can't create a portal," Paul said.

"Same here! Why can't we create portals?" Eva asked in a panic.

"Edith did something to her portal. It's still open, and I guess whatever she did is preventing other portals from forming," Adam responded.

"No problem. We'll run to you," Eva said.

"Same here," Paul added.

Adam surveyed the approaching group and then looked behind him. Cassian's forces were closing in on them and beginning to fan out to circle them. Even if the other two groups ran, they wouldn't make it to them in time. Also, if he and Oliver retreated, he didn't think they could outrun them, and after he saw Cassian's undead forces, he definitely didn't want to lead those monsters back to the rest of the group. Besides, Paul and Caleb's ranged attacks wouldn't do much against the knights, and they couldn't hold off the entire group for long if they fanned out. Adam also didn't want their backs to Cassian's forces, especially Edith and James.

He looked at Oliver, and he slowly shook his head. Oliver slightly nodded. He knew as well as Adam that there was no escape for them. Cassian planned this, Adam thought. He had Edith walk around the manor yesterday just to get them to divide their forces. This way, he could bring his group through, unmatched. The disrupted portal would ensure there would be no escape...no reinforcements.

Adam knew what had to be done. He hated it, but there was no other choice. He raised the walkie-talkie, took a deep breath, and spoke. "Retreat. I don't even think Plan B would work at this point. I know you can't portal, so just run in the opposite direction as quickly as possible. Oliver and I will hold them off for as long as we can."

"We're not abandoning you!" Eva countered. He could hear Kaylee frantically speaking in the background, but he couldn't understand her.

"We can help," Paul added.

"No! It's too late. We are almost surrounded. You will just be running into a no-win scenario. They will kill each group off as they arrive. Take the dagger and run. Keep everybody safe."

"Adam..." Oliver said. Adam looked up and noticed they were now surrounded by the knights, with Edith and James standing near

Cassian, who stood ten feet behind the knights. There was still a lot of frantic chatter on the walkie-talkie.

"Eva. We have eyes on them now, and Adam is right. They are already surrounded. We won't make it in time," Paul commented.

"We are not leaving them to die!" Eva yelled.

"It's too late to prevent that now," Paul interjected. His comment caused the chatter on the walkie-talkie to go silent. Oliver and Adam glanced at each other, but said nothing. No reaction, for they knew Paul's words were not exaggerated.

"Keep Caleb safe, Paul," Adam calmly said.

"I promise. It's been an honor," Paul replied.

"Yeah, for me too," Adam responded.

"Wrap it up, Adam," Oliver hastily commented.

"Eva...keep Kaylee safe and tell her...it would have been good. Also, to never forget my feelings for her," Adam softly said. His eyes teared up as he forced a smile.

"You will tell her that yourself. We are on our way!" Eva frantically said. Once again, he could hear Kaylee in the background.

"Eva! Promise me," Adam sternly responded.

"Fine...I promise," Eva muttered.

"Last chance. Give me the dagger, or you and your friends will suffer," Cassian directed as he raised his scythe. His voice was different. Like it contained his and other voices, all combined into one.

Adam sighed. "We are out of time. I care about each of you. Don't let our sacrifice be for nothing. Be safe. Please...everyone get out of here now!" Adam crushed the walkie-talkie in his hand before anyone could respond.

As much as it devastated him that he couldn't be with Kaylee, if his final act could be to save her life, then it would be worth it. Adam tossed the walkie-talkie aside before he ran his hand over his face and narrowed his eyes. His focus was now on Cassian and his forces. Adam wondered which of them would charge first.

Oliver stood tall and calm. "Until the end, my friend."

Adam stood tall and calm as well. "Until the end, my friend."

They then stood back-to-back, raised their weapons, and awaited the onslaught.

CHAPTER 23

An evil smile appeared on Cassian's face right before he pointed the skull on his scythe toward them. Adam could smell the rotted flesh of the knights as they raised their broadswords right before they advanced. Their speed was moderate, and their footing was shaky, but they didn't tumble over as they ran toward them. Adam remained unnerved as the loud clanking of the approaching undead army came toward them.

Adam's blade clashed with the knight's blade in front of him. From the impact, it appeared that the undead still possessed their former strength. He slightly ducked as he watched the blade from another knight soar past his head. As it moved past him, he swung his blade at the knight in front of him. His blade deflected off its armor, so he spun around and thrust his sword toward another oncoming knight. His blade slipped through a large crack in its armor and into its ribs.

The knight continued as if nothing had happened and swung its sword at him. Adam grabbed its arm with one hand while his blade was still embedded in its ribs. Then, he yanked his sword out just before the knight punched him across his face. Adam dropped to one knee, slightly dazed, but was able to block its next attack. He countered by quickly standing up and smacking the knight in its helmet with the hilt of his sword. The knight stumbled back from the force of the impact, and as Adam's head turned, he saw another knight about to swing its sword, but Oliver was quicker. With a heavy swing of his axe, he took the knight's head clean off its body. That knight wobbled momentarily before it fell to the ground.

Out of the corner of his eye, he saw a glow from James's direction. Adam blocked another attack from a knight, grabbed it by its chest plate, and flung the knight in front of Oliver. Moments later, two bolts of electricity slammed into that same knight. The impact knocked it into another knight, which caused them to fall to the ground. Adam sent a strong front kick to another knight, and as it stumbled backward, another swung its blade at him. He swatted its blade away but didn't see Edith in time. He grimaced as she sliced his thigh, but was able to defend against her next couple of strikes. He noticed that, somehow, her slice caused two cuts to show up on his leg. He now understood her sword's magical power.

Her attacks were swift, but he finally countered with an elbow to her face when he blocked one of her slashes. She fell, but before he could attack, her distraction allowed a knight to stab Adam in his ribs. He yelled as he grabbed his side. Regardless of the intense pain, he saw an opportunity. As soon as the knight removed its blade from him, he thrust his blade into the exposed section of its neck. He quickly moved his sword side to side before he used his leverage and pried the knight's head off.

As the knight collapsed and its head tumbled away, Adam turned and swung his sword at Edith. She blocked his attack, but the power behind his swing moved her weapon out of position. This allowed him to swing upwards, and as agile as she was, she couldn't fully avoid his sword as it sliced her shoulder. She groaned as she held her shoulder and took a couple of steps back. Without hesitation, he came back down with an overhand swing, which she blocked. He heard a snarl behind him, so he quickly stepped aside and watched a knight's sword narrowly miss him and almost skewer Edith. She avoided it only by twisting her body enough that she fell to the ground. Adam rammed his shoulder into the back of the knight, making it tumble over Edith. He then quickly leaned sideways as two bolts crackled past him.

He then felt an intense heat from behind him. Adam turned to see Oliver projecting flames toward two knights and James. The knights did not falter, but despite James's best efforts to dodge the flames, Oliver was able to burn his left arm. James dropped to one knee in pain. He raised his right arm and tried to shoot another bolt at Oliver, but couldn't get a clean shot. Oliver still seemed to be fighting strong, regardless of the few slash marks he had on him. The only silver lining to the undead army was that their weapons were not magical.

Oliver and Adam rushed the oncoming knights, who had flames sneaking out from under their armor from Oliver's attack. As Oliver attacked the one that reached him first, Adam noticed that the other knight was moving more slowly and seemed disoriented. He saw a large volume of flames roaring from the knight's helmet. It started to swing blindly and wildly, seeking any target in range.

When Adam got close enough, he jumped toward it with his sword raised high into the air. Then, with two hands, he brought the blade crashing down on the knight's helmet with all his might. Firey gunk spewed from the thin eye slot as the knight's head exploded. It dropped to its knees before it fell forward. Adam looked over his shoulder and saw two knights marching toward him with Edith behind them, stalking him with a devious grin. As he was about to engage them, Oliver bellowed in agony.

Adam whipped his head around to see a knight lying next to Oliver's feet with its helmet crushed. His eyes widened when he also saw electricity covering Oliver's body. Apparently, once the knight was out of the way, James had a clear shot.

"No!" Adam yelled as he picked up a broadsword from the ground and hurled it toward James. He had to stop his lightning attack so he could move out of the way of the incoming sword. Adam rushed to the fallen Oliver. When he reached him, his body was charred and almost unrecognizable. He didn't know how much time Oliver had left.

"Oliver, Oliver! Hang in there," Adam frantically said as he went to touch him but stopped in fear of causing more pain. Oliver reached down to his belt and handed him his dagger before he passed out.

"I could wait until he dies to receive my prize, but I'm a gentleman. I will end his suffering, swiftly," James said as he approached. His arm was still injured, so he only wielded one axe. If he had used both his axes, Oliver would have instantly died.

Adam's brow lowered as he steadied his breathing. Determination filled him as he tightly gripped his sword and Oliver's dagger. He had to push his pain aside and defend Oliver...defend his friends. The enemy was wrong if they thought his death would be easy.

"I'm sorry, Kaylee," Adam said to himself. His face hardened as he stood up and raised his sword and Oliver's dagger.

Edith, James, and the two knights rushed Adam from each side. Adam deflected Edith's attack with his sword and then blocked James's attack with the dagger. He then ducked under Edith's blade as it narrowly missed his head again. Adam spun around Edith, sliced her across her back, and then sent a powerful front kick to the closest knight. He held Oliver's dagger up and blocked James's attack again, then countered by swinging his blade toward James's leg. It sliced through his thigh, and as James bent over and grabbed his leg, he kneed him in the face. As James fell to the ground, he swatted the sword away from the other knight and followed up with a slash across its chest, but its armor absorbed the hit. Without hesitation, he rammed it with his shoulder and sent it tumbling to the ground.

He felt a presence behind him, so he instantly jerked his body to the side and dodged Edith's sword that glided past his chest. He jabbed his sword at her, but she sidestepped the blade and sent a sidekick to his ribs. As he took a few steps back, she advanced. Edith ducked under his sword to avoid being decapitated and drove her sword into his abdomen. Adam yelled as he knocked her sword away and held his stomach. His hand could barely cover where the sword entered, but not the second mirror wound that appeared next to it. Blood slowly poured out as his face crinkled and his jaw clenched. As much as it hurt, he was glad the wound wasn't too deep, or else he would be on the ground.

She licked her lips before she swung her sword. Adam turned his blade to point downward, so when her blade hit, he quickly smacked her in the face with the hilt. As she fell to the ground, his sword clashed with a knight's sword while Oliver's dagger blocked the attack from the other knight. His muscles bulged, and he clenched his jaw as he held the two knights' swords above his head. He then dropped his sword arm and spun around the other knight, whom he still had blocked with Oliver's dagger. As he spun around the knight, he rammed his elbow into its back. It stumbled forward before the knights both retaliated.

Adam jumped backward to avoid their attack and then thrust his sword into an opening in the knight's armor closest to him, near its lower abdomen. With his sword still inside of it, he ran forward, rammed his forearm into the knight, and pushed it into the second knight. As the second knight fell, he saw a flash behind the knight he still had his sword in.

James sent an electrical blast that hit the knight, which damaged it, but the current found its way to Adam, and he received a jolt of electricity. He fell to the ground, and his insides felt like they were on fire. Adam's forearm was also burned, but the worst part of it was that his sword was still stuck in the knight's body. At a quick glance, he saw Oliver's dagger off to his right, but he didn't have time to grab it. James sprinted toward him, so he stood up, grabbed James's arm, and hip-tossed him. He was sluggish after being electrocuted, and because of that, he wasn't quick enough to avoid being impaled in his chest, near his left shoulder, by the knight.

Adam's jaw clenched as the sharp pain radiated across his chest, but he had to endure it if he was going to reclaim his sword. He had a firm grip on the knight's arm before he grabbed his sword and yanked it out of the knight. Then, he pushed himself away from the knight, but Edith slashed his right hamstring before he could steady his feet. He dropped to one knee and rolled forward to avoid her and the other knight's attack. That is when he noticed James had staggered to the fallen Oliver.

"Now, to collect my prize," James said as he raised his axe over his head.

Adam raised his sword behind his head and was about to hurl it toward James until he noticed James's head snap back. His body then fell backward, and he landed flat on his back. That is when he saw a golden bolt lodged deep in James's right eye socket.

He looked to his right and saw Paul lowering his arm. Paul turned his head and nodded at him. Adam returned the nod and was relieved, but that feeling was fleeting. He saw Caleb standing a few feet behind Paul with his shield raised. Adam also saw Eva and Kaylee rushing toward him with their weapons in hand, about fifty feet behind them. As much as he wanted their help, he wished they had been long gone. Most importantly, safe.

A new problem presented itself when he saw the blueish flames cover James's decayed body, which meant that not only did Oliver need protecting, but Paul would soon need it as well. The two knights and Edith charged at Paul, but Caleb held them off with the wind from his shield. However, it wouldn't take long for Edith to figure out that the wind was concentrated, and all she had to do was distance herself from the knights to avoid the gusts.

Adam whipped his head around when he heard Cassian yell and watched as he slammed the bottom of his scythe into the ground. The blackish flames within the skull and his eyes intensified as he stared into the battlefield. That is when Adam noticed a blackish ball of flame appear around the heads of the fallen knights, and for some of them, the flame replaced their heads. They stood up and marched toward the direction of his friends. He panicked, for he didn't know what to do. There was no way he could catch up to them in his state. Then, he realized what his only option was.

He used his sword to help himself stand up. Adam watched as the blueish flames engulfed Paul, and then Paul began to scream. His eyes drifted to Eva and Kaylee. "Adam, no!" They both yelled, for they knew what he was going to do. He retrieved Oliver's dagger and then slowly turned around to face Cassian.

Adam put the dagger in his belt, raised his sword, and quickly hobbled toward him. His body was damaged and in pain, but he gritted his teeth as his hobble converted to a run. Cassian's blackish eyes now focused on him as the corner of his mouth raised while he walked toward Adam.

They both raised their weapons when they came within range of each other. Adam slashed at Cassian, which he blocked, and to his surprise, the twisted root that the scythe was mainly constructed of did not even chip. Cassian swung the blade down toward his chest, which Adam blocked, and was surprised at how powerful his swing was. Cassian went on the offensive and used both ends of his weapon to target different areas on Adam's body. Adam stayed on the defense and could only get a few slashes and a thrust in. Of course, Cassian blocked them.

The two battled back and forth until Cassian swept his blade low, close to Adam's shins. Adam jumped and spun at the same time, so when he landed, he struck down hard toward Cassian's head. Cassian raised his scythe above his head, with his hands near each end of his weapon, and watched as Adam's sword slammed into the center of his scythe. Adam strained as he tried to overpower Cassian, but he didn't budge as his soulless eyes stared back at him. A slight smirk appeared on Adam's face. Cassian slightly grinned back, and that was when Adam knew it was just a matter of time. He just needed to be patient.

Cassian pushed upward, and as his sword was lifted higher, Adam spun around. When his back was to Cassian during his spin, he grabbed Oliver's dagger in his left hand. Cassian brought the blade of his scythe barreling down, but Adam blocked it with the dagger. It absorbed the impact, so Adam was able to thrust his sword toward the now-vulnerable Cassian.

The blade pierced Cassian's heart. He gasped as his eyes grew wide. Adam twisted the blade that was still deep inside his chest, hearing the bones crack as he did. Cassian yelled before his eyes slowly closed. Adam pulled his sword out of his chest and watched him fall to his knees and then to his side. He noticed Cassian's skin turned gray as decay began to take over.

He scoffed with amazement. Cassian was dead. He smiled as he turned around and noticed the knights had ceased attacking, even though the blackish flames were still present. Paul and Caleb looked fine, and Kaylee and Eva had some cuts on them, but were fine.

As they rejoiced, Adam turned around and noticed the skull still had some flames within it, so with an overhead swing, he shattered the skull with his sword. The flames vanished, and the roots that most of the weapon was made from appeared to wither slightly. When he turned around, the knight's blackish flames had disappeared right before the knights toppled to the ground.

His friends cheered even more. His smile grew, but quickly disappeared as he noticed Oliver was still lying on the ground. He hobbled toward him but then wondered…where was Edith? He scanned the area and noticed she was standing near the flickering portal, behind a tree to avoid Paul's bolts. He continued toward Oliver, knowing that his friends were watching Edith, and at this point, he doubted she would attack. He knew it was a matter of time before he would receive Cassian's mark.

"Where do you think you're going?" Eva called out to Edith as she walked in her direction, with Kaylee behind her.

Kaylee looked at Adam and smiled, but her eyes drifted behind him, and her expression changed. Her eyes widened, and her jaw dropped as she pointed behind him. "He's not dead…he's not dead," Kaylee shouted. Now, all eyes were looking behind Adam. He turned and saw Cassian standing up. His skin color was back to normal, along with his eyes, and even the wound in his chest was gone.

"I told you. You can't kill me," Cassian said with a sinister look. He looked past Adam to his fallen knights, then down at his scythe. His brow furrowed, and his face hardened. "Do you realize how difficult it was to acquire that? For your insult to me and the destruction of my scythe, you will suffer." He reached behind him and pulled out his great sword. A sword that was meant to be held with two hands…he easily held with one.

Without hesitation, Adam attacked. Cassian swung his mighty sword, but he blocked it with Oliver's dagger. Once again, the dagger absorbed the entire impact. Adam went to slice Cassian across his midsection, but Cassian caught his arm. Adam couldn't break free of his grasp, and he had to make sure the dagger remained close to Cassian's blade, which was still looming over him.

Cassian yanked Adam by his arm, which caused him to stumble to the other side of Cassian. Swiftly, Cassian immediately spun around and laterally swung his sword. In his off-balanced position, Adam had no choice but to block it with his sword. The impact knocked him to the ground. He wasn't sure if it was Cassian's strength or the sword's magical power, but if he didn't know any better, he could have sworn Cassian hit him with a truck.

Adam shook his head to regain his focus after the impact, and as he began to push himself up, Cassian stomped on his back. He tried to break free, but he was trapped under Cassian's foot. Then, Adam bellowed as he felt an immense, sharp pain through his chest. Cassian had rammed the blunt end of the scythe so hard into him that half of it was in the ground. He tried to move, but he was pinned.

Cassian knelt beside him. "You will not die today, but you will wish you had after I'm done dismantling your friends," he whispered into Adam's ear before he stood up and walked toward them. Adam tried to get up but screamed. The weapon was too firmly lodged into him and the ground. He coughed up blood as the intense pain from his chest spread everywhere. Any words that he tried to express didn't make it past the blood in his mouth.

"Stick together," Eva yelled as they banded together.

"I can feel the dagger's presence," Cassian announced as he continued to walk toward them. As he did, his attention turned to Caleb. Fear coursed through Adam's body. Caleb must have talked Paul into letting him hold the dagger.

His vision began to blur, but he could see enough. Caleb raised his shield as Paul raised his crossbow. Kaylee combined her daggers into a sword and aimed the hilt toward Cassian. The obsidian shot out, but Cassian deflected it with his sword. Paul sent a few bolts at him, and he deflected most, but not all. However, he easily pulled out the bolts that had struck his body. Adam desperately wanted them to retreat, but it didn't seem they would.

"Edith," Cassian called out, but never looked in her direction. Adam couldn't turn his head enough to get a good look, but he saw her pull the pouch that contained the powder substance and head toward the portal.

Eva and Kaylee charged Cassian. His sword collided with Eva's spear, which almost knocked it out of her hands. He did the same to Kaylee, who attacked right after Eva. While they were both out of position, he swung his sword laterally at Kaylee, and she blocked it. However, the impact drove her sword, along with his, into her stomach. She screamed until his fist slammed into her head, and she fell hard to the ground. He saw Cassian tilt his head as he looked at

249

Kaylee lying on the ground. She looked at him, but seemed unable to get back up. He quickly turned around to grab Eva's spear, which she had thrust toward him. Then, in one motion, he yanked her forward and into his blade. It pierced her ribcage and exited the other side. While she was still impaled, she screamed as he lifted her up and flung her off his sword. She tumbled across the ground until she stopped a handful of feet away.

Cassian continued forward, so Caleb aimed his shield toward him and unleashed a fury of wind while Paul opened fire at him as well. Cassian rammed his sword into the ground to keep himself from being blown back. Paul stopped shooting his bolts since the wind made it nearly impossible for them to find their target. However, he kept it aimed at him, but not for long. His attention was now drawn to Edith, who came at them from the side. He was able to keep her from advancing, but his bolts could not find their target due to how agile she was.

Then, to Adam's surprise, Cassian removed his blade from the ground and allowed himself to be blown far away from Caleb. He tumbled across the ground until he finally came to a stop. There was still wind where Cassian was, but it was tolerable. He stood up, created a portal, and raised his sword. Adam couldn't figure out why until he noticed a portal form right behind Paul.

"Paul!" Adam yelled, but between the howling of the wind and the blood in his lungs, Paul could not hear him. He began to push off the ground and screamed as his body slowly slid up the scythe. His blood ran down the scythe as he did, but he had to push past the immense pain he felt. His friends were in danger, and he had to do something. At this point, Kaylee and Eva were still trying to get up.

Cassian rammed his sword through the portal and into Paul's chest so hard that most of the long blade went through his chest. Paul convulsed as Cassian walked through the portal. Once through, he flicked his blade down. Paul's body slowly slid off his sword while his eyes focused on Caleb.

"Paul! No!" Caleb screamed. He went to reposition his shield to face Cassian, but he didn't realize that now, with Paul dead, Edith was behind him and left unchecked. Adam noticed this, and with one hand on the ground to brace himself, he grabbed the portion of the scythe that was under him and tried to snap it. He could feel it bend, along with his insides, but he couldn't muster enough strength to break it.

Edith cut her finger with her sword, smeared her blood onto the blowgun, aimed it at Caleb, and blew into it. The dart hit Caleb in his neck, and once it did, his concentration broke, and the wind stopped. He grabbed his neck and looked over his shoulder to see Edith smiling before she bit her lip. Caleb pulled the dart out but seemed dazed. Cassian, unfazed by the blueish flames that surrounded him, approached Caleb.

"No!" Eva, Kaylee, and Adam yelled. Adam screamed and pulled with all his might. Finally, he broke the bottom part of the scythe. However, he could not reach behind him to pull the rest out, and now there was even more blood pouring out of him. He wobbled to his feet and walked unsteadily toward Caleb. He didn't know what he could do, but he had to try something. He just had to hold on long enough before his body gave out.

Caleb turned and went to aim his shield at Cassian, but Cassian blocked his progress with just the hilt of his sword from his outstretched arm. He then snatched the dagger from Caleb's inside jacket pocket.

Cassian looked at Caleb's neck before his eyes drifted back. He grinned. "You're dead already." Caleb's brow crinkled before Cassian shoved him aside.

Edith skipped over to Cassian and created a portal. "This could have been avoided if you had only given me what I desired. You killed them, not us. Remember that," Cassian announced before he and Edith entered the portal. The portal closed, and silence filled the air. As much as he hated that Cassian took the dagger, he was more concerned about his friend's well-being as he pushed forward. He had no idea what the dart contained, but if Edith was involved, it couldn't be good.

"I don't feel right," Caleb said after he took a few steps forward.

CHAPTER 24

E va and Kaylee rushed to Caleb as fast as they could, even though they were slower due to their injuries. Adam tried to rush to Caleb, but he had trouble moving. Each step he took felt like a step closer to death. He became increasingly light-headed with the extensive blood loss, and the more he moved, the more it felt as if Cassian stabbed him again with his scythe. It took all his might to remain on his feet and keep his vision clear enough to focus on his friends. He gritted his teeth, and his face crinkled from the pain he endured trying to make it to Caleb. Kaylee reached Caleb first.

"I'm sorry. I didn't mean for him to take the dagger. I'm sorry," Caleb said, teary-eyed.

"It's okay. Don't worry about that now. What doesn't feel right?" Kaylee asked as she rested her hands on his shoulders.

"I feel drained, and my body feels like it is becoming heavier and stiffer," Caleb explained.

"Okay. Just breathe. Stay with me," Kaylee responded. At that point, Eva arrived, but when Caleb went to turn toward her, he couldn't.

"I can't move my legs. I feel them, but I can't move them. That dart must have been tainted with magical poison. I don't want to die. I don't want to die," Caleb pleaded as his eyes welled up.

Eva stood next to Kaylee. "It will be okay. Just keep your mind off it. Think about when we went to the arcade," Eva said as her voice cracked. She quickly wiped her eyes when Caleb wasn't looking.

"Yes, think about that and the fair," Kaylee added as her voice cracked as well. Tears rolled down her face, but she didn't hide them. Both Eva and Kaylee smiled through their sorrow.

Caleb seemed to calm down and even smiled, but it was short-lived. Panic reappeared in his eyes as he looked down at his hands. Adam squinted, and if he didn't know better, Caleb's hands turned a metallic brown color...like bronze. "I can't move my arms. I can barely move at all! What's happening to me?" Caleb cried as his breathing quickened.

"Whatever it is, there may be a cure...or maybe it's temporary. Stay calm," Eva replied as she rubbed his back.

Caleb steadied his breathing, but tears continued to roll down his cheeks. "I love you guys." He turned his head toward Adam. "All of you." Adam crossed his arms over his chest and mustered up a smile. He mouthed "I love you, too," since he could barely talk because of his injuries. Tears began to form, for he was about to lose another person close to him, and he knew he wouldn't make it to him in time. This made him upset, but also frustrated because there was nothing he could do.

"I love you, too," Kaylee and Eva said as their tears became uncontrollable.

Caleb put on a brave face as the bronze covered the rest of his body. Caleb, his brother, had turned into a bronze statue. Eva and Kaylee broke down and hugged the statue. Adam wept, but he became dizzy and started to stumble uncontrollably.

"Adam!" Kaylee called out. He didn't respond and collapsed as the world faded away.

He abruptly woke up on a cot in one of the many spare bedrooms in the manor. Kaylee and Eva were sitting on the chairs near him. Kaylee rushed to him as Eva remained in her chair. He looked out the window and noticed it was dark outside.

"I'm so glad you are awake," Kaylee said as she knelt beside him and gave him a tight squeeze. Her warmth put him at ease. She gave him a quick peck on the lips and glanced over his body. "Are you okay?"

"Yes, I seemed to be entirely healed," Adam responded. He spoke the truth about his body, but his mind was a mess.

"You're lucky the magic left his scythe when you smashed the skull, or else you wouldn't be here with us," Eva solemnly commented.

A knot formed in his stomach. "Oliver?"

"Alive...barely. We put him in the room next door and made him as comfortable as we could. We have some medical supplies, but we are not a hospital. All we can do now is hope his healing works faster than the rate he is dying," Eva replied.

Kaylee sat next to his cot and held his hand. "His coin is with him, just in case. We debated about one of us killing him so he wouldn't suffer and the coin would bring him back to life..."

"But since there is no proof that the coin would work, it was safer not to test that theory," Adam completed her sentence. Kaylee nodded. He felt relieved that his friend was still alive and hoped Oliver would recover soon. That, and he hoped the coin's legend was true.

"What time is it? What day is it?" Adam inquired.

"It's the same day, and it's ten o'clock," Eva answered.

Adam felt nauseous about what he was going to ask next, but he wanted to know. "Where are Paul and Caleb?"

"We moved them to the crypt out back," Eva replied, emotionless, as she stared at the floor.

"How did you move everybody?" Adam asked.

"It wasn't easy, but we were creative and found ways to do it," Kaylee responded. Her eyes became teary.

Adam pulled her in and held her. "I know today was horrible. Just know that I am here for you if you need anything."

"Thank you, but Eva and I spent hours processing our emotions once everybody was moved, but if the need comes up, I will come to you. Enough about me. What about you? You just lost two people that you have known for longer than I have been alive, multiple times over," Kaylee responded as she rubbed his back.

Adam felt his emotions roaring inside of him. The pain of their loss outweighed the pain he felt during the battle. His eyes became glassy, but he swallowed his emotions. He didn't feel it was the right time to discuss his feelings. Even though he was immortal and understood why it was a curse, it was still difficult to accept the fact that being immortal didn't mean you were guaranteed to live forever. "I think I need time to process this, but whenever the time comes, I will talk to you," Adam replied.

Kaylee hugged him. "I hope so." She stood up. "I'm going to check on Oliver." She then left the room.

"I have a confession to make. One that you will not like, but I promised Kaylee I would tell you. Especially since she was against what I did."

"What did you do?" Adam carefully asked as his brow lowered while he stood up.

Eva swallowed hard before she answered. "I took Oliver's coin and placed it on Caleb."

"You what?" Adam asked. The anger was evident in his voice.

"It wasn't my finest moment. Everything just happened, and I was a wreck. Oliver was still alive, so I did it. I know it can't bring people back to life, but maybe this was different. Obviously, the coin didn't work on Caleb," Eva responded. Her eyes were unable to meet his.

"I miss Caleb just as much as you. He was like a brother to us, but you don't trade one life for another. Even if it's someone you are not fond of," Adam sternly countered.

"My displeasure with Oliver has lessened over his stay here. Especially today, when he stood and fought side-by-side with you. All while against my plan. I just wasn't in the right state of mind. I know what I did was wrong, yet still, I had to try. The coin is back in his pocket," Eva said as she wiped her eyes. Adam sighed as he processed what she had confessed.

Eva stood up. "I'm sorry for my actions, and even though I am not showing it right now, I am delighted you are alive." She started to turn around, but Adam grabbed her hand and pulled her into a hug.

"I forgive you. Who's to say what I would have done at that moment, regardless of knowing how wrong it was? Also, I know you won't believe what I am about to say, but I will say it anyway. You are not responsible for what happened today," Adam softly said.

"I can't believe I'm going to admit this, but Oliver was right about everything. Lives were lost today. Even worse, they died for nothing. Cassian took the dagger. If only we had gotten rid of it, or gone back to the diner and given it to Cassian. They would still be alive. How can it not be my fault?" Eva asked in a wavering voice as she continued to hug Adam.

"Everyone knew what they were risking when we decided to stand with you. They didn't die in vain. They died for the cause they believed in and the people they cared about. I get it. I blame myself, too. I can't help but wonder if the outcome would have been better if I had made different choices during the fight, especially when everyone else arrived. You can't let the guilt consume you. We have lived long enough to see what that does to the person and the people they care about. Just remember that you are not to blame for this and that I am always here for you," Adam said.

It took every ounce of his strength to keep his voice free of the emotional turmoil he felt. His goal was to comfort her and to stop the guilt that was growing inside Eva before it devastated her. It would be easy for her to slip down that rabbit hole, so he wanted to do what he could to prevent that. Eva didn't respond, but he did feel her hug him tighter. Shortly after he let go, she quickly turned around and left the room. He hoped she would remember his words.

Adam walked to where Oliver was, and it was only him there. He guessed Kaylee had done a quick check on him and left, so he walked over to his cot. It appeared that they bandaged the second and third-degree burns and left the first-degree alone, minus whatever ointment was rubbed on it. They had his axe and dagger propped up against a nearby wall. Most of his clothes were cut so they could bandage his wounds.

"I'm sorry, my friend. Heal fast. You don't want to keep the 'women of the world' waiting," Adam said as he briefly grinned. He's never seen Oliver, or any immortal, so badly injured from a magical attack and still be alive. Adam felt horrible that Oliver was in this predicament and hoped his friend would pull through. He couldn't bear to lose anybody else. He wanted this horrific day to end, so he went back to his room and showered. After he was done and had changed, Kaylee came into his room. From her appearance, she had done the same thing. She kissed him before wrapping her arms around him. She then stepped away and slapped his arm.

"Do you have any idea how scared you made me earlier today?"

"You've been hanging around Eva too much," Adam said as he rubbed his arm.

"It's not funny! You were really going to sacrifice yourself today, weren't you? Heck, if we hadn't arrived when we did, you would have received your wish," Kaylee countered as she crossed her arms.

"It wasn't my wish. You have no idea the pain I felt knowing I would not see you again, but it was rivaled only by the image of your death. I had to do whatever it took to prevent that. I didn't want any of our friends to die, but the thought of losing you was unbearable. Besides, it's not like Cassian gave me and Oliver much of a choice," Adam responded.

Kaylee sighed. "I understand, and as mad as I am at you, I can't be because if I were in your shoes, I probably would have done the same thing. I...I care about you deeply, and the thought of losing you was too much to handle. I couldn't just leave you to die." Her lip quivered. Adam didn't respond. Instead, he hugged her as he rested his chin on the top of her head. Their embrace lasted a while before she finally let go.

"Can I ask you something? I was going to ask Eva, but the timing wasn't right. It still isn't, but I feel more comfortable asking you," Kaylee said as she slightly cringed.

"Sure. What's on your mind?" Adam asked.

"Do you think Caleb could still be alive? Nothing happened after he turned to bronze. No lights or anything," Kaylee asked.

Adam sighed. "Unfortunately, no. There are rare times when one immortal kills another, and nothing happens. A few things could cause that. One being the type of weapon used to kill the other immortal. Another reason is that the immortal is not around to receive the mark. In this case, both happened. I never witnessed it, but rumors about what happens to the mark do exist. Some say the immortal receives the mark later, but without the theatrics. Others say that no one receives the mark, and the power just fades away. Ironically, Edith would know, but I don't see us asking her."

"I see," Kaylee responded as her head lowered.

"I'm sorry," Adam said. It wasn't an easy question to answer, and he felt bad for how she felt, but he didn't want to give her any false hope.

Kaylee sniffled before she ran her hand across her face. "It's okay. I figured that would be the response, but I wanted to be sure. We need to change the subject. I still can't believe you thought I would listen and abandon you like that. Heck, that any of us would just leave you two out there to die. Don't forget, you still owe me a trip to Alaska," Kaylee playfully said.

Adam chuckled. "I won't forget. It's on the top of my list once we get past this mess. However, leaving now and hiding from this is tempting." Adam went along with her change in demeanor since he knew she didn't want to start crying again.

"It does, but speaking of plans, what is our next course of action?" Kaylee inquired.

"We will clean up the area from the battle and have a ceremony for Paul and Caleb. We need to grieve for them, as well as honor them. After that, I don't know yet," Adam replied.

They went to bed, and Kaylee fell asleep quickly from exhaustion. On the other hand, Adam was drained but not tired since he was "dead" for most of the day. Unfortunately, that left him plenty of time to painfully go over the battle, multiple times, in his head.

He replayed different scenarios of what he could have done differently. As he did this, he couldn't stop seeing his friends hurt and slain in front of him. The thoughts would not stop, and even when he fell asleep, the images of Paul's decayed body and Caleb pleading for his life before he turned into a statue haunted him. He woke up multiple times, screaming and sweating as he did. Kaylee was there to comfort him. Come to find out, she was also plagued with her own dreadful images. Since sleep wasn't going to be an option, they eventually got up early in the morning and started the day.

Oliver remained unconscious, so Kaylee and Eva took turns checking on him while Adam went outside and dealt with the aftermath of the battle. He procured a wheelbarrow and moved the knights, including their armor and weapons, one at a time, to a location deeper within the property. There, he burned the bodies and planned to move the remaining cooled armor and weapons to the forge to be melted down in the future. The smell of the burning, rotted flesh was almost unbearable. While waiting for the fire to burn itself out, he moved to the crypt.

It was a medium-sized stone building that could house a couple of dozen individuals. With the addition of Caleb and Paul, it was half full. Adam noticed Kaylee and he weren't the only ones who couldn't sleep. Eva spent the night creating the marble markers for them and even wrapped Paul in a sheer white fabric. Adam fought back the tears and the images banging on the door to his mind so he could move his friends into position.

He placed Paul onto a wooden plank designed to slide a person into their burial spot along the wall. The wall was stone, but the inside was marble. With only him, it took him a while to get Paul lifted and slid into his final resting spot. He then placed the marker and his golden crossbow near him for later. His next task was Caleb. His statue was heavy, but he managed to slide it to a short, stone pedestal in the corner of the room. However, he had to relocate the decorative statue that was there and place Caleb on it. Afterward, he placed Caleb's marker and shield next to him.

Adam's eyes met the bronzed face of Caleb, and that was when his mental dam collapsed. "I'm so sorry this happened to you. I wish I could have found a way to save you. You did not deserve to die. Neither did Paul, and one way or another, the two of you will have justice. I just hope wherever you are, the rides and games are endless," Adam said through his tears. He laid his hand on Caleb's shoulder, trying to force a smile.

He then jerked his head around to see Eva and Kaylee standing at the entranceway, both with watery eyes. "How long were you standing there?" Adam asked as he wiped his face.

"Long enough," Eva replied. Kaylee rushed over and hugged him. Adam immediately felt at ease while he was in her arms. "I wasn't planning on doing this until later, but we are all here and already upset, so might as well," Eva added.

The three shared happy memories of Paul and Caleb, laughing as they wiped the tears away. The entire time, Kaylee held Adam's hand. The stories lasted a long time…until their eyes were finally dry. They then said their goodbyes to Paul and Caleb. That was when the markers were affixed before they left and closed the doors. Adam quickly removed the remaining metal from the burn pile while Kaylee and Eva covered any remains with dirt. It was dark by the time they made it back to the manor. They stood in the foyer in silence until Kaylee spoke.

"Now, what do we do?"

Adam glanced at Eva, who nodded. He knew she had to be on the same page as him. A page that he was certain Kaylee was on as well. "We get the dagger back and make sure Cassian doesn't harm anyone ever again."

CHAPTER 25

Kaylee smiled with approval. "I'm all for it, but how, and an even better question, where do we start? Cassian could be anywhere in the world right now, and he's invulnerable...even more than your typical immortal."

"Nothing is invulnerable. There must be a way," Eva countered.

"Maybe there is a clue in Caleb's books?" Adam suggested.

"I don't see the point. He would have told us everything," Eva said.

"I'm sure he did, but what if there is some obscure detail that he missed or seemed unrelated? We must try because that's our only hope," Adam responded.

"I'm in. At the very least, it is a welcome distraction," Kaylee added.

Eva shrugged. "Sure, why not?"

"First thing tomorrow, we'll gather any materials related to Cassian. Even if it's indirectly related, it will be included," Adam suggested. Eva and Kaylee nodded. "Good. I'm going to check in on Oliver."

Adam walked to Oliver's room and noticed he hadn't moved yet. He rearranged Oliver and the surrounding blankets and pillows before he changed his bandages. As unpleasant as his wounds appeared, he noticed they had slightly improved. Adam smiled since that was a step in the right direction and hoped Oliver would continue to improve. He cleaned his wounds before he reapplied the ointments and bandages. He wasn't sure if Eva had given him any medicine earlier for the pain, but since he seemed peaceful, he didn't give him anything. "Get better soon, my friend." Adam was exhausted, so he left the room and headed to bed after he was done. However, he made sure to meditate before he slept to help him deal with the loss of Caleb and Paul.

Early the next morning, he and Kaylee met Eva in the kitchen for coffee before they started their task. Eva informed them that Oliver's health was still the same when she checked on him earlier. Once they had drunk their coffee and had a chance to wake up, they headed to the library. Caleb's room was mentioned, but it was too difficult for anyone to enter just yet. Besides, Caleb usually kept only his personal collection in his room. The three entered the library and searched for anything that could be used. They grabbed books related to Cassian, the ritual, other original immortals, and rare magical weapons. Of course, most of these books were from Paul's contact. This process alone took a while to sift through the large collection of books, and when they were finished, there were a dozen books on the table.

"It's only twelve books, but they are thick, and not all of them are translated. This is going to take a while," Kaylee commented.

"It looks like it. I'll grab some notebooks and pens for us to take notes," Adam said. His eyes narrowed when he pulled open the desk drawer. He reached in and pulled out a large envelope marked "Cassian" and revealed it to everyone.

"What's that?" Eva asked.

"Only one way to find out," Adam said and then opened it. He scanned through the few dozen pages, and the more he did, the bigger his smile grew.

"Something good, I hope?" Kaylee commented.

Adam nodded. "I would say so. Caleb had already done the work and summarized it within these pages, including the translations. What would have taken days will now take only hours, if that."

"Way to go, Caleb!" Kaylee exclaimed.

Eva scoffed with amusement. "Even when he's not here, he's still helping us."

"He certainly is. Thanks, buddy," Adam added. The three of them studied the pages for the next couple of hours. During that time, they referenced the books to research anything that caught their attention.

"There's nothing in here that he hasn't already informed us about," Eva huffed. The three sat in silence until Kaylee spoke.

"Maybe we are going about this the wrong way?"

"How so?" Eva asked.

"We are trying to figure out how to find and stop Cassian, but maybe there is someone who could help us. Someone who may know him way better than us," Kaylee replied.

"If you are talking about Edith, then that won't work. Trust me," Eva countered.

"The other original immortals," Adam slowly said as the idea sank in.

"Exactly. Presuming they are not all monsters like him, maybe one of them could help?" Kaylee replied.

"That's great, but aren't they all dead?" Eva mentioned.

"All but two. Cassian, of course, and there is one more. The notes don't mention if the other one is alive or dead. It's like she just vanished from history," Adam commented.

"Katsumi," Kaylee added.

Eva's eyes lit up. "I remember seeing that book." She rifled through the books on the table until she got to hers. "There must be something in here. Some hint to where she may be," Eva added as she flipped through the pages.

Adam and Kaylee were on the edge of their seats over the next hour while Eva carefully went through the book again, taking notes while she read. Finally, she closed the book and glanced at her notes.

"Well? Do you have any idea where she could be?" Kaylee inquired.

Eva sighed. "She vanished over a millennium ago, so I don't have a location." Kaylee and Adam's shoulders dropped in defeat. "I have four locations," Eva added, and then a smile slowly formed.

Adam couldn't believe what he had just heard. "How?" He glanced at Kaylee and saw a smile appear.

"The other originals' stories all had an abrupt end when they died, but hers was more of a disappearance, which could mean death, but I doubt it. This book mentioned four places more than once, and quite fondly, too. All within her native country, Japan," Eva responded.

"And they are?" Kaylee asked.

"Iya Valley, Shikoku; Kita Alps, Honshu; Kamikochi, Nagano; and the Izu Peninsula," Eva responded.

"It's a long shot, but it's all we got. How will we search? Do we just go to each area and explore? I'm unfamiliar with the areas, but I'm sure they are not just a small town that we can quickly go through," Kaylee mentioned.

"After over six hundred years, you learn how to maneuver easily around those types of obstacles. Excuse me," Eva said as she winked before she left the room.

"What did she mean by that?" Kaylee inquired.

"It means she will call her contacts who would be most familiar with those regions to help narrow the search. Once she does that, it will greatly enhance our chances of finding her if she is still alive. Over the years, even if the region is vast, you learn where to look and who would most likely have the information you seek," Adam explained.

"I hope she can narrow it down. Until then, what do we do?" Kaylee asked.

"We continue to look through the books for anything else that could be useful," Adam said as he shuffled closer to her on the couch.

Kaylee smiled as she leaned on him. "Just like studying for the exams." She gave him a quick peck on the lips before they continued their research. A couple of hours passed, and there was no sign of Eva. With no additional luck from their research, they ate lunch before they checked on Oliver. He was still unconscious, but his wounds appeared to be healing.

"I'm back," Eva announced as she entered Oliver's room.

"Hopefully, with good news," Adam remarked.

"I called a few of my contacts, including the one who used to live in Japan. The same one who also loves Japanese folklore. That particular contact had an interesting story. One that involved an ageless princess living in solitude, but occasionally, she would make an appearance. Typically, she joined the celebrations with the townspeople during festivals and helped her fellow natives. This ageless person is seen throughout Japan, but mainly in a small village within the Izu Peninsula," Eva said with a smug look.

"That's perfect. Finally, something goes our way. Great job," Adam exclaimed as he hugged Eva.

"That's great. When do we leave?" Kaylee asked.

"It's a fourteen-hour time difference, so as much as I want to say we leave in a few hours, I suggest tomorrow at five in the afternoon. It will give us time to rest, prepare, and make sure Oliver is situated for us to be gone for an extended time. Also, Eva needs time to study the area so she knows where to portal. With her familiarity with the country, it makes sense that she is the one who creates the portal. It should work out because it will allow us to start bright and early at seven in the morning over there," Adam suggested.

"Bloody hell. Am I the only one around here who understands the value of sleeping in?" Adam, Kaylee, and Eva's heads whipped around to see Oliver awake and struggling to sit up.

"You're awake!" Kaylee exclaimed.

"With all this yapping, how could anyone remain asleep?" Oliver remarked.

"It's good to finally have you back," Eva said as she leaned down and hugged him. Kaylee was next in line.

"Ouch, ouch, ouch," Oliver groaned.

"Sorry!" Eva said as she and Kaylee backed off. With their backs turned to him, Oliver looked at Adam and mouthed the word "progress."

Adam scoffed with amusement. "It's good to see you again, old friend."

Oliver smiled, but then it slowly vanished as his eyes scanned the room. "What did I miss?"

Adam's eyes briefly dropped as he sighed. He then proceeded to tell Oliver everything that happened after he got electrocuted by James, including their current plan. Oliver remained quiet the entire time as Adam caught him up.

"I'm sorry, mate. They were good people. So, who's going to carry the puke bucket for Adam when we leave tomorrow?" Oliver said as he struggled to move.

"You aren't going anywhere," Eva responded.

"What do you mean? Cassian needs to pay for what he did!" Oliver countered.

"And he will, but not with you," Adam sympathetically said.

"He's right. As much as we need the help, you can barely move, and time is of the essence," Kaylee added.

"That's absurd! I can move. Just give me a moment. My body is just sore from being still for so long," Oliver rebutted. He tried to move again, but was only able to move slightly and just with his arms. He was barely able to move his legs.

"I'm sorry. If you make a miraculous recovery before we leave, then sure. If not, you will stay here," Adam said.

Oliver strained again to get up but didn't make any progress. "Maybe you're right. I'm sorry." He lay back down after his failed attempts.

"Don't be sorry, just get better," Adam responded.

The rest of the day was spent planning the trip. This included what supplies to bring, what to wear, and where to portal based on Eva's suggestions. Eva and Adam caught Kaylee up to speed on Japan's customs and even procured some Japanese yen. Also, during this time, they each took turns checking on Oliver. There wasn't much progress, so they prepared his room for when they departed tomorrow. They made sure everything was accessible and close to Oliver and even found crutches for him to use. By the time Adam and Kaylee made it to bed, it was after midnight. This was intentional because they planned to sleep late to help offset the time difference when they traveled.

Kaylee snuggled with Adam. "I know this is a serious mission, but is it bad that I'm excited because I'll be in Japan tomorrow? I know we aren't going sightseeing, but just the fact I will be in Japan is wild...and exciting."

"It's perfectly normal. Even though we won't be visiting any of the popular locations, the local areas can be just as intriguing and beautiful. Yes, we will be on a mission, but still, take the time to enjoy where you are. I've been to Japan but never to this area, so I'm intrigued as to how it will compare to where I've been. Of course, it's been a hundred years, and it was a quick trip, so it will be fun. My Japanese is rusty, but luckily, Eva's isn't. Random, but do you want to know another perk about this trip? We don't have to worry about the hassles of traveling. We will be there in seconds," Adam added.

Kaylee smiled. "I know. That's wonderful all by itself. Free, quick travel. I can't believe I will be in Japan tomorrow!" Kaylee's expression changed as her brow crinkled. "Oh...I just realized you will have to deal with the portal sickness thing. Sorry."

"Yeah...I'm not looking forward to that, but it's over in a few minutes. It's another reason why Eva has us further out of the village we are headed to. So people won't hear me vomiting," Adam joked. Kaylee laughed.

After she had stopped laughing, the two locked eyes. Adam could feel himself mesmerized by her gaze, and never felt so close to her as he did there. The two kissed. It started slowly and gently, but as they continued, it became more intense and passionate. After some time, they managed to tear away from each other. Regardless of how much he yearned for things to go further, and suspected she did as well, he still wanted to honor her wishes. Besides, he didn't want their physical actions to be the result of the pending doom. They remained tightly cuddled with each other before they drifted off to sleep.

The next day flew by fast. They each had a backpack and, of course, their weapon. Since they were unsure how long they would be gone or what accommodations they would find, they packed extra items into their large backpacks. They left their backpacks in the foyer as they went to see Oliver. When they arrived in his room, to their surprise, with the assistance of the crutches, he stood next to his bed.

"I'm glad to see that you can stand now," Adam commented.

"Yep. Is there any chance you can stall leaving for a week or at least a few more days? That, or I can go, and by the time the real action starts, I'll be ready," Oliver suggested.

"I'm afraid not. Sorry. Besides, I don't know how the terrain will be, and I doubt it will be 'crutches friendly,' my friend," Adam responded.

"I figured you would say that, but here is my counter-proposal. How about..." Oliver stumbled as he tried to walk. He fell into

Adam, which almost knocked him over, since he wasn't prepared for Oliver to fall.

Adam got him to his feet. "You were saying?"

Oliver sighed. "I guess my counter-proposal will be that I am here if anyone needs me."

Adam smiled and laid his hand on Oliver's shoulder. "I know if you could make it, you would. Stay here. Get better and stay safe." Oliver partially smiled and nodded.

"He's right. You need to focus on your recovery. I hope you feel better soon," Kaylee added before she carefully hugged him.

"Everything is ready and set up for you, so you should be good while we're gone," Eva remarked.

"Thank you for everything," Oliver replied.

Eva smiled. "I hope you recover quickly, and we'll see you soon." Eva carefully hugged him before the three made their way to the door. When Adam was at the door, he turned and saw Oliver lying on his bed.

"Make sure you always keep your coin with you. Just in case you, unfortunately, take a turn for the worse, or Cassian sends Edith or himself to finish the job. You need that coin as your backup. Especially with you alone and not fully healed," Adam mentioned.

"I always do," Oliver responded. He flashed his coin at Adam before putting it back in his pocket.

"I'll see you soon," Adam said as he grinned and left the room. He met up with Kaylee and Eva in the foyer. He couldn't help but worry about Oliver.

"He'll be okay," Kaylee reassured.

"I hope so," Adam replied as he put his backpack on.

"Is everyone ready?" Eva asked. Kaylee and Adam nodded.

Eva turned around, created the portal, and walked through. Kaylee looked at Adam and smiled before she entered. Adam smiled at her excitement, took a deep breath, and walked through the portal.

271

CHAPTER 26

As soon as Adam made it through the other side, a wave of nausea washed over him. He took a few steps off to the side, put his hands on his knees, and vomited. He wiped his mouth with his arm and tossed a mint into his mouth as he waited for the dizziness to pass.

"Oh, sweetie, are you okay?" Kaylee asked as she rubbed his back.

"Yeah. More embarrassed than anything else. Welcome to Japan," Adam responded as he gestured forward.

Kaylee and Eva walked away while Adam took a few minutes to feel better before joining them. As he walked, he noticed the green grass that covered the landscape and the different fall-like colored leaves that were still on the trees. When he caught up to them, they were standing near the edge of a cliff, looking out. In front of them were the still blue waters of the bay. Further out in the distance was a snow-capped, dormant volcano. The air was brisk, but he knew it would warm up as the sun rose.

"It's so peaceful. I can't believe we're actually here," Kaylee said as she took Adam's hand. The only thing he admired more than the majestic view was Kaylee's smile as her eyes scanned the area in wonder.

Eva pointed. "There. That village is the only one around here for miles. That's where we'll start."

"We're pretty high up. If we start moving now, we will be there by lunchtime," Adam suggested. The group agreed and began their journey.

The walk down to the village was easy but long. When they arrived, it was a quaint village with small houses and stores. Some buildings were white, while others had red, teal, orange, and green accents. There was a small market with various colored tents throughout the street, selling everything from crafts to food. Depending on whether they were on a hill or not, Adam could see the water near the village. There were even a couple of small fishing boats floating in the bay. As they entered further into town, more eyes followed them.

"Why is everyone staring at us?" Kaylee whispered.

"I'm guessing they aren't used to seeing Westerners in this area, especially unannounced," Adam whispered back before he turned his head to Eva. "Time to work your magic."

Eva smiled, approached one of the street vendors, and began to speak Japanese. As she spoke, Adam noticed the others around them were listening intently. During the conversation, Adam observed the people around them smile and inch closer to Eva. The lady and Eva began to laugh as they continued to talk, and now, a few others joined in the conversation.

"What are they talking about?" Kaylee quietly asked.

"My Japanese is a little rusty, but from what I can gather, she is saying that we are travelers and how much she enjoys their village…how lovely everyone is, and so forth. I think she even made fun of us for not knowing their language. Of course, Eva has made friends with everybody," Adam replied.

The vendor handed Eva six skewers with food on them, which Adam and Kaylee helped hold while Eva paid the vendor. They walked off and found a secluded grassy spot to sit, relax, and eat.

"Okay, we have yakitori and dango…one for each of us," Eva announced as she happily began to eat.

Kaylee examined her food. "I can tell the yakitori is grilled chicken, but what are these pink, white, and green balls on a stick?"

"They are a type of dumpling. I think you'll like them," Adam responded as he took a bite of his. Kaylee first ate a piece of chicken, then one of the dumplings, and smiled. The food was quite delicious, and the cool breeze from the bay was relaxing. They finished their food, washed it down with the water from their water bottles, and sat for a moment before Adam turned to Eva.

"So, did you find out anything?"

"Not yet. I didn't want to immediately start asking questions. That would be rude. I figured I would go back and browse the market again. It would be easier to ask questions now that they are at ease," Eva responded.

"Hopefully, they will know who Katsumi is," Adam commented.

"Yeah, and hopefully, she is nearby as well," Kaylee added.

"She's closer than you think," a woman's voice said from behind them. They turned around and noticed a woman leaning against a tree. Adam's eyes widened when he saw the immortal markings covering her arms. They quickly stood up and reached for their weapons.

"I wouldn't if I were you. It's a public area, and I have no intention of having to uproot because I had to kill three immortals who are clearly outmatched," Katsumi casually responded.

"That's a bold statement, considering the company you are in," Eva countered.

"Is it?" Katsumi replied as she smirked.

"How did you know we were here?" Adam inquired.

"News travels quite fast in a small village like this, especially when Westerners are involved," Katsumi responded as she strolled closer to them. Adam gestured for them to stand down.

She wore a red silk blouse with black pants, and her medium-length black hair was pulled behind her head and braided. He also noticed a silver bracelet with a sapphire, the size of a quarter, on top of it. She was around the same height as Eva, but it was her kind brown eyes and absence of weapons that put him at ease. As she stood in front of Adam, she looked at Eva to his right and then at Kaylee to his left, but when she looked at Kaylee, her brow crinkled. She looked Kaylee up and down before her eyes drifted back to Adam. However, he noticed Kaylee had become uncomfortable as she crossed her arms and looked away.

"What's wrong?" Adam asked.

"Nothing…it's just…" Kaylee trailed off.

"Just what?" Adam inquired.

"Cassian looked at me the same way she did," Kaylee replied. When she mentioned his name, Katsumi quickly took a few steps toward her.

"You've seen him?" Katsumi asked as her eyes narrowed. Adam stood closer to her since he was unsure of her intentions.

"Yeah. He attacked our home the other day," Eva commented as she also stood closer.

"And killed people who were dear to us," Adam added.

"And during that, when he passed me while I was lying on the ground, he gave me the same look as you just did," Kaylee remarked. Adam watched as her timidness faded away when she stood up straight as she faced Katsumi. "Interesting, isn't it?"

"So, you don't have an allegiance with him, or here to cause me harm?" Katsumi asked.

"No," everyone said in unison.

Katsumi briefly looked down at her bracelet. A smile formed. "Good, follow me. We can talk more at my place."

"Pretty trusting of you to invite us. It seems almost too easy," Eva commented.

Katsumi held up her arm. "The bracelet detects lies. If it turned red, all of you would be dead, and I would be relocating. Now, you obviously know my name, but I don't know yours." They each stated their name.

"Nice to meet you. Now, let's venture to my house before we add more fuel to their gossip. Follow me." She turned around and walked down a path that led away from the village. The three looked at each other and shrugged before they followed her. Adam glanced around and noticed a few villagers talking as they watched them leave.

As they walked in silence, Adam was both relieved and nervous. It was wonderful that they found Katsumi so quickly, but he wasn't sure what they were about to walk into. He didn't get a bad vibe from her, but his judgment wasn't always perfect. Still, they had no alternative but to follow her and see where this led. He also wanted to channel Caleb and ask her numerous questions.

"You're quiet. The rare times I meet other immortals that aren't out for my head, they are quite chatty," Katsumi commented.

"Trust me, the urge to pick your brain is hard to resist. I have numerous questions floating around in my head, accompanied by the desire to hear your take on history. You have been around for all the major events throughout time. Heck, you are the personification of history," Adam responded.

"I understand. If I had met myself, my curiosity would have been piqued as well. How about this? Let's get past the initial reason why you are here. After that, and time permitting, feel free to ask me anything. Deal?" Katsumi asked with a hint of a smile.

"Deal," Adam replied as he grinned.

They reached the outskirts of the village, and to his surprise, she entered a house that looked like all the rest. Adam expected her house to be further away and to look more... ancient.

"Welcome to my home. Please, come on in," Katsumi said as she gestured for them to enter. As Adam entered her home, he noticed that it was modest. Typically, older immortals lived in extravagant homes or at least showed their wealth in one way or another. Even if they were trying to lay low, there were signs. It was odd for someone over six thousand years old not to show any signs of their age. Adam lightly grabbed Kaylee's arm and motioned for her to take her shoes off. They left their shoes and backpacks near the front door and continued.

"This area is so beautiful and peaceful, and I like your home," Kaylee mentioned.

"Thank you. First time in Japan?" Katsumi asked.

"Is it that obvious?" Kaylee said as she cringed.

Katsumi smiled. "Yes, but that's okay. You are a young immortal, aren't you? Before you ask, yes…it's obvious. If you have been around for as long as me, you tend to pick up on cues quickly."

"Right again. Only a few years. Honestly, I didn't even know what I was until recently," Kaylee responded.

"Well, it's good that you have your boyfriend and close friend here to help guide you," Katsumi said. She then turned and headed to the next room.

"Wait, how did you know?" Adam asked.

"I didn't. It was just a guess," Katsumi said as she looked over her shoulder with a smug expression. "Come along."

"I'm beginning to like her," Eva remarked before she followed her. Adam and Kaylee shared a look and smiled before they followed her as well.

They entered the room to find Katsumi easily pushing aside a bulky dresser. Underneath was a stone trap door that blended in with the rest of the house. She lifted the thick door with one arm and climbed down the stairs.

"I feel like this is how horror movies start," Kaylee whispered.

Adam scoffed with amusement. "I hope you're wrong."

Eva went down first, followed by Kaylee, and then Adam. His jaw dropped when he saw the well-lit, vast area hidden underneath her house. Beautiful wooden floors held various relics from not only the Japanese culture but from all over the world. There were vases, weapons, furniture, elegant scenery pictures, silk fabrics of various colors, journals, and some old black-and-white photos on a table.

"This is amazing," Adam muttered.

"Thank you. This is just one of multiple locations I have in Japan. I am here now just because I enjoy the area during this time of the season. So, what brings you to my side of the world?" Katsumi inquired.

"Long story short, Cassian wanted a particular dagger, and after hearing his reputation was tarnished, to say the least, we did our best to keep it from him. He attacked Eva's home with a couple of followers and a small undead army. The battle ended with him obtaining the dagger, two of our close friends dead, and one friend still so injured that he could barely move. I even stabbed him in the heart with my magical weapon, and he didn't die. We want to get the dagger back before he does anything horrible with it. Also, honestly, to avenge the ones he took from us," Adam explained.

"I can't believe it," Katsumi said as her eyes drifted away, deep in thought.

"Why is that dagger so important? I know it was used in the ritual, but I don't understand why he wanted it so badly," Eva commented.

Katsumi sighed before walking over to a small chest. She unlocked it using pressure points on the chest. "You don't know the full story." She reached in and pulled out the dagger.

"The dagger was for you all along, wasn't it? Cassian retrieved it for you!" Eva said as she, Adam, and Kaylee reached for their weapons. A knot formed in Adam's stomach. She led them into a trap.

CHAPTER 27

Katsumi turned around and was unfazed by their reaction. "Settle down. I'm not working for Cassian, nor do I have any allegiance to him. I mean you no harm. It's time that you now hear the origin story of immortals. The full, real version from someone who was there."

"How can we trust you?" Adam asked. His hand was on his weapon, ready to activate it.

"This bracelet works both ways. Watch," Katsumi said as she lifted her arm. "My name is Kaylee." The sapphire turned red. "See. It will stay red until the truth has been spoken by the individual who spoke the initial lie. My name is Katsumi." The sapphire turned blue.

"I am not immortal," Adam said, eager to see if it worked for everyone. The sapphire turned red. "I am immortal." The sapphire turned blue.

"Are you satisfied?" Katsumi smirked as she lowered her arm.

"Yes. Sorry. It's been a rough few days for us," Adam responded. Katsumi smiled and nodded in response.

"We know about the warlock that invited you, Cassian, and four others with the promise of riches. Then, after explaining how evil each of you was, you still desired what was promised, so the warlock cursed each of you with immortality. We presume the dagger was used in that ritual. So, what are we missing?" Eva asked.

"So much," Katsumi remarked. "The stories about us were true. We were monsters, and some of us stayed that way after the ritual. However, some tried to change their ways, like Cassian and I. Before the ritual, none of us had met each other. We only knew each person by their reputation. After the ritual, Cassian and I vowed to make our immortal lives worthwhile and to view it as a gift, not a curse. Our bond grew over the centuries as we did everything we could to kill off any evil immortal we encountered. In addition to that, we used our riches to help poor communities thrive. For a time, we were so happy. We were in love. It wasn't until he killed an original that I noticed a change."

"So, an original can be killed?" Eva asked.

"Yes, by the very object Cassian took from you," Katsumi responded.

Adam's eyes grew. "That dagger can kill an original?" Eva and Kaylee scoffed as their shoulders dropped. Clearly, they felt the same frustration as Adam did.

"Yes, there were six daggers, one for each of us. I stood in the middle of the pentagram while the others stood at the points. His magic forced me to slit my own throat, followed by the others. You see, nature needs balance, and it won't allow any creature to have the power to live forever, so the daggers used became immortal, and the only thing I've seen kill an original," Katsumi replied.

"That explains why he wanted it so badly," Adam muttered.

"One reason," Katsumi said and raised her hand when Adam tried to speak. "As I was saying, once Cassian killed an evil original, I could see his light dim. He wasn't the same, and I begged him to stop, but he swore he could handle it. In fear, I killed the next evil original, and once I did, I knew he wasn't being truthful with me. I could feel my soul darken and my hunger for power grow. I had to meditate daily for a long time to push that aside. To take in so much evil can change an immortal to their core. Typically, only originals can harbor evil to that capacity. This is partially due to the sheer number of immortals we've killed over our vast lifespan. It also has to do with the power received from a slain original. It's much more potent than receiving the mark from a regular immortal."

"That's good to know you can prevent the evil from taking over," Kaylee commented.

"Yes, but it is not an easy endeavor. It takes great willpower and determination to overcome it," Katsumi remarked. Adam noticed Kaylee slightly grin and was glad to see it. He knew that topic made her nervous...and understandably so. There was a slight pause before Katsumi continued.

"So, under the disguise of good intentions, he hunted and killed another original, and that is when the Cassian I knew died. He tried to kill me afterward but failed. I had this dagger to his heart, and all I had to do was push, but I couldn't. The centuries of memories of the love we shared prevented me from following through, so I disappeared. When he couldn't find me, he went after the only other remaining original, one who was our friend and tried to do good with his life. Cassian killed him as well, but he didn't get his dagger. He didn't know that our friend gave it to me to hide. That was the dagger that Cassian took from you. I originally hid it in the same graveyard where my fallen friend's family was buried, but over the years, grave robbers must have unearthed it, and it trickled its way down to your possession. Now, my dagger is the only one remaining."

"What happens when he retrieves all the daggers?" Kaylee asked.

"If he has my dagger, that means he would have killed me. In that case, he would have the power of all the original immortals, along with their daggers. He would be unstoppable. Nothing to kill him, and with immense power coupled with his new necromancy...he would plunge this world into darkness. He's already tried over the centuries. Each time, I have either prevented or mitigated his plans. Plagues, wars, undead creatures, and other unspeakable acts. He wants power and for the world to suffer. Also, with all the daggers, he could harness the dark magic within them to increase his necromancy abilities. For example, he wouldn't need an additional power source, like his scythe, to control the undead. He could do it himself and on a greater scale," Katsumi explained.

"Actually, I destroyed his scythe the other day," Adam added.

Katsumi scoffed with amusement. "I'm sure he wasn't pleased, but that's good. That would cause a significant delay in his plans, but at some point, he would find another source...or my dagger."

"Can you help us stop him?" Adam asked.

"I can help, but I can't kill him," Katsumi responded as her eyes drifted down.

"Why not?" Eva inquired.

"For the same reason why I couldn't kill Kaylee or even you. No matter how evil any of you had become, I couldn't do it. Regardless of how much time had passed since I last saw you," Adam commented.

"He speaks the truth. I know what he has become and that there is no redemption for him now. With that knowledge, I still can't deliver the final kill stroke. I will give my dagger to you and allow you to use it on him, but I can't do it. I don't even think I can witness it without inadvertently stopping you. However, know this. Whoever kills Cassian will absorb all that he is...all that evil will become yours. So, I promise that whoever kills him, I will make your death quick. If not, Cassian's plan will prevail," Katsumi said as her eyes met with each of them.

"Won't you turn evil then?" Adam inquired.

"After thousands of years of discovering various ways to achieve inner peace, I will be able to handle it," Katsumi replied.

"So, one of us must die. I don't accept that! There must be a way. Some way!" Eva exclaimed.

"I'm sorry," Katsumi replied.

Kaylee held Adam's hand, but they didn't look at each other. Adam's heart sank into his stomach. The idea of having to watch Eva or Kaylee die made him sick to his stomach, so he vowed to himself that he would find a way for it to be him.

"It has to be me," Kaylee said as she held Adam's hand harder.

"No, it doesn't," Adam quickly retorted.

"Yes, it does. That explains why my mark was in that book with the ritual and Cassian. It's like my destiny, or something," Kaylee said.

"It doesn't make any sense. Why you?" Eva inquired.

"Wait. Your mark was in a book?" Katsumi asked, but then she gasped. "I can't believe it."

"Believe what?" Adam asked.

"I was the first to die, so I was the first to become immortal. With that, not only am I the most powerful of the originals, but I also inherited knowledge that no other immortal possesses, not even Cassian. Some of it I dismissed or figured it wouldn't come true any time soon." Katsumi walked up to Kaylee as she unbuttoned her blouse halfway. Adam looked away. "It's okay. Everyone needs to see this. Kaylee, show me your mark." Katsumi said.

Kaylee nodded and unbuttoned the few buttons she had at the top of her shirt. They both revealed their marks. Eva and Adam leaned in, and their jaws dropped when they noticed they shared the same mark, but inverted.

"It wasn't the same mark but inverted in the book, it was two different marks. What does that mean?" Adam asked.

A smile grew on Katsumi's face. "It means I am the beginning, and Kaylee is the end."

CHAPTER 28

Kaylee's brow crinkled as she looked at Adam and Eva. "What do you mean...I am the end? I was right, I'm destined to kill Cassian. I knew it. Six thousand years ago, my story was written, and I don't have any say in it." Kaylee's face was red while she fixed her shirt. Adam rubbed her back to comfort her.

Katsumi smiled as she fixed her blouse. "Yes and no. It means that you are the last immortal. The cursed family lines have been depleted. Therefore, no other immortal will be created after you. Kaylee, you are more powerful than you realize. You are not destined to kill Cassian, but all immortals."

Kaylee's brow lowered. "Is that supposed to make me feel better? My destiny is to kill every single immortal, even the ones I care about. That's not happening. I would rather die!"

Katsumi laughed. "Don't worry. You will not become a hunter that immortals will fear. If so, that would have happened as soon as you became immortal. It only means you will have the capability. Call it nature's backup plan in case the daggers were lost forever. You have many gifts. For instance, you can kill an original with any magical weapon. It doesn't have to be with the dagger. In addition, you can kill a non-original immortal with any weapon, magical or not." For a moment, they were speechless after her revelation.

"It now makes sense. That's why my wound took longer than it should have to heal after she and I trained," Eva commented.

"And no offense to you, but regardless of how great your teaching methods are, did it not surprise you how quickly she picked up on everything?" Katsumi asked. Eva and Adam looked at each other and shrugged. "It's because the ability to fight is engraved within her. This includes learning how to use any magical weapon at an exponential rate," Katsumi mentioned.

"Does that mean I will become a fierce warrior and defeat Cassian if I accept who I am?" Kaylee asked.

Katsumi chuckled. "I'm afraid that's not how it works. You don't have an inner warrior to unlock. Your gifts are powerful, but they are only there to aid you," Katsumi replied.

"It still doesn't erase the fact that I will become the next Cassian," Kaylee commented.

"Not exactly. Think of it this way. Each immortal has a bucket, and as we kill other immortals, that bucket fills. At some point, the bucket will overflow and change who we are at our core. Originals' buckets can hold more, but your bucket is even deeper. It's another gift. You may be able to handle killing Cassian and still remain who you are," Katsumi explained. Adam smiled, but it wasn't as big as Kaylee's at the news as she hugged him. It was the hope they needed.

"I like our odds. We have an original, the dagger, and our secret weapon, Kaylee," Eva commented.

"You do, but don't forget that Kaylee can die just like any other immortal. Even worse, whoever absorbs her power will gain her abilities. This includes her ability to kill an immortal with a non-magical weapon. Also, Cassian is smart, it won't take long for him to figure out that Kaylee is unique and then react to that. That look he gave her, the same one I did, was because I felt a sensation similar to whenever I'm near this dagger. We may have an advantage, but Cassian is not one to underestimate," Katsumi added.

"Understood, but our next problem is how do we find where he is located?" Adam inquired.

Katsumi smirked. "As the first immortal, I have the ability to find any immortal." Everyone smiled.

"You are becoming more and more my favorite person," Eva said.

"So, you just know where everyone is?" Adam asked.

"If I have something of theirs, then I can find them. If not, even a good memory of their appearance will work as well," Katsumi replied.

"You have memories of him," Adam stated.

"And a ring he left behind, so I will have no problem finding him," Katsumi said. She then walked to a different area of the room, reached into a drawer, and pulled out a ring.

From what Adam could see, it was a dull, gold ring with a thin clasp at the bottom that hooked together once placed on the finger. The top of it appeared to be a face with a mask covering mainly the eyes, with long hair on the sides.

"As the last immortal, you share the same gift as I," Katsumi commented as she walked back to them.

"I can find any immortal?" Kaylee asked as her eyes widened.

"Yes, but it's a skill that takes some time to learn. Not only would you have to learn the proper techniques to pull off such a task, but your focus must also be strong. How is your meditation?" Katsumi asked?

"I haven't really tried that yet," Kaylee responded as she cringed.

Katsumi smiled. "Work on it. Once you've mastered that, then you will be ready to learn this skill."

"I will," Kaylee replied.

"I need a few minutes of silence so I can concentrate. You can remain here; just don't make a sound," Katsumi said. They agreed, so she sat down on a pillow and crossed her legs. She held the ring, palm side up, in front of her and placed her other hand over it. Then, her eyes closed. The silence was so awkward that he kicked himself for not leaving earlier and returning when she was finished. Then, his eyes grew wide when a white light formed within her hands. Kaylee and he shared a look while this went on. Not too much longer, Katsumi abruptly snapped out of her trance. Adam waited anxiously for the results. She seemed uneasy about what she saw.

"What did you see?" Kaylee asked.

"He is in Tibet. More specifically, in one of their lesser-known monasteries located at the top of a mountain," Katsumi responded.

"There's more, isn't there?" Adam asked.

Katsumi nodded. "I received images of blood...rivers of blood. That means that he slaughtered the inhabitants of that monastery. Even worse, I felt like he sensed my presence. Something that hasn't happened before. I guess the additional dagger has made him even more powerful."

"I presume that isn't good," Kaylee commented.

"It's not. Knowing Cassian, he would have already fortified the monastery and would soon be on the hunt for me. Now that he knows I am aware of his location, he will be waiting. If we wait too long to attack, he will find us," Katsumi replied.

"So, do we relocate to one of your other locations and prepare for his arrival?" Adam asked.

"No, we bring the fight to him...soon. The more time we give him, the more time he has to find another way to power up his undead army or to find additional followers. At this point, he may just come himself," Katsumi replied.

"When do we leave?" Eva inquired.

"I like your spirit, and I suggest soon. We just need enough time to plan and mentally prepare for the events to come," Katsumi directed.

"Sounds good. Where do we start?" Adam inquired.

"Well, we can't just portal directly there. Cassian is too smart for that. He would have blocked the area for portals," Katsumi mentioned.

"How does he do that? We saw one of his followers, Edith, blow some dust into an open portal, and it prevented us from using ours," Adam remarked.

"If you crush and grind a portal key down to powder, you can use the powder to disrupt a portal. Once it is in a state of flux, the disturbance radiates out for about a mile and will remain until more portal key dust is blown into the portal. Until that happens, no portals can be created, closed, or used. Even the portal in a flux state cannot be used," Katsumi responded.

"That explains it," Kaylee commented.

"I forget that there are a lot of secrets that immortals such as yourself do not know," Katsumi remarked.

"You wouldn't happen to know the cure for portal sickness, would you?" Adam inquired, not expecting an answer.

"Ah, a rare condition. You are one in a handful of immortals I've ever known to have it. Unfortunately, there is no cure," Katsumi responded.

"I figured so," Adam said, defeated.

"But…there is a remedy for its symptoms," Katsumi added. Adam lifted his head and raised his brow with interest. "Chew on fresh mint leaves as you enter the portal. If you do that, you will not feel the symptoms when you emerge on the other side. However, it must be fresh mint leaves…nothing artificial and no substitutes."

A huge smile appeared on Adam's face. "Are you serious? That's the big secret. That's so easy. I can't believe I didn't think about that!"

"Sometimes the easiest solutions are the hardest to find. Luckily for you, I have some mint in my garden," Katsumi added.

"Thank you so much! I really appreciate it!" Adam exclaimed. Kaylee hugged him from the side while his smile remained firmly in place.

"You wouldn't happen to know a cure for a person who has turned into a bronze statue?" Eva asked. Adam's smile left him, but he leaned in and intently listened. He hoped that Katsumi had an answer for this as well.

Katsumi's brow crinkled as she thought for a moment. "Was your friend hit by a dart that was shot from an ivory blowgun?"

"He was," Eva answered.

"Hephaestus's sting. Either the legend of Hephaestus is true, or a witch used the idea to craft that weapon. Regardless, Hephaestus, the Greek god of blacksmithing, crafted the blowgun out of the horns of unicorns. Then, he used the same bronze that created Talos, a bronze giant, to make the darts. It needs the blood of something impure to activate its power. Any living thing that the dart hits will turn to bronze. Similar to Medusa and her gaze. I'm sorry, but there is no cure for that," Katsumi replied.

"It was worth a shot," Eva said as she hung her head. Kaylee put her arm around her to comfort her. Adam contained his emotions as he looked away. It felt like they lost Caleb all over again when the hope of his return was lost.

Adam cleared his throat. "So, do you suggest we portal over a mile away from the monastery and hike our way up?" He hoped the change of subject would help distract her from the upsetting news.

"Yes, but in two different locations. You three will go to one location, and I will go to another. He will expect me to hide as always and clean up whatever mess he makes. This way, I can sneak in while your team takes a different route. Then, we can join forces at the end," Katsumi suggested.

"So, we're bait?" Eva abruptly asked.

"No, bait would suggest that I expect you to die. On the contrary, I want you to live. I will have this dagger, and Kaylee is your dagger. We will have the element of surprise with Kaylee and me. He also doesn't realize Kaylee can kill him. Just be careful along the way. I don't know what he may have in store, but I do know the quicker we react, the less time he has to prepare," Katsumi explained. Adam glanced at her bracelet throughout her explanation, and it remained blue.

"Fair point, and it makes sense. We can look at a map before we go to see where the best locations would be," Eva suggested.

"Let us look now. I can pull up the area on my computer," Katsumi mentioned. Their brows crinkled. "Hey, I may be ancient, but I am current with technology. Even living this far from the big cities, one must stay current with the times." They smiled, and Eva left with Katsumi.

"Are you coming?" Eva asked.

Adam and Kaylee looked at each other. "We'll stay here. Just let us know what you determine when you get back," Adam called out. Eva nodded and walked away. As soon as they left, Adam pulled Kaylee into him and kissed her long, yet gently.

"I'm not complaining, but what was that for?" Kaylee asked afterward.

"With everything happening so fast, I wanted to make sure that important part of the plan was not skipped," Adam responded and then winked. Kaylee smiled and pulled him in for a quick kiss and a long hug.

He took in every moment with her. How soft her lips were, the warmth of her hug, and the joy he felt whenever he was with her. They stayed embraced until they heard footsteps coming their way. It took longer than he expected, but he was fine with that. It just meant he was able to spend extra time with Kaylee.

While they were gone, Katsumi changed clothes. Similar to Kaylee and Eva, and to some degree Adam, she wore jeans, a tight-fitting shirt, and boots. She had the dagger sheathed in a small scabbard on her belt on her right side. On her left side was a katana, sheathed within her red saya, blade side up. The handle was black, however, there was a white sculpted dragon's head at the end of the handle.

"We have the locations," Eva mentioned.

"Please accept this gift. Inside is fresh mint. A pinch per portal trip should suffice," Katsumi said. She presented Adam with a small, airtight metal container…no bigger than a couple of inches long. She did so using both her hands, followed by a slight bow.

"You shouldn't have, but thank you. That is gracious of you," Adam replied. Keeping with the tradition, Adam accepted the gift using both his hands and made a slight bow. He also didn't open it in front of her. Instead, since his front pockets were full, he placed it in his back pocket.

"We are going to leave the backpacks here, so if there is anything you need, get it before we leave," Eva instructed.

"I can't remember the last time I mentioned this to anyone, but if anything were to happen to me, the locations of my other houses are in that drawer over there. Currently, I am the only person aware of them, and I would hate for them to be lost forever, or even worse…pillaged. I would rather have my possessions in the hands of good people. There are sentimental items, as well as items that range from minor to immense magical power. In addition to that, I have chronicled thousands of years' worth of knowledge and experiences that should be passed along. As you know, as the years pass, it's hard to remember everything, so I wrote it down. Please feel free to use anything that will be of great use to you," Katsumi said.

For a moment, Adam thought about Caleb and his chronicles. He could only imagine Caleb and Katsumi exchanging notes, and hopefully, he wouldn't talk her ear off in the process. "I hope it doesn't come down to that, but if so, thank you. You and your items

291

will be handled with respect and care," Adam responded. Katsumi smiled.

They left the lower level and sealed it shut. Then, they grabbed whatever else they felt they needed from their backpacks and put their shoes on while Katsumi gathered what she needed from the other room. Once everyone was ready, they gathered in the central room.

"I will go first, followed by your group. Once you are there, make your journey to the monastery as quickly as possible. Don't delay, and remember, he will be focused on your group. Also, we need to reach him simultaneously so we can attack him together. It's our only chance," Katsumi directed.

"The main entrance to the monastery is at the end of a long flight of stairs, straight to the front door. To save time, we will portal about halfway up. That's how long the stairs are. Katsumi will take that route but will use stealth and only engage if necessary. There is another way…a small path that winds around and will get us to the side of the building where we will find a way in. It's not technically a path. From the looks of it, the path naturally formed over time. It will require some climbing, and some areas will be rocky, but it can be done. Cassian may know about it, but if his resources are slim, he will focus his defenses on the main points of entry," Eva explained.

"Japan and China all in one day. Your travel card is filling up quickly," Adam remarked to Kaylee.

Kaylee scoffed. "It is. Maybe someday I can revisit these places without the threat of an evil original immortal." Adam smiled and rubbed her back.

"Are you sure you can do this?" Eva asked Katsumi.

"I don't know if I can deliver the final kill stroke, but I know I won't stand in your way. I would hand you the dagger now, but I want Cassian's focus to be on the person who holds the dagger…me," Katsumi replied.

292

"We will do our best so you don't have to be the one to kill Cassian," Adam said.

"What does Cassian's sword do?" Kaylee inquired.

"His sword amplifies his strength tenfold," Katsumi replied. Adam now understood why his strikes were so powerful.

"And your sword?" Kaylee asked.

"It is like Cassian's, but it amplifies my speed and agility when I'm using the sword in combat," Katsumi responded. Everybody then took a quick moment to explain what their weapons did.

"Here, take this pouch," Katsumi said as she handed Kaylee one of the two pouches she had.

"What's this for?" Kaylee inquired.

"It's filled with portal key dust. If you come across a portal in a flux state, blow as much of this dust into it until it vanishes," Katsumi instructed.

"Will do," Kaylee replied as she hooked the small pouch to her belt loop.

"I wish each of you good luck," Katsumi added. Everyone wished her good luck as well. She then opened a portal and left.

As soon as her portal closed. Eva turned and gave everyone a group hug. She then smiled and opened a portal. Adam steadied his breathing. He needed his mind focused if he was going to keep everybody alive.

"Mint," Kaylee mentioned.

"Thanks. I almost forgot," Adam replied and quickly retrieved the container. He took a pinch of the chopped mint out and put the rest back in his back pocket. He chewed it as they entered the portal.

As he stepped through, he stumbled on some loose rocks but regained his footing quickly. He looked at Kaylee and Eva and smiled from ear to ear. "I don't feel sick."

Kaylee kissed him. "And you're minty too."

"I'll take her word for it," Eva said and then winked.

The air was brisk but tolerable. He peered up the mountain and saw the large white building with a red roof. Far to their left, almost out of sight, were the stairs. "Welcome to China," Adam remarked. Without delay, they began their journey. Eva led the way, followed by Kaylee and then Adam. Minus a few spots, the climb was easier than expected, and for most of it, they walked normally, especially once they got past the steep section. The area was full of trees and some boulders, with smaller rocks around it. Then, they heard a moan.

To their right was an undead monk staggering toward them with his hands reaching out. He had a gash across his chest. Adam and Eva activated their weapons while Kaylee pulled out hers. Adam glanced around and didn't see any others.

"I got it," Eva said as she approached it.

"I guess Cassian found a way, but this one seems different. Not strong and controlled like the others. As if he just jump-started it and let it loose," Adam commented.

"I wonder how many more of these are wandering about?" Kaylee asked.

They watched Eva aim her spear and ram it through the head of the undead monk, instantly killing it. Adam caught movement out of the corner of his eye, and when he looked, he saw Edith off to the left of them. She had the blowgun aimed at Kaylee and was about to use it.

"Watch out!" Adam yelled as he shielded Kaylee with his body. That is when he felt a sharp pain in the back of his shoulder that made him grimace. His eyes grew big, for he knew what had happened. He looked at Edith, who had a devious grin on her face. His eyes then moved to Eva, whose face was painted with horror, before her brow furrowed. She screamed and charged at Edith.

"What happened?" Kaylee said out of panic as she twisted Adam around. He turned his head and saw her eyes instantly tear up as she pulled the dart out of his shoulder.

Adam looked back when he heard Eva scream again. She was spinning her spear in front of her as she charged Edith, deflecting any darts that came her way. Edith backpedaled past a hill, and the two fell out of sight.

"What did you do? What did you do?" Kaylee exclaimed while tears flowed down her cheeks.

"I couldn't let you die. You mean too much to me," Adam replied.

"I'd rather have. I can't watch you die. You can't leave me," Kaylee said through her tears.

Adam knew he didn't have much time. He could feel his body becoming heavy, and it was almost impossible to move his legs. He hated to see her upset, but his time was near, and there was nothing he could do to prevent it. As much as it devastated him to know that in a few moments, he would never see her again, he had to make that time count. Adam buried his emotions the best he could, raised his sword to his face, and concentrated.

"What are you doing?" Kaylee asked. Her words were almost hard to understand at this point.

The sword was deactivated before he handed it to Kaylee. "I transferred the sword to you so you can use it quicker. Once I die, obtaining ownership of the sword is a longer process. It will now obey you." Adam responded. He could no longer feel the connection between himself and his sword. It felt odd, but the feeling was outweighed by his muscles tightening. "Listen. I don't have much time left, so we need to make this count."

"But you were supposed to take me to Alaska," Kaylee said pitifully.

Adam wiped his eyes. "I'm sorry. I won't be able to keep that promise." Kaylee began to sob. "But you will go on. You will live. You will defeat Cassian and go on to live many years, happily. You will travel, especially to Alaska, and as long as you keep me in your memories and heart, I will always be with you. You are the most amazing and wonderful person I have ever known. You are strong. I know you can do this. You are the hero of this story, not me."

"I don't want to be the hero. I want you." Kaylee wiped her face. "How can you have so much faith in me?"

"The two things I am certain about in this world are your ability to conquer everything and that I love you with all my heart and soul. In over five hundred years, I have never loved someone as much as I love you," Adam said as a tear rolled down his cheek. He smiled, for he didn't want her last image of him to be one of sadness.

More tears ran down Kaylee's face as she lunged forward and kissed Adam. He kissed her back and poured every emotion he felt into that kiss. Being their last kiss, he wanted to be sure she felt how much he loved her. At that moment, he could barely move as he could feel the bronze taking over his body. It was even becoming harder to breathe. Kaylee stepped away, smiled, and quickly said, "I love you, too." Adam smiled right before the darkness took him.

CHAPTER 29

Kaylee stood there in silence, staring at a bronze statue that used to be the love of her life. She slowly backed away from the statue before she screamed in agony, for the pain she felt was unbearable. Her crying was interrupted when she heard a scream, followed by blue lights. She combined her daggers to form the sword and aimed the hilt toward the light, unsure of who had won the battle. She wiped her eyes and focused. A few moments later, Eva appeared at the top of the hill. She had some slash marks on her, all grouped in pairs, but she obviously won the fight. Kaylee lowered her weapon.

Eva's eyes looked past Kaylee and began to water as she covered her mouth and slowly shook her head. Kaylee walked up to Eva and hugged her, and the two cried in each other's arms. When Eva let go, Kaylee looked down the hill and saw Edith's decayed body...decapitated. Next to it was her sword and the blowgun, in pieces. Kaylee wiped her eyes and glared at the monastery. She could feel a burning rage building inside of her...one that was quickly replacing the agony that once filled her.

"You may have gotten revenge for Adam's killer, but she was just a puppet. I want the puppeteer," Kaylee coldly commented as she continued to glare.

"So do I," Eva responded. She, too, glared toward the monastery.

As much as Kaylee didn't want to leave Adam, she wasn't about to let his death be for nothing. She was only able to tear herself away from the statue of Adam since revenge had now replaced the devastation she felt moments earlier. Kaylee's eyes narrowed before she bolted the rest of the way to the monastery. Even with the occasional undead monk she encountered, she effortlessly dispatched it without losing momentum. Memories of Adam's bronze face fueled her determination as she finally reached the building. She kicked open a side door, which echoed throughout the hallways.

"Cassian!" Kaylee called out.

"Quiet. We need the element of surprise. Let's find Katsumi," Eva said as she trailed behind the fast-walking Kaylee. She didn't respond to Eva's comment and kept moving forward. She wasn't sure where she was going. She didn't care. At some point, she would find him. Eva caught up to Kaylee. "Hey. I want him dead just as much as you, but we need to be smart about this, or Adam's death will be meaningless." Kaylee remained quiet as she marched forward. "Do you hear me?" Eva asked as she grabbed her shoulder.

Kaylee spun around. "Yes, I hear you, and guess what…change of plans. If I can kill him, then I am going to do it. Everyone else can either help or get out of my way!"

"Adam didn't die saving you, so you can get yourself killed!" Eva countered.

Kaylee shoved Eva. "Don't you even dare try that on me," she said through gritted teeth. Eva stood her ground as her eyes flared. Kaylee's hardened face eased as she took a breath. "I'm sorry. It's just…I must do this. Adam believed in me…sacrificed himself for me. All because he loved me. I will not throw my life away because that's not what Adam would want. That is the way I honor him. I have the power to stop this once and for all, but I won't cower behind plans and the help of others. Eva, we lost three people in just the span of a few days. It stops here. Cassian is a monster, and I can't let him take any more away from me...from us. So yes, I'm pissed and I have so much hatred for Cassian. I will harness that hatred when I go to kill him."

Eva put her hand on Kaylee's shoulder. "I get it, and I'm all for it. Just don't let this blind rage cloud your judgment. That's all I am trying to get at. I don't care what some original told us. I'm with you. If you want to take him on, with or without help, then fine. I will have your back. Just be smart about it."

Kaylee nodded. "I will."

"Good and if you ever shove me like that again, I will put you on your butt," Eva responded with a slight grin.

Kaylee scoffed with amusement before she turned around and continued. She kept her sword raised in front of her as she maneuvered her way down the hallways until they reached a vast, empty room. The large windows along the perimeter gave it natural light, which displayed the beautiful ceiling and walls. Some areas were sculpted, and other areas were painted with bright colors, all showcasing the monks' religion. It seemed like a room meant to hold large gatherings for events.

"Over there," Eva said as she pointed with her eyes. Kaylee looked and saw a portal in a state of flux in the back corner of the room.

"I'm on it," Kaylee said as she rushed to it. She carefully emptied the pouch into her hand and blew the fine powder into the portal. It took most of the powder to close it. Kaylee wiped her hands together and walked back to Eva.

Then, they both quickly turned in the direction of the clapping echoing throughout the room. It was Cassian, smiling as he slowly walked toward the center of the room. Kaylee's brow furrowed as she held her sword in one hand. Then, in her other hand, she activated Adam's sword. Kaylee glanced down and saw the symbols on the sword quickly change. Her eyes began to water as another painful reminder of Adam's death presented itself. She closed her eyes tightly, took a deep breath to compose herself, and then redirected her attention back to Cassian. Her stare could have burned a hole through him.

His smug look made it difficult for Kaylee to control her emotions. Her hatred of him was eroding the thin wall of reasoning that prevented her from charging. Since he was not wearing his coat, she could see five daggers sheathed along his waistline. Of course, his great sword was strapped to his back. Eva stood beside Kaylee with her spear ready as she glared at him.

"Congratulations! You found me; now what do you plan to do with me?" Cassian asked.

"We were thinking of confiscating our dagger, along with the others, too," Eva announced.

"But not before we kill you for all the misery you've caused," Kaylee added.

"You two suffer from such hubris, even after you witnessed my power," Cassian responded.

"I think I like our chances. You can't hide behind your followers and your undead legion now," Kaylee said with a smug expression.

Cassian's brow furrowed, which internally made Kaylee happy because she knew she was getting to him. Then, the corner of his mouth lifted. "I recognize that spectral sword, but it had a different owner."

Kaylee gripped both swords tightly as her brow furrowed. "He's messing with your mind. Don't let him," Eva loudly whispered.

"Your friend, along with Edith, is absent. Tell me, was it harder to watch your friend die than the kid back home? Maybe, when I'm done here, I'll fetch your friend and use him to hang my coat," Cassian added as his smile grew more sinister. Kaylee began to tremble the more he spoke, and by the time he finished, she couldn't handle any more. She screamed right before she charged at him.

"Kaylee, no!" Eva yelled, but she didn't listen. All she knew was that Cassian must die.

Cassian's smile remained as he pulled out his sword. Kaylee was fearless as she continued toward him. She swung her sword and immediately followed up with Adam's sword. Cassian blocked her sword with his and caught her other arm. His grip was strong, and she couldn't free herself. Then, his eyes looked over her shoulder, and that is when she took the opportunity to knee him in the stomach. It felt as if her knee had hit a wall, but his grip did loosen enough for her to break free. Cassian dodged Eva's spear and turned to face the two of them.

They both attacked Cassian with a fury of strikes, most of which he blocked, but not all of them. When Cassian blocked Eva's spear, Kaylee swung Adam's sword across his stomach, leaving a gash. He grunted, held his stomach, and swung his sword toward her head. She ducked and sliced his leg with her sword. He groaned before he thrust his sword toward her. She narrowly rolled out of the way of his counterstrike.

With Cassian's attention diverted, Eva stabbed him in the shoulder. Before he could react, she pulled her spear out, sliced his other leg, pivoted around him, and cut him across his back. Unfortunately, the wounds she caused seemed to be more of a nuisance than the pain that Kaylee inflicted on him.

"Enough!" Cassian yelled. He caught Kaylee's arm as she tried to slice him across his chest, but before she could counter with Adam's sword, he smacked her in the forehead with the hilt of his sword. The world was spinning, and the pain was intense as she wobbled backward. She could feel herself about to collapse when she saw him swing his sword at her. She barely got both swords up in time to block, however, the impact sent her soaring back against the wall. As her body slammed into it, her head whipped back and slammed against the wall. She slid down to the ground and held her throbbing head. Her vision was blurry between the blood that slowly flowed down into her eyes and the thunderous pounding she felt inside her head, but she did witness Eva block an overhead swing from him. The force drove her to the ground.

Cassian dropped to one knee behind Eva, grabbed her hair, and sat her up. She was so dazed that she couldn't fight back. He looked over to Kaylee, and his sinister smile appeared again. He put his blade to her throat. "Now, you get to watch another one of your friends die."

"No!" Kaylee screamed as she wiped the blood from her eyes and slid her way back up the wall. She fought with every ounce of strength she had left to push the pain aside. Then, her and Cassian's attention was diverted to something that rolled in front of him. Kaylee squinted and noticed it was the head of a monk. Both she and Cassian looked in the direction from which it came.

"Too subtle?" Katsumi said with a smug expression. She stood ten feet away from him, on the opposite side of Kaylee. Her katana was stained with blood as she stared at him.

"Katsumi," Cassian muttered. Kaylee could hear the disbelief in his voice.

"Surprised to see me?" Katsumi asked.

Cassian slammed Eva's head on the floor before he stood up. The sound of the crack as her head met the floor made Kaylee cringe. "Surprised, yes. Delighted...undeniably, yes." Kaylee looked and saw Eva unconscious, with a small pool of blood forming around her head.

"You're losing your touch. Those undead monks barely put up a fight," Katsumi remarked.

"Without my scythe, I can't control or channel my strength to them. However, with the recent addition of another dagger, I was able to harness enough dark magic within me to animate their bodies. How nice of you to bring me the final dagger. With it, I won't need

302

another scythe…or anything. My power will be infinite," Cassian responded.

"Well, I took care of your creations, so it's just you and us girls. We have no intention of letting you have my dagger," Katsumi countered, still with her smug expression.

Cassian looked at his stomach and leg before he glanced back at Kaylee. "While we are on the subject of daggers. I find it interesting that my wounds from the blonde have not fully healed. Any wounds I receive heal almost instantaneously, yet the wounds caused by her do not." Kaylee could see Katsumi's smug expression disappear. "You're hiding something from me," Cassian said calmly. It was enough to make Kaylee cringe.

"You're delusional. The magic in some weapons can be more potent than others," Katsumi retorted as she strolled toward Kaylee. Her movement caused Cassian to stop and follow her with his head.

"Am I? I've had the pleasure of being cut by some of the deadliest weapons known to man, including that spectral sword she wields, yet none have left the same type of wound that I have here, except for one," Cassian responded. His eyes and hand drifted to the daggers on his belt. "Furthermore, you are too good a soul to allow others to go into a battle they cannot win. She's special, isn't she? I would wager that her blood would amplify my powers exponentially." His eyes then drifted to Kaylee, who moved to meet Katsumi in the middle of the room. She regretted not waiting for Katsumi.

"Give us the daggers. I will even allow you to keep yours, but please, hand over the other daggers. Don't make me kill you," Katsumi pleaded.

"You can't kill me. You had plenty of opportunities over the years, yet you just couldn't do it. You still see the weak Cassian you fell in love with many moons ago. That person is long gone, and your attachment to my former self will be your downfall today," Cassian replied.

303

"One could say the same about you. You've had your fair share of chances to kill me, yet here I stand. Funny how your quest for the daggers hasn't involved me. You want to know why?" Katsumi asked.

"Enlighten me," Cassian responded. He raised his hands to the sides of him and took a few steps closer.

"It's because deep down under all that darkness is the man I knew and fell in love with. The man who wanted to do good in this world is still inside there," Katsumi gently said as she lowered her weapon.

"See me as I am today and not as I once was. I've killed thousands…tens of thousands. Men, women, children… entire families from infants to the elderly…tortured and killed together. I will kill you," Cassian said, coldly.

"How can so much love turn into so much hate?" Katsumi yelled.

Cassian smirked. "What you see as hate, I view as power."

"Then, if the person I once knew is truly gone, your reign of terror ends today," Katsumi said as she raised her sword.

"If you kill me, you become me. I hope your soul is ready for mine," Cassian responded as he raised his sword.

Kaylee raised her sword as well, but lost her balance and almost fell. She shook her head as she tried to regain focus. Her head was still throbbing. Katsumi turned to Kaylee. "You're still recovering. Let me handle Cassian. He is my responsibility. It's something I should have done eons ago."

"Can you kill him?" Kaylee softly asked.

Katsumi's eyes drifted down. "No." She looked up, and then her brow lowered. "But you can. Together, we can stop him, but you must wait until I get him to his weakest point. I'll call your name when that happens, but you must promise me you will wait, no matter what. Okay?"

"I promise," Kaylee uneasily responded. Katsumi smiled before she turned to face Cassian.

The two squared off, but no one made the first move. Instead, Katsumi stared him down while Cassian's sinister smile remained. Then, Katsumi bolted toward him so quickly that it caught Kaylee off guard. He was able to block her first two slashes but couldn't avoid the third as she spun around him, ducked under his blade, and sliced his leg.

Before he could reposition his sword, while still crouched down, she twirled in front of him and did an upward slash that cut him from his waist to his chest. Her attack even nicked his chin. She immediately followed up with a downward slash across the other side of his chest. As he grimaced and stumbled backward, she thrust her sword at his head. However, Cassian was able to raise his sword and block her attack.

He countered and swung his sword laterally at her, which she flipped sideways so her entire body flowed just over the blade as it soared underneath her. As she was about to land on her feet, she twisted her body and sliced him across his right side. Cassian drove the hilt of his sword down and smacked Katsumi on her forehead, and as she stumbled backward, he grabbed the top of her shirt, lifted her up, and slammed her into the ground behind him. Her eyes grew big as she looked up and saw him swinging his sword down at her like an axe. She rolled out of the way as his sword smashed into the floor, leaving behind a large crack.

She quickly got back to her feet and leaned back to avoid his next swing at her. She raised her sword, but instead of striking at his chest, she rolled under another swing of his sword. Once she was behind him, she twirled around on one foot and sliced the back of both his knees.

He grunted as he dropped to his knees but quickly held his sword behind him, which blocked her attempt to slash him across his back. He used his strength to lift himself up by using his sword as a crutch, but as he turned to face her, she thrust her sword past his guard and into his abdomen. It would have been his chest, but he was able to push it down with his hand before it reached him. With his free hand, he grabbed her arm and raised his sword into the air.

She struggled to free herself from his grip, and her sword was still lodged inside him. He smiled as he sent his sword down upon her. She leaned to the side just in time to see the sword narrowly miss her. However, she moved in the direction that caused him to release his grip, or else he would have chopped his arm off. She then bent her back as she stood up to avoid his next attack, and as soon as she saw his sword narrowly miss her again, she pulled her sword out of him and slashed him across his chest before she tumbled behind him. When she was behind him, she turned around and slashed him across his back, but she couldn't avoid his surprise move when he blindly thrust his sword under his arm, behind him. Her face cringed with pain as the blade caught her in her left shoulder.

"Predictable, as always," Cassian said as he turned around. His cold eyes and even colder smile made Kaylee shiver. He then removed his blade.

Katsumi held her sword up in defense. "I guess I will have to find a way to remedy that."

Cassian raised his sword high in the air and swung it down toward her. Katsumi raised her blade to block, but right as his blade was about to make contact with her, she sidestepped out of the way. When his blade crashed into the ground, she brought the hilt of her sword down on his sword hand. The move made him drop his sword. She quickly grabbed her dagger with her other hand and, in a hammer motion, drove the dagger's blade toward his chest. However, she stopped right before it pierced his shirt.

Kaylee watched in anticipation and so desperately wanted to help. However, she remembered what happened last time she didn't stick to Katsumi's plan, so she chose to remain where she was. She glanced over at Eva and noticed she was up on one elbow, watching as well. She was thankful she was doing better, but her attention was quickly diverted back to Katsumi and Cassian. She was about to call out to Katsumi to kill him, but she didn't. She knew if that were her and Adam, she wouldn't be able to do it.

The dagger trembled in her hand as her face was pained with the decision she had to make. Cassian was deadpan the entire time until he grinned. Then, in the blink of an eye, he used his free hand to grab his dagger and drove it into her heart. She gasped as she dropped her weapons and placed her hands on his arms. Kaylee's jaw dropped. She couldn't believe what she had just witnessed. Even worse, what was she supposed to do now?

Cassian leaned close to her face. "Like I said, predictable."

Katsumi smiled and weakly responded, "Ironically, I was also counting on you being predictable." Cassian's smile left him, and his brow crinkled. Katsumi turned her head toward Kaylee. "Now, Kaylee!" As she spoke her final words, her eyes closed, and she fell to the floor. At first, Kaylee didn't know what she meant. Why attack now? Then, she noticed Cassian turn his head toward her, and his eyes grew large as he took a few steps back from Katsumi. It was the first time she ever saw him nervous. That is when Kaylee realized that receiving an immortal mark from an original would weaken him.

She wasn't sure if it was because she was an original or if it was because she had killed so many immortals over thousands of years, but the passing of her mark seemed different from what she had seen in the past. Katsumi's entire body glowed so brightly that she couldn't see her anymore.

The blue light engulfed her as the bluish flames grew tall around her, Cassian, and a large portion of the room. Then, the bluish flames closed in on Cassian and swirled around him. Suddenly, her light shot into him as bluish lightning burst around them. Crumbles from the ceiling fell as the room shook while Cassian screamed and dropped his weapons. Kaylee and Eva shielded their eyes and braced themselves since it felt like there was a storm within the room. Then,

Kaylee's brow furrowed as she gritted her teeth and tried to power her way toward Cassian.

"Kaylee!" Eva cried out, but she didn't turn back. She knew what she had to do. She realized this was Katsumi's plan, and she wasn't going to let Katsumi's sacrifice be in vain. Also, she wasn't about to let Cassian live. Adam believed in her...now she had to believe in herself.

She knew she had to act quickly. Cassian would only be weakened momentarily. Once he recovered, not only would he have all the daggers, but he would also have Katsumi's power within him, making him nearly impossible to defeat. However, despite her determination, she was still battling her head wound, and the wind was too strong for her to make any progress. She strained to move, but her focus didn't waver. Thoughts of Adam flowed through her head, followed by Caleb, Paul, and even Katsumi.

She willed herself to be stronger...to keep moving forward, and that is when she felt her original mark begin to burn, but it didn't hurt. Instead, she felt her head wound heal, and she felt more powerful...enough to take continuous, strong steps toward him. When she was about halfway there, the event stopped, and Cassian crumbled to the ground. Kaylee sprang forward. She raced toward Cassian, with her and Adam's swords on either side of her.

Cassian weakly grabbed his sword and struggled to get to his feet. She noticed that his and Katsumi's daggers were out of range of his grasp. Furthermore, Katsumi's body was reduced to ash. Kaylee leaped into the air and came down with both swords, but Cassian was able to make it to one knee and raise his blade over his head.

Their swords collided. Her face crinkled as she pushed with all her strength. To her surprise, she was pushing his sword toward his head. His dumbfounded expression fueled her confidence as she continued to drive his sword back. Kaylee felt an unfamiliar power coursing through her veins. However, just as she was about to make her next move, she noticed her progress had ceased. That is when Cassian's face hardened, and her swords began to draw closer to her.

"It appears Katsumi's faith was misplaced," Cassian said. A sinister smile appeared as he slowly began to rise. To Kaylee's dismay, his strength had returned.

CHAPTER 30

Kaylee strained as she attempted to overpower him. She tried to draw from whatever power was within her, but her strength was no match for his. If anything, he seemed even more powerful than before. At that moment, Kaylee remembered something from her training. She smiled, which made Cassian's brow lower with curiosity. She angled her sword enough and fired a shot from the hilt into his leg. He grimaced as he dropped back to one knee. Immediately after, Kaylee deactivated Adam's sword just enough to slip past Cassian's guard before she reactivated it. Adam's sword pierced Cassian between the eyes.

"Use your weapon's special abilities to your advantage," she commented. Cassian's body convulsed until she deactivated Adam's sword. She strapped his and her sword back to herself as she watched Cassian's body fall to the side. Blood poured from his head as soon as it hit the ground. "Thank you, Adam," she whispered to herself.

"Girl, you did it!" Eva screamed. Kaylee turned her head and smiled. In that moment, she felt the weight lift from her chest, even though she was still in disbelief that Cassian was dead. Eva used her spear to help her stand up, but she didn't walk far before she stopped. Her jaw dropped, and her eyes widened.

Kaylee looked at Cassian's body, and the same bright blue glow that Katsumi had…now consumed Cassian. She could feel her body tingle, and her breath quickened. As the blue flames surrounded her, she could feel a sense of hope, but a sense of hatred and rage quickly overcame it. Then, the bright blue light entered Kaylee, and the blueish flames swirled around her…even wider than before. The entire building shook as lightning crashed all around and through her. Large pieces of the roof began to crumble and fall around Kaylee, but she couldn't move. Regardless of how much she screamed because of the pain, she felt more powerful with each second that passed until it finally stopped. She dropped to her knees, gasping for air, and Cassian was nothing but ash.

Once it was over, Eva hobbled as quickly as she could toward the weapons while dodging falling chunks of the ceiling. She gathered all six daggers, Katsumi's sword, and Cassian's sword…placing them anywhere she could on her body. "Come on, we must go. This whole place is falling apart."

"Not without Adam," Kaylee mumbled.

"My head is too fuzzy to visualize where he is or anywhere near him. We could wind up on the side of any mountain around the world. Same if you tried. Listen, I don't want to either, but we are in a remote area. We can return as soon as it's safe and I've recovered." Eva responded, but Kaylee didn't respond or look up at her. "Come on, we have to go!" Eva yelled and grabbed her shoulder. Kaylee grabbed her wrist and stood straight up. "Ouch…Kaylee, you're hurting me."

Kaylee felt nothing but burning rage flowing through her veins as she pulled her sword and held it to Eva's neck. Memories of their friendship were quickly fading away as her brow furrowed. "I see you got your weapons. It's probably all you wanted. You never cared about me, Adam, or anyone except yourself! Just leave. I will go and retrieve Adam."

"You know that's not true!" Eva countered.

Kaylee scoffed. "You know what...maybe Cassian had the right idea. There is so much wrong with this world that people need to be purged from it. Maybe I'll start with you," Kaylee said as her eyes narrowed. Then, she slowly moved her blade closer to Eva's neck.

"This isn't you, Kaylee," Eva responded as her eyes bounced between the sword and Kaylee.

"Maybe this should have been me all along. You can't feel pain when all you feel is hatred and power," Kaylee responded.

"That's Cassian's mindset, not yours. Katsumi is inside you as well. Take her goodness and harness it to fight off Cassian. Don't let him win," Eva pleaded. A sinister smile formed on Kaylee's face as she raised her sword above her head. As she was about to strike, Eva blurted out, "What would Adam think?" The comment made her face crinkle as the blade shook above her head.

"Adam would want you to live and be happy. To be at peace, not turn into some monster. Remember all the good times you shared with him...all the strong feelings you felt for him, and channel that into yourself. Focus on that and push everything else away. Just breathe in those thoughts and exhale the rest. Concentrate on him, and only him," Eva said.

Kaylee wanted to kill Eva with every fiber in her body, but the memory of her first date with Adam at the boardwalk popped into her head. It was the one beacon of light that began to shine so brightly, it pushed the darkness away. As more light filled her, more memories poured into her mind. Their time spent together in college and at the manor illuminated a path to the fond memories of them that warmed her heart. A smile broke through as a tear ran down her cheek. She then shook her head and realized what was going on. She sheathed her blade and pulled Eva into her.

"I'm so sorry. I didn't mean it. I wasn't in control," Kaylee said as she hugged Eva tightly. Then, a large chunk of the roof fell near them.

312

"I understand, but we should continue this later unless we just want to be a stain on the floor," Eva responded. Kaylee stepped back and nodded. "Okay then. Create a portal and take us home. We can figure everything else out later."

"Okay," Kaylee said before she got her portal key. She created a portal, and they stepped through just as the entire roof collapsed. They arrived on the porch of the manor at night.

It was quiet. For a moment, Kaylee and Eva stood in silence as they caught their breath. Then, Kaylee turned and hugged Eva again. No words were spoken; they just stood there and hugged. Whether she was in control or not, Kaylee felt horrible for how she had acted. In addition to that, the events of the day had taken their toll. Even though they won, they experienced so much pain…mentally and physically. After a few minutes, they separated.

"How's your head?" Kaylee asked.

"I'm a lot better than before, but I'm still a little light-headed, and it still hurts. I'm sure once I go to sleep, I'll wake up as good as new." Kaylee didn't realize how exhausted she was until Eva mentioned sleep.

"I'm going to check on Caleb. I know it's a long shot, but maybe somehow when you broke the blowgun, it broke the curse," Kaylee said as she shrugged.

"It wouldn't hurt to be sure," Eva replied.

They walked toward the crypt. On their way, they noticed a light in the guest house, so they peeked through the window and saw Oliver asleep on the couch. His crutches were next to him.

"It appears he is still improving," Eva commented.

"Should we wake him up?" Kaylee asked.

"Why, so we can tell him that even though we won, his best friend is dead. I don't think I am ready to have that conversation yet. Let him rest. We can tell him tomorrow," Eva suggested. Kaylee agreed, so they continued to the crypt.

They reached the doors, and as they opened them, Kaylee could feel a knot form in her stomach. She hoped to see either no statue or Caleb in the flesh. As they reached the area, the moonlight reflected off the bronze statue of Caleb. Kaylee pressed her lips together to hold back her emotions. Even though she knew it was a long shot, it still hurt. Eva rubbed her back before they turned around and left. As they entered the manor, it felt lifeless. Kaylee turned and noticed Eva's eyes welling up.

"Talk to me," Kaylee gently said as she laid her hand on her shoulder.

"We're immortal. Every time we leave to go somewhere, we know there is a chance we won't make it back. Because of that, we said our goodbyes once, and then after that, it was just understood. We hoped to see our friends again, but knew it wasn't guaranteed. With that said, I made one of the biggest mistakes an immortal could make, and that was to think that Adam was truly immortal." Tears began to run down her cheeks, which caused Kaylee's eyes to water. She was still in disbelief that he was gone, but hearing Eva mention it brought it closer to reality. Eva wiped her face and continued.

"Over the centuries, we have grown so close to each other and spent more time together than any other immortal. I just took it for granted that he would always be there. Now that he is truly gone, I'm painfully reminded again that immortality is not a gift…"

"But a curse." Kaylee finished her sentence and wiped the tears off her face. Eva nodded. "So, what do we do now?"

Eva took a deep breath to compose herself. "We start the grieving process. As painful as it may be, we must. The longer we delay, the harder it will be for us to move forward, and Adam wouldn't want us to be stuck in one place because of him. He would want us to live life and be happy. I know that will take time. Honestly, I don't see myself being happy for a long time. But one day, the fake smiles will become real. We just have to keep his

314

memory with us. For now, I am going to go to my room and mourn him. I suggest you do the same."

"Okay. Just remember that I am here if you need me," Kaylee said. Once again, she fought back emotions from the unfortunate truth that Eva spoke.

Eva smiled. "Same here." They hugged one more time before parting ways.

Kaylee began walking toward her bedroom, but felt compelled to go to Adam's room. It was so quiet that she could only hear her footsteps as she walked. Each step closer to his room made her chest feel heavier. When she reached his room, his door was closed. A faint smile appeared. "He finally remembered to close his door," Kaylee said to herself.

She reached for the doorknob but froze before she was about to touch it. Her eyes became glassy, and her breathing became erratic. She knew what was on the other side of that door...nothing, which frightened her. A reminder of the harsh reality she would have to face. She made a fist and controlled her breathing. Once it became steady, she opened his door.

No matter how much she prepared herself, it meant nothing. The reality of his death smacked her in the face as the door opened to an empty room full of memories. Her breath trembled as a few tears rolled down her cheek. She placed her hand over her heart and walked in. The silence pierced her heart as her eyes drifted around the room.

Every memory, regardless of how precious it was to her, hurt. She pressed her lips together and tried her best to be strong, but the tears kept finding ways to escape. As she passed his bed, she saw the shirt he slept in before they left for Japan. She picked it up and smelled it. His scent brought her comfort...enough to bring a slight smile to her face. As she sniffed it, more memories of them together rushed in. She continued to walk around his room until she reached

315

his memory box. She had never thought about creating one until now, so she opened it to see what items he had inside.

Her attention was immediately drawn to the item lying on top, upside down. She picked it up and turned it over. It was the strip of photos from the boardwalk when they first met. Her lips quivered as tears burst from her eyes. She began to cry uncontrollably as she fell to her knees. Her bawling was a mixture of crying and screaming, for the pain of his loss was unbearable. It was as if someone had just torn out her heart and soul. All she wanted was to be with him. To hear his voice, to feel his touch. The pain was overwhelming. She couldn't imagine a day without him, but an eternity was even more dreadful.

The curse of immortality cut her deep. She squeezed his shirt against her as she lay on the floor, curled up. She continued to cry, letting what seemed to be an endless supply of hurt, anger, and pain leave her body. She had no idea how long she had been lying on the floor, but as soon as her crying turned into a whimper, she climbed into his bed. Even though the bed was empty, it was filled with many fond memories of all the times they talked, laughed, and cuddled. She felt closest to him during those times. With his shirt still with her, from sheer exhaustion, she fell asleep.

During the night, Kaylee woke up and turned over. She gasped before a huge smile appeared. To her astonishment, Adam was lying beside her. He was looking back at her with a gentle smile. "You're alive!"

"Of course. I would never leave you," Adam responded. Kaylee reached out to pull him closer to her, but as soon as her hand touched him, he turned to bronze.

She woke up, sweaty and screaming. Her head jerked to Adam's side of the bed, and it was empty. Kaylee wiped the sweat off her face before she sobbed. Sleep would not come easily after that, for she was plagued with images of Adam's bronze face every time she closed her eyes.

Even though she was exhausted and mentally drained, the idea of being awake outweighed the horrible images she had witnessed while asleep. She didn't want to get up, but reluctantly dragged herself out of his bed and into the kitchen. Silence still ruled the house.

As her coffee brewed, she stared at the strip of pictures from the first day they met. She never knew he kept them. In the past, she would have fussed at him because she looked terrible in those pictures, regardless of what he said. Now, she was beyond thankful he kept them.

Kaylee remembered she had never looked at Cassian's mark when it was branded on her right shoulder. She pulled her sleeve up far enough to view it. For such a small mark, it caused such devastation. On any other day, she would have tested the new power and knowledge that she received, but not today. All she wanted was to be with the man she loved. The thought of never seeing Adam again made her nauseous, so she didn't grab any food. She only took her coffee and left the kitchen.

She made her way to the couch where they sat while he massaged her the other day. Kaylee took a few sips of coffee before she placed it on a nearby table. She looked at the pictures from the boardwalk again. Memories of that day began to bloom in her mind, enough for a hint of a smile to appear. She remembered how great of a time they had together and how they instantly clicked. Kaylee also wondered if he knew how much she had liked him from the start.

It amazed her how a simple coffee accident had led her down the path she was on now. Regardless of how it turned out, she would experience the pain she felt now again and again if it meant she could be with Adam. Her mind then wandered further down the path of memories of that day. Memories that she would cherish forever.

"You know. It's not polite to go through other people's stuff without asking them first."

Kaylee's eyes shot wide open as she gasped and whipped around. There, standing just past the doorway, was Adam, smiling. She pinched herself to see if she was dreaming, and the pain she felt assured her she wasn't. Her eyes welled up, and it felt like all the air around her was whisked away. She was speechless and doubted her eyes. He took a few steps forward, and that was when Eva came in. Kaylee's eyes diverted to her, looking for reassurance that what she was seeing was real.

Eva, whose eyes were pink from crying, smiled and nodded. Tears of joy ran down her face as the weight was lifted from her chest. Kaylee let out a short burst of laughter, laced with crying. A smile formed from ear to ear before she ran toward Adam and threw herself at him. He caught her and spun her around before he placed her back down. She hugged him tighter than ever before as joy filled her heart. His voice…his touch…healed her.

CHAPTER 31

Kaylee pressed her lips firmly against his but then pulled back as her eyes investigated his body. Her fingers roamed anywhere that she could find skin. She seemed worried that she was going to find an area of bronze.

"I'm fine, I'm fine. Besides, Eva already checked me over. I'm bronze-free," Adam reassuringly said. He felt selfish because even though he could only imagine what emotional turmoil they experienced, his overwhelming happiness at being reunited with Kaylee surpassed it. He thought he was never going to see her again. To never feel her touch, to see her smile, to hear her laugh, or to feel the peace and happiness she brought him whenever they were together.

Kaylee looked back and forth between Eva and Adam, trying to get any words to leave her lips, but all she could say was, "How?"

"I could barely sleep, so I left early to bring Adam home. I even brought a dolly in case he was too heavy to transport. When I arrived, he was gone. At first, I thought I was at the wrong destination, but then I saw the crumbled monastery, so that couldn't be it. Then, I feared someone had already found him, but to move a statue like that, they couldn't have gotten far. So, I searched the area, and that is when I stumbled across him, searching through the rubble," Eva explained.

"I wasn't sure what happened, and I feared the worst when I noticed the crumbled building. I could see the devastation from halfway down the mountain. I had my mint but not my portal key because I typically don't carry one. Therefore, I couldn't come here to see if you made it back. So, presuming that if you two were alive, one of you would eventually come and retrieve me, I decided to keep myself occupied and investigate the monastery. Just in case my worst fear came true and you weren't alive, I retrieved Edith's sword first to be safe. Eva found me while I was searching the rubble. After she made sure I was actually me, she filled me in on everything that happened after I turned to bronze," Adam added.

"Yeah, but...how are you alive?" Kaylee asked.

"I have a theory. Follow me," Adam said. Eva and Kaylee looked at each other before they followed him outside to the guest house. He could see Oliver reading a book while he lay on the couch, so he knocked as they entered.

"Bloody hell, mate. That was quick. Is everything okay?" Oliver asked as he sat up.

"Yeah, we retrieved the daggers, and Cassian is dead," Adam responded.

"Daggers...there was more than one?" Oliver inquired.

"Yeah, and Eva or Kaylee will fill you in on the details since I missed most of it," Adam said.

"Letting the women do all the work...that doesn't seem like you," Oliver jested.

"Well, I had no choice since I was dead on the side of a mountain before I ever reached Cassian or the daggers," Adam replied. Oliver's brow lowered. "Let me ease your confusion. Edith tried to turn Kaylee into a bronze statue, but I stepped in front of the dart. I ended up becoming the bronze statue instead."

"Well, it doesn't surprise me that you would play the hero role and sacrifice yourself. But, how are you alive if Edith got you?" Oliver asked.

Adam smiled. "You know, I had the same question when I came to until I felt something warm in my pocket." He reached into his front pocket and pulled out a round disc that appeared to be charred. Adam could see Kaylee and Eva's jaws drop, but Oliver seemed unfazed.

"What's that?" Oliver inquired.

"Don't play coy with me," Adam countered, but his smile didn't leave him. Oliver shrugged. "It's your coin."

Oliver scoffed. "I think you still have some of that bronze in your brain because my coin is right here." He pulled out his coin and flashed it to everyone.

"Wait," Adam blurted before Oliver could put it back in his pocket. He then extended his hand. Oliver rolled his eyes and handed it to him, which Adam's inspection of it didn't take long. "This isn't your coin. Is this…a toy?"

Oliver sighed. "Yes, I found it in a cereal box many years ago when cereal boxes came with toys. That toy is a pirate's coin. At a quick glance, I discovered it could pass as my coin, so I kept it in case I ever needed it. I had a bad feeling you wouldn't make it back, most likely dying to save Kaylee or Eva, so I slipped it into your pocket when I pretended to stumble and fall into you."

"I don't understand. When we asked Katsumi if there was a cure for Caleb, she said no," Eva commented.

Kaylee slowly began to grin. "Because there is no cure, but there is a way to prevent it." Her eyes drifted to the charred coin. Eva scoffed with amusement.

"Why? I didn't think you would ever part with your coin." Adam said in disbelief.

"Most people say 'thank you' when someone saves their life," Oliver responded as he grinned.

Adam shook his head. "Thank you. You saved my life. Not only that, you gave me a second chance at life. To be with the ones I cherish and to finally start my life with the person I am in love with."

"Love?" Both Eva and Oliver blurted out.

"I'll tell you about it later," Kaylee said to Eva. She blushed before she looked at Adam and smiled.

"I owe you a debt that I can never repay, but I will always try," Adam added.

Oliver stood up. He was slightly off-balance, but he maintained his footing. "You owe me nothing. If anything, I finally paid my debt to you." Adam's head tilted slightly as his brow lowered. "You've stuck by me all these years. You were my friend when no one else would be. From my viewpoint, you saved me all those centuries ago when you didn't kill me, then you saved me time and time again with your friendship." Adam smiled and hugged Oliver.

Once he was done, Kaylee rushed to Oliver and hugged him as well. "Thank you. You brought Adam back to me and saved me from an eternity of misery."

"Well, I wouldn't be a gentleman if I stood between my best friend and the love of his life," Oliver said as his eyes cut to Adam while he smirked. Adam scoffed with amusement. Kaylee smiled and hugged Oliver again.

"You risked your life, even when you disagreed with my plan. Then, you put your life on the line when you gave Adam your coin. You saved Adam's life, and I don't know how I could ever repay you," Eva genuinely said.

"Well, the free room and board is always a perk," Oliver joked.

Eva smiled. "You are always welcome here, in the guest house, or inside the manor. I'm sorry for how I've acted toward you. I like this Oliver." She kissed him on the cheek before she hugged him.

As they hugged, Oliver looked at Adam and smiled. Adam began to smile as he mouthed the word "Progress." Oliver winked.

Adam had to press his lips together and turn his head so he wouldn't laugh.

Afterward, Eva caught Oliver up to speed with the events of their trip. Kaylee filled the gap during the time when Eva was unconscious to complete the story for Adam and Oliver. Even though Eva had already informed Adam of almost everything he had missed, he still listened intently. The story was just as amazing and interesting as the first time he heard it. Then, Eva, Kaylee, and Adam decided that coffee and showers were definitely needed, so they returned to the manor. Once they were cleaned up, Kaylee met Adam in his room.

"I believe this belongs to you," Kaylee said as she handed Adam his sword.

"Thank you. From what I heard, it served you well," Adam remarked. However, when he went to activate it, nothing happened. "Um...I think you forgot something."

"Oh my gosh! I totally forgot to transfer it back to you. How do I do that?" Kaylee asked. Adam walked her through the steps, and in no time, the sword worked for him again. It was like reuniting with an old friend. He also noticed the symbols changed back to what they were before he transferred the sword to Kaylee. Afterward, they got into bed and snuggled.

"You have to promise never to scare me like that again," Kaylee said.

"I'm sorry you had to go through that, but I'm here now, and I have no plans of leaving," Adam said. He kissed her on the top of her head. She squeezed him tightly. "Unless you keep squeezing me like that," Adam added in a strained voice.

Kaylee quickly let go and laughed. "Sorry, I'm still getting used to all this added strength."

Adam laughed. "It's okay. So, how does it feel to be the strongest immortal in the world?"

"I have a better question. How does it feel to be dating the most powerful immortal in the world?" Kaylee asked as she smiled and looked up at him.

"Sexy and terrifying all at the same time," Adam teased, which made Kaylee snort. That caused them to laugh. "You're still the same Kaylee to me. I love you." He gently lifted her face toward his and kissed her.

"I love you, too. Can we just lie here like this forever?" Kaylee asked.

"We could, but it would be hard to go to Alaska that way," Adam responded.

"We're going?" Kaylee asked as her eyes lit up.

"Well, I did promise you. I figured we would go right after the holidays. That is, if you still want to go," Adam teased.

"Yeah, I still want to go!" Kaylee exclaimed and then kissed him again.

"But for now, I think staying in bed is a good option," Adam added. They snuggled, and Adam felt at peace.

He was so happy that he couldn't control the goofy smile that formed and wouldn't disappear. He was thankful that Kaylee's head was resting on his chest. He could only imagine how much worse she would make him blush and smile if she noticed. Eventually, he regained control of his smile. Adam looked forward to what their future together would bring. Besides cherishing every moment with her, he knew he wanted to make her as happy as she made him. She deserved nothing less. Soon, her gentle breathing began to make him sleepy, and shortly after, he fell asleep.

CHAPTER 32

The four of them stayed at the manor during the holidays. They each helped decorate the entire manor, which was a chore by itself, but it looked beautiful when it was done. They enjoyed each other's company as laughter filled the halls, feasts were devoured, and presents were exchanged. Oliver ended up moving into the manor, which, of course, was "progress" in his mind. Adam noticed Eva warmed up to him, but Oliver had a long way to go. Most likely a lot further than he knew or wanted to admit. Adam and Kaylee grew even closer together during this time, emotionally and intimately. There wasn't a day that passed when Adam wasn't grateful for his second chance at life…a second chance to be with the woman he loved.

They each took time during the holidays to honor the ones they lost. For Paul, they decided to have a friendly competition at a local go-kart race track. Adam and Kaylee were clearly the better drivers since Eva and Oliver's preferred method of travel was portal keys. Afterward, they went back home to the outdoor training range. They used a spare crossbow to have another friendly game of target practice. Apparently, none of them were a good shot. They competed while they shared stories about Paul.

As for Caleb, the way to honor him was simple and fun. They all decided to take a day and play nothing but online games. They trash-talked each other as they laughed at how horrible they were at the games. They ended up playing into the early morning hours without even knowing it. They enjoyed it so much, especially since their gameplay improved, that they played it again the next day.

Even though they didn't know her well, they also wanted to honor Katsumi. In a short time frame, she had such a substantial positive impact on them, as well as sacrificed herself to stop Cassian. Using the pond on their property, they lit a few floating lanterns, and each said something nice about Katsumi. Then, they placed the lanterns on the water, gently pushed them, and watched them slowly float away until they burned out.

Then, they visited her house in the village on the Izu Peninsula. Through the information she left behind, they found each of her homes, and to honor her wish, they moved all her personal, valuable, and magical items from each location through the cover of night. This included a volume of chronicles that even Caleb would envy.

They started at her house in the village first since they feared someone would stumble upon it, especially when they realized it had been vacant for an extended period of time. Some items they brought back to the manor, and others they stashed at her other home in the Kita Alps. Of all her locations, this was the most remote and nearly impossible to find unless you knew exactly where to go. They found a picture of her in her belongings, so they took that and her sword and placed them in the crypt. Once this was done and the holidays were over, including putting the decorations away, it was time for Adam and Kaylee to take their long-overdue trip to Alaska.

"Our private cabin is ready," Adam announced as he walked into the foyer with his luggage.

"I can't believe today is the day we finally leave for our trip. I hope I didn't forget anything," Kaylee said as she scanned her luggage. She was giddy with excitement.

"I think you packed almost everything you own," Adam teased.

"Hush. It's good to be prepared," Kaylee playfully countered.

"You realize you can portal back here if you forget anything, right?" Adam asked rhetorically.

"I know, but once I'm there, I want to enjoy myself and not have to step away for any reason," Kaylee responded.

"I get it. Besides, I hate for you to be away from me for any amount of time," Adam added before kissing her.

"Bloody hell. Just go. I don't know how much more of this I can take," Oliver huffed. Adam and Kaylee smiled.

"Shut up. I think it's adorable," Eva said as she walked in behind Oliver. They helped Kaylee and Adam take their bags outside.

"I'm going to miss you two. Don't be strangers," Eva said as she hugged and kissed each of them on their cheeks.

"Have fun and remember, luv, if he gets out of line, you can easily straighten him out," Oliver said and then winked.

Kaylee laughed. "Will do. Try to stay out of trouble while I'm gone."

"Now, where is the fun in that?" Oliver said as he smirked. Kaylee smiled and hugged him. As she did that, Adam reached into his bag for the small tin box filled with mint. Instead, he found Oliver's fake coin.

"Why's this here?" Adam inquired.

"I don't need it anymore, so I figured I would give it to you. Something for you to remember me by," Oliver responded.

Adam smiled. "Thank you." He shook Oliver's hand and gave him a quick hug. "Still, I'll need that mint."

"No worries, mate. I got it right here for you," Oliver said as he handed the tin box to Adam.

"Thanks. I'd hate for the first memory of Alaska to be of me puking my guts out," Adam commented.

Oliver scoffed with amusement. "That would be memorable; however, not as memorable as, oh, I don't know…stealing a motorcycle after a bar fight." A smile appeared as he arched his brow.

"I knew there was something!" Eva exclaimed as she smiled.

Adam's eyes widened. "How did you know?" He then looked at Kaylee.

"I didn't say anything," Kaylee said as she raised her arms in defense.

"The bartender told me. She and I are…close," Oliver responded before a devious smile formed.

"Of course, you two are," Kaylee responded as she grinned and shook her head.

"Wait, how did the bartender know about us stealing the bike?" Adam inquired.

"She didn't. She only heard about the bike being stolen. I had my suspicions that you just confirmed," Oliver responded as his smile grew. Adam sighed and shook his head. A smile followed.

"It's too bad I couldn't witness the moment when Adam sank to my level. Tell me, what was worse? Finally, seeing my point of view, or stealing the bike?" Oliver asked as he continued to smile.

"Both were equally unpleasant," Adam replied. This caused everyone to laugh.

"That has to be one of the most satisfying things I've heard in a long time. Try not to steal any snowmobiles while you are away," Oliver jested.

Adam chuckled. "I'll be sure to monitor my behavior, especially at bars. Take care, and I will see you soon."

"Sooner than you think," Oliver responded. He patted him on his shoulder and smiled. Adam and Kaylee grabbed their luggage and took a few steps forward.

"Are you ready?" Kaylee asked as she smiled.

"I'm ready," Adam responded. He gave her a quick peck on the lips before he reached in and put the mint into his mouth. He then got his portal key out, concentrated, and created the portal.

This adventure they were about to embark on would be one of many, and nothing made him happier than being side-by-side with the woman he loved. Just the thought alone was bliss, and he knew that each day they were together, he would show her how much he loved her. They held hands, smiled at each other, and entered the portal.

Eva turned to Oliver after the portal closed. "Aww, look… you're smiling. Someone is a closet romantic."

"It's not that," Oliver responded.

"Then what?" Eva asked as her brow crinkled.

"I switched out his mint with basil leaves. I finely chopped them up and coated them with mint extract," Oliver responded with a crooked grin.

Eva's face was stern for a moment before she burst into laughter. "You're evil."

"I know," Oliver whispered loudly.

THE END

Thank you for reading my book! I appreciate your support, and I hope you enjoyed it!

You can find me on social media at:
Facebook: Author Brian Marotto
Instagram, Twitter, and TikTok:
@MeBrianNotBrain

If you enjoyed my book and would like to rate it, and even leave a review, I would really appreciate it! I would also really appreciate it if you recommended my book to others!

My books can be found at:
https://linktr.ee/AuthorBrianMarotto

DON'T MISS

THE AWAKENING

THE DECEPTION

THE IMPRISONED

THE CREATURE WITHIN
TRILOGY

Made in the USA
Middletown, DE
01 July 2025

77703472R00202